THE OTHER SIDE OF SANCTUARY

The Other Side of Sanctuary

A novel

by

CHERYL CRABB

Adelaide Books
New York / Lisbon
2019

THE OTHER SIDE OF SANCTUARY
A novel
By Cheryl Crabb

Copyright © by Cheryl Crabb
Cover design © 2019 Adelaide Books

Published by Adelaide Books, New York / Lisbon
adelaidebooks.org

Editor-in-Chief
Stevan V. Nikolic

For any information, please address Adelaide Books
at info@adelaidebooks.org
or write to:
Adelaide Books
244 Fifth Ave. Suite D27
New York, NY, 10001

ISBN-10: 1-951214-56-0
ISBN-13: 978-1-951214-56-2

Printed in the United States of America

For all the ones that got away

Prologue

June 30, 2010

Laura locked the door of her grandfather's Chevy before she began the hike west toward Lake Michigan. She wasn't sure exactly where the trail would lead, but soon found her rhythm as she treaded softly in her moccasins over the loamy soil. Shaded beneath the canopy of hardwoods, she didn't notice the fawn step out of the shadows until they were inches apart. The little whitetail, with two rows of spots down its back, stared into her eyes like a soothsayer. It should have known better than to get too close. She should have known better than to encourage it. And yet, drawn together, there, in the trillium-laced forest, they lingered. For just a second or two, when sunlight filtered through the leaves like the stained-glass in a cathedral, she sensed they were kindred spirits.

Once the fawn bounded off, Laura continued up the winding trail that sloped gently, at first, until it slanted toward the bluff. A mile later, when she reached the edge of the dense woods, she could feel her heart thumping. Sweating, even in her flowing skirt and bikini top, she wanted to rest. Then, in the distance, she caught a glimpse of the Great Lake. Parting the ferns that spilled over the trail, she came out into the full afternoon sun high above the open waters that filled the vast divide between Michigan and her native state of Wisconsin.

Eager to get a better view, she hurried across the top of the bluff until her moccasins filled with sand. She stopped to dump them out. It almost seemed to her as if the sand was deliberately weighing her down. After she slipped her moccasins back on, she at last continued toward the lookout point where towering dunes met water that shimmered like hand-blown glass grooved with subtle ripples and hidden pockets of air.

Around her, a steady breeze swept fine grains of sand from the shoreline that stretched for miles in either direction. Ahead, the lopsided humps of the Manitou Islands popped up as if treading water like the two lost cubs of the legendary mother Sleeping Bear who stood guard on the mainland along with the lighthouse at the public beach in Sanctuary. Laura stared into the Manitou Passage, the deep but narrow channel that ran between her and the cubs. Long ago, the Ojibwa ancestors of her mother and grandfather, both now gone, had spoken of it as a gateway for supernatural spirits of good and evil.

The wind gusted, casting spirals across the dunes and stirring childhood recollections of stories her grandfather passed down about the Great Spirit, Gichi-Manidoo. As leader of the manitous, Gichi-Manidoo had the power to connect with humans and other spirits through plants, animals, and various natural phenomena. Though often beautiful, these occurrences could sometimes be dangerous, and, in rare cases—deadly.

Standing above the passage, Laura planted her hands on her hips and took in the sweeping view of Lake Michigan. One after the other, the waves, coming in from afar, picked up speed before crashing onto shore. Suddenly, the sand shifted from beneath her. Laura's chest tightened and her arms flew up in the air as she fought to regain balance. Instead her feet slipped out. Unable to defy gravity any longer, she fell forward—teetering over the edge, staring down into water far below—until she dug in her heel and found something solid. Laura pushed off with her foot and then arched backward. Finally, she caught herself in the sand.

She sat there and brushed herself off realizing, only then, that she'd lost one of her moccasins. Cautiously, she leaned over and spotted it lying upside down twenty feet below. "Frick." There was no way she could reach it from here. Laura looked out at the water to help her think. In the channel, seemingly out of nowhere, a strange figure armed with a long paddle had appeared. She watched him maneuver through the powerful currents above a graveyard of shipwrecks. Standing balanced on his wide surf board, he moved with a ferocity she'd never encountered on the inland lakes around Eagle Ridge in Wisconsin where her grandfather had worked as fishing guide. She'd loved him like a father.

Now, perched on the dune, she remembered the words he'd whispered to her with a soft lisp as she'd sat by his deathbed. "Fly free, my bird. Gazaagin."

His message, delivered with great effort, came a few seconds before he'd drawn into himself and folded his wings. *Gazaagin genii nmishoomis. I love you, too, grandfather.* She'd wanted to respond. Instead, she choked up with grief. Spoke the words only in her head. There was no time to express her gratitude to him for taking her under his wing after her mother died. He'd sacrificed his own freedom for hers, staying at the fish camp, though Laura knew that her grandfather's hatred for her father ran as deep as the dark lake they'd fished together. Her own anger and resentment toward her father remained submerged there still.

Only a month had passed since his death. At first, without him, she'd been stuck. He alone, in the absence of her mother and sister, had been her guiding eagle—the one who supported her and encouraged her to explore her true heart. Somehow, after enduring her eighteenth birthday, she'd searched within herself and found a way to draw on her grandfather's quiet strength. Managed to finish high school. Then, against her father's wishes, she'd left for good. It helped that her grandfather had given her his car, or her father would never have let her go.

Earlier in the day, when she'd reached the turnoff point on the highway and saw the bald eagle circling, her mind had begun to turn. Sensing her grandfather's spirit, she'd followed the bird toward the lake to its nesting place high in the crux of an old oak. Found Sanctuary. Maybe here, she'd thought, possibly, she could figure out how to truly belong.

Now, at sea level far below, the sound of the waves slapping against the shore carried up the dunes. Her mind tricked her into hearing the flapping of wings. She wasn't superstitious but couldn't help feel a little overwhelmed by the natural forces at play. She slipped off her other moccasin and stood, watching the tall figure paddle on the water a moment more, until the soles of her feet burned in the sand. Without further hesitation, she leaped off the edge, not fearing the heights, and latched onto her lost moccasin with fingers like talons, before she flew as free as an eagle over the steep, sinking sands toward the lake.

When she reached the shoreline, she kept running straight into the water. Refreshed by the chill, she lifted up her long skirt and waded up to her knees. From here, she could get a closer look at whoever it was paddling out there beneath the blazing sun. With a lean build and a shock of red hair, he mimicked a mass of molten energy. Then, without warning, instead of continuing along the coast, he made a sharp turn as if he was paddling straight toward her. She backed up a few feet.

With the sun behind him, he approached like a moving shadow. She feared they were on a collision course and retreated onto shore where she waited, watching him, until they nearly could touch. Just then, in the shallow surf, he hopped off his board, caught it under one arm, and faced her. He stood there, water dripping from his board shorts onto his thighs. She watched it snake down his muscular calves, never having been so instantly attracted to someone or as embarrassed in the same moment. She couldn't think of what to say and hugged her arms around her waist. He ran his hand over the coarse whiskers on his chin. *Why didn't he just say something?*

Uncomfortable with the delay, she adjusted the bikini top she'd crocheted night by night beside the fire on her journey through the Upper Peninsula, stitching her way from campground to campground, until today, when she discovered this hidden pocket in the northwest corner of Michigan's lower half. His eyes fell to her chest, which made her nervous and secretly excited. She couldn't bear any more silence between them. "Pretty rough out there?" she asked.

He glanced up at her and, for the first time, their eyes met. After a second, he tilted his head toward the water. "Yeah, but you can catch a smooth ride if you wait for it." Then, as if she'd given off some signal, his attention turned to the drawstring skirt she'd lived in since leaving her father's fish camp a week earlier. "Got any bottoms on under there?"

"Excuse me?" Now, he was pushing it. She propped her hands on her hips. "I don't even know your name."

He wedged the end of his board in the white sand and held it out to one side. "Excuse me. I'm Rob." A smile cracked from the corner of his mouth.

Laura forced back a grin. "Rob—?"

"Sorry, Sanders. And you are—?"

"Laura. Laura Warner."

Rob moved behind his board. "Nice to meet you, Laura, Laura Warner. I was just asking if you were wearing a swimsuit because, I thought you might like to go for a ride."

She'd never seen such a big board, much less ridden one, though she did have good balance and knew how to paddle. "I'm pretty good in a canoe."

Whatever she'd just said had come out all wrong. Her cheeks felt hot; they were probably turning as red as his hair. He chuckled under his breath. "I'm not sure how that works, but I can show you how to do it on my board."

"Very funny." Laura shook her head, grateful for the long strands of hair that fell across her face to hide her blushing cheeks. She approached the paddle board he was displaying for her inspection. Ran her palm down its spine. It was solid. Though it had appeared smooth at first, the rough finish reminded her of the birch bark canoe she'd help sand down with her grandfather. She wondered, if he were here now, what would he have to say?

Rob, if she had to guess, was probably a couple years older than her. He poked his head around from the opposite side of the board. "So, how does it feel?" Out of the corner of his eye, he shot her a glance as piercing as the glacial-ice that carved out the lakebed tens of thousands of years ago.

She acted unimpressed. "About what I'd expect."

She took a step back, not entirely sure if she could trust him but not distrustful of him either. He tried to come off as all cool though, by the way he maneuvered through the water with such conviction, she suspected he had depth—the kind of guy she'd bond with if they ever got past the surface.

His hand brushed lightly against hers. "Want to give it a try?"

Goosebumps ran up her arm. She wanted to say *yes*, and find out all she could about him. Instead, she resisted the urge. She didn't want to send the wrong message. After all, they'd just met. Having worked at her father's fish camp with her big sister, Shenia, Laura had plenty of experience with men who took one thing to mean another and made unwanted advances, especially when they thought they could get away with it. She'd learned to trust her gut. Better to take it slow. "Maybe some other time." She pointed at the lighthouse and made up an excuse about having to go back to the beach and pay the meter.

"How about tomorrow?" he asked.

"We'll see."

A wave washed in, pooling around their feet, before Laura turned and waved good-bye.

PART I

Chapter 1

July 2, 2016

Rob leaned up against the breakwall and looked out toward the water where a red safety flag flapped in the wind. He just wanted to kickback for another minute and relax before going into work. Instead Laura came over from the picnic table and tugged him by the hand onto the beach. He'd grown up on this remote stretch of white sand, wedged between Lake Michigan and the dunes, though now he felt out of place among the tourists with his wife. He should never have let her talk him into staying here to watch the sunset after their son's birthday party. Nate had blown out all five candles a half-hour ago and, by now, was probably halfway home with his grandparents on the new scooter they'd given him.

Laura and he could watch the sunset any night, although they never did. Ahead of them, right in front of the red flag, a woman waded into the water as blue as the streaks in her dark hair. When she took a step deeper, the bottom of her cover-up floated around her waist like a fishnet. The waves, rolling in one after the other, knocked her back. Didn't she realize it was too dangerous to swim? He kept an eye on her, just in case, as he and Laura continued on together down the beach. Then a band of light broke through the cloud bank on the horizon.

They stopped to watch for a minute when the sun descended into view and hovered like a fireball branding its image onto the Great Lake. Behind them, a group of rowdy tourists cheered at the sight. Laura, apparently caught up in the excitement on shore, squeezed his hand. "Isn't it beautiful?"

He winced from the electrifying pain that spread into his fingers—remembering then the heated exchange with his landlord when he'd lost his cool and slammed his fists on the bar. "Yeah, sure." He wanted to share her enthusiasm, but he really needed to get back to work. Rob pulled away from her and shook out his hand. Couldn't she get it? This was peak cottage season. On top of that, all the tourists were in town for the holiday. At the end of next month, once the summer people returned to their real lives in Detroit and Chicagoland, Sanctuary would again become a ghost town until Memorial Day. This was their time to cash in.

Her failure to understand his predicament was partly his fault, he knew. He should already have told her about his landlord's ultimatum from that morning: "Robert, my friend, you're gonna have to make some big changes around here, or there won't be another July Fourth at Sanders." He wanted to punch him in the mouth. Instead he just stood there behind the bar, nodding as if he agreed, until the cocky bastard was out the door. Then he slammed his fists down, so hard that his wedding ring dented the soft cherry wood.

Rob noticed his knuckles on both sides were a little swollen, though the damage he'd done to his own property pained him more than the injury. He and his dad had refurbished that bar by hand. Once again, he found his eyes drifting back to the woman in the water. She didn't look like she was from here. Yet there was something vaguely familiar about the way she ran her fingertips across the surface. He paused for a second with his feet in the water, wondering if she would be okay, but then he and Laura kept walking. He had enough problems without looking for any.

Far offshore, in the Manitou Passage, a lone paddle boarder thrust his oar into the sun's reflection. Rob immediately recognized his old friend's short, quick strokes. Andre. The last time they'd spoken was four years ago when, after thirty months in prison, Andre was released. Rob still couldn't believe Andre had been convicted of involuntary manslaughter when everyone in town knew Sandra's death was a terrible accident. Andre and Sandra were close, as close as any big brother and little sister in the same high school could possibly be. That's what the jury must have misunderstood. He'd never meant to kill her. Isn't that all that should matter?

Rob lengthened his stride to prevent himself from sinking into the wet sand as Andre propelled himself with the prevailing current like a demon on the water. He was the last person Rob expected to see on the lake that mid-summer night. Why would he ever come back to Sanctuary?

The gulls circled around and started squawking. Rob squeezed his eyes shut. There was so little from the snow day he remembered. *He'd fought so hard to forget.* After all this time, he knew only one thing for certain: If it weren't for the snow day, Sandra would still be alive. In his head, which had begun throbbing, he replayed the recorded message on his parents' home answering machine from eight years ago. "This is a notice from your school. Due to inclement weather, Sanctuary High will be closed today: January 13, 2008. Thank you. Stay safe."

If only he and Andre had listened back then. Before the accident, they'd been like brothers. A wave crashed onto the beach, splashing ice-cold water on Rob's shorts. The undertow washed the ground away from beneath his feet. "Hey, you.

Doing all right there?" Laura smiled at him with teasing eyes as if they were once again young lovers preparing to watch the sunset for the first time. "I thought we could stop here." She pointed toward a secluded spot in the dune grass.

Rob averted his eyes from hers. *Oh, Lord.* How he wished he could be in love with her again in the carefree way they once were early on in their marriage, when he was still paddle boarding competitively, before they became the parents of three kids and took on debt from the bar, long before he couldn't pay the bills and they were evicted from their apartment. He stepped over a dead fish the gulls were pecking at. The thought of all five of them stuck in the attic living with his parents made him sick. How could he have let it happen? He'd never imagined being washed up at twenty-six. And, from now on, it looked like he'd have Andre getting in his face. Even at this moment, it almost felt as if Andre was tracking him.

Rob felt something sharp prick his foot. Then the lake turned warm. Laura's eyes widened as she peered into the water. "Rob, are you okay?" When he looked down, he saw the blood pooled around him. The ball of his foot began to sting. Laura cradled his elbow and helped him cross over the stones onto shore. He hobbled a few yards further toward dry sand and sat down. He glanced at his gaping wound. The sight of his own blood turned his stomach.

"Let me see." Laura gently examined the jagged cut in his sole. "Looks pretty nasty, but hard to tell how deep. You should give it a few minutes. Stay there."

As she went to spread the blanket, he sat there watching the sunset like a tourist—trying not to think about his bloody foot, which slightly throbbed. Out on the water, directly ahead, Andre turned around his board. Now he'd have to paddle in the opposite direction against the current. *Good luck with that.*

It would be a long trip back to the lighthouse for everyone. Though, at this rate, Andre would probably make it back to town before them. That bum should never have returned to Sanctuary.

Everything was different then—and now. Rob was a husband and father not some reckless teenager. Unlike Andre, he had responsibilities and didn't have the time to waste messing around on a paddle board. These days, he was lucky to put his feet in the water with the kids. Running into Andre, unexpectedly, like this, had churned up powerful memories that Rob wasn't sure he could keep a lid on. It would only be a matter of time before Andre would try using the past against him for his own gain. But Rob knew better now. He wouldn't get taken. He wouldn't play along with his manipulative games. No matter how Andre tried to provoke him, he wouldn't react. He couldn't afford to. His family needed him to stay strong. Rob made himself a promise: This time, he would take charge.

From a short distance behind, Rob heard Laura's footsteps coming his way. At least she hadn't recognized that it was Andre out there. Rob couldn't take being badgered right now. Instead, she bent down and kissed his cheek. "We're all set. Come on, I'll help you over there. It's not far." She offered him a hand up.

"It's fine, I got it." Though it hurt his knuckles, Rob pushed himself up onto his good foot. It was a lot easier than trying to explain how he'd screwed up his hands and, pretty much, everything else at the bar. He didn't need her getting sore with him too. She wrapped her arm around his waist and guided him onto the blanket. He shifted over beside her to get more comfortable.

She held up a gray stone in the sunlight until the mottled pattern of six-sided fossils appeared. "Look, I found the perfect one for you." She pressed the Petoskey stone, fresh out of the bottom of lake, into his palm. "Do you remember what you told me?"

He turned it over a few times, recalling the evening they'd shared six years ago on this same stretch of beach soon after they met. "Of course." He'd given her a similar stone before explaining that legend says they carry *sunbeams of promise*. That's what he'd given her when he'd been vulnerable and willing to share his emotions. Now he didn't say another word. Part of him wanted to throw the stone she'd given him back in the water. Instead, he just sat there and let her rest her head on his shoulder. For the moment, as the sun slowly melted into its own image, he tried only to think about her. Once, she'd been everything to him. Laura and the kids needed him. That's what he needed to remember. If he wanted them to have a future, he needed to move on and forget about the past.

Ahead, at the shoreline, Laura's friend Chelsea jogged past with her husband, Brett. Chelsea waved at Laura, who sat up and gave her the peace sign. Rob nodded at Brett, who always seemed to have the time and energy to exercise, plus the money to afford a membership at the new health club on Main Street where Patty had started working as a personal trainer. Rob had been so shocked to see her there, when he'd walked by earlier this week, he'd needed a double take. She looked toned, arguably even hotter than she was in high school when they were a thing. Brett had said that she now went by Patricia. Patty or Patricia, regardless, Rob wasn't sure if he could forgive her for ratting on him and Andre to the police. He still didn't trust her.

Lowering on the horizon, the sun beamed straight into his eyes and left him seeing spots. Laura nudged him in the side. "It's so beautiful here. Do you ever feel like you're not living up to it?"

At first, her question made him laugh. "Living up to what?"

"Shouldn't we be living a beautiful life?"

When he considered this, his stomach turned as it had when he'd stepped over the dead fish. He tried to ignore the sour aftertaste of the hot dogs they'd grilled for dinner at Nate's party. "People come here when the beauty of the landscape matches the way they feel. They see what they want to see. It's impossible to live like that all the time. Lake Michigan has good days and bad days. Most people don't stay long enough to realize that it can turn on you."

A whitecap crested at the sandbar in front of them. He hugged his knees into his chest. Not being from Sanctuary or growing up on one of the Great Lakes, Laura couldn't judge for herself. She hadn't seen the dire consequences like he and Andre had in high school when they guarded this this beach. In the variable currents, swimmers were often carried under. Drowning wasn't uncommon. Neither was death from hypothermia. The steep dunes held their own dangers. He'd lost count of the number of times rescue crews were dispatched to assist out-of-shape tourists who climbed down only to discover they didn't have the stamina to make it back up, or, worse yet, had a heart-attack along the way.

His thoughts returned to the foreign-looking woman he'd seen wading into the water. She'd seemed so defiant. Or, then again, had he sensed her desperation? Part of him regretted not sticking around to see if she was okay. Then again, everyone had their own free will. There was nothing he could do to change that.

Rob stood from the blanket. He knew Laura hadn't meant to upset him, but he couldn't sit around waiting anymore. Even though his foot still hurt. "We can watch the sunset on our way back."

Just then a flock of gulls soared toward them. "Aren't they beautiful?" Laura asked.

Rob shielded his eyes with his hand. "Yeah, unless they shit on you." He checked his watch. "You know I've got to work."

When she reached for his hand, urging him to stay together a little longer, he pushed it aside and began limping away toward the parking lot.

Chapter 2

July 3, 2016

One by one, Laura traced the letters of the tattoo inscribed between her sleeping husband's shoulder blades. PERSEVERE. After more than five years of marriage, she knew the contours of each letter needled into his flesh, though the underlying significance of the word remained a mystery to her.

"That was before your time," he'd always say when she asked him about the tattoo he got when he was seventeen, before she came to Sanctuary. "You saved me." From what, she'd always wondered.

Now, as sunlight spread through the attic, his body heat radiated through her fingertips, momentarily reawakening the nerve endings that had progressively gone numb since they'd moved in with his parents. Their relationship had changed so much in the handful of years since they'd had kids, she almost couldn't remember how it felt when they were falling in love. Lately, she'd started to feel more like a burden. She didn't think things could get any worse. Then last night, after Rob went to work, Chelsea had texted her. *OMG. Andre is back. He and Patricia got engaged.*

Laura wondered if Rob knew. As soon as he woke up, she'd have to ask him. Andre had spent some time in prison, she'd heard, for accidentally killing his little sister. Over the years, she'd learned to be careful when she spoke to Rob of his friendship with Andre. But now that Andre was back in town, Laura wouldn't be put off with excuses. *That was before your time* was no longer cutting it.

She didn't like the idea of Rob's ex- hanging around town either, even if Patricia was getting married. Laura scooted over his way, wishing she could postpone the real world and stay in bed with him. She missed holding hands and spooning, never mind the lovemaking that happened naturally and often early on in their marriage. Instead they were cooped up in the attic with the kids. Other than sneaking in an occasional quickie every couple weeks when nobody else was around, their physical contact had dwindled. Something had to give. She wrapped her arm around his waist and flattened her whole body against him, stretching herself until her toes spread against his soles. Then, she brushed up against the scrape from the previous night.

Rob moved further onto his side of the bed. She rolled out the other way feeling rejected and questioning why she'd even bothered trying to be intimate with him. More and more often, he seemed like he'd rather be left alone. Laura worried, could she and Rob persevere like his tattoo?

They really needed to talk, but there never seemed to be any time for that either. He'd worked until after closing and wouldn't be up for another couple of hours. It was almost eight. She must get baking. Since opening the stand last summer to make some extra cash, she'd developed a group of regular customers who had come to depend on her. Today, for the parade, she'd need to bake a double batch of scones. She was counting on making fifty dollars. The baby, Biyen, was down to his last diaper. Ella, covered in freckles like her father, would fry without more sunscreen. Nate was always begging for Superman ice cream.

From across the room, she peeked through the slats of Biyen's crib. It looked like he was still asleep. Right now, she didn't dare wake him. He hadn't nursed since before bed. Once he woke up, her little chick would be peckish. She stepped softly toward the rocking chair beside him and slipped on her old tie-dyed skirt. Stretched and faded after seven years, it had long outlived its natural lifespan but was still her go-to.

She cinched the drawstrings around her waist and glanced out the front window overlooking Main Street. There were no cars, other than the tourists' SUVs lined up on both sides along with the rusted-out delivery van her father-in-law parked at the end of the driveway. A relic now, the yellow Ford Econoline they referred to as the Mystery Machine dated back to the seventies when Sanctuary was a quiet summer hideaway and Rob's dad, Art, had opened his gallery.

A few empty chairs were arranged along the sidewalk. No one had yet ventured outdoors, apart from the frail neighbor across the street who lived alone and doted on her hostas as if they were grandkids. Today, in her housecoat and orthopedic pumps, she stepped gingerly between her little dears, watering them one by one with the garden hose. Afterward, she turned on the oscillating sprinkler for the patch of front lawn.

In an hour or so, the sidewalks would overflow with people lined up for the July Fourth parade, which was always held on the third in Sanctuary. Back in Eagle Ridge, when she was growing up, celebrating Independence Day on any day other than the fourth would have been considered an act of treason. But in this village, which depended on tourism dollars, attitudes were always shifting like the sand. If extending the holiday brought in more visitors or lengthened stays, so be it. That seemed to be the mayor's philosophy.

Laura looked down at her empty stand in the front yard next to the sidewalk. She'd better get to work. Tiptoeing away from the window, she passed the crib and circled around Rob until she reached Ella asleep beyond the door. With her small hands pressed against her cheek, she looked as if she were praying. Laura studied her daughter's serene expression a second more, remembering three years earlier, when Ella was the one in a crib, and they all were living in the apartment. Back then, she and Rob would watch in awe over their little angel. They were all on different schedules now. She'd almost reached the attic doorway when, abruptly, she stopped. Nate's bed, at the far end of the room, was empty.

Laura tossed the pile of sheets. Why was he up already when he'd stayed up past his bedtime after his party? He never went downstairs without waking her first. She ran down the staircase and didn't bother checking the house. Her heart racing, she passed through the hall into the kitchen and went out the side door onto the wraparound porch, which was damp with dew.

Nate's scooter was gone from the place it had stood, propped up against the side of the house. She hurried to the front of the porch for a better view of the sidewalk and looked both ways. There was no trace of Nate, though Rob's mother, Helen, was seated cross-legged in the wicker loveseat with the newspaper on her lap. Laura's heart-rate steadied somewhat with the knowledge that her mother-in-law was supervising him, though usually they would have agreed on it in advance. "Good morning, Laura."

Laura hunched over beside her, next to the tippy side table where Helen had set her morning coffee. "Where's Nate?"

Helen met her eye for a second, then tucked a loose strand of her silver waves neatly behind her right ear as if seated behind her desk at the historical museum contemplating plans for a new exhibit. "Listen."

Laura wanted an answer, not some riddle. But Helen hadn't given her much of a choice. Laura shut her eyes and focused on using her own ears, though apart from the neighbor's sprinkler pattering on the sidewalk, her own heavy breathing was all she heard. She held her breath until, after a few seconds, she detected a faint clatter and pop on the sidewalk. It sounded like Nate was making his way over the cracks and only a block or two away. Still, she wished Helen would actually watch him—with her eyes.

Laura opened hers. She strained to see down the street where the sound was coming from but her view was blocked by the bushy spruce that took up half the front yard. She didn't like the idea of him disappearing on his own. He wasn't even wearing a helmet. Laura knew Rob's mother meant well, but she wasn't sure if Nate was responsible enough for a scooter. Nate loved to go fast. Even on foot when they hiked in the forest, Nate was the kid who couldn't stay on the path. Instead he'd hurdle the wildflowers, his eyes always on the lookout for the next thing to explore.

Helen should have asked her and Rob before choosing this gift, though she reminded herself, they were in no position to complain. They couldn't afford any expensive presents themselves. They should be grateful to Rob's parents, even if Helen and Art weren't always all on the same page as them.

"He came down and got me out of bed a half-hour ago. He was so excited about the scooter." Suddenly, Helen rolled up the newspaper. "I'll let you take over my shift. I need another cup of coffee."

Helen raised her mug off the table and began to push herself up from the chair. Laura wished she could strap her down. She had to find Nate and make four-dozen scones before Biyen woke. She looked to her left, closer to the beach, where the chairs were lined up on the sidewalk. A handful of touristy types with their Tom's slip-ons and preppy red, white, and blue attire were window shopping. The parade would start in two hours. She didn't like asking her in-laws for favors, but she'd spent her last ten dollars on ingredients and couldn't afford to lose any sales. "Would you mind watching him another few minutes? Just so I can get the scones in the oven?"

Helen frowned and pursed her lips with indecision, as if she were trying to avoid the booby prize. She stared into her empty coffee mug. "All right, then." She sat back down and handed over the mug.

Laura couldn't stand by another second. "I'll bring you a refill!"

Once in the kitchen, she gently tipped the carton of wild blueberries over the edge of the bowl and poured half of them into the chilled batter she'd made yesterday along with Nate's birthday cake. As soon as she began folding them in, Helen appeared. "Isn't my coffee ready?"

"I'm sorry, the coffee maker shut off. I nuked your mug. I was just about to bring it." Laura tilted her head over her shoulder toward the microwave. "Where's Nate?"

Helen reached for the coffee. "In the driveway. I told him to ride his scooter there where you could see him."

Why had Helen let him ride in the driveway? Laura thought they'd agreed that he'd come inside once he returned. Sometimes it seemed as if her mother-in-law was working against her. When Rob proposed, he assured her that he wasn't asking her to marry him out of a sense of duty. Laura believed him, though she suspected Helen still resented her for getting pregnant.

She sidestepped to the window over the sink that faced the driveway. "Where?" Laura glanced behind her, expecting to see Helen, but she'd already left with the coffee.

Laura craned her neck until she saw the end of the driveway where Nate had pulled the scooter onto the sidewalk. Didn't Helen just say she'd told him to stay in the driveway? Laura dropped her metal spoon and knocked over the carton of blueberries onto the floor around her bare feet. On her tiptoes, she ran out the kitchen door onto the porch. Nate was waiting behind Art's parked van. With the intensity of a motocross racer, her son gripped the handlebars and pretended to rev his red Razor. She rushed down the steps onto the driveway. "Nate!"

Helplessly, she yanked on her side braid as if that would make him stop. He must not have heard her yell for him— or, more likely, he'd chosen not to listen. All of a sudden, he pushed off with his left leg straight into the road. She ran after him knowing, already, it was too late. Before putting him to bed the night before, she'd said, "Nate, now you have to remember. Are you going to cross the street without a grownup?"

"No."

"Not ever?"

"No, Momma," Nate had sworn.

By the time she reached the curb, Nate had made it across to the other side of the street and was riding through the puddles from the neighbor's sprinkler acting as if nothing out of the ordinary had happened. Laura wanted to scream. *Come back here. If you're not old enough to follow the rules, you're not old enough to ride a scooter!*

Behind her, in the kitchen, the oven-timer dinged. This time, he'd really set her off. She had better things to do than chase him around all day. The scones were ready to go in the oven. But she needed to bring him home for a timeout. From a block away, his friend Jacob, Chelsea's son, was waving from the driveway for Nate to come over. Chelsea, dressed in a crisp white dress, was lining both sides with patriotic pinwheels. She was always one step ahead and not only managed to stay on top of the children's activities but found time to decorate for every holiday. Nate was almost there. Once Chelsea noticed him, she looked down across the street at her. Laura stood there waving until she remembered the stained shirt she was wearing. She crossed her arms over her chest. Chelsea gave her a thumb's up. Laura nodded back casually like she had everything under control. As usual, compared to Chelsea, she felt inept—literally, a block behind.

Jacob handed Nate a pinwheel with stars and stripes on it. Nate watched it whip around in the lake breeze; he always seemed happiest when he was at Chelsea's house. That bothered her. She wanted their home to be a happy one. A place where each of them could be themselves and relax. Yet, as long as they were living at Rob's parents' house, they were just pretending, trying to conform with Helen's and Art's expectations of how everyone should behave. After this morning's mishap, Laura wasn't sure how much longer she could stay in her lane without getting disqualified by Helen. It was totally stressing her out. For everyone's sake, and the sake of their marriage, she and Rob needed to find their own place as soon as possible.

Lost in thought, Laura had almost forgotten about the scones. Nate was okay. That's all that mattered right now. There was no need to make a scene in front of Jacob and Chelsea. She could go home, put the scones in, quickly change her shirt, and come back for Nate after.

Laura passed her empty stand. By the time she reached the kitchen, it was eight-fifteen. The oven timer had stopped dinging, but the blueberries she'd spilled were scattered all over the floor. She grabbed the broom and dustpan and began to sweep, imagining how irritated Helen would get if she saw her kitchen in such a state. Then again, Laura wondered, had Helen's life never gotten messy.

Hopefully none of the customers would notice the scones were missing half the usual amount of fruit. She hated to disappoint anyone. Laura spooned the lumpy batter onto the baking sheets, popped the trays in the oven, and set the timer for twenty minutes. She rushed upstairs for a clean shirt. At the top of the steps, Rob's snoring rushed into the hallway like a rogue wave. By the uneven sound of it she suspected he must have been drinking, though she hadn't remembered smelling alcohol on his breath earlier. She approached their bed, trying her best to avoid waking him as she put on a bra and changed her shirt. He was as cranky as the kids if he didn't get enough sleep.

Lately, he'd grown so testy, there was no telling what would set him off, like the previous night when they were sitting at the beach. One minute he was talking about Lake Michigan and by the next he'd lost his shit. Why had he gotten so angry with her? By the time she'd finished gathering the blanket, he was halfway to the van. He wouldn't even talk to her on the way home. It had taken her by surprise, especially since they'd gotten along so well earlier in the evening at Nate's party. He'd never treated her so coldly before.

Across the room, Biyen cried out. She put her finger over her lips. "Sssh." Laura scooped him up from the crib, instantly soothed by her little chick with the squinty eyes and smushy cheeks of her Ojibwa grandfather who, though a tribal elder, was simply known as Peter. She'd chosen Biyen, an Ojibwa version of the name Peter, to honor her grandfather's legacy and recognize his quiet strength. She would always miss him.

Laura carried Biyen out of the attic. As soon as she shut the door, he nuzzled into her breast. She felt an urgent pang and hurried downstairs. There was nothing she could do now other than feed him. She doubted Chelsea would mind if the boys played a few more minutes, though Laura didn't want to take advantage of her willingness to help. She should probably send her a text. Then she remembered that she'd left her cell phone by the bed. She'd have to get it afterward. She went onto the porch and wedged herself in Helen's loveseat. Hidden behind the monster branches of the spruce, she could feed the baby in privacy and still keep an eye—and ear—out for Nate, just in case.

As soon as she lifted her shirt, Biyen latched on. "That's my boy." She caressed his smooth scalp, flecked with wisps of dark hair, and tried to relax in spite of the clouds that were converging. Soon the sky grew overcast. It couldn't rain. Just then the timer dinged. "Finish up." She hated having to cut him off; he was such a good baby. Nate, who'd always been strong-willed, would have made a fuss if she'd rushed him. Was there no one around here who could lend a hand? Then she realized that Helen must have taken her coffee and gone back into bed with Art. They were both probably reading the newspaper. Laura had almost forgotten how it would feel to lie in bed and read.

She hurried to the kitchen, slipping on a hot pad before removing the scones from the oven with Biyen on her hip. The aromas of baked blueberries, buttery cinnamon dough, and a hint of lemon zest, intermingled. He whimpered. She pulled out the trays and set them on the counter to cool. His saliva dripped down her arm. After a couple minutes, his whimpers switched into a steady whine. He must still not be full, though his diaper definitely was. She wished she didn't always have to wait to change him until his diaper resembled an overfilled water balloon. But that was a luxury they couldn't afford. Even generics came to fifty cents apiece. She went to the cabinet in the bathroom and whipped out the last one from underneath the sink. Laura knelt over him on the dingy mat covering the linoleum and quickly fastened the plastic tabs around his belly. She prayed he wouldn't poop until she made some money and could go to the store for a new pack. A car's horn blared from down the street.

She took the baby carrier off the towel hook on the door and made her way toward the living room. She'd already strapped the carrier onto her chest when Rob shuffled in wearing a wrinkled pair of cargo shorts and a frown.

"Your phone is blowing up. How am I supposed to sleep?"

Chelsea was probably trying to reach her. "Sorry. I meant to bring it down."

She wondered why Rob wouldn't have thought to bring it with him but didn't say anything, or she knew they'd argue. Instead she opened the sling. "Hey, could you slide Biyen in here? I'm late putting the scones out, and I have to get Nate from Jacob's house."

Rob arched his back and stretched his arms over his head. Laura came a step closer. Without a word, he took the baby off her hip and faced him outward in the carrier.

"When did you get home last night?" she asked.

"Worked until one."

"Did you go out after?"

"Sort of. Andre and Patricia came in to hang out after I closed. We did a few shots for old times' sake."

"Seriously?"

"Why does it matter? You were asleep."

Rob had never stayed after work before. Given the family finances, he was in no position to give away free drinks. True friends would know better. "Rob, we really need to talk—"

"Jesus, Laura, before a smoke?"

"I didn't mean now—just sometime. Soon." Laura tightened the straps around Biyen. Rob explained he was going back into work. Since when did he work the day shift? "I need tip money, if you've got any left. Biyen is out of diapers."

Rob ran his palm over the patchy stubble that had sprouted up along his jawline overnight and already looked half-dead like the native vegetation tourists stomped on without realizing it. "Let me get a shirt on and I'll go with you. I'm all out of cigs."

She would never understand his facial hair or his logic. Now they were both going to the store? She wished he could handle it on his own, so she could focus on other things. "I have to put out the scones before I go."

"Just do it when you get back." Rob left for the attic.

Laura left for the kitchen and grabbed the trays off the counter. It's not like she needed his permission. He'd been up less than five minutes and already seemed pissy. Now she was too. "Bring my phone down." She called after him before walking out. Behind her, the screen door slammed shut. The basket lined with aubergine-colored napkins awaited. She loved the way the purple hue accentuated the blueberries swirled into the scones. Laura lifted the tongs from the shelf under the stand. One by one she placed the tasty morsels into the basket. When they were all tucked in, she folded the cloth napkin over the top as if she were swaddling a baby. There, there.

She set out the covered coffee tin for payment next to the basket. Though Sanctuary was a tourist destination, and some of her customers were people she didn't know, so far, she'd never had a problem with the honor system. From behind, Rob wrapped his arm around her waist and pressed himself against her backside. "Let's bounce." He squeezed the muffin-top she hadn't been able to lose since she'd *popped out* their third child, as he liked to say.

"Why do you always have to remind me?"

"Come on, I was just teasing. You know it turns me on."

She couldn't think of a bigger turnoff and was in no mood to kid around. Laura loosened the drawstrings on her skirt. Everything had been so easy in the beginning, when it was all about sex. Before she'd had one, two, three, babies each in July.

As they walked toward the sidewalk, Rob passed her the phone. "You should keep this with you. It looks like Chelsea called and texted."

Laura flipped over her phone and read the message on the screen. *Come here now.*

"Did you see this?" she asked Rob.

He looked at her askance. Laura's chest tightened. Just then her phone rang. Chelsea.

"Oh my god, Laura, something awful has happened."

Chapter 3

July 3, 2016

Laura paused and clutched the phone to her ear. "What—"

Chelsea choked up. "Nate's been hit … an ambulance is coming."

For a second, the whole world came to a stop. Laura couldn't speak.

"What's wrong?" Rob asked.

"Nate's been hit. By a car, I guess." Tears washed out her vision. She shook her head at him and pointed across the street toward Chelsea's house. He took off running down the center of Main Street where a black car had spun sideways. She followed him, Biyen weighing on her like a brick. It seemed like everyone was moving in slow motion—except Rob. In a matter of seconds, he'd reached the car in front of Chelsea's driveway, the pinwheels twirling frantic in the wind which carried the odor of burning fuel. A crowd had gathered on the sidewalk. Everyone was looking at her. Where was her boy? In the gutter lay the handlebars of Nate's scooter. In the street in front of her lay its rear wheels. Laura forced herself to step over them, unable to hear or feel anything. Her lungs emptied of air. Her body went numb. She watched Rob dart around to the back of the car. She zigzagged after him as Biyen, jostled in the carrier, cried out. Her whole body tightened up when she came to the black Mercedes that blocked both lanes. She swallowed hard, trying to contain herself, not wanting to imagine what might have happened to their son. *Please let him be all right. Please. Please.* But from the knot in her stomach, Laura knew Nate was in trouble. Serious trouble.

Her mind went blank as she came around the driver's side after Rob. With two hands, she braced Biyen against her chest in the carrier as if for protection. *God, please let Nate be okay.* Just then she looked down. A few strands of Nate's hair poked out from behind the car. Suddenly, she remembered. *He wasn't wearing a helmet.* Laura, realizing the possible ramifications, drew back for a second. Was he still alive? She wanted to scream, but no sound would come.

Rob dropped onto all fours and crawled under the car frame. Without delay he gave a tug and pulled Nate's limp body out by his armpits. He brought him onto his lap. The lower half of Nate's left leg was covered in blood. Laura fell to the ground and moved around to face her son. Apart from the grease marks, his face was pale. She pressed her hands to his cheeks. He was unresponsive and growing cold. Where was an ambulance? She looked around but saw only blurred faces in the crowd. She slumped over her son's small body and squeezed her eyes shut. "My baby." She heaved. "No. No. No."

She pushed herself up and craned her neck. "My God, help him. Somebody help him." She started to hyperventilate with Biyen, rocking in spasms, on her chest. "Please, somebody. Our boy is dying."

Just then a drop of water landed on her forehead. It wasn't from the sprinkler. A few seconds later, the sky opened. The crowd scattered as people ran for cover around them. She watched them leave. Helpless, she looked to Rob, hoping he'd know what to do, but he just sat there trembling.

Rain spattered on the pavement. A streak of Nate's blood ran across the blacktop. She sat there. Staring. Frozen. Unresponsive to her baby's cries. The rain poured down. Nate's blood washed into the drain. She felt sick. An ambulance siren sounded. Someone was coming. She had to reel herself in. *Don't give up.* But Nate still wasn't breathing. She must do something. "Nate, this is Momma." She gripped his arms, which were getting colder. "You've got to stay with me. You've got to fight." She leaned forward, wrapped her arms around his shoulders, and rubbed vigorously as if she was drying him off after a bath. She just had to keep him warm for a minute more. "Rob, come on, help me."

He hunched over Nate's body and blocked the rain. Laura spoke as if Nate could hear her. "Stay with us, baby. Only a few more seconds. The doctors are coming. You're going to be all right."

A female EMT approached her from behind. "Please, miss. Let us take over now."

Rob pressed his lips to Nate's forehead before he inched back and lowered their son's small head and shoulders onto the street. Laura leaned over him, the rain pounding on her back, and cradled his slack jaw in her hands. Everything seemed to stop. What had she done? Laura bent over and kissed his cold lips.

The EMT placed a hand on her shoulder and drew her away from her son. Laura latched tighter to the boy in her arms. She should never have measured them up against each other earlier on the porch. They would both always be her babies. How could she take one and leave the other?

When the EMT checked Nate for a pulse, her body stiffened. "Hurry!" A few seconds later, the EMT's male partners swooped in, set a stretcher beside Nate, and started chest compressions. Laura leaned up against Rob, gripping onto his arm as the men tried to resuscitate their son. After a couple minutes, they gave up and instead put a collar around his neck and covered the rest of his body with a blanket. All three put her son on the stretcher and then carried him toward the ambulance. A high-tech gurney was positioned behind the rear doors, which were already open. Laura, with Rob on her heels, followed close behind the woman who'd first responded. Once Nate was moved to the gurney, she tapped the woman on the shoulder. "Can we ride in the back with him?"

"There's only room for one of you." Rob nodded definitively for her to go. Laura unstrapped Biyen from her chest. The ambulance doors shut. "We've got to move."

Laura handed Biyen off to Rob. "I'll meet you in the ER," he said.

She followed the EMT around the side of the ambulance. Once Laura stepped in, the woman came in behind her. The ambulance siren sounded and they were moving. The trip to Harbor City usually took about twenty minutes, but Laura suspected it would be significantly quicker. Beside her, Nate rested under the blanket with an oxygen mask over his face. As the EMT checked him for a pulse, Laura smoothed his damp hair with the palm of her hand and recalled how he'd sped down the sidewalk on his scooter so fast that his curls were straightened by the wind. If only he'd listened and hadn't crossed the road. If only she'd trusted her instincts and brought him home for a timeout. Ever since he'd been able to walk, it seemed, all she did was run after him. She'd known he needed more discipline for his own safety. Her scolding and timeouts only went so far. Yet Rob never backed her up. When she'd explained that riding a scooter was a big responsibility—instead of showing Nate that the Mom and Dad team was tight—Rob had told her to relax right in front of their son. Couldn't he see how it weakened her position in their son's eyes? Then again, she'd assumed there would be endless opportunities for them to teach him.

Now it was left up to the doctors to save him. The ambulance flashed across the countryside up and down the two-lane highway, forcing her to hold on, yet Nate didn't move. His face was covered with an oxygen mask, so she couldn't tell anything for sure, yet he still didn't appear to be breathing.

It was almost impossible for her to comprehend, but Laura feared that her son was dying right in front of her. She began counting to five with her fingers and thumb for the EMT. "One hand. That's all he is. He deserves a second chance. You've got to make him live. Please."

The woman reached across the stretcher and gave her hand a firm squeeze. "I promise you. I'm doing everything I can."

The EMT kept checking him. Laura felt cold and empty. This was all her fault. She needed Rob. There must be something more they could do. When the ambulance finally pulled into the hospital, it jerked to a stop at the emergency entrance. Just then the EMT, who had hovered over Nate the entire trip, sat upright. "I got a pulse."

Pacing back and forth in the emergency waiting room, Laura remembered the EMT's pledge. Nate arrived at Harbor City Hospital with a pulse, which had given her hope that he would soon regain consciousness, but that was more than two hours ago. Since then, no one from the hospital had told her or Rob a thing, except that their son was in surgery. What was going on? She needed some answers from the doctors, though she still had questions about how the accident happened in the first place.

As far as she knew, Chelsea was the only one who'd seen it. During the brief words they'd exchanged after Nate was wheeled away behind closed doors, Chelsea tried to explain. Nate and Jacob were standing in the driveway when Nate suddenly took off on his scooter and didn't look before starting to cross the road. When Chelsea saw the Mercedes coming toward him, she screamed: "Stop!" But the driver was going too fast. That's all Chelsea had said on the phone, other than sorry. She'd been an apologetic disaster.

Laura tried not to picture what might have happened next. She continued to pace outside the doors that led to the operating rooms. She should have made Nate come home after he'd crossed the street without permission. So what if the scones would have been ruined? Who cared about fifty bucks anyway? What the hell was wrong with her? She almost couldn't bear waiting here, wondering about the unthinkable.

When the ER doors opened, Laura approached the doctor coming toward her, but he walked past her without any acknowledgement. She turned around and looked to Rob for backup, but he was seated with his mother by the window staring out at the harbor. She couldn't look at her. Helen never should have bought that scooter. Nate shouldn't have been allowed to ride it without a helmet. If only they could have talked things through.

Rob texted someone. Laura knew there were people she should text. Or call. But she could not make herself. She'd even avoided checking in with Art to learn how her other two kids were doing. He'd never watched them on his own before. Ella would be worried about her big brother. But what would Laura say to her? She felt paralyzed. She couldn't think about anything or anyone except Nate. He was her big boy. Five years old. The one his little sister had chased after up the dunes and his baby brother worshiped with his eyes from the safety of her hip during the birthday party the previous night at the beach. It all seemed long ago, almost as if it never happened. Now, she was stuck here. Not being able to see him. Not being able to touch him. Not being able to relieve his suffering in any way.

These feelings reminded her of how helpless she felt visiting the hospital before her mother—a small, tan figure against harsh white sheets—passed away. Lois. Her beautiful mother. It had been ten years. At the time, she never imagined anything could be worse. There had been nothing she could do to save her from the cancer that had spread throughout her abdomen when she was only thirty-seven. Laura gnawed at her thumbnail. There had to be something she could do for her son. She needed to see him, even if he couldn't hear her.

Laura approached the nurse's station. She swallowed hard, trying to channel the calm, assertive spirit of her grandfather. Almost no one ever said no to him. "I need to see my son, please." She kept her shoulders back.

The nurse looked up from the paperwork on her desk, but didn't speak. Laura placed her palms on the ledge. "The EMT said she found a pulse on our way here. Has something gone wrong?"

The nurse winced and picked up her phone. "Let me see if I can get the doctor."

Laura waved Rob over to join her, as if his mere presence would help to improve their odds. Before he could reach the station, the nurse set down the receiver. "Dr. Azzi will be out to see you soon."

"Soon?"

Rob stepped up beside her and slid his hand into hers. Tears seared the corners of her eyes, and she reached for a tissue box. "We've been waiting more than two hours." She dabbed at her face with the tissue. "We need to see our son, now."

"Please, give us a moment. They're finishing up in the operating room." Rob squeezed her hand. "The doctor will be right out to talk to you."

Rob pulled her to the side of the nurse's station, but Laura couldn't stay there and wait. She began to pace outside the doors. A few minutes later, when the secured doors opened, a stocky man came forward wearing blue scrubs and a mask over his nose and mouth. He pulled the mask under his chin. "Mom? Dad?"

After they both nodded, he reached out to shake Rob's hand and then hers. "I'm Dr. Azzi, head of the ER, sorry for keeping you waiting. I understand you must be anxious. We're doing everything we can."

At the sound of that phrase, Laura's stomach dropped, yet her attention remained fixed on the doctor.

"Your son has suffered significant trauma. It's taken this much time to assess the extent of his injuries," he said. "All we know for certain is that he has a head injury, along with first and second-degree burns, and a breakage of the left ankle."

The doctor's explanation wasn't clear to her. "But he's going to live, right?"

Fleshy wrinkles lined the forehead of Dr. Azzi, who looked about forty. "Your son's injuries are significant. I will update you as more information becomes available. I think we've almost got him stabilized. You can come see him then. I'm hoping for the best."

Hoping for the best. What did that mean? She needed a guarantee. Nate must live. She wouldn't let herself think about any other possibility. She took hold of his arm. "I need to see my son, now."

The doctor's shoulders tensed up. She let go of him. "I'm sorry. But this might be my last chance. Please."

"Fine, you can see him through the window in the door, though it will have to be quick. Follow me."

Laura rushed up behind him, and Rob followed on her heels through the automatic doors and down the bleach-fumed hallway to the OR where Nate lay on a gurney. Tubes ran up his nose and an IV-line, bandaged and double-taped, ran into his tiny wrist. His head was wrapped with gauze. His legs were covered in blankets. His arms rested at either side. A woman, wearing scrubs and a mask like Dr. Azzi's, stood beside him and checked a monitor. From where Laura stood with Rob, the red numbers and lines were blurred. But the fresh blood on the gauze on the floor, the blood on the scalpel and the other instruments strewn over the cart, was all in clear focus.

She clasped her hands and covered her mouth. It should have been her blood shed. She was responsible. If she hadn't been so distracted—worried about the scones—Nate wouldn't be here. Under the dim lights, through the tiny diagonal panes in the small square window, he looked peaceful.

"He seems so calm."

The doctor tensed as he had before. "That's because we've induced a coma."

His words knocked the wind out of her and she leaned against Rob to steady herself.

"Why?" No one had asked for their permission. She eyed Rob, but he looked glassy eyed with shock. Shouldn't they have been informed?

"We had to make a judgement call on the spot." The doctor pursed his lips. "It's only temporary—to relieve pressure on his brain. The hope is that, with the swelling relieved, the pressure decreases and some, or all, brain damage may be avoided." He pointed to the monitor. "He's hooked up to a mechanical ventilator, which is doing his breathing for him, and we're watching his brain activity closely on the EEG. Once there's improvement, we gradually withdraw the medicine and allow the patient to regain consciousness. Essentially it's a reversible coma."

"How long will that take?"

"Hard to say, but he's making progress, so we're hoping just a few more hours—though I can't promise anything."

Questions flooded her head. *Had he ever regained consciousness?* She opened her mouth, but the doctor interrupted her before she could speak. "His vitals are moving in the right direction." He nodded with finality. "I'd really much prefer if you returned to the waiting room."

Rob took her hand. "C'mon, babe. Let them do their job."

Laura followed him as if in a trance. Once they stepped back into the waiting room, Laura felt assaulted by all the commotion. Someone's cell phone rang. On the seat by the door, a baby wailed on a woman's lap. Laura walked the other way until she saw Rob's mother still sitting there by the window, waiting calmly, as if she was here for her annual check-up, though now she was talking with a young couple. Helen didn't seem to have noticed her come out, but when Laura got close enough to recognize the couple, she went stiff. What the hell? Andre and Patricia. More than ever, she wished they'd never moved back. They didn't belong here now.

Laura nudged Rob in the side with her elbow. "What are they doing here?"

"I texted Andre about Nate being operated on. Guess he decided to come for support, or whatever."

She didn't get it, and now felt as if someone was choking her. "Well, you can tell them all what's going on, I'm going outside for some air."

She walked toward the circular doors that led out front of the ER, hoping that, despite what she'd said, Rob might follow her, if only to have a smoke before breaking the news to everyone about Nate's condition. For once, she wanted one too.

Laura took a seat on an empty bench in the emergency valet loop. It was eerily quiet, though *really much preferable* to hanging out with everyone else in the noisy waiting room. She didn't like the way Dr. Azzi had spoken down to her. She and Rob deserved an explanation. Their son's life was at stake. She wished Rob would have been more assertive.

She blew her nose into her ragged tissues before deciding to text her older sister, Shenia. She and Shenia—who went by her Ojibwa name against their father's wishes—had lost touch, but Laura still thought she should know about something this important. *Nate was hit by a car and is in a coma.* She wasn't sure if Shenia would even respond, it had been years since she'd heard from her. Laura didn't blame her for leaving their father's fish camp, even if it was for a froo froo job waxing and plucking at the brow bar at Ulta. But Shenia, before she'd skipped town with her boyfriend, had been cold to her, treated her more like a passing acquaintance than a little sister, and never made plans to stay in touch. That's what really hurt.

A few feet ahead, a black car pulled into the loop. Its tires screeched before it stopped in front of her. The image of Nate lying beneath the black Mercedes came crashing back. The urge to pray came over her suddenly, though she hadn't been to church in almost ten years since her mother died. Laura gazed at the passing clouds and asked with her heart for God's help. *Please bring Nate back. Only you can give him a second chance. Don't punish him for my mistakes. He's innocent.* Laura begged through her tears. She made God a promise. If Nate came back to her, one thing was certain: she wouldn't let him down. She would do everything in her power to put him back together.

Chapter 4

July 4, 2016

Laura slept at the hospital in fits and stops between the bursts of fireworks from nearby beach houses. She woke up, groggy, at the first slivers of dawn. Rob was still asleep, grinding his teeth the same as he had been all night. Slowly, she lifted her head off his shoulder, her neck stiff. Her breasts, hard and heavy as cannon balls, burned like someone had just lit their fuse. She hadn't nursed or expressed any milk since she'd fed Biyen the previous morning on the front porch. The clock above the nurse's station now read 6:05. She almost couldn't wrap her head around Nate's accident. This time yesterday, she and Rob were lazing together in bed. If only she'd gotten going earlier, and taken control of the situation as a mother should, none of this would have happened. How long must they wait for an answer about their son?

Dr. Azzi should have told them something. Nate should have come out of the coma by now. The doctors should have asked for her permission before inducing it. Helen should have asked for her permission before buying Nate the scooter. No one ever asked for permission. Laura couldn't stop her mind from going around in circles. How could Chelsea have lost sight of him? Why hadn't Jacob told his mom that Nate was leaving. Someone should have stopped him. She should have never let him go. Laura wasn't sure how much longer she could hold out in the waiting room not knowing.

When she stood up to go use the restroom, Laura noticed that she'd leaked through her bra. She'd have to ask Helen to bring a clean shirt. Rob's mother had stayed until after midnight waiting to hear something more about Nate's condition, but when the night shift came in and gave them all the brush off, Helen had finally called it quits and left. She was probably exhausted. Laura was too.

She crossed her arms over her chest but, didn't get very far before, someone tapped her on the shoulder. "I think you should wake your husband," Dr. Azzi said without any inflection. She wasn't sure if that was a good sign, or bad.

She felt as if a school of minnows were circling inside her stomach. "Wake up, honey." She patted Rob on the thigh.

He swatted her hand away. "What?"

"The doctor wants to talk to us."

Once Rob saw Dr. Azzi, he shot up from the chair. She took his hand and held on as if without it she might be washed away. He was her anchor. His hand began to tremble along with hers. She tightened her grip around his fingers. She was his anchor too. No matter what the doctor told them, she wouldn't let go.

"So?" Rob asked.

The doctor's narrow eyes widened, and the pitch of his voice lifted. "We've been working on your son all night. He's finally awake. I can take you to him now. He's waiting for you." The doctor adjusted his stance. "I'll give you a few minutes with him, and then we can talk more."

Rob cried out and raised their hands in the air. Laura jumped into his arms and felt as if she'd taken flight. Her prayers had been answered. Nate was awake and alive. Once her feet were back on the ground, she went to Dr. Azzi and bowed to him in gratitude. "Oh, my god. Thank you!"

"Nate is a fighter. I can tell you that." Dr. Azzi bowed back at her.

She collapsed against Rob. Then, as they followed the doctor, she rushed to send a group text to close friends and family as well as her sister Shenia: *Nate is out of the coma.*

Moments later, she and Rob entered the dim room where Nate rested with his head sideways on the pillow. Side by side, they took a step closer to the bed. Nate blinked slowly, his eyebrows lifting for an instant, once he saw them, before dropping back into an uncertain place beneath the bandages around his head. He looked like a little mummy. She smiled—as she knew a mother should smile to make him feel better—yet the sight of him, so small and helpless, with his leg suspended from a strap in mid-air, made her want to shrivel up and burst apart at the same time. Her poor boy. How could she have let this happen?

Slowly, she leaned over and held him in her arms, praising heaven and earth—including every EMT, doctor, and nurse—for bringing him back to her. He'd come back to life; he could have just as easily been dead. She wanted to hang onto him forever.

Dr. Azzi cleared his throat. "Mrs. Sanders, can I please speak with you and your husband for a minute?" Laura gave Nate another big squeeze before she gradually peeled herself off him like Velcro. With Rob standing behind her, she sat completely still. They braced themselves for the doctor's prognosis. "I have some good news. His brain scans show no signs of permanent damage."

Rob placed his hand on her shoulder. Somehow Nate had been spared. She almost couldn't believe that she'd heard correctly. It was such a great relief.

"Yes, this suggests the effects of the coma will be temporary as we'd hoped. Now it's just a matter of waiting for the drugs to wash out of his system. Then we can gauge things better."

"And his leg?" Rob gave her shoulder a sharp squeeze. Laura looked up at Dr. Azzi, who suddenly seemed haggard. "I'll be back with you soon."

Anxious for more time with Nate, Laura tried to shrug off the change in the doctor's demeanor once Rob had questioned the condition of Nate's leg. Rob sat across from her on the bed. Through his tears, he smiled at Nate. "I knew you could do it, bud." Rob gave him a fist bump though Nate didn't move his hand, so small and frail, from the sheet that covered him up to his chest. He was too weak. She was reminded. They'd been so close to losing him.

Just then, Dr. Azzi cracked open the door. What could he possibly need to tell them in private? They were lucky. Nate was alive. She almost couldn't break herself away from his side. "I love you." She pulled up the sheet under his chin.

Rob leaned over and kissed his forehead. "We'll be right back."

Once they were in the hall, the doctor explained that Nate's ankle injury was complicated. "With any type of injury, especially one involving road rash and burns, there are concerns. We must try to save the limb and avoid infection. Once the burns stabilize and swelling goes down, probably in a week or two, he'll need surgery. The good news is that we won't have to amputate."

Laura hugged her arms into her chest. All this time she hadn't realized that the ankle injury was so serious.

"My main concern, going forward, is that we restore strength and mobility."

Rob looked at her as if he'd missed something. He then turned to Dr. Azzi. "Or what?"

He stared at the ceiling for a few seconds before clearing his throat to address them. "Or there's the possibility, I'm afraid, that he may never walk again."

She felt as if the wind had been knocked out of her. When she turned to Rob, he looked like he'd been sucker-punched. "How would you know so soon?" he asked.

"I don't know anything for certain. I'm only saying, it's possible."

Dr. Azzi continued talking, but she couldn't take in anything else. *Nate never walk again.* That couldn't be possible.

PART II

Chapter 5

July 6, 2016

Nate could have died or suffered permanent brain damage or lost his foot entirely. But he hadn't. She should be satisfied with that alone. Yet, though two days had passed, she still couldn't accept Dr. Azzi's prognosis that Nate might never walk again.

When the nurse arrived to change his bandages, Nate was resting upright. One by one, the jagged row of stitches emerged in a line that ran down the back of his scalp all the way from the top of his skull to the nape of his neck.

"Don't worry, air will help them scab over," the nurse stated with a nod of certainty.

"How long ... ?" Laura paused to clear her throat but had difficulty breathing, and soon found herself gasping for air as if she'd punctured a lung. She looked toward the window, wishing she could open it, until she remembered that they were all sealed.

The nurse raised an eyebrow at her. "Do you need some help?"

She shook her head, No, then tore out of the room. Rode the elevator down. Streamed through the revolving doors into the parking lot. The hot and muggy air was stifling, yet it came as a relief from the climate-controlled hospital, which had become overwhelming and claustrophobic when she'd started to feel, so unlike herself, trapped there in the room with the nurse. Beyond a sea of cars, the leaves of a tall tree rustled in the warm breeze as if calling her to join them for some respite from her suffering. She scurried along the edge of the pavement like a squirrel hiding away an acorn, moving as quickly as she could without making eye contact, until she collapsed against the thick trunk of the tree. Gulping for breath between sobs, she fought with herself. What kind of wretched mother would have let this kind of damage be inflicted on her own child? Filled with deep self-loathing, she closed her eyes and squeezed herself up into a ball of dark shame. She should have never let him ride that scooter without a helmet. She should have made him come home once he crossed the street.

She lost track of time as she dug deep into the dirt of her mind in search of a place to bury the accusations she kept firing at herself. She'd failed to protect him. How could she ever forgive herself? After forty-five long minutes, she still had no clear answer, but she'd managed to stop crying and breathe on her own again.

She made her way back into the hospital through the revolving door. Unlike Rob, Laura had never been squeamish around blood. Yet, the sight of Nate's stitches had ripped her apart.

Now, as she waited outside the elevator that would take her back up to Nate's room on the third floor, Laura took a cleansing breath. This was her last chance to get herself under control before Rob and his parents brought Ella and Biyen for their first visit. Laura stepped into the elevator and the doors closed behind her. Thank god, they all hadn't been in the room to witness her freak out when the nurse removed the bandages from around Nate's head. Beforehand, she'd thought she felt perfectly fine. The guilt and remorse that welled up within her had caught off her guard, cutting off her breath to the point where she felt like she was incapable of breathing on her own.

Laura stepped off the elevator on the third floor and began walking down the hall toward Nate's room, which was the last one on the right. Her behavior with the nurse was unfortunate, but she owned that now and must pull herself together and get back in there for her son. She was the parent here. Rob was counting on her to stand for both of them until he arrived with the rest of the family.

Nate needed them. All of them. His suffering over the past three days was more than anyone should ever have to endure, much less a five-year-old. It had been forty-eight hours since he'd technically come out of the coma. Yet, even at this moment, he was still very weak and lethargic, and slurred his speech. Only now was she beginning to grasp the severity of the trauma he'd experienced. She must keep his first family visit brief, though she made a secret wish. That, for Nate, the sight of his Nanna and Poppy along with his baby brother and sister, and of course Mom and Dad, might make him feel a little less like a patient in intensive care and a little more like himself.

Laura recalled the last time they were all together at his birthday party on the night before the accident. She'd held onto the glass plate with two hands as she walked barefoot through the sand toward the picnic table where everyone was singing "Happy Birthday." When they were finished, she set the chocolate cake she'd baked that morning, before him. Nate, his tanned face aglow, leaned over the candles as they all chanted: "Are you one? Are you two? Are you three? Are you four? Are you five—?"

He sucked in his breath.

"Don't forget to make a wish," she said. Rob, standing behind her, snapped a picture with his phone of him blowing out the candles. In that moment, celebrating as a family, she couldn't have wished for anything more to come true. Even Rob's parents, sitting together down at the far end of the table, couldn't stop grinning at their grandson as he huffed and he puffed at the tiny flames until—with a little help from his sister—he blew them all out.

By the time she was done serving and took her first bite of cake Nate had finished his and was asking if he could open presents. Rob's mother, usually the one telling Nate to slow down, jumped up. "We have something special for you." Seconds later, Helen reappeared on the sidewalk with a Razor scooter. "Surprise!"

Nate leapt from the bench. Laura followed him, leaving the rest of her cake, to watch as her son admired the red speed machine Helen stood behind. Laura wasn't sure if Nate was old enough for that kind of scooter.

"How did you know that's what I wished for?" he asked.

"Grandmas just know."

Helen leaned forward and wrapped an arm over Nate's shoulders. He hugged her around the waist so tightly she burped. Laura pretended she didn't hear it. Her mother-in-law covered her mouth, though before she could finish excusing herself, Nate grabbed the handlebars and took off. "Looks like a natural," Helen said. Laura shielded her eyes with her hand but soon lost sight of him in the sun. She didn't like him being off on his own.

If only Helen hadn't given Nate the scooter, they wouldn't be in this predicament. Laura took another deep breath before approaching his door. There was no use assigning blame anymore. She would try to do a better job of communicating with

Helen from now. Right now, she needed Helen to help her hold the family together. She'd already seen, after her mother was diagnosed with cancer, how quickly a whole world could unravel. There was no way she'd ever be the catalyst for that cycle to repeat.

Laura knocked on the door. When no one responded, she pulled it open, prepared to face the nurse and apologize. Instead, Nate, glanced over at her from his bed. She couldn't be certain, of course, but sitting up there with his bandages off, his chestnut brown eyes looked a little brighter than before. She sat beside him and gently swept his hair off his cheek. "I have some good news."

When she told him that the whole family was coming to visit, Nate cracked a half-smile that filled her strong and stubborn heart with hope. If they all stuck together, Nate would walk again. The same as he had before. She'd do everything in her power to make sure of it.

Chapter 6

July 11, 2016

Laura rearranged the carnations in the bouquet Chelsea sent. It seemed strange to her that the long stems and ruffled petals still looked fresh, though they'd been sitting on the windowsill for a week along with the rest of the flowers. The roses, wilting now, needed a little more TLC. Laura twirled around a carnation to help it open up, recalling the moment when she'd walked into Nate's room and spotted the colorful distractions. Chelsea's bouquet had been the first to arrive after the text went out to friends and family: *Nate is out of the coma.*

Chelsea always stayed on top of everything and seemed to really care. Shenia had never even bothered to respond to her text that Nate had been hit by a car and was in a coma. Instead she'd left her hanging overnight during those first twenty-four hours—when they didn't know if Nate was going to live or die—and only texted back after they'd shared the incredible news that Nate had come out of it. *Glad he's going to be all right.* That's all she wrote. Chelsea was nothing like Shenia, that's for sure.

Then Laura took a rose from the vase and peeled away its guard petals until she was overcome by a rotting smell. Looking back on the days leading up to the accident, she realized she could have done so many things differently that might have changed the terrible outcome. She should have been more on top of things. If only she'd made the batter for the scones a day ahead of time along with Nate's birthday cake, she wouldn't have been rushing around before the parade. She removed all the roses and tossed them in the garbage can. She'd rather throw them away while they still had some life in them. Right now, she couldn't stand to watch them wilt and die.

She took the water pitcher from the table beside the bed where Nate was sleeping. Half-upright with his left leg elevated, he looked like a crooked letter U. Seeing him in that position made her uncomfortable, yet he didn't seem to have any problem getting enough zzzs. Quite the opposite with all the pain killers. She topped off Chelsea's bouquet with fresh water from the pitcher and poured the rest into the vase of daisies Helen had brought with her from home when they'd all come to visit.

After seeing his grandparents and younger siblings, Nate had perked up for a couple days. Laura had anticipated that he'd make steady progress from there. Instead he'd steadily lost momentum. The only thing that seemed certain about his condition was its unpredictability. It made her uneasy that he still hadn't had surgery on his foot.

She went to the bathroom, refilled his pitcher, and set it beside him. It was eleven, and he hadn't woken up at all. Not even for a drink. Laura wondered what Chelsea would do under the circumstances. She always seemed to have a plan. They seriously needed one. Though Sanctuary was only a half-hour from Harbor City, Rob already was getting rundown making the rounds between the hospital, the house, and the bar. At least Andre had offered to cover for him. That had been a huge help, so far. It bothered her that there was so little she could do from the hospital when she was living there twenty-four-seven. Being forced to wean Biyen bothered her most.

Occasionally, she was going to need some breaks. Confined with Nate to his room and the reclining sleep-chair in the corner, time had begun to blur. She felt as if they were trapped in a macabre kiddie amusement park where, for the most part, they waited in an endless line to ride the roller coaster. Once they reached the front and it was finally their turn, they always took a seat, strapped themselves in for the duration, and slowly made their way up and up the track, anxiously awaiting the thrill of reaching the top, only to throw their hands up in the air for a split-second before plummeting again to the very bottom. The sensation, which seemed to have begun repeating itself, always left her with pounding headache and a sick feeling in the pit of her stomach.

Laura adjusted Nate's pillow, though he probably wouldn't notice the difference. It was better than doing nothing, which made her feel even more useless. She couldn't let herself get down. There must be some way she could help get him back on track. He needed something to look forward to each day. She could use something like that too.

Maybe if Chelsea brought Jacob over for a visit? That would definitely cheer-up Nate. Other than the doctors and nurses, she and Rob were the only familiar faces he'd seen in days. According to Rob, Helen and Art were caught up caring for the other kids. She sat in her chair by the window and texted Chelsea. *Can Jacob come to the hospital today? Nate misses him.*

As soon as she'd sent the text, Dr. Azzi entered. "How's my favorite patient today?"

She forced a smile, not wanting to let him see her down. "He's doing all right."

"All right. You don't sound very convincing."

He may never walk again. Dr. Azzi's prognosis haunted her, yet she was reluctant to share her concerns with him when Nate's surgery was still to come tomorrow. "He just seems so withdrawn. I thought he'd have more energy by now. Do you think he's strong enough for his operation?"

The doctor clasped his hands. "He is—really. Recovery is up and down. When he rests, his body is taking the time it needs to heal. You shouldn't worry about that. He'll come around when he's ready. And, yes, his surgery is still on."

"I was thinking of having his best friend come visit today."

Dr. Azzi stepped toward the door. "That's fine, but there's no need to push it—unless you need the company." He raised an eyebrow.

Shortly after he left, she received a text from Chelsea. They'd be there in an hour, or so, around noon. Laura texted her back right away. *Sounds great. I'll let the nurse know U R coming.*

Nate slept for another forty-five minutes and then partly opened his eyes. She angled his mattress forward and propped pillows behind his back. Sitting up would help him stay awake. He didn't complain, though she wondered how long he could comfortably sit upright with his leg elevated. "I have some great news. Jacob is coming to see you now."

Nate glanced at the bedside table. "Can I have some water?"

"Of course, sweetie." She filled him a cupful and held it to his dry lips. His reaction troubled her. He didn't seem to have heard her say that Jacob would be visiting today. Nate leaned forward and took a sip. Half the water dribbled down his chin onto his hospital gown. "Let's try another." This time, she cradled his head in her hand. He seemed to swallow more than he spilled. "Good job, honey."

She reached for a tissue and wiped around his mouth. She was grateful that Chelsea was bringing Jacob, though—after talking with the doctor and seeing Nate like this—she wondered if it was too soon. Should she have warned them? Nate was so weak. She remembered the long line of stitches running down the back of his head. Today he was again wrapped up like a mummy. She wondered if Jacob would be afraid. She almost wished she could cancel. It was too late for that. By now, Chelsea was probably in the parking lot.

Chelsea was the first friend she'd made in Sanctuary and had always been there to lend a helping hand. At this moment, she needed her friendship more than ever. And yet, other than exchanging a couple texts about the flowers and their brief phone conversation after she'd arrived at the hospital, they hadn't spoken. She must make sure Chelsea knew that she didn't blame her for the accident. What if Chelsea had been beating herself about it this whole time?

A soft knock came from the door. Suddenly, Jacob streamed in with Chelsea trailing behind him with a handful of balloons.

"Well, hello you two," Laura said as she came toward them. "I'm so glad you came."

Jacob walked past her and didn't stop until he reached the foot of Nate's bed where he stood and stared. "Is he alive?"

Chelsea stepped up behind him. "Jacob!"

Laura rushed back to the bed where Nate slept with his head turned sideways like one of the wilted roses she'd tossed into the trash earlier. She caught her breath. "Oh, yes, of course! He's just been on a lot of medication." She adjusted his position so he rested straight back. "Now he'll be more comfortable."

She offered a reassuring smile, but Chelsea's glowing complexion had already taken on greenish hue. "Are you okay?" Laura asked.

Chelsea straightened up and forced a cheerful grin. "I'm wonderful."

Laura cringed. She hadn't expected things to be this awkward. She went to Jacob and patted him on the back. "Thank you so much for coming. You're his first friend to visit. I'll try and wake him for you."

"No, no. That's okay." Chelsea took Jacob by the hand. "We just wanted to stop by quickly."

They couldn't leave already. "Please. He'll be more like himself in a minute." Laura went to the bed and gave Nate's shoulders a gentle squeeze. She cradled his chin in the palms of her hands. "Nate, it's time to wake up. Jacob is here." When she let go, his shoulders slumped and his chin dropped to his chest.

Chelsea gasped. "Laura, you don't need to do this."

Laura sat beside Nate and gently brought him back onto the pillow. "No, really, it'll be okay. He's been looking forward to seeing Jacob."

Jacob ran beside him and held onto the bed rail. "Nate, it's me."

Several seconds passed and Nate's eyes slowly peeled open. He turned toward him. Jacob waved as if he were hiding behind his hand. A smile eked out the corner of Nate's mouth along with a stream of dribble. Laura wiped away his saliva and moved off the bed to give the boys room. She went to Chelsea. "He hasn't talked much. The doctor says that's normal."

The boys stared at each other. Nate raised his chin a notch higher. Jacob raised his too. "You wanna go swimming when you get home?"

Nate blinked hard and gradually gave a nod.

"I'll bring the floats," Jacob said. "And the boogie boards."

Nate swallowed. "My ankle hurts."

Suddenly, Chelsea rushed up from the foot of the bed and stood between the boys. "We brought you these." She thrust the balloons at Nate. "We hope you can come home soon."

He reached for the string that dangled closest to him, but they all slipped through his fingers and floated toward the ceiling. Laura gathered them into her hand. "Thank you for these."

She went to put them by the flowers on the windowsill. Chelsea followed her. "Do you know how long he's going to have to stay here?"

Laura kept her voice to a whisper. "We'll have to wait and see, but the doctor said he'll likely have to stay until the end of the month." She tied the balloons to the back of her chair by the window. "A lot will depend on how his surgery goes tomorrow. One day at a time, I guess."

"I can't even imagine," Chelsea said. "I'm so sorry."

"Thanks. I am too." Laura rested her hand on Chelsea's shoulder. "I just want to make sure you know that I don't blame you for anything that happened. If anyone is to blame, it's me. I should have come and gotten him after he crossed the street. I put everyone in a terrible position. It was all just a terrible accident. The driver of the car that hit him said he feels terrible."

"I'm sure he does." Chelsea began picking off her nail polish. "Are you going to sue him?"

Suddenly, Laura felt as if she'd been struck by something. She was trying to apologize. Why would Chelsea go there? "No. The guy's auto insurance covers most of it, including rehab, and we have our coverage under the Affordable Care Act. Rob thinks it's for the best too. He's not a big fan of the legal system after what happened with Andre. Going to court can just make things worse. And, I mean, why would we bother to go after the guy when Nate's getting what he needs. Truthfully, he did cut right in front of him. I mean, that's what you said happened, right?"

Chelsea looked out the window, for a second or two, and then started picking at her nail polish again. "Yeah, that's right."

"So, I guess the only point in taking it to court would be if the driver was speeding, and we'd have to prove that and by how much. Right now, unless something changes, we'd rather just focus on helping Nate recover."

"Yes, that's the most important thing." Chelsea reached out for a one-arm hug. "Well, we don't want to overstay our welcome."

Laura hugged her back with two. "You're welcome any time."

"Oh, thanks." Chelsea went to Jacob and took him by the hand. Then, she waved over her shoulder. "I really hope you feel better, Nate. I'm so sorry."

Chelsea shuttled Jacob toward the door. "Just text me if you need anything."

Laura stood beside Nate and waved good-bye. "Thanks again for coming."

Chelsea opened the door to leave. "Oh, you're welcome. We'll definitely get the boys together once Nate comes home."

The door shut with a bang behind her. Laura shuddered. Chelsea had seemed so anxious. Laura lowered Nate's mattress into a more natural position wishing, in hindsight, that she'd told Chelsea how difficult things were for them right now. A real friend would want to know the truth. Why had she put on such a show? Nate's eyes were already half closed. She pulled up his covers. "Try and rest, sweetie."

Laura went to the window and stared out into the parking lot where Chelsea and Jacob were almost at their car. Instead of offering reassurance, she'd made the situation worse. She vented the cool air from the AC through the neck and of her gauze shirt. From now on, she must learn to adjust according to her son's needs. Lying flat on his back, Nate looked much more comfortable. She shouldn't have contorted him into a pretzel for company's sake. She went and rested on the bed beside him. Though he'd already fallen asleep, she grasped his tiny hand, letting go of her illusions. Starting tomorrow with his surgery, it would be a long journey to recovery.

Laura stood beside Rob as the anesthesiologist injected Nate with a sedative that would put him under during surgery. She watched Nate's eyelids grow heavy as the liquid passed into his bloodstream through an IV attached to his wrist, unable to stop herself from imagining, for a few seconds, how the doctors might have induced a coma the time before. Rob, as if reading her mind, put his arm around her as sleep overtook their son. "Don't worry, babe. Everything is going to be fine." Laura wanted so much to believe him, but seeing her son sedated so soon after coming out of the coma made her lightheaded. She couldn't help but wonder, *What if he doesn't wake up?*

Laura huddled against Rob and tried to take comfort in having him there as the nurse led them out to the empty waiting room where she offered them seats in front of the TV. At first, Laura sat next to him. However, after a few minutes, her pulse started racing. She had to get up and move around even if it meant walking in circles. Every so often she glanced at Rob, finding it difficult to comprehend how he could just sit there and watch the morning traffic report when their son was being taken apart and put back together again with a metal plate and screws. Altogether, the operation to reconstruct Nate's ankle would take about two hours, Dr. Azzi said. When it was over, they could go in and see him right away. For now, all she and Rob could do was wait. Laura willed herself to stay positive. Nate would come through this one step closer to walking again. She wouldn't allow herself to consider any other alternatives, though she couldn't avoid staring at the clock as she counted down the minutes, which seemed to pass more like hours.

As soon as the nurse came out from surgery into the waiting room, Rob rose from his seat. Laura, feeling as tense as rubber band stretched to it limit, rushed across the room.

"How is he?" Rob asked the nurse.

She pulled down her surgical mask and nodded. "He's out of surgery but isn't awake yet. I'll take you there and you can see him for yourself."

Laura looked to Rob for reassurance, but instead worry lines ran across his forehead. "Was the surgery successful?" He ran his fingers through his beard, which had filled in completely over the past eight days since the accident.

"The doctors will explain everything shortly." The nurse began walking toward Nate's hospital room. Laura took this as a good sign. She wrapped her arm around Rob's waist, feeling like they needed to prop each other up, as they walked in silence to Nate's room without any idea of what to expect once they got there. Through the small window in the door, Laura spotted Nate resting with his eyes closed and his leg elevated above the bed. From the looks of it, he was still under some sedation.

Laura came into the room with Rob a step behind. Nate appeared only half awake but, as soon as they came beside the bed, he started to mumble. "I want to go home."

Just then he opened his eyes as wide as she'd ever seen them. "Momma, take me home."

Laura, feeling like she could burst into tears any second, leaned forward and took his hand. "It's okay, honey."

Rob patted Nate on the shoulder. "I love you, bud. You'll be home soon."

Tears filled Nate's eyes. "Please, Daddy." All of a sudden Nate lifted his head off the pillow. "I'm not staying here anymore."

Just then, Dr. Azzi entered the room. "What's going on?"

Laura found herself shaking. "He's very upset." She and Rob backed away and let Dr. Azzi through. Nate strained his neck toward him. "I'm getting out!"

"Young man, put your head down. You must rest now." Dr. Azzi gently held onto Nate's arms and settled him back into bed. "There is nothing to fight now. Save your strength."

Laura wanted to go calm her son, but Dr. Azzi ushered her and Rob into the hall and the nurse stepped in to assist Nate. "I'm so sorry about that. Drugs can have strange effects on people—even little ones. But I assure you, Nate is doing fine. His ankle responded very well to the surgery. He handled it like a champ. I couldn't have asked for a better outcome."

"That's a big relief." On one hand, Laura felt grateful for operation's success but part of her ached for her son. He couldn't understand everything that was happening and seemed so afraid. He'd suffered through so much already. All she wanted to do right now was comfort him. More than anything, Laura wished that she and Rob could bring Nate home like he'd asked them.

Rob stood beside her with one arm leaned up against the wall. "Does that mean he'll get to come home early?"

Dr. Azzi frowned. "I'm afraid not. But, if we can get those burns treated and stabilize the ankle as I hope, he's on track to be released at the end of the month."

When Rob looked at her and grimaced, Laura felt like she might lose it. Somehow, she managed to hold everything in and nodded at Dr. Azzi. He knew best. For Nate's sake, they shouldn't take any shortcuts even if their son begged.

Chapter 7

July 16, 2016

Rob fastened Biyen into the high chair just as Art set the platter of grilled chicken on the table in front of Ella.

"Bon Appetit," Helen said as she marched in from the kitchen with some boiled potatoes.

"Now we may eat," Ella chimed in.

"Pass the meat," Rob added, feeling like a little kid again.

Ella took a leg and then Helen passed him the platter. Rob reached around the high chair and grabbed it from her with both hands. After serving himself and the baby, he set the rest of the chicken between him and his father in front of Laura's empty seat. Rob missed having her and Nate at home more and more each day. Ella and Biyen missed them too.

Rob wasn't sure what was going on the past few days with his mom and dad. They'd been acting strange ever since Nate's surgery. At first, when Dr. Azzi declared the operation to repair Nate's ankle a success, they'd literally stood up and cheered. However, once it became clear to them that Nate would likely still remain in the hospital until the end of the month, Helen and Art had seemed distant.

Things were only getting stranger. Rob recalled earlier that afternoon when his mother had taken him aside in the hall outside the library as if it was something urgent. "I do not want you to talk about what's going on at the hospital in front of the other kids. It's important not to upset them. I need to get Ella and Biyen into a normal routine."

Rob understood that, in Laura's absence, his mom and dad had picked up a lot of the slack. But asking him not to talk about his wife and son? He'd wanted to talk things over with her some more, but Ella had run in then and hugged him around the knees. "Daddy, daddy! You're home."

Now, seated at the table with everyone, Rob was at a complete loss of what to do or say. If only he could program his brain, so that appropriate thoughts came to him at a certain time like a TV show. *Dinner conversation.* Click. So much of his thinking since the accident revolved around Laura and Nate. Laura tried to keep on a brave face, but the dark bags under her eyes and the deep creases between her brows were signs that she was struggling. They all were. It was difficult to concentrate on anything else, especially now that his mother had told him he was forbidden from speaking of his wife and oldest son. His failing business, he was pretty sure, also would be considered off-limits at the dinner table. Truthfully, he'd been so preoccupied with Nate's condition over the past two weeks, there was nothing much to say about the bar. He'd even given Andre a set of keys. Tonight, he was going in to help him bartend but, for day-to-day purposes, Andre was in charge.

Rob took some meat off the bone and tore it into tiny pieces for Biyen. "Yum, yum." Rob set the meat out on Biyen's tray then started eating his own food. A few minutes later, when he looked over, Rob saw Biyen hadn't touched it. "Come on, little guy, it's time to eat." Rob picked up a bit of chicken from the tray and flew it like an airplane toward Biyen's mouth. "Open up." Biyen smacked his lips, but when Rob tried to land the plane, Biyen kept his lips sealed. Rob rerouted the plane and popped the chicken into his own mouth. "Mmm, mmm." He licked the tangy sauce off his thumb for some additional encouragement.

Ella giggled. "Daddy, you're silly. Chicken can't fly. Only a bird, or a plane, or Superman can do that!"

Superman. Nate loved Superman. If only he were here with Laura. She would know how to get Biyen to eat. Helen, seated on the other side of Biyen, scowled. "Rob, really, have some manners. Please."

At first, Rob rolled his eyes at her until he looked down and saw the drop of brown sauce that had landed on the breast pocket of his white shirt. He took his napkin and dabbed at the spot. Suddenly, his mother jumped up from her seat and ran back with a dishrag and a bottle of blue Dawn. "Stop. You're just going to make it worse."

He squatted her away. "Mom, I'm not five."

She persisted, dabbing at the spot left and right. "You can't go into work like that."

"Fine." Rob put his hands down, figuring that letting her take care of it for him was easier than going upstairs to find another clean shirt, if there was one. He needed to tackle the laundry that had been piling up on the floor next to his side of the bed. Once his mother had finished wiping him up, he looked across the table and saw Ella's plate. She hadn't eaten any of her chicken either. His mom noticed too. "Rob, you need to make sure she eats it."

He knew he should say something but, unable to think of anything appropriate, decided that he really didn't give a shit if she ate it or not right now. He balled up his napkin. He had to get out of there before he said something he'd regret. His mom should have never treated him like a child in front of his own kids—even if he chose to act like one. The kids knew what he meant when he was acting silly. He gave Ella the you-know-better eye. "You be good for your Nanna and Poppy, now. I've got to go to work." He looked to his father for an acknowledgement that he'd heard him. He was the only person who might relate to Rob's frustration as a father, caught by his daughter, being disciplined by his mom. Before he could get a better read, Ella started whining for attention.

"But what about a kiss goodnight?"

"I'll give you one when I come home."

"But I'll be sleeping."

"You better be." He waved a finger at her and stood from the table with his plate.

"I'll see you for breakfast, little guy." He bent over the high chair and kissed Biyen, who had finally decided to eat his food. Hopefully, with a full stomach, he'd sleep well for his grandparents who had moved his crib into their room downstairs until Laura and Nate came home. As soon as they did, Rob vowed, he was moving them into their own place. His parents had done so much, Rob knew he shouldn't get angry at them, but today his mother had crossed more lines than he wanted to count.

She frowned at his plate. "You didn't eat much."

"I lost my appetite." He set his plate in the sink and walked out the door. His patience was shot. Still, he wished he could have kept his cool. None of them needed any more stress in their lives. Instead he'd regressed into a five-year-old right in front of his parents and own kids. Without Laura, he felt unbalanced. He took a couple deep breaths and continued down the driveway toward Main Street. It was only a few blocks to the bar. He could use a stiff drink right about now. Why had they ever moved in with his parents? It was messing with his mind. He would rather live in the woods. Lately, with Nate in the hospital and everything disrupted at home, Rob couldn't deny that his nerves had begun to fray.

He walked a little faster. Up ahead, on the sidewalk, he saw something that made him think his eyes must be playing tricks on him in the sun. He shielded them with his hand until he could clearly make out that the line of people snaking toward him was, in fact, coming from Sanders. The last time he remembered the place having a line to get in was ten years ago, when it was called The Sand Bar, and he and Andre were sixteen and using fake IDs. Rob picked up his pace. He must be mistaken. Something bad must have happened. Had Andre evacuated everyone?

Rob squeezed his way in past the line. There didn't seem to be any problem, other than being short-staffed, as customers jockeyed for position to place drink orders with Andre. Dressed in a fitted, black T-shirt and dark jeans, Andre shook the martini shaker one last time before straining clear liquor into a chilled glass. For Rob, it all looked way too slick to be his bar until he saw Patricia, in a mid-riff top and cut offs, standing behind the register with a credit card in her hand. For a few seconds, he just stood there and watched her run it through the machine—almost forgetting that they weren't in high school anymore—until someone slapped him hard on the back. "Hey, Rob, my friend, it's good to see you here."

Instantly, Rob snapped back to reality. Without having to turn around, he knew that his landlord, Bill, was standing right behind him. Rob forced himself to smile and make it look genuine.

He didn't recognize the fancy cocktail Bill was drinking, except for the sprig of rosemary sticking out like a straw. "I like what you and your friends are doing around here."

Rob shook his hand. "Thanks, Bill."

"Just a reminder for you." He swirled around his ice. "The rent is due in full at the end of the month, or it will cost you a half a grand extra."

Rob felt his pulse begin to race. He wiped his hand down his pant leg where it balled up into a fist. He'd never punched anyone in the face but, at the moment, every muscle in his arm was engaged and ready to strike. "I'm fully aware."

He hadn't expected Bill to make an exception this month. *I mean, why would he, it's not like his kid was in the hospital.* Rob also hadn't asked for an extension—though he was certain Bill knew he could use one—especially since they were closed on the third of July and the Fourth because of the accident. "Yes, of course. I'll have a check for you on July 31."

"You know that's a Sunday, Robert."

Robert. Really, William? If there was one thing Bill was good at, it was pressing his buttons.

"Well, can I get it to you the next day then, August first, once the bank opens at 10?"

"I'm afraid not."

"You know that means I won't have revenue in yet from the last Saturday of the month then?"

"Think of it this way; you'll have a head start on August."

"That's not what I'm worried about right now. You know my son is in the ICU, right?"

"Yeah, I'm sorry to hear about that."

"Yeah, thanks. He was almost killed and might not be able to walk again. But why the hell should that matter to anyone?"

"I know being closed over the Fourth cost you, Rob. I'm really sorry, man. But business is business. And right now, my friend, a lot of folks are champing at the bit for the opportunity you have here. So, I'd hurry up and figure out how to make the most of it like your old pal Andre."

Rob felt as if he'd been run over by a semi-. Then it dawned on him. Bill was angling for Sanders to fail so that he could lease the bar to somebody else who could bring in a higher rate of return or, at least, be willing to pay higher rent. Rob knew he must decide: give in and ask for mercy or stand up and fight. If he sucked up to Bill, he might be able to negotiate a deal to save his dad's house from being taken by the bank due to extenuating circumstances. At this point, there was no telling whether he'd make this month's payment. But then he'd be playing right into Bill's hand. Pumping with adrenaline, Rob's competitive nature kicked in. He felt his voice harden until it solidified into stone. "Excuse me then, my friend."

Bill swished the remainder of his drink and took the last sip.

"Looks like you're empty. I'll have Andre bring you another."

Rob brushed past him without waiting for an answer. At all cost, he must avoid an altercation. Bill probably had his personal liability attorney on speed dial. Rob wouldn't take the bait and let that bottom-feeder crush him. Not legally. Not financially. Not personally. Not now. Not like this. His family was relying on him. His parents were doing everything they could. Andre and Patricia had stepped in and offered to help carry his load. He must find a way to persevere.

Rob came behind the bar just before Andre set a tall glass of spirits and soda on the counter by Patricia. She added a shot that looked more like weak tea than liquor. "What the heck is that?" he asked her.

"Chamomile, helps relax the senses." Patricia winked. "You should try it." Once she left with the drink, Rob went to pour himself a shot of Jack Daniels.

"Hey, bro, while you're over there, grab me the St. Germain." Andre filled up another tall glass with club soda and added a shot of vodka.

Rob took the bottle of Elderflower liqueur off the top shelf, almost surprised that he remembered where it was since he'd never served it to anyone before. He handed it to Andre. "I'm impressed. You really know how to pack 'em in here."

Andre tipped the bottle. "Yeah, it's been a trip."

Rob watched him measure out the pour. "Definitely making up for some lost time." He cocked his head to the side. "You see Bill over there, my landlord?"

Andre glanced over at him quickly. "Yeah."

"Have Patricia bring him another of whatever he's drinking. Just make sure he doesn't try and drink for free. That weasel is trying to drain us."

"Got it, unless you want to handle the register to keep tabs?"

"I'm all in." Rob downed his shot. "Need one?"

Andre shook his head. "I'll wait. Think you can hang after with us?"

Rob took a second to consider Andre's offer. Laura was staying at the hospital. Everyone at home would be sleeping. No one would notice the difference if he stayed after closing for a few drinks. "Sure, why not?" Just then he remembered his promise earlier to Ella. He must remember to kiss her goodnight.

Once they'd locked up out back, Rob turned the corner and began walking home. Arm-in-arm, Andre and Patricia, the lovebirds, disappeared in the other direction toward the beach. In the wind off the lake, their laughter carried through the dark—though it wouldn't be long until sunrise. Rob stumbled down the sidewalk, unable to recall the last time he'd stayed out this late. Maybe back before he met Laura? He missed her now, but felt too old to miss those happy days when they were in love. It had been so long since he'd slipped his fingers through her hair.

It was only a few blocks to home. He longed to be in bed. At least, the wind had his back but oh, god, was he wasted. Since the accident, he hadn't been drinking much, except for a beer here and there. His tolerance must have fallen. Those chamomile cocktails of Patricia's had done a trick on him. He should know better than to let her serve him. He struggled to put one foot in front of the other. It was all her fault. She was an elixir, like, some goddamn fountain of eternal youth. That much he knew. Looking at her made him feel intoxicated. He hated her for her power over him. The way she'd winked at him had made him feel invincible again, almost immortal as if any-thing was possible then and now and forever more—though he knew better. He shouldn't trust her. They were each other's first, and she'd betrayed him. How could he ever forgive her? She'd ratted him and Andre out to police. He must never forget that. Then again, she and Andre were engaged now. If Andre could move on, then why couldn't he?

Rob continued. Only a few more blocks, and he would be home in bed. He couldn't forget, Andre and Patricia were helping him keep the bar afloat for tips alone. Then why did being around them make him feel so uneasy? It was as if they both understood a secret he never would. He couldn't figure it out. Rob replayed his conversation at the bar with Andre in the early hours of the morning leading up to Nate's accident. "So, come on, be straight with me—why are you even here?"

"Relax, dude, you're starting to sound like your dad. I'm just, here, trying to catch some waves."

Andre had laughed it off. And there was no denying that, over the summer, the southwesterly winds had kicked up some of the best waves in years on Lake Michigan—the likes of which Sanctuary had rarely before seen. Regardless, Andre and Patricia could go anywhere. Why here? Why now?

Rob couldn't do it anymore. He needed to sit down and rest for a minute. Up ahead, the clapboard sign at Frank's rattled in the wind. He took a seat on an Adirondack chair beside the door and, closing his eyes, leaned his head back as he often did when he and Laura took the kids for ice cream. She always ordered strawberry and then complained when they never had it. Rob laughed. She couldn't accept that this was Cherry Country. Strawberries were the enemy. She'd get mad at him every time when he tried to explain to her that, around here, some things would never change.

Rob got up from the bench and continued walking. When Laura moved to town, he'd thought that he'd make a clear break with the past. Only now, it seemed as if the past six years had whizzed him by like a shooting star. Was history repeating itself, Rob wondered. For ever since the night of Andre's return, and Nate's scooter accident the following day, Rob felt like he'd been caught up in a rip current. Suddenly, it seemed like he had no other choice but to ride it out by going along with Andre and Patricia's plans. He couldn't stop the flow forward. And if he tried to fight it, he'd soon wear himself out, then be overpowered and left to the undertow—sunk and buried in the sand like one of those shipwrecks at the bottom of the Manitou Passage. His only chance of survival was to give into the current and then wait and see if it spit him out. Only then, could he make his way back home to shore.

Rob stepped onto the porch and unlocked the kitchen door. At the moment, between the alcohol, anxiety, and exhaustion, he wasn't sure whether he was strong enough even to make it up to bed. He tried to be quiet on the back stairwell, but tripped over the last step and landed face first on the floor outside the attic. After a few seconds, Ella poked her head around the corner in her long-sleeved nightgown. "Daddy, are you okay?" She rubbed the sleep out of her eyes. "You don't look so good."

Rob pushed himself onto his knees. "I'm fine, sweetie. Just go back to sleep."

She pouted, "But what about my kiss?"

"I'll be there in a minute." Once she'd returned to her bed, he took a deep breath to help get his bearings. He got back onto his feet and turned the corner. "Good night, I love you." He bent down and kissed her cheek.

"I love you too, Daddy." She began sucking on the ruffled cuff of her sleeve. "Do you miss mommy and Nate?"

He stood there, for a second, reeling at the memory of his mother's request earlier and the possible implications if he failed to be straightforward and honest with his daughter. "Yes, baby, I miss her and your big brother a lot. Don't worry. They'll be home soon. Let's get some sleep."

"Can I sleep in your bed?"

More than anything, at that moment, all he wanted was some space. But, staring into those blue eyes of hers in the moonlight, Rob's heart softened into mush. "Okay, just this once. Get over there, quick, and I'll tuck you in."

Ella fell right back asleep on Laura's side of the bed, but Rob's mind continued to run. He couldn't click off that easily. He needed Laura and Nate to come home as soon as possible. There was no way he could keep up, like this, being caught at every corner.

Chapter 8

July 27, 2016

When the nurse pulled the burn net off Nate's leg, Laura almost had to look away. This was her boy. His shin, pocked with countless raw cuts and scrapes. His ankle and foot, a swollen mass of leathery, waxy-white and black skin charred around the edges. She fought to keep a straight face and not let her discomfort show.

The nurse, who spoke methodically, didn't flinch as she unwound the final layer of moistened gauze and thick dressing. "Burns over skin joints like this will require ongoing therapy to restore motion and strength."

Laura hoped Nate wasn't in too much pain. She nodded at the nurse, and tried to pay attention, though she couldn't bear to see her son suffer. In a few days, once he was able to come home, this would be her job. Rob would never be able to tolerate it.

At the moment, he was leaning away to one side as if trying to maintain his balance on a listing ship. She latched her arm around him. For everyone's sake, they must keep it together. They owed it to Nate, who was straining forward to examine his bare skin. "Look, Momma. I'm peeling."

Laura felt a little nauseous, but forced herself to take a deep breath and view the peeling as a sign of progress. She recalled her panic attack early on during Nate's treatment, when this same nurse had removed the bandages around Nate's head to air out his stiches. Since then, his stitches had healed swiftly and he no longer needed to have his head wrapped. His leg wounds would heal the same way in time, Laura told herself.

She willed herself to suck it up. She had no other choice. Rob's squeamishness around blood was never going to change. He shook his head at her and stepped away from the bed. Laura leaned forward and gently smoothed Nate's wavy bangs off his forehead. Light as sand on top and progressively darker underneath, his hair reminded her of the dunes they'd climbed together at the beach during his birthday party the night before his accident. His hair would grow back in, but would he ever regain his footing like that? She had her doubts. For the time being, she pushed them aside.

Right now, Nate needed her encouragement. She searched deep in her heart until she reached the part of her soul where her grandfather's spirit whispered. *Gazaagin, my bird.* Laura understood then, she could do this. "Don't worry, sweetie. It's just like the bark that peels off a birch tree. Healthy skin will grow back underneath."

Despite how terrible the wounds on Nate's leg looked, he was making steady progress, Dr. Azzi had told them earlier in the morning. Moreover, the internal fixation of the ankle during his surgery had been deemed a success by the orthopedic surgeon. All that said, recovery would still take months. Now it was up to her and Rob to decide whether they could handle bringing Nate home to recuperate, or whether he should remain at the hospital.

Nate could only leave, according to Dr. Azzi, if they agreed to follow his specific instructions. Laura had been confident she could meet any and all requirements. Yet now, as the nurse in pink scrubs demonstrated the care necessary, Laura wondered if she had the skills to fulfill the commitment.

"He's going to need consistent care," the nurse said. "A lot will depend on both of you."

Laura glanced at Rob who was leaning against the back wall with his arms crossed. She straightened up. "I'm ready."

"Good. Let's get started." The nurse proceeded. "His scars will contract, potentially causing further disfigurement and loss of function. Without proper home care, reconstructive surgeries may be necessary."

Laura's neck stiffened at the thought of Nate having another surgery. The notion of him spending even one more day in the hospital was more than she could bear. She wanted to get behind his bed, break him out of there, and run him all the way home. Home. Right now, that's what Nate needed.

She shot Rob a sideways glance, but he looked zoned out, staring off into space. She forced herself to focus as the nurse bandaged Nate's leg and replaced his splints. She couldn't miss anything. Once he left the hospital, Nate's recovery would depend on her. Ongoing rehab would occur at the children's hospital in Big Rapids, the nurse added. Laura looked at Rob in disbelief. Big Rapids was a two-hour drive. They didn't own a car. "How often would he need to go?" Laura asked.

"At least twice a week. Rehab is key." Done correctly, it can prevent or minimize scar tissue deformities, she said, pointing at darkened skin on the outside of Nate's ankle where the worst burn damage occurred. "It also will help recondition the muscles."

The nurse had started to sound like a robot. For a few seconds, Laura lost her concentration. How was she going to get Nate to Big Rapids? The best treatment plan in the world was pointless if the patient couldn't be present to receive it. She considered this, then tried to tune back in. The nurse's monotone voice, sounding as if it were coming through a PA system, registered again as she outlined further restrictions. "Since the pigment cells in the skin may have been destroyed, the patient will need to avoid sun exposure for a year or more. Burned areas might not have the fatty insulation that they had prior to the burn. There is a need to avoid extreme temperatures."

Laura kept standing there, listening the best as she could, though she didn't understand how they'd manage. Michigan didn't have anything but extreme temperatures. Apart from a week or two in early fall and late spring, it was always too hot or too cold. What did they expect her to do, keep him cooped up in the attic? All of a sudden, she couldn't breathe very well. How would they even get him up there to bed? She should have started a to-do list weeks ago. Now, it was too late. She stopped herself and took a few seconds to catch her breath. At the moment, worrying about all the obstacles they'd face once they got home was counterproductive.

The nurse marched to the side of the bed and stood beside Nate. "We want our big guy here to be able to get back swimming and running around, so we're going to have to work those muscles twice a day, Mom and Dad. And give big rewards. Lots of ice cream to strengthen his bones!" She patted Nate on the head and, for the first time, smiled. "Sound good?" Nate gave her a big nod. "Sound good, Mom and Dad?"

Laura waited for a second to see if Rob would respond. However, when she looked over at him and noticed the blank look in his eyes, she knew that there was no point. Instead she stepped forward and shook the nurse's hand. "Sounds perfect!" Then she waved Rob over.

He uncrossed his arms and came beside the bed. "Sounds all right by me."

Laura had always accepted that caring for Nate was going to be mostly up to her, but Rob seemed totally out of it. If his attitude today was any indication, she was going to need to find support elsewhere. Somehow, she'd have to figure it out. Dr. Azzi would always be there if she ran into serious trouble. He'd saved Nate's life and, for the past month, had treated him like his own son. She could never express enough gratitude. She wanted to make him proud with her continuing care. The nurse leaned toward her. "Mrs. Sanders, are you sure you're capable of this?"

Laura looked around for Rob's mother before she realized the nurse was talking to her. Weird. Being referred to as Mrs. Sanders gave her a boost of confidence. "I'll try my best."

She was committed to her son. She would learn to wrap those bandages and work his muscles like a true medical professional. She would find a way to get him to Big Rapids. She wouldn't let him down. Laura took Nate's hand. Rob, without any coaxing, came beside them.

"We're going home soon, sweetie." Laura knotted her fingers around Nate's. Rob cupped his hand over the top of them. For the first time that she could remember since the accident, they shared a fragile smile.

Chapter 9

July 31, 2016

Laura rested her arm out the passenger window of Art's van as Rob pulled into town with Nate in the back seat. A steady wind rustled the leaves of the temperamental old oaks that stood guard along Main Street, including the tallest, where the eagles nested. Still, there was no avoiding the glare of the midday sun blazing down on the storefront windows, so much so that the village antique store appeared to squint. Their neighborhood, once so familiar, seemed strangely surreal as if they were newcomers. After spending the better part of a month at the hospital, it was difficult to believe that they were finally bringing Nate home.

Rob tapped his fingers on the steering wheel and looked over his shoulder at Nate. "I've got something big to show you when we get home, bud."

"What's that, Dad?"

Rob grinned. "You'll see when we get there."

Laura tried to pick up on Rob's enthusiasm. Right now, for Nate's sake, she couldn't let herself get down. She glanced back at him through the rearview mirror. Staring out the window, he seemed lost in thought. She could only imagine what was going through his stitched-up head. *I fought for you momma*, he'd told her at the hospital as soon as the breathing tube came out and he could once again form words. He'd fought to stay alive for her. Now, she must fight for him. Their initial appointment in Big Rapids was less than a month from now. She had to find a way to get him there. Perhaps Art could give Helen a ride to and from work at the museum, and let her and Nate take the Buick? One way or another, she must figure it out.

Up ahead on the left, the bungalow they called home stood in the shadows, the windows dark behind the lace curtains. Laura leaned forward, the back of her thighs sticking to the vinyl seat. In the yard, covered with clover, weeds scaled her warped bake stand. Rob pulled in the driveway until he reached the wheelchair ramp he and his dad had rushed to build. It led up to the side porch where Ella's skateboard was left in the corner along with Biyen's umbrella stroller. An upside-down sand pail and a shovel were scattered by the door. At some point, Helen must have taken them to the beach—unless Art had gone out with them as an excuse for a smoke. Laura was thankful Helen didn't let him or Rob light up in the house. Over the past two weeks, between aligning the planks of plywood and hammering them all together, they'd both been smoking like chimneys, Laura imagined.

Rob turned off the van and continued around back for the wheelchair. Laura, half excited, half panicked, opened Nate's door beside the ramp. The new golden-brown planks running up to the porch glistened in the sunlight. Everything else, by comparison, looked decrepit, including the dried out planter of geraniums beside the door. Shuttling back and forth between the hospital for the past twenty-four days she hadn't noticed how much the house had been neglected until now. It was as if their home, previously budding with life, was now clinging to it.

Suddenly, Laura felt as if she'd aged twenty-four years. Behind the car, Rob wrestled with the wheelchair. "Did you unlock the wheels?" she called to him. A couple seconds later, she heard them pop. If only Nate's recovery were as simple a fix. She'd meant to come up with something special for his return home, but reaching this point had consumed all her energy. Rob came around the side of the van pushing the wheelchair. It was only a few feet from the van to the ramp, but getting Nate there was going to be a challenge given the crumbling concrete in the driveway. Laura rested her hand on his shoulder. "Are you ready?"

He nodded, though his eyes glazed over. He was hardly able to hold up his head and it wasn't yet noon. Meeting with the nurse and getting discharged had taken a lot out of him. It had worn her out too.

Rob, his back covered in sweat, leaned into the car. "Can you come a little closer to me, bud?"

Laura cringed. Though she knew Rob would be careful, it was hard not to tell him what to do. He couldn't knock Nate's leg against anything—much less lose hold of him. Laura held the wheelchair in place. Nate, dragging his leg across the vinyl, scooted toward the edge of his seat and bumped himself up. Rob caught him under the arms and lowered him into the chair. Laura made sure it didn't move wondering how she'd manage when Rob wasn't around.

Just then Ella flew down the ramp toward them and wrapped her arms around Laura's knees so hard that she thought they might give out. "Momma, you're home!" Laura bent down and gave her a quick hug until Helen, who was holding Biyen, waved for everyone to come in. Art was in the living room watching television, she explained. "He's thrown his back out," she harped. "Darn ramp."

Ella rushed toward the door. "Hurry, Daddy!"

Laura, straining a bit, pushed the chair forward. "Here we go." Tilting it onto the rear wheels, she managed to maneuver it over the lip of the ramp. She leaned her weight into the chair and heaved it upwards plank by plank.

The sound of the heavy wheelchair moving over the wooden path reminded her of the last time she'd pushed Biyen in his stroller over the boardwalk by the beach earlier in the summer when she was still nursing him. How she'd longed for her little chick all those days and nights apart, especially on his first birthday. At last they were all home together.

Laura pushed Nate into the kitchen. As if moving in slow motion, she maneuvered the chair across the linoleum floor. With the weight of her son in her hands, it felt like they were entering a whole different dimension. Once, he would have run free. Now, she wondered: Would he ever walk again?

"Poppy, Nate is back!" Ella called into the living room.

Laura's heart pounded faster as she followed her down the hall. Their family was already being pulled apart before the accident. Now that they were back together, everything only felt that much more disjointed. Would their family scatter into pieces like Nate's scooter?

She continued to wonder about this as she wheeled him into the center of the room where everyone was gathered. Art, sitting in the far corner, was engrossed in the news at noon on TV. Apparently, he hadn't heard Ella's previous announcement.

"Poppy, look who's here!" Ella ran over and hopped onto his lap.

At first, Art appeared startled by her, but then he wrapped his arms around her and straightened up in his seat. When he caught sight of Nate, he smiled. "Welcome home. How do you like that ramp I made for you?"

"It's fine." Nate pouted. Laura took a seat on the couch next to Rob. Now that they were home, she hadn't expected Nate to be so down. Ella, who seemed more energetic than ever, jumped off Art's lap and rushed toward her big brother, stopping inches from his leg, propped up in the wheelchair. Her eyes widened as if she were peering into binoculars. "That's a big boo-boo."

Helen winced, moving toward Ella as if she were a police officer about to issue a citation. "What did I tell you?" Ella cowered a little and lowered her eyes. Helen patted her once on the head before shooing her off. "I know you can be con-siderate. Why don't you go sit on the couch by your father and mother."

"I've had to watch this one like a hawk." Helen thrust Biyen toward her like he had a stinky diaper. Rob rolled his eyes. It was apparent from Helen's sharp tone, that she'd run out of patience with the kids. Helen also probably resented her, Laura suspected, for being away for so long at the hospital and leaving her with the other kids. After a second, Biyen squirmed out of her arms and crawled onto the Oriental rug, which covered the wood floor under the coffee table. Helen treasured the hand-knotted rug she'd purchased on an excur-sion to the Far East, which was sponsored by the Sanctuary History Museum where she worked part-time. Unlike many of her friends who were already retired and taking exotic trips, Helen couldn't afford to cut back her hours, not even, for one month. Art, though summer was his peak season, had been forced to cut back his hours and pitch in watching the kids as needed when Rob was at the hospital with her and Nate, or at the bar. Without Andre and Patricia's help, they would have lost the whole month of July. She and Rob owed them all big time, yet they had no way to repay anyone.

At the moment, Biyen, steady and determined, was using the coffee table to pull himself up to stand. She and Rob watched him wobble from side to side. Their little chick, wearing only a diaper, was about to prove himself a toddler. He gripped the edge of the table with his chubby hands and stabilized himself on two feet. He then let go with one hand and raised his heel off the rug. He was going for it. Laura knelt in front of him on the rug and opened her arms. "Come to Momma."

By now, everyone was watching Biyen. He let go with the other hand, spread his arms wide like the wings of an eagle, and took a step toward her with his left foot. His mouth dropped open as he brought his right foot forward and then his left. After a few tentative steps, he leaned forward and collapsed into her arms. Laura, almost breathless, rocked him from side to side. "You can walk, Biyen. You can walk."

Rob and Ella started clapping. Helen and Art joined in the with a round of applause. When Laura turned around, Nate was staring into his hands. "I want to walk," he muttered under his breath. She swallowed the lump in her throat, and held Biyen still.

Helen, grimacing, came across the room and patted Nate on the arm, as if to console him. "You will, you will." She let out a deep sigh and stepped behind the wheelchair. "But right now, how about you help me make us all some lunch?"

Laura sat by and watched her push him out of the room. Art, acting once again as if the lightbulb in his head had been switched off, returned his attention to the television. Laura rolled her eyes at Rob. "Why does everything always get so messed up? It's never …"

When she saw that Ella was paying attention to their conversation, she caught herself.

Rob got up from the couch. "It's going to be all right. Everyone is a little overtired." He scooped Ella into his arms. "Except us. Right surfer girl? How about we go to the beach? You can bring your boogie board."

Ella jumped up and down so hard the floorboards creaked beneath the plush rug. "Can I wear my new swimsuit, Momma?" She looked up at her with a pleading grin, knowing that Laura had told her she must wait until her birthday tomorrow. At the moment, Laura no longer saw the point in holding off. "Sure, honey."

"Thanks, Momma." Ella dashed away.

Rob glanced at her. "Want to come with us?"

"Maybe later." She cocked her head in the direction of the kitchen where Helen had taken Nate. "I think I'll stay and work on things around here." Biyen wiggled off her lap and, with his diaper sagging between his chunky thighs, crawled onto the rug. She needed to give him a change.

"Do what you gotta do, babe. I'm out." Rob bent down and offered her a hand up.

As soon as she was on her feet, Ella was tugging on Rob's arm. Within a few seconds, they were gone. She went to into the hall bathroom for diaper. When she returned, Laura pulled Biyen onto the carpet. Lying on his back, he beamed up at her. But, she wondered, after almost a month apart from each other, did he still recognize her as his mother. Her milk supply had dried up within a week of the accident, though now her chest ached. She slipped off his wet diaper. When she set it aside, he squirmed away and crawled the other direction. She chased after him on her hands and knees. "Come back here you little rascal."

Just then Helen came in the room. "Lunch is ready!"

Laura caught Biyen by one foot. At that instant, pee streamed through the air like a fountain. Drops of urine spattered onto the rug around Biyen's bottom and continued to rain down on her. It wasn't the first time she'd been peed on when changing a boy's diaper, but none of her children had ever gotten away. After a couple seconds, she managed to fasten the new diaper around his waist. Biyen giggled. On another occasion, she might have found the situation humorous, but Helen was scowling at them like never before. Looking as if she might lose it, she held her hand over her mouth and left the room without saying anything.

Laura, ashamed at her own inadequacy as a parent, carried Biyen into the bathroom, which smelled of lingering cigarette smoke and Lysol spray. Art must have just left. At his age, he should already know that nothing could eliminate the odor of nicotine, which had absorbed into the peeling flowered wallpaper and old shower curtain ringed with mildew. She pulled it open, sat Biyen down in the tub, and listened to the water fill the bath. She wasn't sure how she'd ever show her face in the house again.

Ten minutes later, when Laura carried Biyen out into the hallway, dish soap bubbles floated toward them from the living room. She'd planned to take him upstairs for a nap, and avoid Helen at all cost, yet now Laura felt obligated to help clean up the mess she made. Clutching Biyen to her chest, she poked her head around the corner and saw Helen on her hands and knees. She was scrubbing back and forth so hard that the loose skin on her upper arm shook. Laura could only imagine the curse words running through her head. She didn't blame Helen for being angry. It was stupid to have changed Biyen on the carpet. Laura approached her slowly. "I'm really sorry."

Helen didn't look up at her. Instead, she kept scrubbing. "Don't worry. I'll make sure it comes out. You just take care of yourself."

Her instincts told her to stay and help anyway, but she turned and walked into the kitchen where Nate slept in the wheelchair with his head slumped sideways. She passed right by him and crept away upstairs to put Biyen in his crib. Right now, she needed a moment to herself. When she put him down in his bed with his blanket, he rolled over onto his stomach. She rubbed his back for a moment to help him settle, remembering then, her mother had once soothed her the same way. That seemed like another lifetime. Her mother and grandfather were gone.

Chapter 10

July 31, 2016

He'd left the house feeling as if his Tevas were sinkers. But now, walking hand-in-hand with Ella, Rob's mood lightened. He opened his mouth wide and sucked in some fresh air from the wind coming off Lake Michigan. Since the accident, he'd been running on fumes. Ella bumped her hip into the side of his leg. "Daddy, stop that." Her face twisted up like she was half laughing, half scolding him. "You look like Billy Big Mouth."

Rob opened his mouth even wider, imitating the tacky electronic bass that hung above cash register at the bar and sang "Don't Worry Be Happy." He lifted her into his arms and, opening his mouth as wide as he could, pretended to take a bite out of her tummy. "You better watch out or I'll eat you up for supper."

Ella giggled. "Stop, that tickles." She wiggled around until she was near hysterics and he put her down. It felt good to be wild and silly. His eyes began to water. He couldn't remember the last time he'd laughed so hard.

In the distance, beyond the roundabout at the village beach, whitecaps were rolling in as if it were September rather than the last week of July. Rob walked faster, his breath rising and falling with each swell. When they rounded the bend, a familiar form appeared on the water. Squat on his board, paddling hard with short, quick strokes, Andre was on the verge of catching a monster wave. Rob felt a pang of jealousy. He'd give his left nut to be out there training again. He shielded his eyes with his hand. Andre was still using his board, the same one he'd let him borrow four years ago today, the day before Ella was born. The last time he'd been out on a paddle board.

Ella, with her boogie board dragging behind her, tugged him toward Lake Michigan. "Hurry, Daddy, or we'll miss all the good waves."

Rob slipped on her lifejacket before she bolted past the playground onto the beach and straight for the water. By the time Rob caught up, she was kneeling on her board, riding the first line of waves into shore. She glided toward him.

"Look at me, Daddy. I'm a surf champion like you!"

Rob shook his head. "Just be careful." After seeing Andre in prime form, her compliment left a sting. Five years ago, it had been him, not Andre, on top of the leader board. Rob leaned forward and stretched his Achilles tendon. They'd said it would heal itself within a year—with rest—but taking off that kind of time was a luxury he couldn't afford. The injury healed, though the decision to quit paddle boarding still caused him grief. Why had he ever let his dad talk him into taking over the bar? Looking back, he would have been better off if he'd stayed on the circuit and waited it out.

Now Andre was the only one riding the waves they'd once shared. In high school, they'd been tight. He wished they could still be that close. There was a time when Rob believed nothing could come between them—before Sandra died and Andre started blaming him for her death.

At the time, Rob had wanted to die and had contemplated suicide. "You must forgive yourself. It was an accident." Mom forced him to see a psychiatrist. It had taken time to make himself believe it. Paddle boarding helped salvage what little remained of his sanity. Falling in love with Laura was like being reborn. They created a new life together and were now a family of five. Still, Rob wondered, could he ever fully mend his friendship with Andre. If only Andre could understand, it was Patty who'd betrayed them both.

After Sandra's accident and Andre's trial, Rob thought he'd never speak to Patty again. Instead, they were all back here together and she and Andre were engaged. It was crazy. Memories were firing at him from all directions. How was he supposed to live like this? With the passage of time, he'd buried his other self; the reckless teenager inside him was dead. And yet, he couldn't stop the waves of memories rolling in one after the other making him begin to wonder who he was. Lately, it had started to feel like they were chasing after him.

From the looks of it, Andre had his whole life ahead of him. If Andre trained hard, he'd still have a crack at making the cut for the world paddle-boarding competition in Puerto Rico this spring.

Ella caught a wave near shore. "Daddy, watch me!" Rob threw her the hang loose sign. She smiled at him as she rose onto her knees.

Maybe, in time, he and Andre could once again trust each other? He'd already given him keys to the bar. Over the past month, Andre had been a lifesaver by taking his place behind the bar. He'd done a hell of a job too. Right now, no matter where their friendship stood, he should be thanking Andre. Without his help—and Patricia's— he would have lost everything to the bank. Instead, for little more than tips, they'd kept him afloat. He couldn't afford to hold any grudges.

There had been so many times he'd tried to tell Laura about their collapsing finances, but he couldn't bring himself to burden her with more bad news. How low could her opinion of him fall before she'd leave? He recalled the hostility in her voice when she asked for his tips to buy diapers. He didn't blame her. They were already taking on water before Nate's accident. What kind of husband was he to force his wife to live in his parents' attic with three kids? But now they were on the brink, and he had no one to blame except himself. Michigan was a No-Fault state. The other driver's insurance covered almost everything. The rest was covered under the Affordable Care Act. It didn't get better than that.

Still, he hadn't been able to think straight since Andre returned to town. Rob couldn't stop himself from replaying Nate's accident over and over—how he'd pulled him out from underneath the car, how his body went limp in his arms, and how, for a moment—he'd thought they'd lost him. He had to stop playing mind games and get his shit together, or he and Laura would lose everything they had left. His dad should have never taken out a second mortgage so they could borrow money for the bar. Now, if the bank cracked down, they might even lose the house. He couldn't afford to make any more excuses for himself. Water churned at his feet as Ella ran around in circles.

Out on the lake, a hundred feet off shore, Andre was chasing another wave. Rob had all but forgotten those days when he too had harnessed the power of the surf. Watching Andre ride his board into shore, Rob wondered what it would be like to go back until he paddled toward them, dripping wet in black board shorts that came down past his knees. When

Andre waved to Ella, she hopped on her board and sped off along the surface in the other direction. "A showoff like her pops, I see."

"Yeah, yeah, whatever, dude. Soon, she'll be showing us both up."

Andre tipped his head sideways and knocked the water out of his ears. "Speak for yourself."

Rob laughed it off. "I'm just kidding, man. You looked good out there. Why aren't you doing the Harbor City race?"

"Waste my time at amateur hour?" Andre splashed at the water with his foot. "Patricia wanted us to hang out here, be like a normal couple and chill at the beach. Tonight, will be our first night off together. You know?"

A deep sense of gratitude mixed with a fair amount of shame came over him. "Yeah, I don't know how I'll ever repay you."

Andre shook his head at him. "Don't worry about it. I know you and Laura would have done the same for us."

Rob got a lump in his throat.

"By the way, when I went into the bank yesterday to deposit the check like you asked, I ran into Bill. He said I could just give it to him instead of wasting my time putting it in the account."

"So, you just handed it to him?" Rob asked.

"Yeah, we were standing there inside the bank waiting. You should have seen the shocked look on Bill's face when he saw me with the check made out to it him. All twenty-five-hundred."

"Ugh."

"What?"

"I don't know. I have a bad feeling about that guy. It's kind of a long story. I wish you would have stuck with the plan to make the deposit. I mean, what if he says it wasn't in the account on July 31."

"I don't see the difference. Isn't in his hand the same as in his account?"

"Forget about it. I'm sure it will be fine. You and Patricia have better things to worry about." Rob looked around. "Where is she?"

Andre pointed to a neon orange tent set up on far side of the boat launch beyond the lighthouse. "She's with some of her girlfriends, you know, other personal trainers from the gym. You're welcome to come over, unless … you're waiting for the rest of the fam."

He wished he could still confide in Andre instead of bull-shitting him. There were times when he just wanted to be one of the guys. More and more he felt trapped. With Andre, he could let loose. Back in high school they'd shared everything. Maybe Andre had grown up some, now that things with Patricia had gotten serious? No doubt, he'd been there for him over the past month of hell. They'd been friends for as long as Rob could remember. Outside the family, Andre was the only one who might understand.

Rob looked him in the eye and tried to explain. "Of course, it's Murphy's Law, we just bring Nate home from the hospital and Biyen decides to walk for the first time."

"That's great, man."

"I know. At first, we were all amped until we realized Nate was watching the whole thing—from his wheelchair."

For a second or two, Andre looked away at the water; his jaw tightened as it had, so often, during the trial. Then he kicked at the sand. "Your kid is back home with you. Just be thankful for that."

Rob shook his head in confusion. "I get that. I am. It's just hard seeing him—in a wheelchair—and not knowing if he will ever walk again. It's been a long haul for us. Why you gotta go digging at me?"

Andre looked toward the sky where a hawk was soaring over the bluff. "I'm just saying, you're the lucky one." His chin jutted out like the bird's sharp beak.

A couple seconds later, Rob caught on. Suddenly, his chest tightened as it had when he'd been trapped at the hospital, and at the house—and, long ago, on the opposite side of the bluff—when he was left alone with Sandra not knowing what to do next. Sandra. How could he have saved her? Rob couldn't believe Andre had reopened that wound.

Rob's eyes drifted toward the bluff where Andre's gaze was set. Shielding his brow with his hand, Rob watched the hawk soar above the tall dune grasses in search of a meal. Though he couldn't see the scene in detail from such a distance, he'd watched the scenario play out countless times before. He could picture the mouse darting from its hole and scurrying across the sand—its quick movement catching the hawk's keen eye. Now, up ahead, the bird of prey hovered for only a split-second before it swooped in and made the kill. The back of Rob's neck seized up. The hawk took off into the sky with the small ball of fur clasped in its talons, its broad wings flapping hard against the wind toward its nest.

A wave broke near shore and foamed at their feet. Andre picked up the paddle board and held it deliberately at his side. Rob met his eye for a second. He couldn't be certain, but it seemed like Andre was somehow staking a claim, to exactly what, Rob wasn't sure. But he took the bait. "You just gonna keep that board of mine forever?" Andre bit down on his lower lip as if he was about to say something. Rob had a bitter taste in his mouth. Ella bumped against his side.

"It's too rough out here, Daddy. Let's cross to the lake in Sanctuary where it's calm."

Rob took her by the hand. Until then, he hadn't realized how much his palms were sweating. "I'll talk to you later, man. We're going over to the other side."

Chapter 11

July 31, 2016

Laura sank to the floor outside the attic and sat there, for some time, thinking about her relationship with Helen. She didn't want to fight and couldn't understand why there was always such animosity between them. When she finally tiptoed downstairs, the house was eerily quiet. She poked her head into the kitchen to check on Nate, who was still slumped in the same uncomfortable-looking position. On the counter beside him, Helen had left two ham-and-cheese sandwiches, but Laura wasn't hungry. It was probably best, for now, to let Nate be. She just wished that there was some way to show Helen she was sorry.

After a minute, she heard banging from the other side of the hall. Laura stepped toward the library and listened from outside the door. Chair legs skidded across the wood floor. It sounded like Helen was moving around the furniture. Maybe she needed help? Laura raised her hand to knock but held off for a moment and reconsidered. She didn't want to piss her off again. Then a loud thunk came from inside the other room.

"Ouch!"

Laura reached for the knob. "Helen, are you hurt?"

When she didn't respond, Laura opened the door a crack. "Can I come in?" At the far end of the room, Helen stood behind her desk sucking on her thumb. Laura peeked in a little more. "Are you okay?"

Helen shook her head dismissively. "I'll be fine. Just dropped the corner of the desk on it."

The bulky antique with an elaborate marble top was obviously too heavy to move for one person, especially someone Helen's age. Laura peeked up at her. "Let me give you a hand."

Helen arranged herself behind the desk and pointed out where she wanted it placed. Then each of them took hold of opposite ends. "Ready?" Helen asked. She lifted her end and Laura followed. Together they carried the desk from the center of the room and repositioned beside the wall adjacent to Helen and Art's bedroom. As soon as they'd set it down, Helen began clearing books and photo albums from the shelf behind it. "Nate can put his things here. I want to give him enough of his own space. Someone can bring his bed down later."

For a second, Laura was confused until a wave of relief came over her. It was as if Helen had read her mind. "Of course, thank you so much. This will be a big help."

Just then, Helen reached for a picture on the shelf above the one she'd cleared. She brought it down to show her. It was of Rob when he was a boy. In a deliberate fashion, she held it out for her to see. "This is him on the first day of kindergarten."

The library, with its wall of built-in shelves, was Helen's private space and contained her most precious collectibles. Laura had only seen the photo once, long ago, before she and Rob were married. She remembered how his red hair stood out, but now—seeing it again—realized that her husband and Nate both half-smiled out the left side of their mouth. "Rob looks like he's keeping a secret when he smiles like that. He reminds me of Nate," Laura said.

She handed the photo back to Helen, who took a second look. "I see what you're saying."

Laura relaxed, thankful to have found some common ground. "I'm really hoping he can start kindergarten on time and doesn't have to be home-schooled. I guess it will just depend on how much progress he can make with the new doctors between now and Labor Day."

Helen nodded. "Nate is like his father. He's very determined when he chooses to be. But you never know. It's always on their own terms." She pursed her lips. "Rob could be quite a handful too."

Laura appreciated her mother-in-law's candor. "And Biyen, apparently. I'm sorry about the carpet. I never thought—"

Helen waved her finger. "There's no need to explain. You're always so busy. I get it now. I'd forgotten how it was with toddlers, though there was only ever the one." Her hand trembled as she set Rob's picture back on the shelf. Suddenly, she leaned against the wall as if for support.

Helen didn't seem like herself. Laura worried she'd overdone it. "Is something wrong?" She placed a hand on her shoulder. "I didn't mean to upset you."

Helen waved her off and bent down to pick up one of the photo albums she'd taken from the shelf. When she stood, she opened the album to the first page where there was a photograph of her when she was pregnant. Laura smiled. "You look beautiful. How far along were you with Rob, then?"

Helen ran her fingertips over the photo. "This was me with our first. It was when Art and I started finishing off the attic. Rob was my second pregnancy. I miscarried this time and, again, when Rob was two."

Helen closed the book and clasped it to her chest. "We hadn't planned for him to be an only child. I always imagined he'd have a brother or sister running around like we have now with your kids."

"I'm so sorry, I never knew."

Helen's shoulders slumped. "You couldn't have, Art and I never spoke of it to anyone—not even Rob." Helen's fair skin turned blotchy and tears welled in her eyes. Laura put her arm around her. Helen, who rarely showed emotion, wept in her arms. For the first time, after all these years, Laura felt like she'd met the real Helen. Finally, she'd lowered the fortress door and let Laura inside. "We tried not to treat him any different. Let him have responsibility. We didn't want to hover, not realizing, until it was too late, how easily his friends could manipulate him."

Just then, Helen straightened up. "But Rob is a grown man; there's no point in keeping it a secret anymore."

Laura had never imagined that the secrets from *before her time* were not just holding her and Rob back, but Helen and Art too. She had so many questions she wanted to ask about Andre and Patricia. From the sound of it, Helen wasn't a fan of theirs either.

"Are you talking about Andre and all that happened with his sister?" Laura asked. "I've tried to ask Rob, but he avoids the subject."

"I know. I'd like to forget too. Partly, I blame myself." Helen sat in the desk chair and smoothed back her hair before she continued. "It was a snow day. They were all supposed to stay home. But, as it turned out, none of them did as they were told. First Andre and his sister came over here. Then Rob left and went to Patricia's. But everyone called her Patty back then. She told police Rob was drunk and high when the girl died."

Helen clasped her hands together. "I should have checked on them. Art should have too. He knew better than to trust Rob and Andre together. Andre bossed him around. Rob never should have let Andre use Art's snowmobile to take his sister home."

Laura's temples throbbed. She struggled to imagine the trauma for Rob. It must have been devastating. He was only seventeen.

"The hardest part for Rob, I think, was that he found her, but it was already too late." Helen stood. "It was absolutely terrible. The guilt. We got him professional help, but the whole thing changed his mindset. He was so unfocused. It ruined his chances for college. I mean, I hadn't necessarily seen him following in my shoes all the way to the University of Michigan, but I'd held out hope that maybe he'd study art somewhere not too far from home like Northern. Instead he made his way into paddle boarding and traveled outside the country. Competing helped him cope, but he really didn't seem to come out of it and regain happiness—" Helen took her by the hand. "—until he met you."

Laura appreciated Helen's acknowledgement. Her mother-in-law hadn't been fond of her when Rob had first introduced her. Laura realized that after all the turmoil Rob had suffered through, Helen had been trying to protect him from making another mistake. If only Laura had known, she could have helped him. After the death of her mother and being abandoned by her sister, Laura understood loss and betrayal.

She'd come to Sanctuary and found Rob. Though a fierce competitor, he was a gentle soul. Laura had been certain of it since the day she first saw him paddling in the Manitou Passage, maneuvering through the currents with long, smooth strokes, as if he were trying to appease the forces of nature.

He'd helped her forget those last two years of high school. She wished he'd been able to confide in her, but at least she better understood. They needed to be able to support each other especially now that they were trying to help Nate recover.

Helen paced back and forth. "I must admit, I wasn't thrilled when Andre came back here, or Patricia for that matter. It was terrible the way they both turned against Rob during the trial—Andre insisting Rob could have saved his sister when he should have just been grateful Rob managed to save him." Her mother-in-law paused in the middle of the room, before returning to Laura's side. "Still, it was an accident. No one ever thinks … it's just human nature. You can't keep punishing people or yourself. It's hard to forgive but you have to, if you want to move on. Don't you think?"

Laura was overcome with emotion. Helen had shared so much, and offered her an olive branch, a chance for them to build a closer relationship. "Rob and I are really thankful for all you've done to support us, especially since Nate's accident. We're really trying."

Helen shifted her weight against the desk, and Laura worried she'd said the wrong thing. Would her mother-in-law once again put up her guard? Laura needed someone to confide in. Helen lowered her eyes and her face took on a pained expression. "I can't tell you how sorry I am for buying that scooter. I had no idea they were so dangerous," Helen said. "I want to help you, if I can?"

Laura's shoulders relaxed. She hadn't realized they'd been scrunched up to her ears. Helen's apology meant a lot as did her willingness to work together for Nate's sake. "I want that too. Sometimes, I feel so inadequate."

Helen cupped her hand over Laura's and squeezed. "Welcome to the club."

"Thanks." Laura managed to laugh. "I think."

Helen moved away from the desk, pulled her shirt down over her trim waistline, and straightened up to her regular posture. "I'll finish up in here. Why don't you take the kids and meet Rob at the beach?"

Laura hurried upstairs. After talking with Helen, she felt a new sense of possibility, though she'd still need time to sort through all she'd learned about Rob and his upbringing. She gathered Biyen from the crib and went downstairs him in the carrier. When they entered the kitchen, Nate stirred. Laura gently rubbed his shoulders. "Hey, did you have a good nap?"

"I guess so."

She patted him on the head. "How about we get some fresh air?"

When Nate shrugged, she took it as a yes, and put the sandwiches in plastic baggies. "Let's roll." She pushed him onto the porch, sank her weight into her heels and slowly maneuvered him down the ramp for the first time. Gravity pulled her forward, reminding her of the moment when she and Nate stood atop the dunes on his birthday. They ran down the soft slope together, the sand kicked up from the force of their feet as they leapt into the air. He would be running down the dunes at the beach again one day, she reassured herself. Right now, they were just starting the climb.

As they started down the sidewalk, she tried to convince herself it was a good thing that they were walking. For on a sunny day like this, the beach would be packed. The parking lot was probably full, the same as it had been on the day she pulled into Sanctuary driving her grandfather's Chevy Malibu when she and Rob first met on the beach.

Laura laughed at the memory of how she'd come across Rob on his paddle board. She'd been so into him, but had tried so hard not to let it show—even making up an excuse about having to go back to the parking lot and pay the meter. It had taken her a half-hour to walk there along the beach. Then she had to turn up Main Street, and go all the way down the gravel road to reach her car at the trailhead, which took another thirty minutes at least. Finding Rob had made everything worth it. She'd met up with him the next day at the same spot.

Even back then, Laura had sensed Rob kept secrets, though she couldn't have known to what extent he guarded his emotions. That realization came over time. She thought he'd open up about his fears as their relationship developed. Instead he kept that part of himself *before her time* closed off. Earlier in the library, Helen had hinted at the source of Rob's anguish. Andre had been manipulating Rob his whole life. Though Rob was vindicated in the death of Andre's little sister, he still seemed to carry guilt. She wished he'd let her in. He shouldn't have to suffer alone. She understood from experience how to hide the hurt. Be strong. Not let it show. But if they were going to help Nate recover, and rebuild their family, she and Rob needed complete trust. She couldn't do it alone. She had Helen's support, now Laura needed Rob's. How could she get him back?

If only it were as easy as releasing the drawstring around her waist and revealing the skimpy crochet bottoms she hadn't meant for anyone to see—until she met him for the second time. She recalled the way he looked at her with adoration and desire when her violet skirt fell to her feet. A few weeks later, after meeting at the same time and place each day, they'd stayed until after dusk and made love in the sand. Married love was different. Most of it had nothing to do with sex. Laura wasn't sure she understood how it was supposed to work. But if she and Rob were going to make it through this crisis, and keep their family together, she must figure it out fast.

By the time Laura passed the roundabout for the beach, Biyen was kicking his way out of the carrier. Like any other toddler, he wanted to be on his feet. She stopped on the sidewalk across from the playground, stabilized Biyen with one hand, and searched the pocket of her dress with the other until she palmed her cell phone. When she pressed Rob's number, Biyen kicked his heel in her side. Rob didn't pick up. He and Ella must have gone for a swim. She was about to give up. Just then, he answered. "Hey, babe."

It was comforting to hear his voice. She sensed that their relationship had changed significantly in the few hours since he'd left with Ella. They agreed to meet at the swimming hole on Sanctuary Lake where the only waves were the ones made by the kids. At the crosswalk, she pushed Nate to the other side of the street, feeling a sting between her two big toes where the skin had worn raw from her plastic flip-flops. She slipped them off; they weren't made for heavy-duty walking. She needed a pair of sturdy shoes like Birkenstocks. Yeah, right. To afford those, she'd have to sell a truckload of blueberry scones.

Since the accident, she hadn't been able to bring herself to open the bake stand. Maybe she could start making jam again instead? It would be good to get back to work. She could put Ella on the job of foraging for hidden delicacies. If the girl used half the energy collecting nuts and berries as she did mucking around in the water like her father, her help would be priceless. Wild ingredients set Laura's products apart, and silverberries were coming into season. Thank goodness Ella had a keen eye.

Ahead on the sidewalk, coming toward them, Ella held her boogie board against her chest like a shield. Funny how a pretty piece of foam could make a little girl feel so powerful. It wouldn't be as simple with Nate. Laura parked him beneath the Norway maple on the sidewalk beside the little beach. Nate straightened himself up in his seat and looked around. In front of them, at the water's edge, Jacob's yellow and black skim board was angled away from the shore. In three long strides, Jacob approached with his jaw set and eyes intent on where he'd land his feet on the board. Nate watched as Jacob leapt on like a pro and took off across the water. Nate slumped back in his chair.

Across the beach, Chelsea waded in the shallow water next to the floating dock that stretched into the lake. She held out an inner tube for her twin girls as if she were mothering a pair of ducklings. Laura watched them a moment more. The girls looked so cute in their matching swimsuits with pink and purple stripes. Chelsea looked over at her for a second and then turned her head the other away. Was Chelsea really going to pretend she didn't see her and Nate sitting in the shade.

Sweat pooled under Laura's arms, which had gone as limp as over-boiled spaghetti. Why had she thought coming here with Nate would be a good idea? She could have left him home with Helen to rest. In the shadows of the ancient tree, her son turned his attention away from the water and gazed up at the leaves with sad puppy dog eyes that had lost their innocence. His elbows jutted out from his wheelchair in keeping with his bony knees. He'd lost so much weight that his shorts and T-shirt were now two sizes too big. A broken boy, hidden in the shadows, he almost seemed too small for his skin. Laura approached him and pulled one of the sandwiches from her pocket. "Nanna made this special for you."

Nate frowned at the sandwich inside the plastic baggie. "I'm not hungry."

Laura got it. Nate wanted to be in the water playing with his friends. Before the accident he'd never been introverted. The new Nate craved attention in ways that were hard to pinpoint. He acted like he was alone in his own dimension. From the way Chelsea was ignoring her, Laura too felt like a shade of her former self. Laura opened the baggie for Nate. "Come on, just a couple bites for Nanna."

Nate wouldn't touch it. Biyen, anxious to get out of the carrier, gave her another kick. Laura stood from the picnic table and let him out to put his feet in the sand. His back was soaked with sweat. Poor little guy. He must have been roasting in there. She propped him up on the bench so he could cool down.

Soon afterward, Ella and Rob arrived at the table. Rob eyed the ham and cheese on Nate's lap. "That sandwich looks good. Why aren't you eating? Saving it all for me?"

Laura looked on. For a second, Nate met his father's gaze, until he stared back at the lake where Jacob and his other friends were swimming. Rob noticed them too. Laura's stomach twisted into a knot. She caught Rob's eye.

Ella tugged on Rob's shorts. "Come on, Daddy, let's swim." She pointed to the kids jumping off the end of the pier.

Rob raised his finger at her. "Just a second, I need to talk to Momma."

He took off his old Hurley T-shirt and tossed it onto the picnic table. Laura wished she'd worn her swimsuit under her dress, so she could strip off a layer and at least put her feet in the water. Not that it really mattered to her. She was here to keep Nate company. He couldn't put his feet in the water. They could get their sweat on together. She pulled the other sandwich out of her pocket and handed it to Rob. "Your mom made it."

Just then, Biyen fell onto his bottom in the sand. When he started to whine, Rob picked him up. "I got this." He leaned over and kissed her on the cheek.

Laura felt a little flush. "What was that for?"

He smiled out of the side of his mouth like he had in the kindergarten picture Helen had just shown her. "I'm just happy you came," he said.

Laura was too. She smiled back at him. "At first your mom seemed really stressed, but then we started to talk." She didn't want to ruin the moment by unloading all the details on him. Instead she pointed to Biyen's diaper. "We sort of had a little accident on the rug when I was changing him."

"I wouldn't worry about it." Rob swatted away a fly with his Tigers' cap. "A little pee never killed anybody—"

His careless words trailed off. Then he cocked his head toward Nate. "He should eat."

"You're right, but it's just kind of weird being here," she said. "I don't think he has much of an appetite."

A few yards ahead of them, Ella splashed around on her boogie board. Out further in the water, Jacob swam with the other boys Nate's age. Rob took a bite of his sandwich. "Speaking of weird, Ella and I just ran into Andre who was surfing … on my board. He made some weird comment."

"And that's weird?" Laura said half-joking.

Rob stared down at his feet. "Seriously, why can't you ever cut the guy some slack? He kept the bar going the whole time we were at the hospital." He shook his head at her. "You know, you should just be happy our son is alive."

The wind gusted in her face. She rocked back onto her heels in disbelief until the anger hit. He'd never attacked her that way. "Oh, so now I'm the one who—" She stopped herself, remembering Nate seated downwind from the conversation.

Rob threw the rest of his sandwich onto the picnic table. "I'm sorry. Just never mind."

Ella grabbed him by his board shorts. "Come on, Daddy." When he didn't budge, she pulled harder.

"All right, all right. I'm coming, I'm coming."

Rob left and didn't look back. *Great*, Laura thought. Thanks to Andre, she and Rob were pissed at each other, again. She'd have to talk with Helen some more and figure out what the hell was going on. She couldn't live like this. Like some outsider looking in. Overhead, the leaves rustled in the wind. If not for the breeze, she and Nate would have melted by now, like the ice cream of the girl in front of them.

Laura remembered the nurse's orders. There were other ways to get calcium than cheese. "Hey, want to get some ice cream?"

Nate sat forward and planted his hands on his hips. "Yes, I want Superman."

Once Nate said it, she remembered the blue, red, and yellow swirls that had always been his favorite.

"You know it has super powers," he said.

Laura nodded before swallowing the lump in her throat. If only it were true. She couldn't get emotional. Nate didn't need to see Mom in tears, not when they were going to get ice cream. She looked toward Rob who stood with his back to her and was watching Ella run for the end of the dock. With Biyen in the crux of his elbow, he waded out into the shallow water. "Ella. No diving!"

Laura chided herself. He tried to be a good dad. She should know better than to say anything against Andre. For better or worse, he and Rob went way back. She and Rob must try and get along. Fighting wouldn't help her determine why he was so troubled. To heal their relationship, she needed to understand what had happened in Sanctuary *before her time*. Laura was determined to find out. Their marriage depended on it.

She left the baby carrier on the picnic table for him. He'd be fine with Biyen and Ella for a little longer. For Nate, on his first day back home, a half-hour at the beach was enough. "Come on, let's bolt." When she gave him a push, the blister between her toes burned as if she'd been bitten by a snake. She stopped and adjusted the straps of her flip-flops before starting again down the sidewalk toward town.

It might not be as easy to connect with Nate, but she would bring her adventurer back to life—even if he would never walk exactly the same. She would help him face down any demons and recover the boy with the glint in his eye, the one who'd challenged her every step of the way since the day he was born. She was ready for a battle.

But first, she had to stop again and fix her shoe. When she looked up, Andre was coming toward her. He glanced sideways toward the car beside him. It appeared as if he hadn't seen her. However, if Andre was as manipulative as Helen suggested earlier, Laura figured he'd spotted her long before she'd noticed him. Andre rolled back his shoulders. In his muscle tank, there was no mistaking that he was ripped, but his baggy sweatpants made him shorter than he was in actuality. Still, he was probably an inch or two taller than her. She stared at the sidewalk as he came closer. Maybe she could still avoid eye contact? Andre's Quicksilver slip-ons looked new and comfortable. He must have just bought them, most likely, with the cash he'd made at the bar when Nate was in the hospital. When they were about to cross paths, her gut told her to run. He was probably still mad about whatever he and Rob had argued about earlier.

Just then, Andre raised his dark eyes. Laura suddenly recalled the nightmare she'd been having repeatedly over the summer. It dawned on her for the first time. *The shadowy reflection glaring at her from the mirror above the sink in the mysterious motel room was Andre. He was holding a knife and pointing it at her.* Laura tightened her grip on the handles of the wheelchair and forced herself to keep moving in his direction. The pale skin on his shoulder, now within inches of her, appeared as smooth as the underside of an animal hide that had been skinned and newly preserved. Their eyes met for a split-second. "Hey, beautiful," he whispered.

His hollowed-out voice made her shudder. Was he coming on to her? She looked at him askance without saying a word. *What is your problem?* He shot her back a harsh look and didn't flinch. Unable to withstand his cryptic glare, she blinked before continuing past him, the strap of her flip-flop cutting deeper between her toes with each step.

Chapter 12

July 31, 2016

Rob waded into the water with Biyen on his arm once Ella took her place in line behind the older boys. Jacob, with running start, leaped off the end of the dock hollering, "Geronimo!" The other boys followed his lead, running and jumping off the edge in rapid succession. "Geronimo!" They each yelled one after another before making their big splash. The swimming hole hadn't changed a lick since Rob and Andre were boys. Near the end of the dock, Ella wiggled and fidgeted as she waited for her turn. *A showoff like her pops.* Who was Andre to talk? Until the bastard became a father, he should keep his trap shut. Rob dug his toes in the muck. Calling him *the lucky one.* Rob glanced over his shoulder across the parking lot. He looked past the lighthouse toward Lake Michigan. The waves were still rolling in, but Rob didn't see Andre. Sweat trickled down Rob's forehead. He wanted his damn board back. Andre always found a way to gain control. Rob hadn't been this pissed at him since high school—on the snow day. Damn him.

Now, at the end of the dock fifty feet ahead, Ella bent her knees and leaned forward with her hands pointing down. What was she doing? He'd just told her not to dive. Rob gnashed his teeth as she disappeared headfirst under the cloudy water. He craned his neck to see around the dock. As far as he could tell, Ella hadn't popped up. He tightened his hold on Biyen and waded out further until he was waist deep and could see the spot where she'd gone under. Why hadn't he forced her to wear her lifejacket? She hadn't surfaced and with all the sand kicked up by the string of boys before her, there was no way to see below. Biyen splashed with his feet. Rob's heart raced. He couldn't go out much more, much less swim to the bottom to find her.

"Daddy!" Ella called from far beyond the dock as she doggy paddled toward him. "Did you see how far I swam underwater without taking a breath?"

Rob sighed with relief. When Ella came within reach, he hooked his arm around her elbow. He'd have done the same thing at her age. He'd been a royal pain in the ass to his parents. Still, Rob had never pictured himself being anything like his dad. Dad was the bad guy. Dad enforced the rules along with Mom. Now the parental burden was on him and Laura. He wished someone would shoot him with a tranquilizer gun and put him out of his misery for the rest of the afternoon. Instead he dragged Ella toward shore without another word. Kids never listened.

When he was a boy Mom had never really seemed to get that angry. Even eight years earlier on the snow day, she'd simply stated her rules and expectations. On her way out the door for work she raised a finger at him as if he were seven instead of seventeen.

"Just stay inside and get some homework done. Don't do anything stupid."

Rob smiled in the usual way, acknowledging that he'd heard her, though that usually didn't mean much. He and

Mom both understood he did as he pleased. It had gone without saying until last week when he and Andre were busted for drinking by Dad. If Dad were still home, Rob would have gotten another lecture. "I'll be fine, Mom."

Rob waved good-bye to her, knowing she wouldn't be back from the museum until five o'clock and Dad never left his gallery before six. Praise the Lord, they were both workaholics. Eight hours of freedom. "Amen."

He flopped on the living room couch, rested his feet on the coffee table, and watched the snow pile up on the front windowsill. At that moment, he could think of no one he loved more than Mother Nature. He thought about it again. Patty, and all her soft curves, placed a close second.

He flipped on the TV and didn't give a crap what channel he watched. Anything was better than Chemistry and Geometry, the first two periods he'd miss. His phone buzzed. He reached for it off the table. It was a text, from Andre. *Hey dude, I scored. Be over in fifteen. Explain when I get there.*

Rob wasn't positive, but it sounded like Andre had weed. This day was getting better and better. He went to his room, threw on a pair of jeans over his boxers, and pulled up the tube socks he'd worn to bed. He rifled around in the hamper until he found his gray sweatshirt. He leaned into in the mirror above his dresser and deliberated whether to take a shower. Other than the hair sticking up on the back of his head, he looked presentable. He spat on his palm and tamped down his cowlick.

Nighttime buildup coated his teeth. He cupped his hands over his mouth and exhaled. Major halitosis. He thought about brushing until he heard a firm knock on the kitchen door. Andre. He walked down the hall a short way into the kitchen and yanked it open. Frigid air burned his lungs. He coughed a few times. On the porch stood Sandra, her teeth chattering. Against the white backdrop her pale skin practically disappeared, leaving him face to face with her deep-set, blue eyes and alarmingly red pout. A vision of Snow White with a streak of the evil queen. She looked at him confused and a little perturbed before pulling back the hood of her parka with the faux fur trim. Black curls unfurled over her shoulders. "Are you going to let me in, or what?"

Rob moved out of the way. Sandra stomped the icy snow off her Payless combat boots onto the doormat. Andre hustled past and kicked his snowmobile boots onto the linoleum. Rob shut the door. Why had Andre brought his little sister? Well, actually she wasn't that little anymore. He remembered last year when she was a scrawny, bookish freshman—before she'd hit puberty and transformed herself into a Goth.

Andre rubbed his hands together. "Man, it's freezing."

Rob tipped his head toward Sandra and gave Andre the eye. *WTF?*

"Sorry, Ma didn't want her home alone. I had to take her with me. She'll be out of here at ten."

Sandra smirked. "After you give me a hit like you promised."

Andre pulled a dime bag out of the front pocket of his puffy coat and dangled it in front of her. "Yeah, but that's it."

Andre's jaw clenched and he turned to Rob. "Can't believe she almost busted me with Ma."

Sandra brushed a piece of lint off her black T-shirt. "I told him he should hook me up with his dealer and let me buy my own. That way he wouldn't have to worry about sharing or me telling Ma."

Rob pretended to ignore her comment. Andre would kill him if he showed Sandra any sympathy, though Rob couldn't help but feel sorry for her and a little protective. She shouldn't be smoking pot. She'd always seemed like the most stable person in the Donato family. As Andre told the story, their dad left them two years ago and hadn't made contact since. "No child-support. Nothing. I guess he's still mad Ma got to keep the house." That's all Rob remembered Andre saying. Mrs. Donato had always been a heavy drinker. Now, she could hardly stay sober long enough to drive to and from her job doing nails at the resort. He didn't understand why she even bothered showing up this time of year when there were so few vacationers. Today, there would likely be no one. Rob felt sorry for her and Sandra, and maybe even a little for Andre, though pity was the last thing his friend wanted. Pity wasn't cool.

Sandra and Andre followed him into the dining room. Rob cracked open the window, which made it feel like the North Pole, but he had no choice. He couldn't risk trapping the pungent odor. Now that Mom and Dad had wised up to his "alcohol and tobacco use" they were always hunting for clues to bust him, though they had no idea he and Andre smoked pot on a regular basis. If they found out he used illegal drugs, he'd be grounded from everything forever.

Andre took the head seat at the far end of the table where Dad usually sat. Sandra perched herself in Mom's chair at the other end, closest to the kitchen. Rob sat in his usual place on the side with his back facing the window along the driveway. He crossed his legs and tried to look casual as Andre rolled a fat one, though he kept close watch to ensure his friend didn't leave a trace of evidence. Mom was paranoid as it was about scratching the wood; she'd notice even the slightest residue.

Rob rested his hands on his abs and glanced out of the corner of his eye at Sandra. He couldn't deny she was hot for a sophomore, though she hadn't fully bloomed, unlike Patty who'd matured into a woman by the end of eighth grade. They were complete opposites: Sandra, a standoffish introvert; Patty, a popular party girl.

Sandra tapped out the theme song from the "Lone Ranger" on the table with her black nails. "Are you going to take all day? I'm supposed to be at Mallory's."

Andre bit the inside of his cheek the way he always did when he was searching for a clever comeback. "I'm supposed to be at Mallory's," he said in a whiny imitation of his sister. "Give it a rest."

As far as Rob could tell, Sandra was way smarter than her brother. Another secret he'd have to keep. Andre licked the edge of the rolling paper, sealed it down, and held up the joint for their mutual admiration. "Now that's what I call a breakfast burrito."

Rob nodded in agreement, realizing they would need a flame to light it. He grabbed a book of matches out of the dining hutch and tossed it over to Andre, who didn't waste any time. Andre took a long drag. Within seconds, a trail of smoke rose toward the plaster ceiling and away from the open window into the kitchen. At the moment, Rob didn't give a shit. Everything would air out by the time Mom and Dad came home. Without thinking, he smiled at Sandra. Sandra smiled back.

Andre poked Rob's forearm, frowning at him as if he was an idiot, and held up the joint. Rob took it between his peace fingers, closed his eyes, and inhaled the herb's medicinal effects.

"Hey!" Sandra motioned for him to pass it along.

He did, staring at her chapped lips before his eyes moved to her chest, which lifted as she inhaled. She seemed to be moving in slow motion.

Andre rapped his knuckles on the table. "That's enough."

Rob snapped out of his daze. "What?"

Andre, staring down Sandra, tipped his head at the door. "Why don't you run along and make some snow angels."

She stood in a huff, sticking out her pierced tongue at her brother, before taking one more hit and passing him what was left.

Andre glared at her. "Ma will be home at five. I'll see you there."

Sandra glared back at him. "Don't boss me around." She gave Rob a flirty wave. "Bye."

Andre cursed under his breath. "Such a pain in my ass."

Seconds later, the side door slammed shut. Rob glanced over his shoulder long enough to see Sandra, surrounded by a blue aura, skipping down the icy drive, kicking up snow as she went along.

Now, from beside him on the beach, Ella kicked up sand at him. "Stop that, right now." Rob tightened his grip and let Ella have it. "I told you no diving. It's dangerous. Plus, you went out way too far. No more swimming today."

"But, Daddy. I'm fine."

"This time. You got lucky."

Mom should have been firmer with him and really punished him. If he'd known there'd be harsh consequences if he failed to follow her rules and expectations, maybe then he would have listened and nothing would have happened to Sandra. Instead he and Andre had been stupid. Everything they'd done that day was stupid. Much worse than stupid. He was only beginning to understand now.

Rob spanked Ella on the butt. She ran off crying and screaming for her mother. He went back to the picnic table. For once, Laura should approve of his parenting. He'd put his foot down like she'd been asking him all summer. Rob finally understood. They must stick together. But, where was she?

Chapter 13

July 31, 2016

Laura's blisters had started bleeding, but she kept hustling the other way from Andre. "Momma, don't go!" Laura stopped and turned around. Ella, with tears blurring her freckles, caught her by the knees. "Daddy told me I can't swim. He spanked me too."

Laura put her arm around her. "Why?"

Ella didn't answer. Rob had never hit any of the kids before, as far as Laura knew. She didn't believe in spanking the children. Rob must have thought he had a good reason. Under the tree by their picnic table, he was wringing out his shorts. Biyen squirmed to the ground. She watched as Rob propped him up against his knees and held onto his hand. Biyen wiggled his tiny toes, staring at them as if they were the most fascinating things he'd ever seen. There was no way Rob was going anywhere, right this second, or Biyen would throw a fit.

Rob lifted his chin and caught her eye as if waned to explain what was going on with Ella. Laura turned around the wheelchair and started walking toward him with Ella on her heels. When they were about a block away, a group of women, two in highlighter-colored bikinis and another in black, surrounded him. She recognized the perky butt of the peroxide blonde in the orange bottoms as that of his ex. Patricia circled her pointer finger around Rob's tattoo. Laura understood they were on better terms now. But Rob was still her husband. Why did Patricia think it was okay to touch him like that?

Laura came closer. Rob bent down and lifted Biyen out of the sand acting like everything was cool. No uncomfortable twitch. Nothing. Did she need to post a street sign with an arrow to make things clear? *Wife Here.* Laura doubted Patricia would notice. Standing next to Rob with her eight-pack abs engaged, she raised her hands in the air and waved her friends in for a close-up view. One, who had auburn hair and wore ruched bikini bottoms, leaned forward and exposed half of each butt cheek in the process. The other, who had dark hair with blue streaks in it, kept her distance. Laura thought she might have seen her at the beach once before.

Ella tugged on Laura's dress. "Momma, why can't I swim?"

Laura, her eyes focused on Rob, couldn't concentrate on her daughter. "Just a minute, honey."

Laura adjusted the waist of her dress. "Ella, wait here with Nate. I'll be right back." She approached the group a few yards ahead of her. No one appeared to notice.

"Rob was on the national paddle-board circuit before Andre," Patricia said. Again, Laura noticed her checking out Rob's abs, which were hidden under a modest layer of fat. Though, for a twenty-six-year-old dad who'd traded in paddle boarding for bartending, his gut wasn't that bad.

"But now I own The Second Sand Bar. Most people just call it Sanders. It's a few blocks from here, at the corner of Main and Beach. You should come by. First round's on me. I'll make you one of those energy cocktails of Patricia's—if she'll ever share her recipe."

Patricia shifted her weight and placed her hands on her hips. "Every lady has her secrets." She winked at Rob before patting his belly. "But if you come to the gym, I could share some tips to help you fix that spare tire."

Patricia giggled along with her friend in the skimpy bikini. Laura had seen enough of their flirtation. She stepped beside Rob and took their son from his arms, pretending not to notice the women encircling her husband like a harem. She bounced Biyen on her hip. "Hey, sweetie. We're going to get some ice cream, if you want to join us."

Rob barely made eye contact. "Oh hey, Patricia was just introducing me to her friends. They all work together as personal trainers at the gym."

Laura nodded at each of them. "Hey, I'm Laura, Rob's wife."

Patricia rolled her eyes at her friend in the highlighter bikini, who forced a fake smile. The other woman, in a black netted cover-up, extended her hand. "Hi, nice to meet you, I'm Rosa. Actually, I am not a personal trainer. I work in the locker room."

Laura shook Rosa's hand. "It's nice to meet you, too, but we have to get going. The kids are melting down." She wrapped her free arm loosely around Rob's waist. "Come on, babe."

He looked down his nose at her. "I still need to talk here. It's business," he whispered. "I'll catch up with you in a few."

Patricia grinned smugly as if she'd known all along who he'd be more interested in hanging out with at the moment. Laura couldn't totally understand his change in attitude toward Patricia. He hadn't spoken to his ex in years until she moved back to town a month ago. Certainly, he couldn't have forgotten how she'd betrayed him to the police to protect herself. Why did he trust her again now?

"Whatever works." Laura wrapped both arms around Biyen and tried to walk away with her dignity but tripped over her dress in the thick sand. Behind her, she could hear Patricia's muffled laughter. Laura drew her shoulders back and tried not to let her humiliation show in her labored steps as she carried Biyen toward the picnic table where she gathered up the children's things. How could have been such an insensitive dick?

Laura didn't look back at him as she approached Nate, who was waiting on the sidewalk beside Ella. "I want to swim, Momma."

Laura wanted to scream at her to stop whining. Instead she took a deep breath. Someone had to be an adult. She must send a clear message to their daughter. Actions have consequences. She could talk to Rob later about the spanking. Laura patted her head. "No. Your dad is right. No diving. That's the rule. It's for your safety. Now, take your Boogie Board and let's go. Girls who start following the rules can still earn back ice cream."

Laura shook the sand out of Biyen's diaper and, just when she was about to strap him in the carrier, Patricia's infectious laughter carried down the beach along with the cackling of the other women.

"What's so funny, Momma?" Ella asked.

"I couldn't care less," Laura said.

Then she heard Rob's deep belly laugh. He seemed to have no clue as to the rules. Laura envisioned the sand under Patricia turning into a sinkhole. Being a mother wasn't glamorous. Still, she wouldn't entirely abandon her dignity. She slipped on her Aviator sunglasses. No one had to know they came from Five and Below. She wheeled Nate away. Ella followed a few steps behind and for once didn't put up a fuss. Though she was too young to understand, her little girl sensed things and seemed to recognize that something was very wrong with the picture.

Once they were back on Main Street, Laura pushed Nate past the bar without a pause, her heart pounding so hard she worried it might disturb Biyen, who'd dozed off. *Talk business.* Yeah, right. The placard for Frank's Frozen Kingdom clapped in the breeze. Nate sat up and leaned forward. "Momma, hurry. We're almost there."

Ella ran up beside them and twirled. "Ice cream. Yummy."

Laura sped up. Only a block to go. The Adirondack chairs sat empty on the sidewalk under the sun. Everyone was probably crowded inside under the ceiling fan in the parlor. She glanced in through the screened door. Most of the tables were free, apart from one to her right where two women talked in hushed tones. One of them was drinking a milkshake. "I just saw them at the beach. Terrible what happened to their son," she said. The woman, seated with her back facing the door, had a shrill voice Laura didn't recognize.

Then, the other woman sat forward. Laura peered through the door at Nicky, one of Rob's high-school classmates who now worked at the bank as a loan officer. She'd helped facilitate the lease agreement for the bar. "Yes, but when you think about it ... it's not that hard to believe. I mean those two trying to run a business and raise three children here. Didn't she come from some Indian reservation? She should go work at the casino. And Rob, of all people, running a business. Seriously, he never even went to college. I'm giving him six more months, tops."

Laura, her knees wobbly, took a step back and leaned up against the front of the building so they wouldn't see her. In this corner of Michigan many, like her with Ojibwa blood, considered themselves the hidden people. Now, safe in her hiding spot, she wanted to find out what people really thought—even if it was tough to hear them pick her apart.

The other woman sucked down her milkshake through her straw. "I guess so, but Andre seemed to know what he was doing the other night. I almost felt like I was at a casino. He made me a killer cocktail."

Nicky cleared her throat. "After what he did to his sister, I'm not surprised."

"Come on. That's not fair. It was an accident."

"But he went to prison for it. Either way, I'm just sayin', I wouldn't trust him with a dime."

"It must be hard for their family right now. I just hope she opens the bake stand again. I really miss her blueberry scones."

Beads of sweat pooled along Laura's hairline and dripped into her eyes. She pushed Nate toward home. She had to get away from Nicky and that petty woman. Who were they to judge? Her eyes began to sting.

Nate cocked his head. "Momma, where are you going?" he asked. "You said we were getting ice cream."

Ella wrapped her arms around Laura's forearm and jumped up and down in protest. "I followed the rules like you said. I want ice cream."

Laura, unable to stomach going in there with those women, kept walking. "Nanna can take you."

"No, Momma. You promised." Nate blinked back tears. She couldn't let down him or Ella. They deserved their ice cream. She turned around and ordered the treats to go from the outside window—a Superman for Nate, a cookies and cream for his sister, and a strawberry for herself.

The teenage boy behind the screen frowned. "I'm sorry, mam. The closest we have is tart cherry."

"That's fine." She took a lick of her ice cream. It was pink like strawberry, though not nearly as sweet. She'd eaten plenty of cherries from local orchards, and liked them fine, but she wished she could have gotten the flavor she really wanted instead of what was popular around here. She was beginning to wonder; would it ever be possible for her to belong in Sanctuary.

Chapter 14

July 31, 2016

Rob left Patricia at the swimming hole with her friends and walked across the parking lot toward Lake Michigan where the beach stretched for miles ahead of him along the shoreline. He knew he should catch up with Laura and the kids for ice cream, but he lengthened his stride in the other direction. He couldn't face her and the family. Not right now. Laura couldn't understand. When Andre and Patricia moved back to town, everything changed. In a village as small as Sanctuary, Rob couldn't continue pretending that the past didn't exist—especially when Andre wouldn't let it go. Rob had to figure something out. How could he adapt? For some reason, he kept thinking of Rosa. He'd realized this afternoon that he'd seen her once before, right after Nate's birthday party. She was the woman wading into the water as if she might do something terrible. Rosa was a "dreamer," Patricia had told him in confidence, brought here illegally by her mother from Mexico when she was six-years-old. Rosa had legal work papers under a federal program, but her mother—who worked nearby for years at the Sleeping Bear Resort—had recently been deported after ICE raided the place. He could only imagine how alone she must feel here now. It was weird; Rosa reminded him of someone. He couldn't put a finger on exactly who, yet. But he wanted to find out. Maybe he could help her? And, given her family circumstances, she might be willing to work for cheap. He desperately needed the help. Now that Andre and Patricia were moving on with their lives, Rob was really stuck.

He felt lost in time as if the past, present, and future were converging like the towering cumulous clouds. He walked on, flattening the soles of his feet in the thick sand, and fell into a rhythm. For the next ten minutes, he emptied his mind and just breathed until he reached the turnoff into the forest.

Here, where the dune grass came thigh high, Laura had emerged from the forest six years ago almost to the day. When she first appeared on the bluff overlooking the beach with her windswept hair, he thought she must be a mirage. Then she came closer and things got real. They'd discovered each other. At the time, he believed that Laura had come to this sacred place, so near to where Sandra died, to help him heal. Her arrival was a sign for him to move on.

Now, as Rob climbed the dune, he was plagued with doubt about his way of thinking. Nate's accident had altered his perspective. He'd failed his son. Seeing him trapped under the car had brought back the old shame and guilt. There was so much about himself he'd kept buried in the sand. So much he wanted to forget. Somehow, the trauma of the accident had stirred up those memories like the powerful forces of nature that turned over Lake Michigan each winter.

With the waves of memory bearing down upon him, Rob froze. The snow day, January 13, 2008, came back. He'd never been good at taking care of anything, not even himself. And after smoking pot all morning with Andre, Rob received Patty's call. "Mom got called into work. We have the house all to ourselves," she said. How could he refuse? By mid-afternoon, between the pot, beer, and sex, he felt chill enough to fall asleep and hibernate until spring. He peeled himself off Patty, and rolled onto the other side of her bed, every muscle in his body spent. "Gotta love a snow day," he said. She murmured softly in agreement and closed her eyes. He closed his along with her and drifted off, absorbing the good vibes they'd created. Then, from the bedside table, a familiar tone buzzed in his ear. Rob reached for his phone. The home number appeared on his caller ID. It was already four o'clock. He shot up. Mom or Dad must have come home early. *Shit.*

Did he have to answer? He turned toward Patty's side of the bed and wanted to ask for her opinion, but she seemed to have dozed off. *Sound casual.* That's all he could do. Rob pressed the green button to speak, praying it was Mom—not Dad. Suddenly, he felt like he had to take a crap. Rob clenched every muscle in the lower half his body. On the other end of the line came a gruff voice. Rob held the receiver away from his ear and prepared to get reamed.

"Hey, dude?"

Once he realized it was Andre, his bowels settled back into order. "What's up? I can't believe I'm still stoned. That was some good shit you got." Pulling up the covers, he leaned against the headboard and tried to get comfortable again, until he remembered where Andre was calling from. He was supposed to be long gone. "Why are you still at my house?"

"I'm sorry, dude. I got the munchies after you left, and then I had a couple beers and passed out. I need to borrow your Dad's snowmobile to get home. You can drive it back."

"No way." Rob, suddenly feeling sober, wanted to punch him. There was no way he'd let him touch the machine, even if Patty's house was just down the hill from Andre's. Dad was already pissed at them. Told them last weekend specifically not to use the snowmobile. He'd kill them both if he found out.

"Have you looked outside?" Andre asked.

Rob opened the blinds. His breath created a fog on the inside of the window. He wiped his hand over the glass like a windshield wiper. The window, encrusted with ice on the other side, made it difficult to get a clear view. He got the gist. The dirt road he'd walked in on had disappeared beneath a blanket of snow. It looked like a complete white-out. Soon it would get dark. Visibility would drop to zero.

Andre swallowed on the other end of the line, still waiting for an answer. He cleared his throat. "Sandra's here with me. She was afraid to walk home alone. Dumb chick doesn't even have real boots."

Rob remembered how she'd strutted into his house like she owned the place and stomped off the snow and ice caked onto her boots at his door. She was clueless, usually in a good way, though not this time. Under these conditions, combat boots wouldn't cut it. She'd have frostbite by the time she was halfway home. Still, Sandra was Andre's problem. Why did that bonehead have to get him involved?

As usual, Andre really hadn't left him a choice. "Go ahead, take it. But hurry. I'll meet you at your house in twenty minutes."

Rob pressed the red button on his phone to end the call, wishing he could kill Andre—and Sandra—for that matter. Why did Andre always have to fuck things up? He switched on the bedside lamp.

Now, squinting up at the bluff, Rob was nearly blinded by the sun. It had been more than eight years since the snow day, and yet he'd never learned from it. Instead, all this time, he'd fought the truth. He'd thought Patricia had been asleep when he and Andre were talking on the phone, bragging about being drunk and high, but she'd heard the whole thing. The police had every reason to believe she knew something and pressured her into talking. *They said they were getting the phone records.* That's what she'd said, Rob remembered now. Patty, her eyes swollen, begging him to forgive her. Instead he'd walked away.

Up until now, he couldn't make the connection between January 13, 2008, and July 3, 2016. Again, he tried not to picture Nate on his scooter, pushing himself off with his left foot, and speeding across the street—trying to get back in time for the parade. But, this time, he couldn't fight the truth.

The accident might never have happened, he realized just then, if he'd supported Laura when she'd asked him for help with Nate. Instead of acting like a real father, he'd been more interested in scoring a cigarette than tracking down their son. He'd left that up to her. Watching the kids was a mother's job, or so he'd told himself that morning and all others prior. God, he'd been hung over. He'd thrown back more than a few the previous night at the bar, once he officially closed the place to the public, and made the call to let Andre and Patricia bartend. He could still recall the mix of spicy cinnamon and creamy Kahlua in Patricia's Slippery Nipple shot. Why did he always regress when he was around them?

He should have backed up Laura when she'd told Nate the rules. No. 1: Do not cross the street. No. 2: Stay on the sidewalk. Instead, he cracked a joke, something about how she'd become one of those nagging Tiger Moms. What had he been trying to prove? He'd noticed, after he said it, how the skin around her mouth sagged. His comment had hurt her. Yet Laura, once again, had found a way to forgive him.

Rob turned around. He had to make things right again between them. He didn't want to lose her. Rob ran down the dune onto the beach. In the distance, at the water's edge, sat Andre. His back hunched, his chin jutting forward, he carried himself like a guy who'd been through hell. Andre was right. Rob was a lucky man. He owed his friend an apology for being such a dick about the paddle board earlier. Rob picked up a jog and kept going until he was within a stone's throw of Andre. When he came within a few feet of him, Andre glanced up. "Come for your board?"

Rob took a deep breath. "Hey, I'm sorry about before. You can keep the board as long as you want." Andre lowered his chin and kept his head down. "Seriously, it's the least I could do. I mean, you were like my savior helping out with the bar. The landlord has been riding me. It's rough." Rob thought back to when they were boys with nothing better to do than comb through trash cans on garbage day. "Not like when we were kids—remember when we found that old paddle board at the curb?"

Andre nodded. "Uh, yeah. It didn't even have a rudder."

Rob laughed under his breath. They'd lugged it all the way to Sanctuary Lake and used a long stick as an oar. Together, on the same board, they'd paddled around in circles for hours. Eventually, they learned how to steer it straight. Growing up in the same town, failing the same classes, playing the same sport, and now—dating the same girl—they'd developed an inexplicable bond that Rob couldn't fully understand. Andre, who sat next to him in kindergarten, seemed to him a fellow comrade on a secret mission with an unknown objective that would only be revealed if they took appropriate steps. Unlike Rob, Andre believed change was progress. Andre wanted to change Sanctuary. He was determined to make a comeback and seemed to have direction. There was something about him when they were together that lifted Rob's spirits and made him feel like he too could accomplish something. Yet, on another level—after coming out of prison—Andre seemed as lost as Rob. They were both trying to figure out how to fit in and find their place in life. One thing Rob knew for certain, they'd been friends for too long to give up on each other.

Andre pointed his chin up at Lake Michigan. "When's the last time you were out there?"

Rob eyed his old board. "The day before I gave you that."

Andre tilted it forward. "Want to take it for a ride? Might help you chill."

Rob ran his hand over the surface, remembering the length and feel of his board on the water, its rough texture like coarse sandpaper on the soles of his feet and the smooth underside, generating the fluidity that powered him across the waves without any friction. He wondered where Andre stored it at night. Rob wouldn't admit it out loud, but he loved that board. Without it and the water, he felt as if he'd lost his own rudder. He couldn't help but wonder what he could have accomplished if he would have stuck it out on the SUP-boarding circuit instead of trading places with Andre. As it stood, his memory and a few Internet blurbs were all that remained of a career that had taken off unexpectedly and peaked in the pros. It had happened almost too quickly to appreciate. Had he quit before his best years arrived? Like a lot of professional athletes, he hadn't quite given up hope that somewhere there would be another opportunity to kick butt and once again know glory. Rob took the board by the rails.

Andre looked up at him with a wry grin. "Have at it. I'm going to enjoy this."

Chapter 15

July 31, 2016

Nate licked off the red, yellow, and blue drippings around the edge of his cake cone as Ella picked out bits of cookie from the cream. Laura eased Nate over a hump in the sidewalk where the roots of an old oak forked into the soil. The tree had been growing there long before the concrete was poured, Laura thought, perhaps when her Ojibwa ancestors inhabited these lands—long before Sanctuary was settled, long *before her time here,* or Rob's for that matter. Six years seemed like a long time to know someone, but she sensed that they were only just beginning to understand each other.

"You saved me," he'd told her the night he proposed. After talking to Helen earlier in the library, Laura finally was beginning to comprehend. She'd brought a new perspective to town. When Rob fell in love with her, he took another step toward putting the trauma of Sandra's death behind him. At that time, early in their relationship, Rob had put her first.

Laura thought back to the New Year's Eve, six months after they met, when she was eighteen and three months pregnant. They'd walked arm-in-arm into the dining room of The

Sleeping Bear Resort. Laura chuckled at the memory. How out of place the two of them must have looked entering on the red carpet. The hostess hadn't quite been able not to stare. Laura, self-conscious of showing, took care to smooth the wrinkles out of her not-so-little black dress before she went up to the buffet where the savory aromas of roasted meats and vegetables reminded her of the Eagle Ridge Supper Club back home, though the resort's white linen tablecloths and crystal chandeliers didn't exude the woodsy charm she once cherished on cold winter nights when she'd sat cuddled between her mother and sister in the corner booth beside the fire.

Seated across from Rob, Laura began chowing down as politely as possible. Maybe it was because she was pregnant, and her morning sickness had passed, but she couldn't recall a time when food ever tasted more delicious. She couldn't wait to try the chocolate-covered strawberry but, when she bit into it, juice dripped onto her baby bump. Laura just sat there and stared at the mess she'd made until Rob gently dabbed the spot on her belly with his napkin. "I would have licked it off, but the maître d' was watching."

"It would have been a good show," she said. They shared a good laugh. Then he kissed her with unexpected urgency. He went back to his seat and they finished dessert. But, after that, she could tell that he was anxious to leave.

When they arrived at his parents' house, Rob eyed the living room couch and suggested she have a seat. As soon as he sat down beside her, his eyes looked as if they'd begun to water. Then he presented her with a scroll tied in a black ribbon. The paper was as white as the bloodroot petals that first emerged from the partially thawed soil each spring. Although her heart was racing, she carefully took both ends of the ribbon between her peace fingers and pulled them apart.

Laura flattened the scroll on her lap to reveal her own profile inked in black and white. Her chin rested on her left hand and, though her head was turned, Rob had managed to capture the look of a free spirit in her eye. The portrait, signed Robert Sanders, showed his steady hand, though Laura most appreciated his ability to portray subtle nuances, including the hollow groove beneath her cheekbone. Apart from the ring drawn around her finger, the sketch was realistic. She teared up, along with him, though she wasn't entirely sure what to make of the gift. "It's so beautiful. I had no idea you could draw."

Rob reached for her left hand and held it between his calloused palms. "I made it for you as a token of my love. I'm still saving but, by the time our little one is born, I should have enough to buy you a proper ring. I promise."

More than anything, she wanted him to ask her to marry him, but only if it was out of love rather than duty. "You don't have to do this."

His bottom lip trembled. "I know, Laura. I want to." He got down on one knee. "Laura Warner, I think I've loved you since the moment you first told me your full name." From the corner of his mouth cracked a smile. "Will you be my better half and take me as your husband?"

She promised to love him forever. He fell into her arms. They'd been so intimate. At the time, she couldn't imagine any love more real.

Now Laura felt a tug on her dress. Beside her, Ella licked off an ice cream moustache and held out the last of her cone. "I saved you a bite."

Laura chuckled. "Thanks, but you can have it." Ella skipped up the ramp to the side door and Laura followed with Nate into the kitchen. She pushed him down the hall toward the living room past the same couch where Rob had proposed to her. Once considered fine furniture, the fabric on the cushions was stained and threadbare. Helen walked out from the library. Nate took a last bite of his cake cone.

Helen smiled at him. "Superman seems to have thoroughly enjoyed himself." Then she eyed Laura and tipped her head toward the library. "Your Mom and I have something special to show you."

Laura led Nate inside where his bed was set up by the bookshelves they'd cleared. However, now it was covered with a new comforter. Nate spread his arms. "It's a bird, it's a plane, it's …" he paused and looked across the room. Laura followed Nate's gaze toward the doorway where Rob was hiding around the corner.

"What's going on in here?" Rob, with his hands shoved in his pockets, poked his head in.

Nate sat forward and pointed at the bed. "Dad, look. It's Superman!"

Rob came beside him. "This looks like a different place."

"It is, Dad. It's like we're back on Krypton before it was destroyed—before anything could hurt Superman."

Rob ran his hand down the thick whiskers on his chin as he always did when he was thinking. "That sounds like a pretty cool place, bud. But then, Superman had to figure out how to live on earth."

Ella wrapped her arms around Rob's leg. "I'm sorry for not listening to you, Daddy."

"I understand. We all make mistakes." He patted her on the head. "All we can do is try and learn from them."

Laura glanced at Rob as he put his arm around their daughter. Then, he raised his eyes. "Sorry it took me so long."

She swallowed the lump in her throat. He'd come back, but she sensed his past was tugging him away like the undertow. With Andre and Patricia around would it ever be possible for her and Rob to come together and move forward?

PART III

Chapter 16

August 9, 2016

Laura finished wiping the crumbs off around the toaster. Just then she heard a thud on the window above the kitchen sink. Ella ran in from the dining room. "Momma, what was that?" Laura had a sinking feeling went she followed her out on the porch to see. "Oh, no. Momma, look." Ella pointed to the cardinal lying on its side. Its wings were twitching. She peered over at the broken bird with the tiny beak and timid eyes. "Its legs aren't moving."

Laura cringed. "Let's go inside now, and give her some space. We don't want to scare her." She took her daughter's hand. "Maybe she's only stunned?" Laura pulled her away and Ella followed along halfheartedly. "Why don't you go finish coloring."

Ella seemed to pick up where she left off, yet Laura remained troubled by the bird suffering outside her door. Though what could she do, really? She wished someone else were here to help decide, but Rob was at the bar taking inventory and Helen was at the museum. Art had taken Biyen for a stroll to the beach, which also meant he would be having a smoke or two. So, there was no telling when he'd be back.

Nate was here. Good thing he hadn't heard anything. She poked her head around the corner of the family room where he was watching TV. She followed his eyes scroll down the medal count from the Rio Games. Laura was grateful for the distraction. Ever since the end of Opening Ceremonies, he'd been obsessed with watching the Olympic athletes reach new records—swimming faster, diving sharper, flipping higher, spiking harder, or running at the speed of lightning like Jamaica's Usain Bolt.

Now, observing him in his wheelchair, she saw a boy broken like the cardinal that crashed into the window. The bird didn't have anyone to protect it. She should have protected her son. Kept him safe so that one day he could soar. Dr. Azzi's prognosis haunted her: *He may never walk again.*

For several seconds, her legs went as stiff as the bird's. What had she done? What could she do about the bird, her son, or anything? She went upstairs to make the beds. When she entered the attic, stagnant air overcame her. Last night before she went to sleep, she'd opened the front window as far as it would go. Apparently, it had done no good, though she'd caught a glimpse of the Perseid meteor shower when a star trailed past. Piece by piece the universe was breaking apart around her. She had no idea the sky could fall so close to home.

She threw the tattered quilt over the lumpy mattress she and Rob shared and turned up the fan on his side of the bed. She stood with her back to it and tried to catch a breeze as she filtered out all the negativity in the household and the outside world. A woodpecker tapped on the pine tree in the front yard, which came as a welcome change from the buzz of cicadas. For now, at least, the terror attacks from earlier in the summer had ceased and the conflicts over questionable killings of black youths and white police officers had simmered down. Both candidates' toxic political conventions were over. Amen to that, though none of it was much consolation. She'd never imagined there would be a time when everything would feel so unstable. She lifted her hair and let the air whir around through the thin strands on the nape of her neck taking comfort from the relief it provided. There was always something to be grateful for, she reminded herself.

When Laura went back downstairs, she found the bird in its same position. Suddenly, she understood what to do. Laura took a brown paper grocery bag from the recycling bin and called to Ella. "Could you poke some holes in this?"

Ella raised a colored pencil like a mighty sword and went to work. "I did it." She grinned at her as if she'd won a pivotal battle.

Laura brought out a fresh washcloth from underneath the kitchen sink. Together they approached the bird. Laura opened the washcloth and gathered up the cardinal. The bird fluttered her wings, but then eventually stayed still. Ella held open the airy bag. Laura gently set the cardinal inside and loosely taped shut the top of the bag. "She'll stay in the basement overnight as our guest. This way she'll be away from predators. Maybe she can recuperate."

The next morning, Laura brought the bag outside onto the dried grass in the backyard. Ella helped cut off the tape. Laura removed the little bird in the washcloth and placed her on her side facing the rising sun. Ella set a saucer of water beside the bird's beak. Within a few seconds the cardinal opened her eyes. In them, Laura saw no fear. The bird raised her head and tilted it toward the sun. Suddenly, it hopped to its feet and flapped its wings. Laura held her breath. Ella's eyes glistened at first. Though, after a few seconds, the bird stopped moving.

It became clear that the cardinal could no longer fly. Instead the bird skittered toward the bushy pine in the back corner of the yard. Laura put her arm over Ella's shoulder. Together they stepped away toward the porch.

Tears trickled down Ella's flushed cheeks. "Momma, why couldn't we save her?"

"We did all we could," Laura said. "You should feel proud about that."

Laura went back into the kitchen and observed the cardinal as it slowly disappeared into the trees and laid itself to rest in the shade where it blended in with the reddish-brown pine needles fallen in the summer heat. In the end, the cardinal had relied on herself. Died on her own terms. In that, Laura found dignity.

The cardinal had succumbed. Nate had a chance to recover, though there were no guarantees. His foot and ankle were badly burned and broken. There was nothing she could do to change that. She must help him heal and keep up his spirits even when hers were low. She couldn't let him down again. They must find a way to rebuild.

Chapter 17

August 22, 2016

Laura dug in her heels as she pushed Nate's wheelchair up the hill toward the children's center in Big Rapids. Tired as she felt after the two-hour drive, she kept a steady pace toward the building that towered ahead. Nate wouldn't be late for his first appointment with the physical therapist. They'd been waiting for this day for almost a month, ever since he was released from the hospital. Laura glanced at the massive white grids strung like kites across the exterior. Big Rapids Children's Health Center was even grander than the pictures of it posted online. She couldn't deny that she was a little intimidated—until the glass doors parted and she and Nate entered a sunlit dome that looked more like a botanical garden than a medical facility. She tapped Nate on the shoulder and pointed up at the clear panels over their heads. Nate's eyes widened in wonder.

"It's almost like we're still outside, though you can't get a sunburn in here," Laura said. "Isn't that cool?"

Nate nodded, and Laura could tell by the way his wrists relaxed over the edge of the armrest, that her son was comfortable here. She pushed him toward the directory on the far wall where Back on Track Physical Therapy was listed in Suite 201. They came around to the elevator and she stopped beside the arrow pointing Up. "Nate, can you get that?"

Soon they were on their way to see the therapist. "I wish we had one of these at home," Nate said.

When they exited the elevator, his eyes were focused on the office at the end of the hall. Her palms began to sweat as they approached the door. "Ready?"

Once they were inside the waiting room, elephants, tigers, and tropical birds surrounded them. He turned from right to left, as if he couldn't decide where to explore first. "This place is awesome," he said.

The receptionist poked her head out from behind the check-in desk and waved to Nate. "Glad you're here. We don't get too many from up in your neck of the woods. See anything familiar?"

Nate gazed at the mural as if he were out on a safari. "You guys need some bears."

The woman chuckled. "Thanks for that suggestion. I'll look into it." She turned her attention to Laura. "I like his spirit. He's gonna do great." She motioned for Laura to take a seat. "Keshya, your therapist, will be right out."

Laura sat at the end of the row of chairs. She reached over and squeezed Nate's hand. "I have a good feeling about this place."

"Me too, Momma."

After a few minutes, a young woman with a bright smile and goddess braids greeted them. "You guys can come on back."

When Laura pushed Nate through the doorway, it seemed as if they were entering a professional gym. Barbells, medicine balls, and a set of parallel bars were lined up in separate areas. Keshya led them into a small room with a window facing the equipment. "We like to call this our VIP box," she said. "From here, you can see all the action."

Keshya, who wore a loose shirt and black leggings, eyed Nate's Detroit Tigers T-shirt. "I'm a baseball fan too."

Nate was so engaged in the conversation that he didn't seem to notice as Keshya helped him up onto the examination table. "Even when we're working in here, you can see everything." She swept her hand across the exercise area where a boy, who appeared to be in middle school, was lifting weights over his head. A girl, who looked about ten, was riding a stationary bike. "Does any of that look fun?"

Nate leaned forward. "I want to ride a bike."

"That sounds like a terrific goal." Keshya positioned herself in front of Nate with a clipboard. "I'm going to jot it down." She held up a chart that said one hundred percent at the top. "Today, we're going to begin our sixty-day challenge, so we can measure how far you can go. Sound good?"

Nate nodded enthusiastically. Laura, who took a seat along the wall, hadn't seen him so excited since the accident. "Yes. Nate's a natural athlete and competitive like his Dad."

"Oh, yeah. What sports does your Dad play, Nate?"

"He used to paddle board on the national team, but not anymore. He quit."

Nate lowered his chin to his chest as if he were embarrassed. His reaction made Laura uneasy. Is that how Nate saw Rob, as a quitter?

"I used to play competitive volleyball, until I went back to school so I could become a physical therapist and help people like you." Keshya squinched up her face at Nate and made him giggle. "Now I just play with my friends for fun."

Nate nodded. "My dad paddle boards with his friend too."

Keshya turned to Laura. "What does your husband do for a living?"

"He owns a bar."

"That's a big change. Does he like it?"

Laura shrugged. "That's a good question."

Keshya seemed genuinely interested in learning about their family, though Laura couldn't explain much at the moment. "It's been kind of stressful, especially under the circumstances. My husband has been pulling double shifts. But we're committed to coming here and making this work for Nate."

Keshya made another note. "Great. Having a positive attitude is key to reaching goals. We like to say: When you believe, you can achieve."

It sounded similar to the mental coaching techniques Rob subscribed to when he was on the SUP-boarding circuit. Laura had never set specific goals, tracked her progress, or used slogans to help think positive, but she was happy to go along with the plan for her son. *Believe to achieve.*

Keshya gently lifted Nate's left leg and began to move it up and down and from side to side. Laura hugged her arms to her chest and forced herself to keep her mouth shut. They'd just met Keshya. So far, everything made sense. Laura didn't want to interfere, but physical therapist or no, the woman didn't yet understand the extent of her son's injuries—not like she did. With daily dressing changes, Nate's wounds had healed significantly since he'd been home. Many of the abrasions from the road rash had scabbed over, but his skin was still somewhat raw from the burns, the scar tissue made everything sensitive, and his ankle was held together by metal pins. They couldn't risk reopening any wounds.

Keshya reached for Nate's left foot, and ever so slightly began to flex it. Laura stood from her chair and came beside him. "I wouldn't try to move his ankle."

Nate frowned at her. "Momma, it doesn't hurt. I'm fine."

Keshya remained focused on Nate's movement. "We are going to take things as slow as necessary. But each time we're together, we'll try and move forward little by little." She rested Nate's leg on the table and patted his other thigh. "We want to maintain strength in this guy too, so both your legs will be strong. Can you lift it?"

Nate straightened his right leg with ease. Next, Keshya put her hand around Nate's bicep. "Make a muscle for me." Nate made a fist and raised his knuckles toward his chin. He twisted his neck to see his bicep bulge. "Wow! You're going to be able to help your Mom move this wheelchair real soon and learn to get around more on crutches—not just back and forth to the bathroom." Keshya chuckled. "How about that, Mom?"

Nate smiled and Laura patted him on the shoulder. She would help him recover. They were a team. Laura believed they could achieve, along with help from Keshya. She showed Nate a few more stretches, and demonstrated the exercises he was required to perform at home before his next appointment. She handed Laura a packet of paper that listed each exercise step by step. "And remember: get plenty of calcium."

"Momma, can we go to Frank's on the way home?"

Keshya raised an eyebrow at Laura. "Frank's?"

Laura chuckled. "It's his favorite ice cream shop, but I'm not sure we'll be able to make it there before dinner. We'd have to hurry."

By the time Laura wheeled Nate into the dining room it was quarter after six. The aromas of tomato, garlic, and basil escaped from beneath the aluminum foil that covered the casserole dish in the center of the table. Rob, who was seated between Ella and Biyen, put a heaping forkful of lasagna in his mouth.

"Sorry we're late." Laura pushed Nate into his spot beside Helen next to the kitchen. "It smells delicious." She took a seat beside him.

Helen rose from her chair to serve them. "That's all right. We waited five minutes, but then decided to just go ahead since we weren't sure how long you'd be. Everyone was hungry." She sliced them each a piece of lasagna. "I made it with extra cheese for Nate, so he can get his calcium. How was your day?"

"Great!" Nate said.

Ella, seated across from him, squinted. "What's on your face?"

He licked around his lips, which were stained red, yellow, and blue. "Oh, Momma got me Superman."

A wave of embarrassment washed over Laura.

Helen raised her eyes in disapproval. "Before dinner?"

Laura's cheeks felt as hot as the steaming lasagna on her plate. "The therapist said he needed calcium, sorry. I didn't know you were making this."

Laura also hadn't mentioned to anyone that she felt guilty because Nate had missed the cake and ice cream at Jacob's birthday party this afternoon. Chelsea had brought over the family's old Wii for Nate before he left for physical therapy. They were getting a new X-Box system for Jacob, Chelsea said. "Nate will have to come over and give it a try when he's up for it." Laura wholeheartedly agreed. She'd been wondering why—other than the birthday—Chelsea hadn't invited Nate over since the accident. Laura hadn't said anything, though she sensed a wall had gone up between them. She poked her fork into the layers of noodles.

"I told you what we were having before I left for work, when I called up to you from the kitchen. Remember?"

Laura didn't want to get on Helen's bad side again. She eyed Rob from across the table. Picking up on the cue, he shook his head at his mother. "That was me. *Remember?*" He laughed. "I'm coming down the stairs to go to the bathroom, and there you are eating toast. You hadn't even put in your dentures."

"Or my glasses," Helen mumbled.

Rob leaned back in his chair and smiled at Laura and then at his mother. "All I hear is bwah, bwah, bwah." Rob looked over his shoulder at Art, seated at the opposite end of the table from Helen. "How was I supposed to respond to that?"

"You just nod," Art said, before taking a swig of beer from his tall mug.

"I don't know how I've managed to live with you two—always putting me off," Helen wagged her finger at Art and then at pointed it at Rob. "Rob, you're almost as bad as your father."

Rob snorted. "That's a big almost."

Helen sighed. "Okay, I guess you're right. At least you pretend to listen. Your father just tunes me out."

Rob leaned into the table toward Laura. "I bet she's never told you this. Mom, do you remember when you set Dad's newspaper on fire?"

Helen leaned back in her chair and placed a hand over her heart. "Oh, my goodness; don't bring that up in front of the children."

Rob waved her off. "Come on, it was years ago—before they were born."

Helen threw up her hands in apparent surrender, and then cast a glance at Laura. "You know how men are—we needed to decide about whether to take out a second mortgage on the house." Helen pointed down the center of the table at Art. "He refused to talk about it and just pretended he was reading the newspaper and couldn't hear me. Just like he's doing right now, playing with his food."

Laura tried not to stare at her father-in-law who was moving the wide noodles around his plate.

"So, then what, Nanna?" Ella asked, her jaw hanging wide open.

"I struck a match." Helen spread out the fingers on both of her hands "And poof!"

Helen's faced turned bright red before she buckled over in laughter. Rob started laughing too. Laura sat dumfounded, unable to imagine Helen acting out on impulse.

Across the table, Ella appeared frightened. "But what happened to the newspaper, Nanna?"

"Oh, Poppy just wadded it up and shoved it in the chimney."

"You could have burned the house down," Rob said.

Helen chuckled under her breath. "At least that way we'd have gotten some money out of it from the insurance company."

When Laura looked toward Art for his reaction, the corners of his mouth were downturned, and his paunchy jowls began to shudder. "Enough!" Art pounded his fists on the table and his fork fell to the floor with a clatter. "This house is the only thing keeping us all afloat, goddammit! It's about time someone realizes that and takes things seriously, or we're all going to be on the street."

He stood from the table and wiped his mouth with a napkin. He pointed an accusatory finger at Rob. "I need you at the gallery tomorrow. It's the first day of my sale, and I'm going to need an extra hand with a project."

Chapter 18

August 22, 2016

When Laura pulled the blanket over Nate's legs, he wiggled uncomfortably from side to side. She smoothed the hair back from his forehead, which usually helped him calm down. However, tonight, he wouldn't stop fidgeting. She thought he'd gotten used to sleeping between the bookshelves of the library. Unless something else was bothering him? Going to Big Rapids for therapy was a big change. She recalled the grimace of determination that had spread across his face when he'd made a muscle for Keshya. "I was proud of you today."

Nate stared at her with big, sad puppy eyes. "I'm sorry I made Poppy angry." He tugged the blanket up to his chin and ran the satin edge over his quivering lips.

"Oh, Nate, don't worry. He wasn't angry at you." She gently covered him with his bedspread. Art's outburst earlier at the dinner table had upset her too. Laura felt for him. He'd made a valid point. Money problems didn't solve themselves. Laura just wished he hadn't blown up in front of the kids. He must be under a lot of stress. Nate's accident had taken a toll on everyone, including Art, who had often watched the other kids when Helen was at work. Thinking back, she couldn't recall if Art had made a single sale of his original work this summer. Rather, he seemed to be relying on commissions from the works of other artists he now featured in his gallery. Art's Art wasn't what it used to be. She'd often heard passing tourists chuckle in amusement at the name. Now, for the first time, Art was marking all his paintings forty percent off.

Maybe Rob could try and talk with his dad about it tomorrow? She would have to make sure to ask him. As parents, they needed to talk about what they were going to do to keep things on more of an even keel. "You sleep tight Superman."

"Momma, can I ask you something?"

Laura sat on the bed. "I'm listening."

He pulled the blanket up to his chin. "If Poppy kicks us out like the man at the apartment, will I get to keep my bed?"

Laura cringed when she recalled the eviction—seeing the crib, their clothes, and the rest of their belongings flung in a pile at the curb like someone's garbage. She couldn't believe Nate remembered. She brushed back the hair from his forehead. "You must have super powers of memory. No one is going to let that happen again. Nanna and Poppy love you very much. Dad and I love you too. We all help take care of each other. Okay? Grownups just get worried sometimes and they say things they don't mean. Just like kids do. Remember when Ella took the first piece of cake at her birthday—the one you wanted—and you told her you wished you only had a baby brother?"

Nate pulled the covers up over his head. "Come on out," she said. "I'm not mad at you. Everyone gets angry sometimes."

He poked his head out like a turtle coming out of its shell. She bent over and kissed him on the forehead "I love you."

"I love you too, Momma."

Laura switched off the light and slowly shut the door. She breathed out deeply and tried to calm herself on the way downstairs. Why was Art talking about losing the house? Had Rob kept something from her? They couldn't afford any more setbacks. Little by little, Nate was making progress. Similar to the wounds on his skin, his muscles, tendons, and ligaments would take time to heal. A few exercises, a few times a day, would make a big difference.

They must persevere, especially for the next few weeks, to cash in while the tourists were in town. After Labor Day, they could get into their fall routine. Helen had enrolled Ella at the church pre-school. Ella couldn't wait to start. If Nate gained enough strength, he could start kindergarten on schedule with the rest of his class, including Jacob and the other boys he hadn't seen since they were all at the beach. And then Laura could get together again with Chelsea. She missed their friendship. It was all about attitude, Laura reminded herself. Like Keshya said: *Believe to achieve.*

Once downstairs, she knocked on the door of the bathroom where Ella was brushing her teeth. She twisted the knob and pulled, but the door was locked. "Ella, it's Momma. Open up. It's time for bed." The bathroom went quiet. When Ella didn't respond, Laura twisted the knob each way. Ella had never shut her out. "This isn't funny."

Ella sniffled on the opposite side of the door. "I know."

Laura's heart clenched into a ball. "What's wrong?" Ella didn't answer. Laura rapped on the door. "Please honey, let me in." After a second, Ella opened it a crack. Her eyes were blood-shot and the skin underneath was rubbed bright red. Laura bent down and put her arm over her shoulder. "Why are you so sad?"

Ella shook her head and pouted. "I don't want to tell you."

"Why not? I'm your Mom. I'm always here to listen."

Ella stomped her foot. "No, you're not. You left me. You only care about Nate now."

Laura started to get the picture. "Are you mad because you didn't get to come along to the new hospital?"

Ella scowled at her with arms folded across her chest. "And you got Nate ice cream and not me!"

Laura placed a finger over her lips to remind Ella that they must be quiet. "Nate is going to sleep now. He's tired after his long drive and doctor appointment. Ella, do you like driving in the car for a really long time and going to the doctor?"

"No." Ella dropped her chin to her chest. "I like ice cream. You didn't get me any. It's not fair."

Laura's head pounded. She hated it when Ella whined like this and couldn't take any more drama today. They were all overtired. Laura wanted to kick herself. If only she hadn't pushed it and taken Nate for ice cream. She took a deep breath and gathered her daughter into her arms. Once the kids were asleep, she was going to bed too. "You're right, Ella." She kissed her on top of the head. "Do you want to go on a special adventure this fall, just the two of us? The trees are starting to turn."

Ella swiped away her tears. "Where?"

"I'll tell you in the morning, after you get a good night's sleep."

Ella blinked her heavy eye lids. "But I'm not tired."

Laura picked her up and carried her into the kitchen. "I know just the thing to help." She sat her on the counter next to the microwave where Laura warmed some milk. Ella watched the mug go around in circles. Once it was ready, Laura took her upstairs, set the mug beside her bed, and helped her into her frilly nightgown. She took her by the hand and led her toward the bed, remembering herself at the same age, when she and Shenia had been fighting. Often, it had fallen upon their grandfather to calm them down before sleep.

"Gazaagin," he'd say with a slight lisp once they were tucked in. In Ojibwa, it means *I love you* from an elder to a child, he taught them. "It is the eagle that represents love because it has the strength to carry all the teachings. We must take care of each another to love one another."

Now, though she was nearing exhaustion, Laura took her grandfather's words to heart as Ella got into bed. "Do you want to hear a story?" Ella, holding her mug between her hands, nodded. Somehow, at that instant, Laura knew what she wanted to tell her. "Do you remember the legend of The Sleeping Bear?"

Ella sipped her milk, licking her lips a couple times before she nodded. Everyone around Sanctuary knew the local lore of the mother bear, Mishe Makwa, who was driven out of Wisconsin long ago by a raging fire. Swimming through the day and night, she crossed Lake Michigan with her two cubs, only to lose them both to drowning within sight of the Michigan shore. Moved by her sorrow, the Great Spirit, Gichi-Manidoo, created the North and South Manitou Islands to mark the spot where the cubs disappeared along with the solitary dune overlooking them at Sleeping Bear Point to represent the faithful mother bear who still watches over them.

"Well, my story is a little different."

Ella's eyes widened. "How?"

"The cubs live!"

Ella smiled. "That's what I always wanted."

Laura patted her on the head. "Me too. But that's not the whole story." In these confusing days, they all needed stories to help navigate through the treacherous waters facing them. Laura took a deep breath and the storytelling powers of her grandfather stirred within her as she spoke. "When the mother bear grows too weak to finish the journey, these cubs, who are sisters, are cast out onto separate islands beside each other."

Frown lines crossed Ella's forehead. "The mother bear dies?"

"I'm not certain. But, for the time being, the cubs must fend for themselves."

Satisfied with her explanation, Ella took another sip of milk. "Then what?"

"That's for the sisters to decide. Left alone on their separate islands, without their mother, they each blame the other. At the same time, they don't like being apart. They must decide whether to find a way back together."

"Wouldn't that be dangerous?"

"Yes, probably." Laura smoothed back Ella's hair. "What do you think they should do?"

Ella finished the last sip of milk and handed her the mug. "Try."

Laura swallowed the lump in her throat. She and Shenia had communicated only by text and hadn't actually spoken to each other in years. "I think you're right."

She kissed Ella on the forehead and switched off the bed-side lamp. Moon rays filtered in through the attic window and cast slant shadows beneath the crib where Biyen was already asleep. "Good-night. I love you. Gazaagin."

Chapter 19

August 23, 2016

Rob paused for a second on the sidewalk beside the gallery when he saw his dad, seated in front of the window, putting the finishing touches on a painting of a small row boat in a vast lake. Rob had always liked this particular piece, though he and his dad usually saw things differently when it came to art. When he looked up, Rob noticed the sign above the front door was missing.

A familiar trio of bells chimed when he stepped inside. Yet, today, Rob got an uneasy feeling. Art might have given the gallery a lighthearted name, but he'd always considered himself a serious painter. In recent years, Rob had noticed that his dad hadn't been able to keep up with the times. The market Up North had changed. It was big business. Even the paintings were big. These days, customers in Sanctuary came from big cities like Detroit, Chicago, and even New York, looking for the next new thing. Abstract oils portraying artificially vibrant landscapes were in—reality was out. People came to Sanctuary for an escape, not to be reminded of the gritty details, even if his dad found beauty in them. His vision was lost on the tourists who strolled past the gallery with a chuckle and didn't bother stopping in.

Rob stood by as his dad dabbed his brush where a stroke of the oar had funneled into the still water. "Just let me finish up here. I'm hoping the embellished giclee will make it look more like the original. Apparently, regular prints aren't good enough anymore. Everyone wants these limited-edition canvases."

Rob approached his dad's desk covered with stacks of papers and bills. He needed a book keeper, that much was clear. They couldn't make a dent in the backlog today. On the floor behind the captain's chair, a new sign rested up against the wall. Arthur Sanders Fine Art. He hadn't known his dad was even considering changing the name of the gallery. Rob took a seat.

Seconds later, a fashionable couple in their mid-thirties strolled by holding hands. Suddenly, the woman—who wore an oversized diamond ring—stopped and pointed at Art. She tugged on the shirt-sleeve of the man beside her, who Rob assumed was her husband, and led him inside where she took a close look at the painting. "We used to have a row boat at our cottage when I was a kid." She leaned back and smiled. "This fills me with nostalgia."

Rob could relate. He too yearned for the days of his childhood when it seemed everyone else of his generation was rushing toward the future—though in this painting, the vast body of water unsettled him. To him it felt like the unknown, but that didn't appear to trouble the woman.

Art set aside his brush and approached the couple. "What brings you here?" He flagged Rob over before putting his hands in his front pockets.

"We're celebrating our first anniversary," she said. "We drove up from Chicago. It's so beautiful here. Someday we hope to buy a cottage."

Art chuckled. "Well, this print you're looking at—which I've been embellishing all morning—is a lot more affordable than the real estate around here, not to mention the taxes."

Art patted Rob on the shoulder. "Isn't that the truth, son?" Rob, cringing on the inside, smiled politely at the couple as his dad continued. "Robert grew up here. Still lives down the street. They say Sanctuary is one of the most beautiful places in America."

Rob glanced at the couple before averting his eyes. He hated when his father called him by the name on his birth certificate. Where was he going with this spiel?

Art continued. "Well today I can make you a deal on this. It's a limited edition giclee, and with the embellishments, this is the only one like it. I'm trying to part with some of my classic pieces, so I can make room for new work. It's the first time they're on sale. Forty percent off. With the extra touches, it's almost as good as the original, which now hangs in the capitol in a gilded frame just like this."

The woman bounced on her toes. "In Washington D.C.?"

"No, Lansing, our state capitol." Art stared at the floor. "In any event …" he leaned toward the oar of the boat and lightly blew "… it should almost be dry." He took a step back and raised an eyebrow at Rob. "If you'd like, Robert could have it crated and ship it to you in Chicago. It only takes a few days. That way, you wouldn't have to worry about carrying it around with you at the beach."

Art tipped his chin at the woman, who nodded at her husband. The man ran his fingers along the rim of his fedora and took his wife aside. "I'll give you a moment." Art stepped back. Rob, his heart racing, followed his dad's cue and returned behind the desk.

After a brief discussion with her husband, the woman approached Art. "We'll take it."

Art shook the woman's hand. "Wonderful. My son will take care of the payment and shipping."

She approached Rob and wrote him a personal check for five hundred dollars. Her husband leaned over her shoulder. "That includes shipping, right?"

"Sure," Rob said. "I'll have it sent as soon as it's dry. It should be there when you get home."

The man put his arm over his wife's shoulder and kissed her on the cheek. "I love you," he said.

"Love you too."

Rob scribbled their purchase information on a receipt and handed it to the woman, Becky Smith, who was now blushing. Rob, momentarily, found himself caught up in the couple's excitement. "I hope you enjoy your purchase and the rest of your stay in Sanctuary." He shook the man's hand. "I own the bar on the corner up the street if you want to stop in later. Over there, you can call me Rob."

The man waved and took the receipt from his wife. Once the couple left, Art disappeared into the back room. Before Rob could remove the painting from the easel, his dad returned carrying another print of the same row boat painting in a standard gold frame.

Art held it up to the light and blew off the dust. "This one should do," he said. "And next time, you charge for shipping."

Art handed the substitute print to Rob, who noticed a couple dings in the frame. "Are you kidding me?"

Art pointed to the embellished painting by the window. "That frame costs a fortune, more than the print is worth."

"Even one that's embellished?"

Art crossed his eyes at Rob as if her were stupid. "You thought I really was going to sell them one that was embellished at that price?"

"Yes. That's what you told them."

"Rob, those aren't collectors, they're yuppies from Chicago who only buy art to impress their friends. Unlike us, they live in a high-rise apartment and have more money than they know what to do with. Trust me. They won't know the difference."

Rob's temples began to throb. "But we will."

He wondered whether his dad told the truth about the original hanging in the capitol, even the state capitol. He wasn't sure he wanted to know.

Art swept back the loose gray hairs from his forehead. "Rob, the age of King Arthur and the Knights of the Round Table—if it ever existed outside fairytales—ended a long time ago in a land far, far away from here." He stood from his stool. "You have a wife and kids to support. I have to keep a roof over your heads. Those people believe what we tell them. We don't have the luxury of living in a fantasy world."

He drilled his eyes into Rob's before he shuffled past him toward the back room. Dad had taken out a second mortgage on the house to keep the bar afloat, Rob knew. If he lost the lease because he didn't bring in the minimum return guaranteed the landlord, Dad would lose his home.

"Make sure you cash their check, and it clears, before you ship it," Art said. "When you come back, we can hang my new sign."

He'd never heard his dad sound so cynical or bitter. All Rob's life, his dad had been there for him, shown him affection and taught him the difference between right and wrong. Like any good father, he'd set limits. He'd forbidden Rob and Andre from using the snowmobile after he'd caught them drinking. Though Rob disobeyed his dad and had resented him in high school for getting on his case, he'd understood that's what dads were for. If only he'd listened—Sandra would still be alive. Even then, amid the accusations, his dad stood by him. Believed in him. After the accident that killed Sandra, Rob never wanted to disappoint his dad again. He tried to be the son Arthur Sanders wanted him to be. His only son. Rob knew about the others, though his parents never spoke of their loss. Dad was his King Arthur—the one who fought for him.

When had he started acting like a total schmuck? Rob needed to talk about it with Laura, though lately she'd been so focused on Nate that she didn't seem to have any time for him. The last thing she needed was to hear about any more of his problems. He probably was best to keep his mouth shut if he wanted to keep the peace.

Chapter 20

September 16, 2016

Laura helped Nate onto the examination table as they waited for Keshya. Sixty days after surgery, he was starting the second phase of rehabilitation for his ankle. He'd reached an important milestone, which gave Laura a sense of accomplishment. "I can't believe you're doing so great!" She patted Nate on the head.

Just then Keshya came through the door.

Nate, seemingly embarrassed of Laura's affection, rolled his eyes. "Stop it, Mom. Geez."

Keshya smiled at each of them. "Are you ready for this?"

Nate nodded enthusiastically, though Laura was still wary. From now on, Keshya had warned her, his therapy would target the area of injury. So far, they'd focused on maintaining strength in his quads and upper body. He liked to ride the arm bike, for sure, and just last week, he'd learned to ride the stationary bike with his good leg. Today, he would start learning with the other.

"The ankle is a very complex joint, actually it's made up of three," Keshya said. "The stability of the joint is maintained by connective tissue and surrounding muscles. The primary connective tissue is the ligaments, which connect bone to bone to limit excessive movement."

Laura tried to absorb every word, though she doubted Keshya's explanation meant much to Nate. "The muscles of the lower leg, ankle, and foot also help stabilize the ankle joint. So, when the ankle starts to move more than it should in one direction, muscles fire from the opposite way to help stop it. These muscles must react quickly. Our job is to restore range of motion, strength, and control."

Keshya smiled at Nate. "Do you want to move fast?"

Nate bumped his bottom off the table. "Uh-huh."

"Great. Let's start teaching your muscles how to do it then. Believe it or not, this means moving very, very slowly, but with a lot of effort."

"Like a turtle crossing the road?" Nate asked.

"Exactly," Keshya said. "That's how you build strength."

Keshya led him to the stationary bike and set the timer for ten minutes. "Can you warm-up on your own this time?"

"Yes," he said.

Nate pumped his right leg with ease and Keshya nodded for Laura to follow her back to the exam room.

"He's doing great, but this next part isn't going to be easy," she said. "We've got to start pointing and flexing and moving side to side. He's not going to like it."

Laura choked up. "I had a feeling."

"I won't give him any challenge he can't handle," Keshya said. "Do you trust me?"

Though Laura had complete confidence in Keshya, she still wished there was some way Nate could avoid the grueling physical therapy ahead. If only she could do it for him. Accepting that neither option was possible, Laura swallowed the lump in her throat. "I do."

Keshya clapped and waved for her to follow. "Then let's go for it."

Once Nate had finished biking, Keshya handed him a crutch for under his right arm. He hopped off the seat and moved toward a treatment table. Laura observed as he sat with his left leg straightened and his foot positioned over the end of the table. "Now, I want you to flex."

Laura crossed her arms over her chest as Nate gritted his teeth and brought his toes toward him so that they pointed toward the ceiling. The movement was almost imperceptible, but to her it felt as though he'd moved a monster truck. Keshya went up on her tiptoes. "That was great!"

Nate pressed his palms into the mat and slowly brought his toes toward him and then relaxed his foot. "I did it, momma."

The corners of Keshya's mouth turned down and she stared Nate in the eye. "Now we must do it nine more times."

Nate, gritting his teeth, repeated the exercise over and over until he reached five and he said he wanted to quit. Laura, who had broken into a sweat just watching, would have let him stop there, but Keshya wouldn't let him give up. "Come on, Nate. You can do it. Push a little harder."

Nate grimaced and his leg trembled until finally his toes came toward him. Keshya released the band and quickly helped him off the floor. Nate collapsed into his wheelchair. "Momma, it hurts."

Laura wanted to break down, though she maintained a straight face. "It's going to get better, Nate. Trust me."

Keshya gave him a minute break. "I'm really proud of you, Nate. Let's keep going." One by one, she led him through each of his previous stations, including leg lifts, until she'd completed everything. "Today was like a double dose of medicine. You're going to be biking with both legs in no time!"

For the first time all day, he didn't smile back at her. Instead, he gripped the armrests of his wheelchair and scooted back into it. "I'm tired, Momma. Take me home."

Laura pulled onto Main Street. Soon, they would be home. It had been Nate's hardest day of therapy yet. Luckily, she brought along a blanket and Nate had been able to sleep the whole ride. He lifted his head off the arm rest of the door. Just then, a school bus approached from the opposite direction and put out its stop sign across from Jacob's house. Laura waited with her foot on the brake. One by one, Jacob, and another friend from school, crossed in front of the car. She looked behind her in the rearview mirror. Nate's eyes were glued on the boys. Laura followed Nate's gaze up the walkway to Jacob's front door where Chelsea let them in. Chelsea never invited Nate, or her, over anymore.

Laura continued down the street, wondering if she'd made the right decision to home school Nate. She could tell he missed Jacob. Maybe he should be going to school with the rest of the kids? But she'd said "No!" when the principal suggested that he use scooter to get around. Nate wasn't ready for a scooter. Not now. Not ever. He was safest with her pushing him in the wheelchair. A wheelchair wasn't an option for him at school since they didn't have a paraprofessional available to take care of him. Laura wasn't about to take any chances with his safety.

After all his hard work today, Nate deserved a pick-me-up. She passed by the house and parked in front of Frank's down the street. "You know what they say? A double dose deserves a double dip."

"Yay!"

Laura took the wheelchair from the back and pulled it around for Nate, who hopped out the side door and plopped onto his seat, blanket still in toe. She didn't say anything about it and plowed the wheelchair through a mound of sand. Therapy had been grueling, but Nate had persevered. Maybe they were finally getting back on track?

"I've never gotten two scoops before," he said.

"Think you can handle it?"

"Oh, yeah."

Laura smiled to herself. It had been months since she'd heard Nate sound that happy. His voice had been missing that childish joy since his birthday, when they'd surprised him with a party at the beach—the night before the accident. Before dinner, Rob had taken him for a swim. She'd watched from the picnic table as they waded into the calm water until they were knee-deep and standing side by side. That night, Nate and Rob had really seemed to bond as father and son. Like Rob, Nate had always loved being at the water. She'd have to tell Nate about the first time they'd all gone to the beach, when he was only a month old.

Laura gave the wheelchair a shove. They were almost there. Frank, the owner, came to the door and let them in. "Well, thank you," she said.

"Got to take care of my best customers." Frank motioned with his hand around the empty parlor. They were the only customers.

"This is what happens when school starts," Frank said. "Please, Mrs. Sanders, have a seat." Frank knew all of the customers in town by name. She wheeled Nate into the cozy nook by the bay window and took a seat on the angled bench across from him. In a matter of seconds, Frank hurried back with Nate's cone. Nate immediately took a lick. As she'd asked, Frank had made it a double. "Taste as good as it looks?" Nate nodded without taking his eyes off his ice cream. "Superman is my favorite too. This one's on the house."

Before Laura could thank him, Nate tipped his head to the side, stuck out his tongue took a big lick around the blue, red, and yellow glob on the cone. Frank chuckled before he stepped back behind the counter. Laura remembered the rest of her story. "I bet I can think of one thing you liked even more than that ice cream."

Nate raised an eye brow. She pointed to the blanket on his lap. "Did you know we've had that since you were a baby?" Nate shook his head. "You and your dad always used to have tummy time on it. You loved it when he played with you on the sand, even before you could roll over."

Nate's lower lip quivered as if he might cry. "I'm done." He gave her the cone, though he'd only eaten half. Nate always finished his ice cream.

"What's wrong?" she asked.

He straightened his arms and pushed himself out of his wheelchair onto his good leg. Laura jumped up from the bench to catch him. "Nate, stop." He persisted in standing. "It isn't safe." He wriggled out of her arms and tried to take a step. "Please, Nate, why are you doing this?"

"Dad doesn't love me anymore!"

Frank, having heard the disruption, stepped in to help. He caught Nate by the elbow. "Hold on, young man. You don't want to hurt yourself."

Nate flailed his arms and tried to wrestle free. "Yes, I do. I'm no good anymore. Let go of me."

Laura, who had dropped Nate's ice cream, tightened her grip around his arm to prevent him from tipping over sideways. "Nate, you are good. Please, stop. Sit back down in your chair."

His muscles gave out and, with Frank's help, she coaxed Nate back into his seat. Frank helped get him settled. "I'll get some water," he said.

Nate's outburst had taken her by surprise, though she'd increasingly been wondering why Rob was closing himself off when Nate needed all the support they could give. Apparently, Nate had noticed too. Laura, catching her breath, bent down on one knee in front of him. "Dad loves you very much."

Nate clenched his jaw. "That's a lie."

What did he just say? Laura was so puzzled she felt dizzy. It took her a second to steady herself. "Nate, you know I wouldn't lie to you." She stroked his hand. "It's kind of like what I told you about Poppy when he got so stressed. Sometimes when you're an adult love is hard to show."

Chapter 21

October 2, 2016

Nate zoned out in front of the television watching SpongeBob as Laura measured a sixteen-inch strip of gauze dressing. As much as the sound of SpongeBob's laughter irritated her, keeping Nate distracted while she worked was critical. Laura cut the material and dipped it in sterile water. She kneeled on the floor as she wound the dressing between her son's toes. Though she tried not to pressure him, it was crucial he didn't wiggle when she fan-folded. She had to be precise or, the burn specialist had warned, Nate's skin could heal incorrectly. In a worst-case scenario, it would look like he had webbed feet. Laura almost couldn't imagine that the quality of her care, or lack thereof, could lead to a deformity. It didn't seem possible but, then again, none of this would have seemed possible a few months ago.

Laura gently parted his toes, hesitant, at first, to take a peek. Much to her relief, the tender skin in between his big toe and the second was only a little pink and looked like it was healing as it should. She continued bandaging Nate's foot. In a matter of months, the tedious task had become routine, though it still took her full concentration. She didn't hear Rob until he was right behind her.

"Hey," he said.

"Oh, good morning." Laura sat back on her heels. "Or afternoon, I guess."

Rob sat in Art's La-Z-Boy and put his feet up. Nate's bare leg was propped in the wheelchair, and Laura started up his ankle.

"Couldn't you do that in another room?" Rob reached for the remote. "I was going to watch football."

Laura glanced over her shoulder at him and wondered how anyone could be so insensitive. It would take her about ten minutes to wrap Nate's leg to the knee and cover it with the burn net before attaching the splints. "Maybe you could come back after SpongeBob?"

Rob shook his head at her and let out a heavy sigh as he stood from the chair. He'd never been able to watch her change Nate's bandages. She'd tried to be sympathetic to him and had gone out of her way to change the dressing when he wasn't around, but Nate had been home from the hospital for more than two months. It was about time Rob got used to it. He couldn't kick them out of the room for his own convenience anymore. Couldn't Rob see? Nate was the patient; he was the one suffering. No wonder Nate felt "no good anymore." She'd been thinking about how to broach the subject with Rob, since Nate had confided in her a couple weeks ago, but still hadn't found the right words.

Rob was impossible to get along with these days. Laura was so looking forward to getting out of the house and taking Ella with her into the forest to forage. However, for that to happen, she needed his help. "We're almost done here and then you can watch football all day. I promised Ella I'd take her on a little adventure with just the two of us. I thought you and Nate could stay here together. Biyen just went down for a nap."

Rob scowled. "How long are you going to be?"

"A couple hours or so. I'm hoping Ella can help me pick silver berries for that jam you like. Plus, the farmer's market is next weekend. I sold out of it last year. Made two hundred dollars."

"How are you going to have time for that?"

"What do you mean?"

"I mean, you're already going back and forth to Big Rapids during the week. Now you're going to be out on Saturday and Sunday too?"

"I can take the kids with me to the market if I have to. I'm just trying to pitch in and, you know, help out financially like your dad has been saying?"

Rob ran his hands back through his thick hair, which he hadn't cut in months. It now had grown out past his shoulders. "It's going to take a lot more than some jam." He stormed out toward the kitchen. Ella, coming from the other direction, breezed by him in the hall and came beside Laura. "I'm ready to go, Momma."

"I'll just be another minute. You can watch some TV with Nate." Laura finished wrapping the bandages around his leg and left for the kitchen to put away her supplies. When she came into the kitchen, Rob was foraging through the refrigerator. "I don't see how all this is going to work," he said from behind the door.

"Why not?"

Rob slammed the fridge shut. "So, I'm supposed to work all night and then turn around and babysit Nate and Biyen all day. I was going to meet up with Andre and go paddle boarding. Now what? I'm supposed to sit here. I mean, there isn't even anything to eat."

He glared at her as if it were her fault they had little food. Laura felt as if he'd backed her into a bush of thorns. She sprang forward. "Figure something out."

"What the hell are you talking about?"

"I'm talking about you. You are not the victim here. Nate is. Maybe you could try and think about how he feels for once?"

"Oh, so now I'm the bad guy because I want to watch a little football in peace."

Laura felt the heat rise to her face. She was done sparing his feelings. "Do you know what Nate said to me after that appointment a couple weeks ago when I took him for ice cream?"

Rob crossed his arms and leaned back against the fridge. "No."

Laura willed herself to speak the truth. "Dad doesn't love me … I'm no good anymore." She swallowed. "That's how your actions in the other room make him feel."

Her throat burned. "And by the way, I know you spanked Ella. I thought we agreed that we would never hit the children." She'd never been so infuriated with him for his failure to get on the same page as her. "So, yeah, figure something out. Like, maybe go get a haircut. Ella and I will be back in a few hours."

When they came upon the small pond hidden away in the forest, Ella ran ahead to get a closer look. They were only a few miles from the center of town yet, to Laura, walking with her daughter among the beeches, maples, and birches, felt like a secret world where anything was possible. On the still water an eagle feather floated, reminding Laura of her journey from Eagle Ridge to Sanctuary. She'd known to turn off the highway when a bald eagle—taking on the spirit of her Ojibwa grandfather—had soared overhead and led her down Main Street. She'd followed the great bird of prey toward the water until she reached Lake Michigan and could drive no further. She'd needed Sanctuary then, after her grandfather's death. And she needed it now, in her time of family crisis.

She'd turned her back on her father and left her native state. She was a woman. A married woman with three children to look after. She loved her family, though she wasn't sure if she could hold it together without Rob's support. Since Nate's accident, even when they were in the same room, it seemed as if Rob was off somewhere in his own head. So far, he'd refused to acknowledge a problem. Was he overstressed about their finances? Like Art remarked, someone had to take the family's welfare seriously. They needed food. They needed money for necessities like diapers. Something had to change.

Laura didn't want to be a burden. Maybe Rob and his parents would be better off without her and the kids. At times, she still felt like they didn't fully belong here. It shook her to the core. She'd once been so certain. Laura searched for the eagle feather on the water, but it had disappeared. Perhaps she'd misread her grandfather's sign.

She gazed at the mirror images of the trees reflecting off the surface until Ella splashed her hands in at the edge, disturbing it. Laura followed the ripples across the pond. She'd considered taking the kids back to Wisconsin to get to know their grandfather, Heinz, and their Aunt Shenia, though Laura hadn't seen her big sister since Shenia skipped town shortly after their mother's death. She'd invited them both to her wedding, but they'd made excuses. Shenia couldn't miss work. For her father, Michigan was too far. Then again, what did she expect from him. Never had he leaned down to kiss her or welcomed her into his arms for a bear hug. For him, there were no gestures of affection. Not once could she recall even a simple pat on the head.

Her father and Shenia knew about Nate, yet neither of them had never asked to come meet him or his siblings. *Guess Shenia's too busy plucking eyebrows.* Laura didn't like to dwell on her big sister's lack of interest. It saddened her too much. She wondered what Shenia was up to. Someday, she would love to see her again. One day, maybe, Laura would be brave enough to go back to Wisconsin and re-experience at least the memory of home. She missed having a big sister almost as much as she missed having a Mom. The three of them had spent so many fall afternoons in the forest, collecting bushels of berries like the silverberries she and Ella would forage for today.

It was early in the season, though the leaves on some trees around the lake were already changing color. The leaves of the silver birches, shaped like arrowheads with jagged edges, were always among the first to turn. Laura stared into the narrow space between a pair of their peeling white trunks. Her mother had once taught her how to shoot an arrow straight through such an opening. Laura turned sideways, stepped her feet shoulder-width apart, and took aim. Drawing back the elbow of her right arm behind her shoulder, she extended her left arm forward at the same height. Her target came into focus. Between the two trees, a ray of sun streaked all the way to earth. Laura pinched her peace fingers to the thumb of her right hand and released her imaginary arrow. She watched it soar clear through the light.

"Manistee," she whispered in tribute to her mother and the spirit of the forest. In doing so, she sensed she'd also set her own spirit free. She longed to share her connection with Ella, who now was leading her around the pond, yet Laura trailed a few steps behind as they walked through a tunnel of trees among the fluttering locust leaves. Out here, away from the cramped bungalow, she could finally think.

It was a mother's responsibility to hold the family together. Leaving wasn't an option, and neither was divorce. She still loved Rob, no matter what he was going through. She knew, deep down, he loved her too. But she'd had enough of his bad attitude. He acted like such an ass today. They must find a way to get along.

If only they could rekindle the passion and tenderness they'd shared when they were just two young lovers on the beach. If their love was true, they should be able to stick together. She recalled Rob's watery blues eyes when he'd proposed. How could loving one another be so tough?

Laura continued along the path behind her daughter until Ella pointed at a bush ahead of them and ran off toward it. "I think I see some, Momma." She stopped at the final turn beside the birches Laura had noticed earlier. "Look!" A rugged bush with odd red fruits sprinkled in silvery flakes came into view. The bush was so laden with berries that its limbs rested on the ground under the weight. Ella ran over to it and started picking. Laura joined her, holding a cluster over her basket and loosening the ripe fruits with her fingers until, one after the other, they fell in.

Within a half hour, their baskets overflowed. By Laura's estimate they'd collected a gallon. Raising her basket, Ella shared an accomplished smile. Just then, there was movement in the thick brush next to the pond. "What's that, Momma?"

Branches snapped left and right. Laura took Ella's hand and pulled her daughter into her side. *Anything but a bear.* Laura stiffened up when she saw a patch of brown fur. Suddenly, a doe bounded toward them, zigzagging until it reached the sprawling patch of berries. Laura led Ella to the other side.

"There's certainly plenty to go around." They watched as the doe lowered her mouth and nibbled up the fruit.

Ella's eyes sparkled. "Next time we should bring a tarp."

Maybe next time, Laura thought, they could bring home more than berries. Rob could hunt in these woods. Bow season had started yesterday. Maybe he could still get a license. As he'd said, it would take *a lot more than jam* to provide for the family. She still couldn't bring herself to eat any type of fish, and wouldn't serve them to their children, though fish were easy to catch from shore in almost any lake around—not to mention the salmon and whitefish that lurked further out.

A decent size buck could provide for a family of five, or even seven, all winter. Art's Ten-Point crossbow had hung on the rack in the basement beside the clothes dryer for years. As far as Laura knew, Art hadn't hunted since she and Rob were married when his eyesight began failing. However, she'd heard plenty of stories from Rob about how they'd gone hunting when he was a boy. She'd have to talk with him about it. They had a lot of things still to talk about.

Chapter 22

October 2, 2016

Laura set her heavy basket on the counter by the stove. From the looks of it, between her and Ella, they'd collected enough fruit for a double batch of jam. Laura rummaged around in the cabinet before pulling out the largest pot she could find. With a little luck, she could sanitize the jars before dinner. Laura glanced up at the case of the mason jars on the top shelf above the oven. She went over and stood on her tiptoes, realizing then, she still couldn't quite reach it. She wondered, where had Helen put the step stool.

Just then, Rob came in from the hall. "Want me to get that for you?"

She mumbled that she could do it, but didn't complain when he stepped up beside her and took down the entire case.

"Sorry for being such a jerk today about Nate and everything." He shoved his hands into the pocket of his hoodie. "I don't know how you do it. You're so amazing with him." He dug his hands in deeper. "Most of the time, now, I don't even know what to do with myself."

"I'm sorry you feel that way." Laura recognized how squeamish blood made him and appreciated his compliment, but that was still no excuse for his behavior. It would take a lot more than one small apology to make up for all the time he'd neglected them. "Honestly, I can't do it alone. Nate really needs you now. We all do."

"I know. I'm sorry. I haven't been able to tune in."

That much was obvious. She needed a better explanation why. "Yeah, you've been acting really weird. What's going on? Does it have something to do with Andre, or Patricia?"

"I'm not sure but, ever since they came back to town, it's like I'm trapped."

"How is that possible?"

"I can't seem to decide on anything. I don't know where I stand anymore."

"Do you still want to be with me?"

Rob reached for her hands. "Yes. You know that."

"How would I? You push me away? You're pushing all of us away."

"I don't mean to."

"Then why did you hit Ella?" Laura asked.

"I was afraid."

"Of what?"

"Of her getting hurt. I wanted to punish her so that she would listen to me next time. Things just keep coming at me that I can't control and I don't know what to do. Even Dad's thrown me some curves. I'm worried he's going to lose the gallery. That means he could lose the house. I know I need to do more. But sometimes I can't think things through clearly enough so that they make sense. Everything always seems to happen so fast. Like, I didn't entirely mean to spank Ella. It, sort of, just happened."

Laura could relate to some of his confusion. Not to mention his frustration. She'd had similar experiences, such as the awkwardness that had developed between her and Chelsea, which she didn't fully understand. "I kind of know what you mean. Maybe together we can figure out how to deal with this situation we're in—whatever it is. From now on, how about, we try and be more patient with each other and talk things through rather than lash out. What do you think?"

"I think I can do that." Rob wrapped his arms around her waist.

"Me too." She gave him a hug. It was a start. But it would take more than words to change things. At the moment, she could use his help. Laura gave a nod toward the berries. "Want to help me pit these?"

Rob offered up a wry grin. "Oh, babe. You know it."

"Stop that." She handed him a basket of berries and placed two empty bowls between them. "This is for the fruit and that one's for the pit."

They each dug their fingertips into the fleshy fruit and extracted the hard nut at the core. Rob tossed his in the bowl.

"Ella strings those into necklaces."

"Whatever you say. I'm just looking forward to eating some jam."

Now that they were talking food, Laura saw an opportunity. "So, a doe came up right beside us and ate while were picking. It made me think, maybe you could try hunting again?"

He immediately shook his head. "Nah, I haven't done that in years."

"I know, but we could really use the meat."

"I was never very good at it."

"Well, could you get your dad to come and give you some tips?"

"No. He wouldn't be up for it. Hunting takes a lot out of you."

She couldn't argue about that, but she wouldn't give up on the idea just yet. A freezer full of venison could carry them through the winter. They couldn't afford not to try it. Helen had told her that Rob was best to stay away from Andre but, this once, they might have to chance it. After all, he'd pitched in at the bar when Rob needed him. "What about asking Andre?"

"You'd be okay with that?"

Feeling like she had no other choice, Laura nodded. "Sure."

Rob ate a berry from between his fingers. "I forgot how much I liked these. Open up." He popped one in her mouth.

She relished the lemony taste of the fruit, knowing its acidity would mellow out once it cooked. She held out her fingertips to him with more berries. "Me too."

Slowly, he sucked them all in. "Mmm, almost as good as you. Maybe later we could be alone?"

Laura flashed him her sexy pout. Rob could be irresistible when he wanted to be. "We'll see."

Late in the evening, after the kids had quieted down and Art and Helen were asleep, Rob stopped her in the hallway on her way upstairs. He took her hand and pulled her in the opposite direction. "What are you doing?" He put his finger over her lips before leading her out the kitchen door and into the backyard. "Where are we going?" Suddenly, he made a beeline to Art's shed. Once they were both huddled inside, he switched on the space heater, setting the small room aglow. The walls, lined with his father's old watercolor paintings from the "Distant Dunes" series, almost made her feel as if they were at the beach. "I'd forgotten about those."

"Yeah, he's working on some new stuff. Larger than life. More abstract."

Rob threw a drop cloth on the floor and spread it out like a beach blanket. Splotches of lavender, turquoise, and amber melded together like the canvas of a work in progress. He sat down and reached for her hand. When she gave it to him, he took her into his arms and cradled her there. "I really love you, you know?" Gently, he kissed her lips.

A lump formed in her throat, so much so she couldn't speak. She nodded once. "I love you, too."

Then, layer by layer, they removed each other's clothes. Soon they were lying beside each other naked. In the soft light, surrounded by the paintings, the shed disappeared and Laura imagined they were making love on the beach at sunset as they had as teenagers. Afterward, once their bodies were spent, they held one another close. "Thank you … for being patient," he said.

She rested her head on his chest and ran her hand over his soft skin, still troubled, yet as deeply happy as she could be. They might not live a beautiful life, but this was a beautiful moment—maybe as beautiful as they could be. She and Rob must persevere. They loved each another. Wasn't that all that mattered?

Chapter 23

October 22, 2016

Once she'd finished tuning Art's bow, Laura set it beside the kitchen door. It had taken some leg work but, three weeks into the season, Rob and Andre were now licensed and permitted to hunt. They were supposed to meet at the range in six hours. Rob had promised to come home at midnight and, now, it was already was past one. She slipped on her fleece. If he stayed until closing and locked up, it could be another two hours before he made it into bed. They couldn't risk it. His senses must be sharp in the morning.

Laura left the house and hurried down the sidewalk toward the bar. Along the way, she started feeling optimistic. What if he took a twelve-pointer? She began savoring the stew she'd make for Sunday dinner with the fresh cutlets until she yanked open the grimy glass door. Quickly, she slipped off her knit gloves, worn thin from gripping the wheelchair. She must find Rob. Oddly, it was fifteen minutes until closing and the bar was packed. She couldn't see him anywhere. At least, for once, he'd make some good tips. Money had never been so tight. Earlier, when Ella had tried on her snow boots, she'd discovered they were too small. Freezing drizzle was forecasted. Hopefully Rob wouldn't be hunting in that kind of weather, although though he might have to—they couldn't afford to hold off another day. A deer would make all the difference.

Laura took a seat at the counter. A woman with long black hair similar to hers stood behind the register. It took Laura a second but, when the woman turned around, Laura instantly recognized her. It was Patricia's co-worker, the one who had introduced herself at the beach. Except, now, the blue streaks in her hair were gone. At first, Laura couldn't recall her name. Then, she remembered. Rosa. Rob had mentioned something about possibly hiring her. Rosa's mother had been deported, but Rosa was allowed to stay because she was brought into the United States as a child and had protected status. Now that her mother was gone, Rosa needed a second job. Rob said he'd felt bad for her having to stay here alone and wanted to do what he could. Plus, she had bartending experience and was willing to work unpopular shifts for almost nothing.

"Last call." Rosa, who spoke firmly, clapped once. An older gentleman, around sixty, took the stool beside Laura. He raised two fingers at Rosa, who came right over. "What can I get for you?"

"Tanqueray and tonic."

She pursed her lips. "How do you like it, sir?"

"Short and stiff with a lime." The man cracked his knuckles. "Just bring me a drink. I didn't come here to explain."

Once Rosa had walked away, he turned to Laura and muttered so she could hear. "If I were in my right mind, I'd send ICE out here tomorrow."

Laura's pulse raced. "She has legal working status, sir. My husband runs this bar."

He grunted. "Far as I'm concerned, they should all go back to Mexico."

Laura ignored him, but was reminded of why she never came to the bar, especially this late at night. Behind her, in the other room, a roar of laughter erupted from where a crowd had gathered around the pool tables. She elbowed her way over to see what was causing the commotion. A hazy glow emanated from the stained-glass lamp over the pool table, though she couldn't see the players. She struggled to move ahead and stood on her tiptoes in hope of catching a glimpse. A guy with broad shoulders, wearing a flannel shirt a size too small, stepped in front of her. She leaned sideways, intent on determining who and what had captured everyone's attention. She had to get closer. The guy in front of her leaned the other way. Through the opening a few feet ahead, Laura spotted Patricia leaning over the pool table. No wonder the guy in front hadn't budged. Patricia set up for a shot, her clingy scoop-neck T-shirt revealing an obscene amount of cleavage. The crowd fell silent until a man's voice cut in. "Wait up a second, partner." It was the one voice Laura knew better than anyone else's in the room. "You've almost got it."

From the far-right corner of the table, Rob came around behind Patricia and spread his legs shoulder-width apart. Laura's neck tightened up. He reached his left arm down hers, realigned her pool stick, and centered it on the cue ball. Patricia was aiming for the black ball, the only ball left on the table. Laura's stomach turned. It was as if the two of them were back in high school and had never broken up—as if she'd never entered his life.

The crowd went quiet again. "Eight ball, left corner pocket." Patricia squinted at her target, though it was obvious from her posture, that she knew where every guy's eyes were focused. Rob, of course, had her back.

The hulk in front of Laura crossed his arms and almost split his shirt at the seams. "Dude, are you going to hit it for her too?" he asked.

Laughter muffled through the crowd. Patricia giggled along, though she held her position. Rob inched himself away from her and raised his hands up like he'd surrendered. Full-out laughter spread through the room. Laura thought, if only she'd brought the crossbow. For once, she wished Andre were here. If he saw Rob's hands wandering all over his fiancé, he'd have killed him.

Patricia cocked the pool stick and brought it forward in one smooth stroke. Laura didn't bother watching the rest. Of course, *Perfect Patricia* sank the eight ball. The crowd went wild. Laura approached her husband as Patricia wrapped her arms around his neck. Rob playfully smacked her bottom as if they were on the same football squad. Laura winced. It was worse than the beach. She wanted to run out of the bar and never speak to him again, but she nudged her way forward. When she tried to get around the guy in the plaid flannel, he lost his balance and landed on her foot. She felt a sharp pain. "Sorry, I didn't know you were there," he said.

Laura glanced down. The tread of his work boot had made an imprint on her moccasin. "You're not the only one." The guy shrugged and walked away. She limped toward Rob who was waving a wad of bills. Patricia was on the other side of the table surrounded by her hyper-fit friends. Rosa flashed the lights, signaling it was closing time. The signal didn't appear to register with Rob. Neither, apparently, did she, although she was standing right behind him. When she tapped him on the shoulder, he turned around with a guilty grin as if she were a teacher who'd just caught him cheating on a test. "What are you doing here?" he asked.

"I thought you were supposed to be working."

"I made more money on the floor." He flipped through the ones, fives, and tens. "One hundred smackers."

The cash didn't impress her. "You and your old flame put on quite a show."

His cheeks flushed. "C'mon, it was just a game."

Her jaw tightened. She didn't want to hear any excuses, especially after their conversation earlier in the month when he'd said he would try to do better. His ongoing flirtation with Patricia had gone too far. Would he never grow up?

Rob stared at her bleary eyed. "You're not going to get jealous again?"

There was no use trying to reason with him now. "It's past two. I'm going home. Are you coming?"

Rob glanced at the register. "I've got to close out."

"I thought you were supposed to be hunting tomorrow."

"I am."

His breath, reeking of Jack Daniels, burned her nostrils. "Then maybe you should let Rosa close up, especially since you've been drinking."

"I was just trying to have a little fun." Rob shifted his weight to the other foot. "Why you always gotta bust my chops?"

Why did he always make her feel like a nag? "You know how important tomorrow is. I tuned up the bow." She shouldn't have to explain. "I thought we were together on this."

"We are." Rob sighed. "But Jesus, Laura."

He shook his head at her before he returned to the bar. She glanced back at him one last time on her way out the door. Her husband had his eye on Patricia, who had zipped up her leather jacket halfway and was now approaching him from across the room. Laura couldn't watch. He'd obviously made his choice. She turned and walked out. The wind coming off the lake whipped at her face; her hair tangled around her like coarse string. She was too furious and wounded to think.

"Laura, wait!"

She walked faster, feeling as if her predator was closing in. She must flee, but where to? She had no money and no place to go. With three kids, it wasn't like she could just leave and start over.

"Please, Laura, stop!"

She took off in a sprint but, soon after, lost her breath. He was coming closer. Rob's parents' house was next. If she made it there before him, she could run upstairs to the attic and lock him out. Rob caught her by the arm. "Please, hold up."

"Don't touch me." She pulled her arm away and refused to look at him.

"I'm sorry."

"I don't care." She took another step back.

"Come on, Laura. Why do you always get so mad at me?"

Now he was back to blaming her when he was the one breaking his promises. All their arguments blurred into one. "You make me feel like I don't belong here. You make it seem like you want everything to be like it was—before me."

The hard lines between Rob's brows softened. The wind whipped through his bomber jacket. "I'm sorry, I was out of hand. Acting like an idiot. You know I love you, not her. You're everything to me." His words offered little comfort. He hadn't given her any answers. And though she wanted to, she wasn't sure if she believed him. Her teeth were chattering. "Come here." Rob put his arm around her. "Let's go home."

Laura walked the rest of the way home beside him though she kept to herself. She wouldn't push him now. Tomorrow was too important to their family. He must be ready to hunt.

Chapter 24

October 22, 2016

Rob followed Andre along the edge of the woods at the shore-line. The setting sun, hanging low in the gray sky, seemed as heavy as the slush on the surface of the lake. Ahead, in camouflage coveralls, Andre turned off into the forest onto the path that ran near his old house. They'd left the lodge eight hours earlier in high spirits but, with the exception of a rabbit and a couple of squirrels, hadn't seen squat. Rob's feet were numb along with his nose, which had been running all afternoon since they last stopped for lunch. He wiped it with his coat sleeve. Deer had to be out there somewhere, though tracking one at this point in the day seemed like a fantasy. Soon they would have to head in, and admit they'd been out-smarted. Deer could scent them and detect their every little sound. Over the years, since last going out with Dad in junior high, he'd lost his hunter's edge. Admittedly, he'd never had much of one to start.

Still, he couldn't give up today. Laura was counting on him. Traces of her scent, fragrant yet musky, lingered on his skin. He must make up for last night when she'd come looking for him and found him with Patricia. Storming into the bar in her moccasins, she'd reminded him of the free spirit who'd left home in Wisconsin and crossed the UP to find Sanctuary. Now, as he trudged through the stiff dune grass, he recalled the moment when he'd first seen her emerge from between these deep-rooted blades. In all these years Laura's uninhibited passion hadn't faded, though last night—for the first time— he'd sensed her fury. This morning he'd left the house prepared to kill for her out of necessity. He must prove himself to her. Though now, tracking through the wild at dusk, Rob almost felt as if he was the one being stalked.

He continued behind Andre into the forest, where a thin layer of ice covered the fallen leaves and pine needles. He searched the trail for tracks. This was their last chance. It would be dark soon. They should have given up already. There weren't any No Hunting signs posted, but Rob understood that they were beyond legal territory. Not far from here, on the other side of the hill, Andre's old house once stood. His mother sold off the property before she died. For now, Andre continued living off his small inheritance. The new owners from Chicago tore the "shack" down and replaced it with a luxury log cabin. Rob doubted it would be occupied off-season, but he didn't want to take any chances. After all they'd been through here with the cops, they couldn't afford to get busted, not even by the National Park Service, which often had rangers on patrol. Anxious, Rob walked faster to catch up.

He'd lost sight of Andre and instead followed the faint footprints his friend had left behind. Rob kept his eyes on the trail, though his attention gravitated toward the bluff looming to his right. He didn't look up. He already knew what was there. Wind gusted off the lake and sent drops of freezing drizzle down his collar. Rob zipped it up all the way. Had

Andre felt the same anxiety? Or had he passed by the cross and paid his sister no attention? Rob knew it would be wrong not to acknowledge Sandra and the place where she died. He and Andre had erected the cross before the trial in an attempt to hold themselves together when each of them felt the tug of coming undone. They'd labored up the steep slope, carrying wood from the remains of a shipwreck that surfaced on the beach early in the spring following the accident that took Sandra's life. Though one of the many that lie undiscovered beneath the shifting sands at the lake's bottom, this particular wreck held significance to them. He and Andre both failed Sandra. They raised the cross to make amends. When they were finished, Rob stood behind Andre who knelt at the foot of the cross and promised his sister one thing: "I'll never forget."

Rob had made the same promise. Now, as a grown man, Rob lifted his eyes toward the cross hidden among the trees and invisible to the rest of the world. He'd never returned to the site. He swallowed the lump in his throat and scaled the bluff. His lungs burned by the time he reached the top. When the cross first came into view, for a second, he stopped breathing. Cradled in a mound of branches, it had fallen backward, perhaps blown over by the wind. Rob set down his gear. Tiny drops of freezing drizzle landed on his cheeks and stuck to his beard. He closed his eyes and said an Our Father. Hunting so close to this sacred spot was a bad omen. In his head, the hours leading up to Sandra's death eight years ago began to rewind. For the first time, he remembered.

For his seventeen-year-old self, the snow day had been the closest he'd come to total bliss until Andre called him at Patty's and ruined everything. Late that afternoon, when Rob jumped out of Patty's bed, he instantly felt the draft coming from the window. Goosebumps popped up on his arms and legs. He threw on his clothes and left Patty asleep nestled under her down comforter naked. When had his life gotten so complicated? Lately, nothing seemed to go as he had envisioned. Rob didn't even want to imagine the punishment if his dad found out Andre and Sandra had come over, smoked pot, and drunk beer. They'd taken the snowmobile without Dad's permission. He couldn't know about any of it. Rob put on his winter gear, feeling like a criminal as he pulled a facemask over his head.

As soon as he stepped out the back door, ice pelted him from the sky. The wind was coming off Lake Michigan, and its fury hit him full force. It was less than a half mile to Andre's. He could do this. Rob fought his way up the hill; with each step, he raised his thigh to his waist and crushed the sole of his snow boot through the slick coat of ice on the surface. The pines towered, swaying back and forth as he trudged. It was impossible to see through the storm. The sun usually didn't set for another hour, but today cold darkness surrounded him. Rob tucked his chin to his chest. He'd made this uphill climb from Patty's to Andre's countless times before but never under these extreme conditions, which made the stretch of dense forest almost impenetrable.

The snowstorm was disorienting, but he continued straight up the hill in pursuit of his friends, his breath coming hard with each step. Near the top, Rob spotted Andre's front porch light glowing faintly above the door. Only a little further and he'd be golden. He pushed hard, stumbling through the packed snow underneath as he hurried toward the house. He imagined the warm wave of relief that would come over him when Andre let him inside. When Rob arrived at the door, he didn't bother knocking. He reached for the knob and tried to twist it. Nothing. It was locked. He pounded on the metal storm door with his fist. He was staring at the door, cupping his hands over his mouth, when all of a sudden, he remembered. They'd snuck in before. He went around the side of the house. As he suspected, all the windows were dark. There was no sign of anyone. He came onto the back deck and tugged on the sliders. Andre had forced them open without much effort last time, that night when they were being eaten by mosquitos in the summer. This time they wouldn't budge. Summer now seemed like a bitter joke.

The icy wind gusted in his face and encrusted the openings around his mouth, eyes, and nose. At this rate, his facemask soon would freeze to his skin. He hugged his arms into his chest, turned his back to the wind, and huddled against the house under the small awning that usually provided shade. Andre and Sandra should be here by now. It would have been quicker for them to walk. Rob's fingers and toes were so cold they began to burn. He'd be lucky to get back without frostbite. Where the hell was Andre? That crazy bastard. Rob took off his gloves and called his cell, though he already knew Andre probably wouldn't answer. He left a message anyway, teeth chattering. "I'm waiting at your house. Where are you?"

Unless Andre arrived in the next couple minutes, they would all be toast. Dad couldn't find out. Rob pressed himself into the side of the house; impatient, fatigued, he stood frozen, the icy wind lashing at his back. After some time, when the squall passed, Rob pried himself away from his only shelter and scanned the forest for a sign. He soon abandoned the search. It was going to be a long walk home and an even longer night when he got there. He heard nothing, not even the snap of a twig, until the unmistakable rev of an engine echoed through the woods. A distant flash of light, coming from the direction of the beach, caught the corner of his eye. He'd assumed Andre would have taken the road. Rob's instincts told him to follow the light. He set out again into the snow. Step by step, he plowed ahead, thankful at least for some guidance. On the downward slope of the hill facing the beach, a plume of smoke rose between the trees. Gas fumes filtered through the air. Rob's heart beat faster. When he came to the edge of the hill, he grabbed a branch for stability and leaned over to see. Fumes overwhelmed him and smoke clouded the air. Rob coughed and his eyes burned. He blinked hard and tried to make out the scene. About halfway down, a dim light was cast horizontally. He recognized the glow of the headlamp from his snowmobile. "Andre! Sandra!"

Rob sidestepped down the slope toward the light until he saw the yellow Ski-Doo wedged against a tree on its side. Where was Andre? A weak cry for help escaped through the tall trees. "I'm here! Help me. Someone, please help."

Rob rushed down, though he wished he could pull back. By the time he reached the snowmobile moments later, his heart was pounding out of control. His dad's machine appeared to have hit a pine tree and one of the front blades remained wedged between a large branch and the trunk. Rob lunged toward the ignition to turn off the engine and, when he pressed the switch by the handlebars, came face to face with Sandra.

Headfirst down the hill, she was trapped beneath the snowmobile. She tugged with both hands to free her pinned leg. "Get it off me!" Amid the fumes, her breath clouded the frigid air. "I've got to find my brother."

Where the hell was Andre? Sandra was hysterical. Rob had to get her out, but how? The slope was so steep. He had to hurry or her leg would be crushed. She would freeze to death.

Rob looked around and saw only trees, many long-dead, and darkness. The forest had never seemed so isolated. He wanted to call 911, but this far away from the house there would be no service. He had to help her first. His thinking was so cloudy. From the pot or beer? He wasn't sure. He needed Andre; together they could free her. Rob cupped his hands around his mouth and called out to his friend. When he got no answer, his mind raced. He ran around the snowmobile to the place where the blade was hung up on the tree. In a single motion, he got under the machine and heaved it away from Sandra.

"No, not there!" She waved her arms over her face. Terror streaked across her blue eyes. At that instant, with the weight of the machine in his grasp, Rob lost his footing and stumbled backward. The snowmobile rolled forward and came to a standstill on her chest. What had he done?

He kneeled in the snow beside Sandra. Her arms splayed sideways, she'd fallen unconscious after the impact. He ripped off his facemask and pillowed it under her head. He must get help.

When Rob glanced over his shoulder, he saw, twenty yards farther down the long slope, almost at the edge of the path, in the crux of two birch trees, a body on its side in a rumpled heap. Andre. *Oh my god.* Rob made the sign of the cross over Sandra. He had no choice but to leave her and go to Andre. By the time Rob reached him, the snow once again began to swirl. Blood seeped from a hole in Andre's forehead. His condition appeared critical. "Wake up! I'm here!" Andre, semi-conscious, opened his eyes half-way. "Where's my sister?"

"Uphill."

"How is she doing?"

"Not so good."

Andre tugged Rob's coat sleeve. "You've gotta help her."

After a second or two, Andre's eyes closed and he faded out of consciousness. Rob fumbled in his pocket for his phone. Though it said No Service, he dialed 911. Got nothing.

Time splintered in an instant. Rob heard his name being called. Standing at the top of the bluff with night closing in, he took a deep breath and reoriented himself. An unmistakable odor like rotted juniper permeated the air. Andre yelled. "I got her. She's hit. Coming back your way."

Rob, still haunted by his recaptured memory of Sandra, remained frozen. A stick snapped. The sound of thick brush being trampled shocked him back to awareness. A large doe, her nostrils flaring, bounded toward him with an arrow in her chest. A pain pierced his chest as if he too were struck. He came into her sights. The doe's terrified eyes pleaded with him as if screaming for help. Rob knew those eyes, that look. Suddenly, it was again Sandra staring at him. Without his help, she was going to die.

The doe darted the other way down the bluff. He had to follow. Rob picked up his gear and threw it over his shoulder. Groggy and confused, he lost her. His adrenaline surged and, on the move again, he ignored his memories of seconds earlier. What was he thinking? This was the moment they'd been waiting for all day. Fifty feet ahead, the injured doe stood behind a tangle of branches. Rob stepped closer. When he was within twenty feet, she dashed off in the opposite direction. Relying on brute endurance, he charged after her white tail through the woods. She was agile, powerful, captivating. He chased after her as she bounded in ten-foot leaps this way and that among the thick trunks of the old-growth forest. Suddenly,

Andre came at her from the opposite direction. He and Rob closed in. With her wild eyes, she looked from right to left at each of them before she made a frantic leap straight between. Together, they followed her into the forest until an hour later at last she collapsed behind a thicket in the distance. He and Andre, breathing heavily, hearts hammering, paused before they approached to collect their kill. In a few minutes, it would be dark. Rob envisioned the silent body. Nothing was said until they stood over the place where they'd seen her go down. The doe somehow had made off.

They'd both seen the doe collapse. Rob, nauseated and light-headed, hunched over with his hands on his knees, sensing that any second he too would crash.

"What the hell just happened?" Andre asked.

If Andre weren't standing beside him, Rob might have thought he'd imagined the whole encounter. He caught his breath along with a glimpse between the bare trees of the sun setting over the dark lake. Once again, he and Andre were bound in blood. Left with less than nothing. He faced his old friend who so often acted more like his foe. "How could we lose her?"

Chapter 25

October 22-23, 2016

Laura got into bed and pulled the covers under her chin. She closed her eyes and tried to sleep but couldn't silence the mental chatter. What was up with Rob? She rolled onto her side and checked the clock. It was 10:15 p.m. They hadn't spoken since before dawn when he left to hunt with Andre. His text earlier in the evening had sounded weird. *Andre almost bagged a doe. Heading back to lodge. Going into work late.* She'd texted him back but never received a response. Cell service was sketchy on the hilltop around the lodge, though he should have checked in by now. And why had no one answered when she phoned the bar?

She still was so mad at him, but then Laura remembered the tenderness in Rob's embrace the previous night when he'd apologized. She pushed aside the covers. He wouldn't have failed to keep in touch with her today. Something must be wrong. She slipped on the moccasins she'd left beside the bed, hurried downstairs, and threw her fleece over her T-shirt and sweatpants. As soon as she reached the sidewalk, the wind off the lake lashed at her cheeks. Laura zipped up her coat and shuffled along with her chin tucked under the collar until she made it to the corner. She pulled open the heavy door and entered the bar.

Unlike yesterday, tonight, apart from a few old-timers and Joey, the teenage bus boy, the place was empty. Once again, Rosa stood behind the cash register in Rob's place. "Hi, do you know where Rob is?"

Rosa unwound an elastic band from her wrist and pulled back her hair. "I have no idea. He asked me to cover for him— said he was coming in around eight."

Rosa hurried to the far end of the counter where George Bigsley lowered himself off his stool in front of the flat-screen TV where a college football game had just finished. He'd been mayor for decades and was a regular at the bar long before Rob took over. George patted the stack of singles next to his brandy snifter.

"Goodnight, Mr. Mayor," Rosa said. "Have a safe trip home."

The mayor winked, his eyes glassy as usual. Once he'd stepped out, Laura took Rosa aside. "Let me know if he ever gets too fresh."

Rosa nodded casually. "Thanks, I will. Seems like it's mostly for show."

"Well, you don't want to take any chances." Laura tilted her head at the pair of men in wire-frame glasses and saggy jeans putzing around the pool table. "Though I doubt those two will give you any problems."

Over the years, working at the fish camp for her father, Laura had learned to trust her gut when it came to men. They didn't always behave the way they looked. She'd seen it happen with Shenia. One too many of their father's valued guests had felt at liberty to cop a feel as if it were included in the price of their package. Rosa seemed like she could manage the place on her own, based on her no-nonsense response to the mayor's flirtation, but why risk it? "I'm going to try and track down Rob. Why don't you just close now. Keep Joey with you until you lock up. I've got my cell phone, but I'm not sure there's reception at the lodge. Sorry about all this."

"Okay, good luck. Let me know if you need help." Rosa scribbled her cell number on a napkin and handed it to Laura.

"Thanks, I will." Laura hurried out the door. Why did Rob think it was okay to play hooky and leave Rosa like that? Sometimes she wondered if he ever thought things through. Then again, she was starting to worry, what if something had happened to him? The mayor, stumbling down the sidewalk on her left, didn't seem to be worried about a thing. Laura walked in the opposite direction. Up ahead, Rob's parents' house was dark. Laura came in the side door and unhooked the keys for Helen's Buick off the rack. She didn't want to wake her at this hour to ask for her permission. Surely, she'd understand why she took the car this one time when Rob might be in danger.

Laura backed out of the driveway onto Main Street and stayed on it for a few blocks until she passed Chelsea's house. Chelsea had dropped off the Wii for Nate a month ago, yet she hadn't let Jacob come over to play any games with him. It almost seemed like Chelsea wanted to distance herself and her family from them. Laura needed to find out why. She missed their friendship. And Nate needed company from someone his own age—someone who would give him some real competition at Mario Bros. Art tried his best to keep up but, at his age, he'd never really get the hang of it. Not like the kids.

Laura took a left on Old Road. She followed it until she reached the turnoff that led up the hill to the lodge. She swerved right onto the dirt drive. The car rattled and shook.

She could hardly see, so she switched on her brights. The road was full of potholes. When she swerved around them, the tree branches reached into the narrow passageway as if intending to scrape Helen's car. She leaned into the steering wheel and tightened her grip as she reached the part of the road where the shoulder disappeared. She'd only been up here once and that was in the daytime. Laura almost wished she could turn back and sort things out with Rob tomorrow morning, but there was only enough room for one car to pass, and she worried about the drop-off. Helen would kill her if she damaged the car.

Laura slowed to a crawl before rounding the final turn. Then the road opened up into a small dirt parking lot that cornered the lodge. Art's van was backed in by the side door where an old security light flickered above the entrance. As she came closer, she noticed the driver's side door was dented. When she pulled beside the van, she saw the front windshield was missing. She got out of her car. The van's back doors had been left open. Her throat tightened. Clutching her cell phone, she approached the lodge. Nothing more than a wood-sided cabin, it was boxed in by the tall pines that guarded the surrounding hilltop. The area was pitch black, apart from the flickering light over the metal door, which was cracked open a bit. She pulled it toward her, hesitating beneath the emergency exit sign, before she stepped into the paneled hall. Didn't the lodge close at ten? A faint sound came from a room up the hall on her right. She held her breath as she approached. The sound became distinct. Chopping. A streak of light spread into the hall from beneath the door. Laura knocked. "Hello. Rob? It's me." The chopping stopped, but no one answered. "Can I come in?"

Her hand trembled as she slowly twisted the knob and pulled open the door. She peered around the side. Everything in the small room was illuminated by a single bulb dangling on a cord strung from the ceiling above a butcher-block table in the center of the room. The floors, the walls, the table—all appeared as if in black in white. A pungent and sour smell intruded her nostrils. Laura came around the door, unaware of the blood pooled at her feet until she'd already stepped into it. Her leg muscles tightened as she followed the trail of blood with baby steps in her moccasins toward the table where someone had slung a doe. She walked to the opposite end of the table where one of the doe's hind legs hung precariously over the edge; its hoof was inches off the floor. Beside it, she saw a man's bloodied work boot. Laura turned the corner. A few feet behind the table Rob sat on the floor with his back propped against the wall and his head between his knees.

"Rob. Holy shit. Rob." Laura crouched beside him. "What the hell is going on? Are you all right?"

Without looking up at her, he shook his head and kept his face shielded. "I can't do this."

A meat cleaver was on the floor at his feet near the doe's bloody hind leg. Rob must have been swinging at it, though he'd clearly gutted the deer elsewhere before bringing it into the lodge. From the looks of it, he was by no means a butcher. Bits of flesh and fur littered the floor around its mangled leg. For a moment, in the stark room, Laura clutched herself. Something terrible must have happened. She placed her hand on Rob's shoulder. "I understand. It's going to be all right. I'm here now. I'll take care of the butchering."

He pulled away. Goosebumps ran up her arm. She sat beside him shivering. After some time, Rob finally lifted his eyes. He wore a tortured expression, his sockets hollow, his cheeks gaunt. She wasn't sure he recognized her. Again, she placed her hand on his shoulder. "Rob. Why are you acting this way? It's me, Laura." He still didn't seem to acknowledge her. Must be in shock. She had to snap him out of it. She wrapped her arms around him. His body was cold and rigid. "Please, Rob. I'm here for you. Just tell me what happened." She ran her hand in circles around his back. "I can't help you if you don't talk to me."

After a second or two, Rob startled as if he'd been struck by a hundred volts of electricity. "I killed her ... with the van." Rocking back and forth, he turned to Laura. "I was wiped."

"How so?"

"Andre and I came back here and had a few beers. We talked about how we couldn't believe she'd gotten away. Then we were coming home. I was following him down the hill, but he got ahead of me. Dude always drives like a maniac." He held still. "Next thing I know, I'm face to face with her. She has this crazy look in her eye. Then she jumps right into me, smashes onto the roof, and comes in through the windshield. The arrow was still in her chest."

Laura didn't follow half of what Rob said. "What arrow?"

He pressed his hands into the sides of his head. "She's the same damn doe Andre shot. The one that got away. She came back. Tore up her leg. Wrecked half the car. How is Nate going to get to therapy now?" Rob pounded the wall behind him with his fist. "And what the hell am I supposed to say to Dad?"

Laura took his hand in hers. "The truth." She held it tightly for reassurance. "He'll understand. It's not your fault."

Rob pulled his hand away. "Oh yeah, just like Dad understood the truth about the snowmobile ... just like Andre understood the truth when I couldn't get Sandra out from under it." He started rocking again. "Why'd you let her die? That's the first thing Andre said when I came to see him at the hospital after the accident."

Laura shuddered. She'd never seen him suffer such despair. "Andre still blames me. Told me as much at the beach the day Nate came home from the hospital." He hugged his legs to his chest. "Told me I was lucky. 'Your son is alive.'"

Rob was traumatized. He wasn't thinking like himself. Why was he still beating himself up about Sandra's death? He'd done everything he could, just the same as he'd done with Nate. She remembered him pulling Nate out from under the Mercedes. He'd moved so fast to rescue him. "Rob, please calm down. It's over. It's all over. Andre is to blame. He was sent to prison. Some people can never accept responsibility."

Rob turned to her with lines etched across his forehead. "Oh my God, Laura. Don't say that."

She threw her hands up. "Why not? It's the truth!" He turned his eyes away and rose to his feet. Laura stood beside him. "I'm sorry. You know I was trying—"

"You're always trying …" He seemed like he was about to say something more until his deep voice cracked. "Let's finish with this deer and get out of here." Rob looked to the deer on the table, though he didn't make a move. He was acting so strangely, she wondered if they should go to the hospital instead.

"Rob, I'm worried about you. Do you want me to take you into the ER to get checked out?"

"No, I'll be fine."

There was no sense in arguing with him anymore right now. Laura grabbed the meat cleaver off the floor. They had a lot of work ahead of them if they intended to harvest the animal tonight. Rob had been right to bring in the deer; it would be risky to store the carcass in the van with the smashed-out windshield. Laura brought the cleaver to the utility sink at the opposite end of the room, cleaned it with hot water and soap, then returned to the table along with three garbage bags, paper towel, and a roll of plastic wrap she found in a bin stored beneath the sink. Rob picked up where he'd left off earlier, skinning the hide off with his fold-up knife. It was a shame Andre hadn't left his—the serrated one he always carried with the pointed tip. Without a curved deboning knife, it'd be hard to butcher the deer, but together she and Rob would manage. She'd butchered many deer under far worse circumstances as a teenager, once on the forest floor in Wisconsin with her grandfather. He'd complimented her adeptness with the small knife: "You handle that like a surgeon."

Her grandfather, in his quiet way, had taught her well, though she'd never seriously considered becoming a surgeon. If the forest were her operating room, she'd have excelled on the spot. The impersonal, sterile setting at the hospital was not an environment in which she'd ever imagined she could thrive. Did she really have the hands of a surgeon? The hands used not only to cut but to suture and heal. The possibility that she might have some aptitude hadn't occurred to her until Dr. Azzi charged her with caring for Nate at home. She'd been confident she could do it and been right. Nate's burn wounds were healing without webbing and ahead of schedule. Keshya, too, had noted his progress in physical therapy, called it extraordinary. Nate's will to walk was key to his success, yet she, too, had contributed to his recovery so far. It had taken time, patience and some skill.

Once the deer was skinned, she began work butchering the clean carcass, starting with the shoulders. Blood dripped onto her moccasins, but Laura couldn't stop to clean them. She continued her job.

Rob stepped in and helped her prepare the hindquarters, including cutting out the sirloin. Side by side they worked.

Piece by piece they wrapped the meat in plastic and loaded it into the bags. Three hours and ten minutes later they'd processed the entire carcass and Laura was on the verge of collapse. After all he'd been through, how had Rob managed to find the strength? And they still had to clean up the room and themselves. Helen would kill them if they left any blood in the Buick.

They disposed of the hide and bones and hosed down the room. Then they removed their shoes and stripped down to their underwear before hosing themselves off. Laura sealed their outer layers of clothing in a garbage bag so that she could take them home to wash. She sprayed Rob's boots, but there was nothing she could do now for her moccasins, which she slipped back on before she followed Rob to the door. Laura switched off the light and left the lodge with an underlying sense of accomplishment at the meaningful work they had performed together. Their family would eat well in the coming winter.

Chapter 26

October 23, 2016

Laura removed the blanket from the trunk and spread it over the front seat of the Buick. Rob began loading the meat. His long underwear was soaked with blood around the neckline and cuffs of his wrists. They couldn't risk staining the plush upholstery. Freezing her butt of now, she tried to convince herself, was better than facing Helen's wrath in the morning.

Shivering behind the wheel in her bra and underwear, Laura cranked up the heat. Carefully, she maneuvered down the hill through the potholes and prayed that none of the juices from the meat would leak. Her moccasins already had left a mess at her feet. Tomorrow, she'd have to scrub down the floor mats. Still, it would all be worth it—as long as Rob was okay.

Beside her, he sat in silence. The ritual of harvesting the deer had seemed to dull his trauma, though now he was sullen and slumped sideways against the passenger window. She turned onto Old Road and they continued without speaking until she came to a stop at the flashing red light on Main Street. Once there, she was startled by him. He'd straightened up and was staring blankly at the windshield. Just then, he spoke: "I can't be the man you, or anyone, want me to be."

He looked down at his hands and shook his head. She kept her foot on the brake. For several seconds she could barely breathe, much less speak, until she forced out the words. "What are you trying to say?" He didn't answer and began wringing his hands. "Rob, look at me."

Instead, he stared straight ahead. "I've got to go."

"Go where?" She couldn't believe he was saying this. "Why?"

He'd not been acting like himself all night. Hitting the deer had triggered something terrible. Made him question his existence. At the moment, they were both half naked and strung-out. She couldn't stop at the intersection all night. They needed to get home. "Rob, it's late. We're both tired. Let's talk about all this in the morning. Please."

Laura veered right onto the empty street, and they rode the rest of the way in silence. Where had their relationship gone? By the time she pulled in the driveway it was almost 4 a.m. Rob stood up slowly, opened the garage door, and started unpacking the meat from the trunk into the garage freezer. She took the bag with their dirty clothes to the house, slipping off her moccasins on the side porch, before carrying the rest of their stuff into the basement. Then she dumped everything— reeking of dried sweat and fresh blood—into the machine. She ran into the bathroom to take a shower. Ten minutes later, when she came up to bed, Rob—who hadn't even bothered to shower—was already asleep.

She pulled on a T-shirt and got in her side. She was exhausted but couldn't sleep. All night she stayed up tossing and turning. Rob, beside her naked in bed, clicked his teeth as if he were keeping time. It reminded her of the clicking of Nate's scooter wheels along the sidewalk coming toward home. On the morning of his accident nothing had clicked. If only she'd gone out to get him, instead of making the scones, everything would be different.

A dim haze of sunlight spread across the attic. Laura realized she must have dozed off at some point. Behind her, Rob unzipped his suitcase and began opening and shutting dresser drawers. Images of the previous night, including him sitting beside her stone-faced at the red light, came to mind. She rolled over and pretended to still be asleep. Where was he going? A dull pain formed in her left temple. She must think of something to make him stay. Once he walked out of their room, she sat up on the edge of their bed and gnawed at the cracked skin around her thumbnail. The bitter taste of dried blood filled her mouth. How had everything gone so wrong between them?

She pushed herself to her feet, put on some pants, and followed him downstairs— watching from the hall as he entered the living room where Nate was playing Mario Kart on the Wii. Rob paused behind him. Nate, engrossed in the game, didn't seem to notice his dad was standing right there. Rob continued to the front door and reached for the knob. Was he planning to leave without saying good-bye? She couldn't just let him walk out until he gave some explanation.

Nate waved the Wii remote over his head. "Victory!"

Rob turned the lock. At the sound, Nate spun around his wheelchair and beamed at his father. "Hey, Dad, I finally unlocked Rainbow Road. Come play with me."

Laura leaned against the hallway wall for support as Rob's jaw went slack.

"You said you'd play me if I did it," Nate said.

Rob's arms fell to his sides. "I'm sorry. But I have to go."

"Go where?"

Rob opened his mouth as if to answer, but his lower lip trembled when he tried to speak. "All right, buddy." He shrugged and set down his suitcase. "I'll play you one game."

Rob lowered himself onto Art's La-Z-Boy. Within seconds he and Nate seemed fully engaged in the race. Laura, on the verge of tears, stayed in the hallway. They looked as if they were concentrating so hard to stay on the track that the world outside the game didn't exist. "Be careful, Dad. Don't run off the rainbow."

From her viewpoint they were like clones, both hunched over their Wii remotes at the exact same angle, leaning this way and that depending on which way they wanted to direct their player. Why couldn't Rob recognize it?

The game was almost over. Suddenly anger hit like a clap of thunder. What kind of man had she married? They'd agreed to honor one another. There was no honor in this—walking out on her and the kids without any good reason.

Once Rob finished playing, he set down the remote on the side table. She faced him. "So, this is it?"

He nodded once before he stood and glanced down at Nate. "I'm sorry, Laura, I can't pretend anymore."

"Pretend what?"

"To be the kind of man you need. I messed up—really messed up." He put his hands on her shoulders. "It's better this way."

"How?"

His hands fell to his sides. "I can't explain."

"Is it Patricia?"

"No."

"Then what? Just tell me, please."

"I can't."

"I hate you." She pounded her fists on his chest. "You should have told me if you were only in it for the good times." She stepped behind the wheelchair and gripped the handles.

Rob shook his head at both of them and grimaced. "I never planned for this. I love you." He cupped his hand over Nate's knuckles, and squeezed. "But I gotta go."

"Go where, Dad?"

Rob, who didn't make eye contact with either of them, hesitated for a couple seconds. "To the gym." He patted Nate on the head and walked to the front door.

Nate, who had never used the wheelchair on his own, pushed himself forward after him. Laura lost her grip.

"What gym, Dad?"

"You know. The new one."

"But you never go to the gym."

"Well, I'm going now."

"Why?"

Rob picked up his suitcase. "I need to get back in shape."

Nate adjusted his leg on the footrest. He looked up at Rob with conviction. "I need to get back in shape too. Can I come with you?"

Rob shook his head. "I'm not really—"

Nate stared up at him in earnest. "Please, Daddy."

What was going on? Nate never called Rob *Daddy*, except when he really, really wanted something he knew he couldn't have. The last time Nate had begged like that was at the hospital right after his reconstructive surgery. How he'd protested, lying in bed with his leg propped up, shouting at her and Rob: "I'm not staying here anymore!" Nate had appealed to his father to take him home. *Please, Daddy.* Back then, there was nothing anyone—including Rob—could do to give Nate what he wanted. Now Rob had a chance to fulfill his son, if only he were willing.

"Rob, why won't you talk to me? You know I love you."

"You just said you hated me."

"I'm sorry. I really hate that you won't tell me what's going on. I'm your wife!"

"I'm sorry I let you down."

She placed her hands on Nate's shoulders and glared. "You're letting us all down."

Rob raised the suitcase and faced the door. He'd made up his mind.

"Coward." She'd been devoted to him and longed for them to be a real family so deeply that she'd seen only what reinforced that view. It had made her blind to Rob's immaturity. "Fine—if you're not going to talk to me, there's no point— just leave. I'll try and explain to your parents about the van."

"What about it?"

Nate leaned forward and strained his neck sideways to get a view from the living room window. Normally, Art's van would have been parked at the end of the driveway. Nate pulled up to the window and stared out as if the Mystery Machine might appear any second. Rob shut his eyes. Then, Nate pulled on his sweatpants. "Daddy? How are we going to get to the gym now?"

Rob squinted at him for several seconds, and—seeming to come out of a dense fog—set down his suitcase. He planted his hands on his hips and looked Nate squarely in the eye. "We'll walk."

Chapter 27

October 23, 2016

"Welcome to the Jungle" by Guns N' Roses blared through the speakers when Rob entered the gym pushing Nate. He couldn't remember the last time he'd heard that song. Probably around the same time he'd last pumped iron, right before Ella was born, when he'd quit the circuit. He approached the front desk and presented the guest pass Patricia had given him at the beach a couple months before—the day Nate had come home from the hospital. He signed them in as her guests.

Everything had gotten so complicated. Rob patted his gut. He'd sure filled out since fatherhood. Twenty-six and running out of gas, almost on empty. How was it possible to feel this used up? Five years ago, he couldn't have imagined himself in this condition. His body, once a fine-tuned machine, was overdue for service. If he didn't get back on a regular maintenance schedule, he'd soon need an overhaul or end up a junker like Dad's van. What a horrible scene. All that blood embedded in the grill. He couldn't think about the condition the vehicle was in now. The gym was the kind of place where he could forget his problems and focus on something positive. Here, he and Nate could draw strength from each other.

He pushed Nate's chair forward. "This was a great idea, bud. If it weren't for you, I wouldn't be here."

Lord only knows where he thought he was going earlier when he'd headed for the door. He'd never seen Laura more furious. She and Nate had made him really think. Rob wheeled him into the men's locker room and hung up their coats on hooks side by side. He clapped his hands on Nate's shoulders. "Ready to get to work, bud?"

Nate nodded with a wide grin. Rob pushed him toward the free weights stacked up along the mirrored wall in the far corner. He handed Nate a two-pound barbell. "Let's see some bicep curls."

Nate sat up straight and eyed the weight in his right hand. Without looking up, he bent his elbow and lifted it toward his chin. "You look like a pro. Now do three sets of ten with each arm if you can. Just take breaks when you get tired."

Nate kept his elbow at his side and lifted the weight toward his shoulder. "Like this?"

"Yep. You got it, bud." Rob left him to finish on his own, confident he would perform the set with proper form. Through physical therapy Nate had developed discipline and focus. Prior to the accident, Rob had never known Nate to focus on any task. Now he acted with intent. There was no question about his commitment. Rob eyed the nearby weight bench. What about himself?

He grabbed a weight bar from the shelf in the corner, set it on the floor, and loaded it with sixty pounds at each end. He shrugged a couple times to warm up his shoulders before lifting the bar onto the metal stand at the top of the bench.

When his chest was positioned beneath the bar, he planted his feet on the floor and rotated the bar so that his palms were directly underneath. Once his shoulders were locked down, he tightened his grip on the bar, puffed up his chest, and reminded himself to keep his shoulder blades squeezed. He'd forgotten what it felt like to use his muscles until he'd lugged the deer around. Though he ached all over, he wanted more. He remembered: proper form was key to avoid getting hurt.

When Rob removed the bar from the racks, his obliques tightened. He inhaled as he lowered the bar until it hovered above his sternum. He imagined his biceps as springs ready to uncoil and raised the bar. He tried not to shift his feet as he drove the bar upward from his rib cage in a slight backward arc toward his face. His heart hammered. He hadn't remembered this amount of weight being a strain.

He was out of practice, yet he couldn't deny that last night at the lodge had left him stiff and sore. Even with the doe gutted, lugging her into the back of the van and onto the table at the lodge had been a feat of endurance. He inhaled and exhaled to fight through the pain. If Nate could get back in shape so could he. Like Nate, he was a warrior not a victim.

Rob brought the bar to his chest. All of a sudden, he remembered what his dad had said to him when he was seventeen and learned the police were charging Andre as an adult for involuntary manslaughter: *Toughen up, son. It's all in your head.*

"Tell me you didn't give him permission to use the snowmobile," his dad said.

"I was drunk," Rob said.

How his dad berated him and then placed all the blame on Andre. Why did his dad have to press charges against Andre for stealing the snowmobile? He begged him to back off, but he wouldn't take any back talk from Rob.

"Get yourself under control," his dad told him.

Rob raised the bar. *Toughen up. It's all in your head, son.*
The gym's fluorescent lights glared into his eyes like the lights
had at the police station. He squeezed his eyes shut but
couldn't avoid the image of the doe charging at him with
those same terrified eyes—the ones he'd seen with Andre
that afternoon when they'd shot her—though angrier. They
came face to face with only a pane of glass between them. He
tried to swerve before he slammed his foot on the brake and
leaned away from the driver-side window. There was nothing
he could do. The doe's neck strained as she leapt toward him.
Hooves banged on the roof before pellets of glass rained into
the van as she came crashing through the windshield with an
arrow in her chest. Her warm breath shocked him. He sat
powerless. Her back hooves knocked on his door until she
stopped still on the roof with her head hanging over him and
one eye open.

It wasn't in his head. Sandra had come for him.

Rob raised the bar again, feeling like his heart, too, was
punctured as he recalled ducking under her twisted neck and
sliding across the vinyl onto the passenger side. He got away
through the other door then came around front and pried her
off from what was left of the crumpled driver's side. Dragging
her by the back legs, he approached the working headlight,
unable to stop staring at the arrow in her chest. He set down
her carcass. How he feared the gaping wound that would be
left after he removed the jagged tip. It seemed like he would
bleed to death when he pulled it out of her. Why would he
think that when she was already gone? Probably killed on impact like Sandra.

Now, as Rob lowered the bar to his chest, he recalled
bracing himself against her flesh with one hand and yanking
the arrow out with the other. Then he rolled the doe on her

back, unfolded his pocket knife, and gently inserted it beneath the skin. In one smooth motion, he slit her open from tail to throat, swallowing hard at the sight of the innards—vital organs like the lungs and heart—before leaning forward and reaching under the skin around the doe's throat. Then he took hold of the mass of internal organs and tugged with all his might. Blood splattered on his boots.

Rob set the bar in the rack. He strained for breath as if his own lungs had stopped. He was done denying it. His heartrate surged. He held his hands to his chest, which throbbed like a deep wound. The pain was so intense he thought he might be having a heart attack. Wasn't he too young for that? Rob didn't want to think about the doe. He sat up and glanced at Nate, who was lifting his weights with the other arm now. That took a lot of courage. Just then Rob figured out something about himself. He must find the courage to set an example. He and his son were warriors not victims.

Rob got back into position on the bench. He had three more sets. For the sake of Nate and his family he must get himself under control and make himself believe: *I am a warrior not a victim.*

After taking a series of deep breaths his heartrate stabilized. He was lowering the bar toward his chest when a feminine scent, a cross between vanilla and cherry, penetrated his nostrils. Patricia, her hands resting on her thighs, leaned over him from the top of the bench. Her hair, professionally straightened, brushed against his cheek. "Enjoying your workout?"

Oh, shit. For half a second, Rob lost his concentration. His form fell apart, though he managed to finish the lift. He rested the bar on the racks. Patricia had given him the pass, but Rob hadn't expected to run into her today. He sat up. "I didn't know you worked Sundays."

"I don't. I just came in to workout." Patricia adjusted her Spandex bra top, which left little room for imagination. She'd aged exceptionally well since high school. Not that he hadn't liked her when she was soft and curvy—though after Sandra's death, once they'd broken up, she'd ballooned to the point that at Senior Prom, behind her back, her frenemies called her Fatty Patty. "I could really help you work on your form."

Rob couldn't deny he wanted results. Personal training worked. Patricia was living proof. "Normally, I charge sixty dollars for a private session," she said.

Rob chuckled under his breath. "I don't doubt you're worth it."

"But for you, I'd do it for free."

Rob felt a familiar pang as he had when they played pool together at the bar. Suddenly, the room felt inexplicably heavy. After all these years, Patricia could still elicit the same response. Something instinctual. Primal. Ingrained. They were each other's first. He'd loved her once, but that was long ago. Now, he wished she'd stay away. "Maybe another time, thanks. I'm here with Nate. Laura is expecting us home soon. We had a late night."

"Is that why your face is all scratched up?"

Rob had hoped she wouldn't notice or at least have the common sense not to get personal and ask him. Patricia didn't need to know about any of it, though word of his collision would get around. He may as well just say it. "I hit a deer coming home from the lodge."

"That's awful." She leaned to examine the jagged cut on his hairline. "You better keep an eye on that one. Looks like you must have hit the windshield pretty hard. Do you have a headache?"

"It was no big deal. I'm fine." Rob's head hadn't stopped aching since the collision, but that was none of Patricia's business. No matter what Andre said, Rob didn't trust her. He couldn't work with her—not now, not ever. She wasn't the understanding type like Laura. He recalled the way Laura had come and sat beside him at the lodge and tried to listen. Even when he was talking bat-shit crazy and had given up on himself, he could see deep behind her eyes that she still believed she could reach him. Would help bring him back. "You should focus on your paying customers."

Rob resumed his starting position for a third set, his back pressed flat against the bench, his hands gripping the bar, his chest puffed. Patricia took a step away from the bench and crossed her arms. "I'll just wait here, in case you or Nate need a spot."

She paused and glanced at Nate with a toothy grin that seemed unnatural partly because her teeth were so white. When Rob nodded, his eyes landed on Patricia's belly button adorned with a silver ring. He hadn't known she'd gotten it pierced.

"Let me just show you one thing." She leaned forward and ran her thumb and forefinger down his arm from his wrist to his elbow. "Your forearms should be close to vertical at the bottom of a rep."

Back came the familiar pang. Sweat pooled along his hairline, trickled behind his ear and dribbled across his jaw. He inhaled her artificial sweeteners, most likely from the new Bath and Body store. Laura would never wear fake shit like that; she preferred natural essential oils. God, he hated himself. Patricia was standing too close. "Andre has noticed a big difference since I've started training him."

"Yes, I see." He had to get off the bench. "I think Nate needs me."

Rob turned his head and caught their reflection in the mirrored wall. Everyone in the gym could see them, including

Chelsea's husband, Brett, who was climbing the Stairmaster. By the time Patricia cleared the bench, Rob had broken into a full sweat. He grabbed a towel and wiped his brow. His chest burned. The familiar pang was gone.

Rob got off the bench and approached Nate where Patricia was giving him suggestions for training in his wheelchair. "It's okay." Rob stepped between them. "I've got this."

His voice sounded hard as he'd meant it to. Rob turned his back to her. He'd thought they could just be friends—even if she still turned him on—but Laura was right; Patricia was hitting on him and acting like she wanted to be more. He wouldn't let Patricia put his marriage in further jeopardy. Had she forgotten she was engaged to Andre? Rob considered whether he should tell him. He wondered if it was just him, or did Patricia use her body as a selling tool with every guy she gave a free pass? Rob didn't care anymore. He knew what was important. After their workout, he and Nate were going home to the family.

He hoped his dad wasn't too upset about the van. Insurance should cover the damage. If not, he would find a way to pay and have it fixed—unless Art expected him to work for him selling paintings under false pretenses at the gallery. He would never make that mistake again. He was done repeating his mistakes. Rob now understood, even his dad could make mistakes. He wanted to be a better father and husband.

"Want to try some chin-ups, bud?" Rob wheeled Nate away from Patricia to the opposite end of the gym toward the high bar.

"How am I going to get all the way up there, Dad?"

"I'll spot you."

Nate pushed himself up from the chair, leaned forward into Rob's arms, and set his sights on the bar. Rob reached under his armpits and hoisted him until his chin rested on the bar. Once he took hold, Rob slowly loosened his grip. Nate, clutching the bar, clenched his jaw and lowered himself until his arms were straight, then inch by inch pulled himself back up. When his arms began to tremble with fatigue, Rob lowered him back into the chair. When Nate was seated, Rob exhaled and extended his arm for a fist bump. Nate gave him one. "Dad, that was awesome. When I grow up, I want to have muscles as big as you."

Rob wasn't sure what to tell him. After all he'd been through over the past few months, Nate was already tougher than most of the guys in the room. Earlier this morning, he'd shown Rob what it meant to be a man. Heavy stuff for a five-year-old. "It all comes from the heart, bud. That's what I'm trying to work on. From what you're showing me, I know you'll get wherever it is you decide to go."

Nate stared at his injured leg. "You remember when the doctor said I might never walk again?"

Rob recalled the weakness in his knees when he'd received Dr. Azzi's unnerving prognosis. He steadied himself. "What do you think?"

Nate scowled every inch of his small face. "I don't believe him."

"Me neither." Rob now understood their new mission. But first, before he lost his courage, he had to get home to Laura.

Chapter 28

October 23, 2016

Wind off the lake whipped against their faces as Rob pushed Nate home from the gym over the uneven sidewalk. The leaves of the tall trees scattered around them. Ahead, where Main Street and Beach Road met, the church steeple jabbed at the gray sky. His parents were probably at mass. He always tried to avoid going with them. Not that he didn't believe in God. Rather he couldn't come to terms with the afterlife and how it would feel to be somehow both dead and alive—like Sandra. Over the past few months, since Andre moved back to town and Nate's accident, Rob had picked up on an ominous vibe. He hadn't known where it was coming from until the doe collided with him on the way home from the lodge. Now he understood why, more and more, often he felt like he was being watched, even judged, by Sandra. Yesterday, when he and Andre had dared to hunt on the sacred grounds near the cross they'd erected in her memory, Sandra had found him and reached her verdict. Guilty. Later that night, she'd come after him seeking justice.

Now, he couldn't get the image of the doe's terrified eyes out of his head. He couldn't forget the moment after she'd fallen on top of the van and crashed through the windshield—when she took her last breath—before he'd gutted her, literally ripped her heart out. Rob now understood what he had to do. He couldn't keep his lie a secret any longer. After nearly eight years, it was time. He had to tell someone—Laura—the truth about the day Sandra died.

On the frozen sidewalk Rob forged ahead with Nate.

"Dad!" Nate, his neck straining, frowned at him bewildered. "Where are you going?"

Rob loosened his grip on the handles and came to a stop, not realizing that he'd passed their driveway. His eyes had been focused on the church. "Sorry, bud." He turned Nate around, cast aside the images of the doe's anguish, and headed back the other way. "I wasn't thinking straight. I'm wiped out from all that exercise. We should get some lunch."

Rob pushed Nate home and tried to clear his head. Laura would be expecting them. How could he have almost walked out? Laura was right. Only a coward would abandon his family when they needed him most.

He hustled Nate up the ramp and into the kitchen where Laura stood over a mixing bowl at the far end next to the oven. The aromas of brown sugar and cinnamon wafted toward him. The comforting smells of home were so at odds with his jarring memories moments earlier on the sidewalk. How could the two worlds coexist? He realized the dilemma had been eating away at him for months. None of it was Laura's fault, though he'd been taking out his anger and frustration on her.

Laura, her thick hair pulled up in a messy bun, turned and smiled cautiously when she heard them. Without makeup, in her jeans and sweatshirt, she looked beautiful yet fragile.

"Where is everybody?" Rob asked.

Laura glanced at the clock on the microwave above the stovetop. "Your mom and dad took Ella and Biyen to church. They should be back around eleven. Until then it's just the three of us." She winked at Nate but averted her eyes when she came to him.

Rob wheeled Nate to the refrigerator. "I'll get him a snack. He can eat in front of the TV." Then, he faced her. "I have something I need to tell you." Her eyes narrowed. "It's important," he said.

When he returned to the kitchen, Laura was putting a roasting pan with cuts of venison in the oven. Rob's stomach churned. "Please, leave that for now." He took her by the hand. "Come upstairs with me for a minute."

Creases ran across Laura's forehead like an incoming line of storm waves. There was no turning back; Laura's intuition was too strong. Rob led her to the attic, hand in hand, and ran his thumb across her ring finger. His pulse flattened out when he realized this might be the last time she'd let him touch her. Once they came to the door of their room, he let her go. Laura took a seat on their bed. She must have made it when he and Nate were at the gym. Rob choked up. She always took care of everything around the house, including him. He'd gotten lucky. Still was … just like Andre always reminded him. Rob sat beside her. He cleared his throat. All these years later how could he explain to her what he'd done?

"Laura, I've always wanted to tell you this. I'm so sorry. I did something terrible." She looked up at him, blinking with her long lashes that curled upward like Nate's. She'd always expressed such faith in him. After what he had to say now, would she ever trust him again? "Andre was right about his sister," he said. "I want you to know what really happened to Sandra. It was my fault."

Laura cocked her head, seeming not to follow. He went on and tried to explain everything as it had come back to him over the past twenty-four hours. "I lost control." His heart pumped with adrenaline as when he'd first arrived at the scene of the accident. "When I found Sandra, only her leg was trapped under the snowmobile. I tried to pull it off her from where the blade was wedged against a tree. She told me 'No.' But it was too late. I didn't realize the slope was too steep to lift the machine toward me. When I did, my feet slipped out. I dropped it."

She listened, silent and still, until he described how he lost his grip on the icy blade and the snowmobile rolled forward down the hill before coming to a standstill. "It landed right below her chest." The words embedded like shrapnel in his conscience broke free. "It crushed her." He met Laura's gaze. "I killed her."

A tremor of fear appeared to course through Laura like a thin streak of fork lightning. Rob felt weak from the shock of the revelation, never imagining that she'd be afraid of him. She must understand that he would never harm anyone on purpose. "It was an accident." His hands were shaking. "Laura, I am so sorry." He reached for her and tried to stop himself from shaking, but she pulled away. "Please, say something."

"Why didn't you tell me?"

"I couldn't."

Laura pounded her fists on her thighs. "Why not?"

Rob's jaw latched shut. He'd kept his feelings to himself for so long it was almost beyond his power to share them, though he had to let Laura in. "I thought you would hate me."

She hugged her arms into her sides as he described the moments after he dropped the machine. Sandra was unconscious at first. He tried to dig her out, but with the weight of the snowmobile on her chest it was pointless. She didn't appear to be breathing. He couldn't do anything more, and if he didn't act quickly he'd lose Andre too. "I left her and went to Andre."

Laura seized up. "No, no, no."

A draft came through the attic. Laura hugged herself tighter. Rob wanted to stop there. He'd dreaded telling her about the moment he found Andre semiconscious near the bottom of the slope. Now, he forced himself to describe it to her verbatim.

"Andre asked, 'How's Sandra?'

"I said, 'not so good.'"

Rob pulled down the cuffs on his sleeve as he recalled how Andre tugged on his coat and begged. "'You've gotta help her,' he said.

"'I already did,' I said."

At the time, Rob recalled, the tips of his fingers had been so cold they burned. "I thought I'd lost them both, so I got down next to Andre and thought about dying there with him. Then, I felt him breathing. Once I realized he was alive, I hated him so much. If it weren't for him, none of this would have happened."

He rose from the bed, remembering how, fueled by anger, he'd risen from the knee-deep snow. Now he stood behind Laura and reached under her armpits to demonstrate how he dragged Andre down the rest of the hill onto the path. "Stop! You're scaring me." She slapped away his hands. "Stop!"

He did as she asked, though his temples throbbed. "You don't understand. I had loved him like a brother. Up until then, I would have done anything for him." He began to pace. "I kept thinking, we had a plan. Why did he wait around all day at my house until it was too late? He could have gone home

THE OTHER SIDE OF SANCTUARY

when the weather broke and I went to Patty's. He could have walked home with Sandra before it got dark."

Rob pressed his hands into the sides of his head. "Instead, he sits around all day drinking and doing exactly as he pleases. That's Andre. Then, he calls me at Patty's and asks to use the snowmobile when he knows it's already too late. He knew I couldn't get busted again by Dad. Dad had made it very clear that we couldn't use the machine. Andre didn't have anything to lose—except Sandra."

Now, looking back, it still made no sense. "How could he not have known something awful would happen when he drove up the hill? Who gave him the right? Everything was always about him."

Laura tucked her knees into her chest. "So, you turned against him and lied? Blamed it all on Andre?"

"No, it wasn't like that." Suddenly, Rob regained clarity. "As much as I hated what he'd done, I wanted to save him. I needed to save him. I kept dragging him, every now and then stopping to check for a phone signal, but by the time I got one I was more than halfway to Patty's. The 911 dispatcher told me to stay where I was. They met me on the path and carried Andre the rest of the way on a stretcher. It was less than a quarter mile to the road. An ambulance was waiting to take him to the hospital, but it took the EMTs another half hour to reach Sandra.

"She didn't die from hypothermia." Rob looked directly at Laura. "The coroner ruled she bled to death from internal injuries."

Once again, a wave of self-revulsion overcame him as it had hours after the accident, once he sobered up, when Rob understood if he'd been clear-headed he would have made different choices. "I should have been able to get the snowmobile off her another way. I could have dug around her shoulders and pulled her out."

Laura wouldn't look at him. Still, he kept talking. "I walked into the hospital prepared to tell Andre everything." The memory of Andre's accusation came up into his throat like bile.

"Andre asked, 'Why'd you let her die?'

"'She was already dead.' That's what I told him."

At the time, the words had just come out. Repeating them to Laura burned his throat. The bitterest cold he endured that night on the bluff—in the moments after he failed to save Sandra and lived with the possibility of Andre dying along with her—made his bones ache. "After what he did and said to me, I wasn't going to take the blame. Not a chance. I tried to save Sandra's life and instead I caused the injuries that killed her. How do you think that made me feel?"

Laura watched him pace, though she didn't answer him. He felt like a caged animal. "I know I failed, but what about protecting the rescuer? If it weren't for Andre, I never would have been there."

Laura tugged at her wedding ring. "I realize that, but he didn't kill Sandra. You did."

Rob felt his hands shake as they had when he failed to speak up to police and even to his dad. "When I didn't come home, Dad went looking for me at Andre's. He saw the emergency lights on the bluff and came to the accident site. Though Sandra had been taken away for treatment, his snowmobile was still there. He went back and called me from outside Andre's house. I was out on the road by the ambulances. He didn't even ask me what happened, but he made his position very clear. 'When they ask you what happened, you must tell them you were only trying to help.'"

Rob believed what Dad said was true. He was only trying to help. Andre had taken the snowmobile after he'd bullied him into reluctantly giving his permission. Andre drove it into a tree and his sister was killed as a result of the crash. *You've done nothing wrong, son.* Rob always wanted to believe, but deep down knew otherwise. Still, he couldn't bring himself to tell the truth. No one ever asked him whether he'd moved the snowmobile off the tree. "Everyone assumed it had landed on Sandra's chest in the first place. I never corrected anyone."

Laura shook her head. "So, because of you, Andre went to prison for a crime he didn't commit?"

Rob couldn't bring himself to look at her. "Yes."

"Is that why you got the tattoo? To remind yourself to *Persevere* in keeping your secret and lying to everyone, including me?"

It was impossible to take Laura with him back in time. Could she believe him? "I never imagined when I visited Andre at the hospital that he would ever be convicted. I got the tattoo before he went to prison. I never foresaw meeting you and the significance the tattoo would come to hold. Please believe me."

Rob reached for her hand, but she wouldn't give it to him. "After the accident, I wanted to die. That's all. When Andre went to prison, the tattoo was a way to mark myself. A constant reminder that I was chosen to live. If living was hell, well then, it was fair punishment for killing Sandra."

He wished Laura could try to understand how unstable he was that day when she came into town and found him out on the water. "Before I met you, Laura, I was so low."

Back then, armed only with his paddle and board, he'd sought the roughest water and fought for his sanity. Without her smile, her laugh, her kiss, he would have sunk. Instead he buried his memories under layers of thick sand at the bottom of the lake and prayed they would never ever get churned up again. He surfaced only thanks to her. They married. By the time Nate was born, all his memories of Sandra were washed out. In a matter of months, Laura had restored his will to live.

"You gave me back my life. I'm sorry I didn't trust you." He grasped her shoulders. "Do you believe me?" She lowered her eyes, brimming with tears, and edged away from him without a word. "I always planned to tell you. But when you got pregnant it didn't seem fair. I didn't want to upset you or do the baby any harm. I know it sounds lame, but the last thing I wanted to do was hurt anyone again, especially you. I wanted to keep it all behind me. Start us. I thought you wouldn't love me. I wasn't strong enough to accept that."

Laura glared at him through her tears. "So why now?"

"I think somehow I'd repressed it," he said. "But yesterday it all came back. Became real again. Last night, after I hit that doe, I thought I was going completely crazy."

Rob remembered how out of control he'd felt when Laura found him at the lodge. "I didn't know how to tell you, but when I looked into the doe's eyes as she came crashing into the car—I saw Sandra and the terror in her eyes—as if she were staring up at me from under the snowmobile."

Laura braced herself on the mattress. Rob wished he could stop talking and spare her, but this other force was now driving him. "Today, at the gym when I was lifting, I closed my eyes and it was like Sandra told me what I had to do. She wanted me to tell you the truth."

Only then did he remember the last thing Sandra said. "'What have you done to me?' Those were her final words."

Rob knelt on the floor before Laura. She raised both eyebrows. "The doe was like her messenger?" she asked.

Rob nodded. "Please don't think I'm crazy." Then he asked, "Am I crazy?"

She helped him up. "I think you should rest now." With her gentle touch, she lowered him crossways onto their bed. He lifted his feet and adjusted himself. He didn't have the strength to argue. Once he was lying down, she covered him with a heavy blanket. "Just give it time."

He reached for her hand. "Stay with me, please."

Laura, standing over him, withdrew. "I need to be alone for a while."

PART IV

Chapter 29

October 23-24, 2016

Now what? She couldn't risk going downstairs and having to face anyone. Helen and Art would be home with the kids any minute. She sank into the corner outside the attic door and stared at the planks of knotted oak in the ceiling. The last twenty-four hours and Rob's confession seemed almost unreal. He'd finally told her the truth, she believed, but how could she ever trust him again? Sure, he had his reasons, but he'd lied to police and his family— through omission and maybe more. Her heart was angry. Laura closed her eyes and tried to collect her thoughts. Could she stay with Rob after what he'd done? Nothing was certain except that their relationship was forever changed.

All these years she thought she'd known him when, in actuality, he'd been hiding from the past. Unknowingly, she'd helped him run away. Early on in their marriage, when Rob was paddle boarding professionally, their life had seemed so carefree. They'd travelled light with only baby Nate, from one beach destination to the next, with sponsors footing most of the bill. Usually, it wasn't anything luxurious, except for once in Cancun when they had a room with the ocean-view balcony. It had been their favorite except that she'd forgotten to pack her birth control pills and gotten pregnant with Ella. Back then, Rob never spoke of his relationships with Andre and Patricia. He'd said nothing to her even after he dropped off the circuit when Ella was born, around the time Andre was released from prison. Rob had claimed he was quitting because of injuring his Achilles, but then Andre took his place on the team. Rob took over the lease on the bar. Had he sacrificed his spot in an attempt to make amends?

Running a bar had never come naturally to him like paddle boarding. He'd never complained about work until Andre and Patricia moved back to Sanctuary. They'd driven a wedge between her and Rob. Now she understood the source of his flashes of anger, which seemed so out of character, like when he'd lashed out at her after Nate's birthday party for commenting on the beautiful gulls. She finally knew why Rob hadn't talked about what happened *before her time* in Sanctuary. But what did it mean for their family? Should she make him confess to Andre?

Andre deserved to know the truth, though she wasn't sure Rob would ever be able to own up to it. What would happen if he did? Andre had every reason to want to see him thrown in prison. Worse yet, Andre might take justice into his own hands. Hadn't Rob done the same? No matter what, now that she knew, she couldn't go on living a lie. Somehow, Rob must try and right the wrong he'd done.

Footsteps were fast approaching up the stairs. Out of breath, face beaming, Ella appeared on the landing. She held out a piece of paper. "Momma! Look what I made for you." Laura squinted at the crayon drawing of a woman with long hair holding a cross made from two Band-Aids. "Today we learned about the Beatitudes and being motivated by love … like you are when you help fix Nate."

Laura patted her hand. "Thank you."

Downstairs the oven dinged.

"Smells like cake!" Ella said.

Laura had completely forgotten about the coffeecake. The venison was still on the counter. "Okay, could you see if Grandma would take it out for me? I don't think I'm up for eating anything."

Ella's forehead knotted up. "What's wrong? Does your tummy hurt?"

"No, I'm fine."

"Then what are you doing sitting out here?"

"I just need to be alone for a little bit, to think."

"About what?"

"Adult things."

Ella frowned.

"Don't worry." She held up Ella's drawing. "This helps me feel better."

She opened her arms for Ella and wrapped them around her tiny body. In that instant, Laura too felt enveloped by love as if her own mother's presence had entered the landing and sealed their embrace. Laura vowed: she would stay strong for her children—the three of them—so young and dependent upon her. For her sake and theirs, she must take her time to think through the situation before deciding what to do about her marriage. She must get it right.

She didn't talk to Rob the rest of the day or night. Though yesterday, he'd roused himself out of bed and gone to the lodge with Art and retrieved the van. Afterward, he'd continued on to work. She'd gone to bed early, and kept her back to him when she felt him get in beside her around 12:30. She hadn't wanted to be anywhere near him, much less in the same bed, but there was no place else for her to go.

Now, as she went through the motions of a Monday morning, she wasn't sure she could cope. She'd thrown a flannel button-down over the T-shirt she'd slept in, fed the kids breakfast, and made sure Ella was ready in time for Art to drop her at preschool on his way to take Helen to work. What next?

Her thoughts were jumbled. When she'd first discovered Sanctuary, tucked away among the dunes, the beautiful village had instilled new hope in her. Here, she could realize her dreams. She and Rob had fallen in love and built a life together, and she believed that she could hold her family intact against the elements the way loam bonded the dunes. For the first time, she questioned the foundation of their marriage. It felt as if they were trapped inside a sandcastle that could be crushed by one foot or swept away in a single wave. Could they hold it together long enough to work things out?

She pushed Nate away from the living room TV and set him up at the dining table to start his schoolwork packet for the week. She left for upstairs to gather the dirty laundry, tip-toeing between the beds where Biyen and Rob were still asleep.

Laura glanced at Rob, his jaw hanging wide open, as she filled up the laundry basket. Resting on his side with his knees slightly bent, he looked as vulnerable as Nate had on his first night home from the hospital. In many ways Rob was still just a boy. Could he ever grow up and face responsibility? For their marriage to survive, he would have to.

She carried the laundry back downstairs into the kitchen and stopped to retrieve her bloodied moccasins outside the side door. Maybe there was still hope for them? She set them on top of the other laundry and went into the basement to do a load. When she opened the washer, Laura discovered their stuff from the lodge was still wet in the bottom of the barrel. She'd forgotten all about it and wished there was some way to avoid it forever.

A side of her wanted to break down and cry. Instead she got to work and moved her wet things and Rob's coveralls into the dryer as if it were any other load. Once she'd turned it on heavy duty, she set aside her moccasins on the floor and began sorting Rob's lights and darks. Trying to keep her head, she weighed the factors behind his actions as she tossed his black sweatpants into the barrel of the washer and left his white socks and T-shirts into the basket for later. Rob, panicked and confused, had dropped the snowmobile by accident. If only he hadn't lied everything would be different.

Why hadn't he been able to trust anyone? Not even her. That's the question that troubled her most. Laura stared at her soiled moccasins beside the washer. She'd brought them with her when she came from Wisconsin and they were nearly new. Protecting her soles for six years, the worn suede, tattered at the toe and heel, was almost like her own flesh. She bent down and ran the pads of her fingers inside the seam, noticing where the blood had penetrated, leaving her no way to restore them. She set them back down. It was time to let go. She must move forward even if she didn't know her next steps.

Fear had held Rob back. As he told her yesterday, he wasn't as brave as he put on. He'd finally found the strength to tell her the truth. It took courage to admit that he'd caused Sandra's death. Laura imagined how terrified he must have felt as a teenager being questioned by police. Would she have had the courage to be honest, especially if she thought she could get away without being caught? Or escape punishment. Would she ever be so selfish as to allow someone else take all the blame? She recalled being punished by her father when she was ten and she and Shenia had purposefully stayed out on the island in the center of the lake after dark. They'd missed their chores and were late for dinner. They stood before their father outside the door with wet shorts, dirty knees, and little hope for mercy. "You scared your mother to death. She was worried you'd drowned out there in the dark. You should have been more careful. No one would have been able to find you."

They both knew better. He frowned at them with a severe look in his stone-gray eyes. A bolt of fear coursed through her, starting with a spark under her feet, shooting up her legs into her stomach and past her heart until the words escaped from her mouth. "Shenia didn't tell me it was time to go."

At the instant, his furrowed brow softened.

"I did so." Shenia socked her in the arm. "You were the one who ran off to the top and looked out one more time. I had to chase after you."

He shook his finger at Shenia. "You're supposed to be responsible for your little sister. I'm very disappointed in you."

For a second or two, Laura thought she might avoid being beaten. She'd been so frightened that she'd hoped her father would make Shenia take all the punishment. He pointed at her. "Don't you ever lie to me, Laura. You should have listened to your big sister."

He took the wooden paddle from the peg on the wall of the garage outside the kitchen door. He bent them over on the doorstep and walloped each of their bottoms like never before. The first strike shocked her. The second strike rattled her to the marrow of her bones. Still, she held out hope that her father might take it easy on her for the final stroke of punishment. But when he landed the third blow with the greatest force of them all, her whole body shuddered so hard that she thought she'd lost her insides.

"Now, both of you, go to your room and get straight to bed." Father, in a gruff tone, insisted. "Go!"

She and Shenia scurried into their room beside the kitchen and jumped under the heavy quilt of their queen bed. Her sister pulled it over their heads, Laura still trembling, before they each retreated to opposite sides. In the kitchen, their mother turned on the sink faucet. Forks, cups, plates clattered. She'd started doing the dishes without them. Realizing her mom wouldn't tuck her in tonight, Laura began to cry. The best she could do was imagine how her mom sometimes ran her hand up and down her back to comfort her. "It's okay, my little makwa, just try to sleep."

Though Father forbade them from speaking in her mother's native language, her mother, like her grandfather, had secretly spoken it before bed. She'd almost forgotten her mother's Ojibwa nickname for her—makwa—meaning bear, and symbolizing bravery. That night, Laura had been anything but brave. Nothing could take her mind off her burning bottom or—worse yet—her sister's wrath.

"Stop crying, you little baby," Shenia said. "You're such a liar. That's the last time I take you anywhere."

They'd both been afraid. She'd been so frightened that she lied to protect herself with the hope that her big sister would take the blame. She'd gotten her rationalization from their father. *Shenia, you're supposed to be responsible for your little sister.* Laura blamed her mother too. If only she'd stood up to their father and told him, *No.* Mother knew it was wrong to beat children because grandfather had taught her another way. Yet fear had held her mother back and led Laura to lie. From that point on, she now realized, her relationship with Shenia had started to erode because they'd lost trust. Fear was a powerful force. She wouldn't be ruled by fear anymore. What about Rob?

Just then, she noticed a scrap of paper on the floor with a number scribbled on it. She bent down and picked it up, remembering then that Rosa had given it to her at the bar. It must have fallen out of her pocket when she'd come home from the lodge. They'd only spoken a few times, but Rosa seemed like someone who knew herself and would be a good listener. It couldn't be easy for her now either. She might be the only one around here who could understand Laura's sense of isolation. They definitely needed to talk.

Laura left the laundry but carried the moccasins upstairs with her. In the dining room Nate sat at the table doing his homework. He was learning to write and recognize the Letter of the Day: G. She looked over his shoulder. He'd matched it with a picture of a word starting with the same letter— drawn a line to the Good Girl smiling cheerfully in black and white on the page. "Good boy, Nate." She patted him on the head, grateful for the small accomplishment. They were all still learning. Rob was seventeen when the accident occurred. He'd finally found the courage to tell the truth and ask for her forgiveness. That was a start. Would it be enough?

Chapter 30

October 24, 2016

Jarred out of sleep by Biyen's high-pitched cries, Rob raised his head slowly and glanced at the clock. It was past ten. Biyen, standing there in his diaper, rattled the rails of his crib like he was trying to break free of his cell. What was he still doing in bed at this hour? Rob forced himself out from under the covers and went to his son who reached for him with both arms. "Uppy, da-da. Uppy." Rob took him into the crook of his arm and carried him down to the kitchen.

Then he stopped beside the fridge and peered into the dining room. On the other side of the passageway, Nate sat at the table doing his homework. Beside him Laura stared out the windows facing the driveway. She seemed lost in thought. Rob could relate. The last few months had given them a lot to think about. He now realized that though physically present, he'd been mentally absent for months—ever since Andre and Patricia moved back to town—and even more so since Nate's accident and the recent memories of Sandra. Caught up in his own head, consumed with his own problems, he'd been a husband and father in name only. Laura had endured and been there for him. Now it was his turn. He had to bring her back. Prove he was worth staying for, though she had every reason to leave. Almost any other woman would already be gone. Rob came around behind her and Nate.

"Good morning." He glanced at the papers. "What are you two working on?"

Laura nodded for Nate to go ahead and answer.

"Nothing, Dad. My homework was easy. Want to play Wii?"

"I haven't even had breakfast." He gently mussed Nate's hair, careful to avoid the bald patch that finally was filling back in.

Laura looked over her shoulder and broke for a second into halfhearted smile he couldn't read. She hadn't said a word to him in nearly a day. Now he couldn't tell if she was ready to forgive him or on the verge of walking out and taking the kids. The silent treatment was unbearable. Her moccasins, stacked on top each other behind her chair, were in bad shape. Rob stepped around them. God, he needed her to stay with him. What would he have done without her at the lodge, if she hadn't come to find him? Unable to butcher the deer, he'd sat on the floor with the meat cleaver in his hand and thought about killing himself. After she called his name and entered the room he'd set down the knife.

Yet, he'd treated her so badly the next morning. He wouldn't blame her if she held it against him forever. He'd thought it would be best for him to leave to protect her. He'd never wanted to burden her with the consequences of his actions from *before her time* or now. Nate had instilled him with fresh courage. Laura had heard him out. Though in relieving his load he'd weighed her down.

Rob's empty stomach churned. He hadn't eaten since the Sunday brunch Laura skipped yesterday. She always made him breakfast first thing when he woke up on Monday mornings. Today he was so wiped out that he hadn't even realized how late he'd slept-in. She and Nate were probably getting hungry for lunch.

Laura stood from her seat. "I'll try to get your breakfast ready before Nate and I leave."

She started to slip on her moccasins as if by habit and then pulled back. "I need to find my flip-flops."

"Or get some new shoes?" he asked.

"Seems like it, though I'm not sure how we can afford it," she said. "I was going to try and wash them with the other stuff, but then I realized it was no use. They're gone."

"I'm sorry," he said.

"You can't hold onto anything forever." Laura ran her fingers back through her thick hair as if untangling her thoughts about their relationship.

They needed to talk before she made up her mind. Or had she already decided to leave him? Soon, she would take Nate for his first appointment at the new medical complex in Harbor City. Rob wished they could talk beforehand. There really wasn't enough time, though he wasn't sure he could wait until she came back.

"What time will you be home?" he asked. "I was hoping we could talk."

Laura looked away. "Maybe around two or three." She started to walk toward the kitchen. "I'm going to get ready."

Rob couldn't let her leave. "Aren't you going to have breakfast?"

Laura cocked her head. "I don't have time to make anything today."

"I know. Biyen and I are cooking."

Laura's head fell forward. "Are you sure?"

"Yeah, positive. What do you want?" he asked.

She turned around. "Oh, you mean, for all of us?"

Rob pretended as if it were normal for him to do the cooking. "What?"

"Nothing," Laura said.

"Who's ready for eggs and toast?" he asked with an ear toward Nate.

"Dad, I want bacon too."

"We can do that." Rob jostled Biyen on his arm. "Right, little man?"

Biyen sucked his thumb. "Any other requests?" Rob glanced at Laura, who had dark bags under her eyes. "A cup of coffee?"

She looked up at him. "Sure. With a smidge of creamer?"

"Got it." Oxygen poured into his lungs. He'd almost forgotten the boost of energy that came when he was engaged with her and the kids. Laura sat down at the table with Nate. Rob stepped out into the kitchen and reached for the cabinet beneath the stovetop. Now could he find a frying pan? He set Biyen on the floor beside him and opened the cabinet doors into unfamiliar territory. He rummaged around and allowed Biyen to lend a hand. Patience. He would find what he needed eventually; he just had to sort through it all.

Chapter 31

October 24, 2016

Laura hauled Nate's chair out of the trunk of the Buick and locked it into place beside the rear passenger's side door. He hoisted himself onto his good foot and into the seat. When she reached for the handles, he swatted her away. "Momma, I got this." Then, Nate took control of the wheels.

She followed behind as he led the way into the new facility. Other than yesterday in the living room, he'd never used the chair on his own. "Look at you go."

For so long, she'd yearned for him to regain his independence, and yet it scared her that he might soon leave the safety of his wheelchair and take on the even more dangerous challenge of crutches—much less a knee scooter like the principal recommended.

The wind shook the leaves from the trees that lined the cement path to the front door. She flipped up the collar of her shirt. The cold air was raw as her emotions. Since she'd left the house after finishing breakfast a half hour ago, Rob had texted her a cheery message. *Good luck at the doctor.* He was making an effort, but she couldn't stop her mind from drifting back to all the things he'd said. She wanted them to try to stick together, though she didn't know if they could. Each of them was wounded and grieving over the trust and innocence they'd lost. It felt as if they were in the early stages of healing, almost as if they were trying to grow new skin like Nate's, which took time, patience, and willpower. Were they strong enough to recover? She really needed someone to talk about it with—even if she didn't get into details. She'd brought Rosa's number with her.

For now, she must focus on Nate, who was already inside. Three months ago, when he was released from the hospital, she never would have imagined he'd make such progress. She followed him to the elevator where he pressed the up button. No longer the scrawny boy with a gaunt face, Nate was buzzing with energy. His cheeks, which had gotten chapped from the wind, were plump enough to pinch. She couldn't stop herself from just one squeeze.

"Momma, stop that, I'm not a baby anymore."

Nate took off toward Dr. Azzi's new office at the end of the corridor on the second floor. When she met him at the door, he didn't look at her and instead pushed the metal button which automatically opened. Where had this independence come from? Soon after Laura checked in, the doctor's medical assistant took them into an examination room and checked Nate's vitals. Dr. Azzi greeted them a few minutes later. He extended his hand to her. "Nice to see you again."

Laura shook his hand before he and Nate exchanged knuckles.

"How are you doing, young man?"

"I'm a lot stronger."

"Let me see." Dr. Azzi reached for the wrapping on Nate's leg. "Has he been able to put any weight on it?"

She shook her head. "That's what we're working toward. We've been doing leg lifts and a lot of other exercises to keep up his strength. He's almost ready to ride the stationary bike."

"My arms are strong too." Nate sat up tall in his chair. "My Dad took me to the gym yesterday. I can do a chin-up." Nate made a muscle.

Dr. Azzi stared at the chart on his clip board. "I don't see any of that as part of our home care program." He looked up and raised an eyebrow at Laura.

"Oh, no. That's separate. I take care of all the bandage changes at home, and supervise the stretches and exercises on the list to ensure he's on schedule. We've made every physical therapy appointment. Just ask Keshya."

Nate gripped the armrest and bounced in his seat as if it were a trampoline. "Dad's is extra training. We're warriors."

Laura smiled at the doctor reassuringly. "It's more of a male bonding thing. Helps build confidence. I think my husband enjoyed it as much as he did."

"My dad spotted me when I was up there."

Dr. Azzi half smiled and scribbled notes on Nate's chart. "That's fine. As long as they don't overdo it. I'd hate for any kind of … incident to interfere or set him back."

He unwound the wrapping from Nate's leg, ankle, and foot. "Let's see what we've got here." He leaned in for the examination and ran his fingers down his square chin.

She looked over his shoulder at Nate's toes. "Is something wrong?"

He shook his head. "You are the one responsible for this?"

Laura nodded with a shrug. She must have missed something. "I've been doing everything I was told."

He leaned forward and took another close look at Nate's foot. "See here." He pointed at the new pink skin between

Nate's toes. "Pretty remarkable." Dr. Azzi tilted his head to examine it from another angle. "You usually don't see that much regrowth until after six months or more." He turned and frowned at her in disbelief. "Are you a nurse?"

Laura laughed. "No, but my grandfather once said I had hands like a surgeon when I field-dressed a deer."

Dr. Azzi grinned at Nate. "This gives new meaning to the term Doctor Mom."

Nate lowered his chin to his chest. "Sometimes, when it itches real bad, she fans it with her hand and makes it stop."

Heat rose to Laura's cheek, and she knew she'd turned bright red. "Sorry, I hope that's not wrong. It's just to make him feel better. I follow all the proper procedures when I change his bandages."

"Please, don't worry. Based on what I see here, you could teach my staff a few things. Actually, you might want to talk with our office manager and get some information before you leave. We're looking to hire medical assistants."

Laura felt a flutter in her chest until she realized she probably wasn't qualified. "I only have a high school degree."

"That's where most people start. The position would require additional certification though, which you could do online or at the community college. We also offer on-the-job training and tuition reimbursement."

"Really?"

"Yes. Sorry, I sound like an infomercial." His eyes widened. "But you're a natural."

He guided Nate onto the table and moved his ankle up and down and from side to side. "Based on what I see here, I'm thinking he can get rid of the wheelchair and move into a boot and crutches. He should continue with therapy, but could return to school right after Thanksgiving. I would just need you to sign some paperwork today."

Nate clapped. "Awesome!" He bumped his butt up from the table. "Now I can be with Jacob."

"Let's not get carried away," she said.

Chelsea still seemed wary of them, though Laura didn't want to discourage Nate. He'd missed out on so much this summer. More than ever, he needed a true friend. So, did she. Nate and Jacob always went trick-or-treating together. She wondered what Chelsea's plans were.

On the other hand, Laura reminded herself, she had to be realistic. Recovery was a slow process with progress measured in increments. Therapy and working out only went so far. If Nate went back to school with the other kids, he'd have limitations. Laura still wasn't sure she liked the idea of him wheeling around on a knee scooter. So far, she hadn't mentioned the option to Nate or Dr. Azzi.

He handed Laura a pen and held up his clipboard for her signature. "Mrs. Sanders, do you think he's ready to start trying the boot and crutches full-time and then going back to school?"

For a moment, Laura lost her train of thought. She recalled what Nate's therapist had told them. *You must believe to achieve.* Should she ask Dr. Azzi whether he thought Nate should use the knee scooter the principal had recommended? Laura didn't want to hold Nate back because of an irrational fear—of hers. A Razor scooter wasn't the same as the medical scooter he would ride around at school. Dr. Azzi was always so understanding. Laura knew she had no reason to feel uncomfortable about talking openly with him about her concerns. And yet, something was holding her back. Fear. This time the fear was hers—not Nate's.

"Mrs. Sanders?"

"Well, there's one thing. Nate's principal said they have scooters at school for students with mobility issues. She thinks it would be a lot easier for him to ride around on that rather than use crutches. I'm just worried about whether it's safe, given—."

The doctor nodded at her. "I see." Then he turned to Nate. "What do you think, young man?"

"I want to ride the scooter." Nate looked over at her. "As long as my mom says it's okay."

"So, Mrs. Sanders, the decision up to you."

As she thought about it, her eyes started to sting, but she blinked the tears away. She wanted to be brave. At the moment, she wasn't sure whether she was strong enough to be his advocate.

Dr. Azzi cleared his throat. "I don't want to rush you. Today, we can simply sign the paperwork giving him permission to return to school. Then you can determine the best mode of transportation for him once you're ready."

"I think I would feel more comfortable with that plan."

"There's nothing wrong with taking it one step at a time."

Laura left the hospital with Nate feeling optimistic about his possibilities for returning to school and making a full recovery—even it was a gradual process. Yet, as soon as she and Nate were belted up in their seats for the ride home, she froze. All of a sudden, the hope she'd sensed in Dr. Azzi's office disappeared. She and Rob had so much to work through. Would they ever be able to talk openly again? Nate needed them to be his advocates. Returning to school would be a huge adjustment for him. She wanted to do what was best for him but, right now, she was torn.

Once again, she felt alone. She needed to talk to someone about her feelings soon, or she truly might lose her mind. She thought about texting Chelsea, but Laura wasn't in the mood to make plans for the kids. Instead, she took Rosa's number from her pocket and gave her a call. When she didn't answer, Laura was tempted to hang up. Though, once it went to voice mail, she managed to leave a message. *Hi. It's Laura from the bar. I was hoping we could talk.* She wasn't sure if that made any sense, or if Rosa would even respond. But, at the moment, Rosa felt like her only lifeline.

Laura turned on the car and pulled out of the hospital parking lot. Soon after, Nate pulled up his blanket and fell asleep. Laura passed by building after building, her mind wandering. She had to go somewhere, nowhere, anywhere—but home. The thought of facing Rob was making her crazy. On the seat beside her, the phone buzzed. Immediately, she picked it up.

"Hi, Laura. It's Rosa, calling you back. I didn't think I was working today. Is something wrong?"

Laura's hands trembled on the wheel. "Oh, no. I didn't mean to worry you. It's not about work. I mean, I always see you there, but we've never really had a chance to talk."

For a second, the line went silent. "Oh, yeah, about Friday night. I heard Rob hit a deer. Do you want to come over? I'm home now. I live right off the main highway."

Laura glanced in her rearview mirror. Nate would probably sleep for at least an hour. "Okay, if that's all right. I have Nate with me in the back seat. I won't stay long."

"Sure, no problem. I'll text you the address."

Laura hung up. Why had she invited herself over to Rosa's? Now that was crazy. She knew she should go straight home, but couldn't force herself to do it. She had to see Rosa. After about five miles, the mailbox with her address appeared. Laura turned onto a dirt road that led into the woods. Ahead, set off behind a stand of evergreens, stood the small white house Rosa had described with a tin roof and paint peeling off the green shutters. Laura pulled up around the side by Rosa's motorcycle.

She took her purse and left Nate asleep in the backseat. He'd be okay for a little while. She hurried across the fallen pine needles and was half way to the front door when she heard music. It sounded like someone was playing a clarinet or a saxophone. She listened for a moment before gathering the will to knock. After a few seconds, the music stopped. Then, wearing a large instrument strapped around her neck, Rosa appeared. "Hi. Were you waiting long?"

"Nope. I hope I'm not barging in on your practice."

"Not at all. All I do is practice and work since my mom left. I need a break."

"Is that a saxophone?"

Rosa nodded before poking her head out the door. "Whose car is that?"

"My mother-in-law's. The van might be totaled."

"From the deer?"

"Yeah. It was bad. A doe crashed right through the windshield." Laura's mouth suddenly felt dry as sand. "It's been a rough few days."

"Well, come in then. Can I get you something to drink?" Rosa set the saxophone in its stand near the door. "I made a pot of coffee this morning."

"That sounds good. I've been living on caffeine lately. I don't know how you're able to work day and night." Laura followed Rosa into the kitchen.

She poured them each a cup. "Well, that's pretty much what you do, isn't it?" Laura laughed. She didn't expect Rosa to understand.

"Milk or sugar?"

"No, black is great." Rosa handed her the coffee and took a seat at the kitchen table. Laura sat across from her where she could see Nate in the backseat of the car. She took a sip. "Wow. This is amazing. It's so smooth. They should serve this at the bar instead of that watered-down Folgers."

"Thanks. It's from Mexico. My mother sent it to me last week. We always used to drink it before our performances at the resort."

"What do you mean?"

"My mom sang outdoors in the summer on the bluff. It was unofficial, but hundreds of people would gather to hear her. She let me back her up a few times on saxophone."

"What kind of songs did you like to play?"

"Mostly, we played classic songs from the '70s. She had a lot of fans. That's what they wanted to hear. They were really upset when she wasn't there anymore, I heard. I have a contact list of more than a thousand people. Now that she's gone, I'm writing songs of my own, jazz, like my dad."

"That's great. You should play at the bar."

"Oh, I don't know. I'm not sure my music would translate."

"Why not?"

"It's about our struggle. My dad died when I was six. Some people who worked in the competing clubs spread a rumor that Mom had poisoned him. That wasn't true. I think they didn't want her to rise up in his place. They threatened her. When she felt her life was in danger, she fled, and we found our way here. Now, she's back there alone and I worry. I guess that's what my songs are about."

"I'm sorry to hear that. But I'd definitely be interested in hearing you play. It sounds like the kind of music I could relate to. My mom died from cancer when I was thirteen." She gulped her coffee. "To be honest, I always wished it was my father who had died." Laura set her cup on the table feeling like a terrible person and yet, at the same time, so relieved to have spoken the truth.

"Is he still alive?"

Laura nodded. "But I never see him. I have a sister, though, in Wisconsin. I don't see her either, although I'd like to. Since she left after our mom died, it's like I don't exist to her." She stared into her empty coffee cup. "I'm sorry. I have no idea why I'm telling you all this. I just feel like this weekend threw everything off."

"Hey, at least you're being honest. Sounds tough. This summer, after my mom was deported, I was so overwhelmed, I went into the lake and almost—"

Then, Rosa was silent.

Laura recalled how Rob had described Rosa, at the time, when he'd seen her wading into the water. Possibly suicidal. Maybe it had been a mistake to come here? Their conversation had gotten way too deep. Rosa probably wanted her to leave. Laura glanced at her car where Nate lifted his head off the back seat. "Hey, Rosa, please forgive me. I have to go out to the car. My son is awake." Laura stood. "I should get going. Rob is probably wondering where we are."

"Are you sure? Why doesn't your son come inside for a minute? You can have another cup of coffee." Rosa raised her eyes. "I've always wanted to meet him. Nate, right? I have some drinking chocolate from Mexico."

"Seriously?"

Rosa shook the tin of cocoa. "Please, stay. I don't need all this for myself." She puffed out her cheeks. "Help me."

Laura laughed. "Stop. You look like Dizzy Gillespie."

"Ah, the trumpeter. So, you do know something about jazz."

"Only what I've heard on my mother-in-law's stereo."

"Well, it sounds like you might have an ear for it. I'll put some on. It'll be our little party."

Chapter 32

October 24, 2016

Once Biyen was fed and dressed, Rob strolled him to the kiddie park. As soon as they reached the sand, Biyen pointed at the baby swing and babbled. "Da-da." At first, Rob gave him a soft push and then another. Biyen squealed to go higher. "Mo-? Mo-?" Rob chuckled, entertained by his son, until the ride was over. When he lifted him from the swing, Biyen weighed on him, a reminder of all Rob had to lose if his family fell apart. He had to do everything he could to keep it together, starting with earning back Laura's trust. He wished she would check-in, though it was only one o'clock. He looked on his phone to see if there were any new messages from her. Instead one popped up from Andre. Rob's hands shook as he clicked on it. *Bro, Patricia said you hit a deer coming home the other night. WTF?*

He usually responded to Andre right away. This time Rob didn't know what to say. He put Biyen in the stroller and lit up a cigarette. A wave broke close to shore. Now that the truth had come out—even if only to Laura—what was he supposed to do? Another wave crested over the sandbar before it came rolling in. This was the kind of surf Andre lived for. Suddenly,

Rob felt like a target. He and Biyen had to get out of there. What would he say if Andre showed up?

He looked behind him, but no one was there. This whole thing had made him paranoid. Rob hurried away down the sidewalk behind the stroller. By the time he entered the kitchen, it was almost half past one, the time when Biyen usually went down for a nap. Rob filled a sippy cup with milk, changed his diaper, and put him in the crib. As the hour passed, Biyen grew crankier, but wouldn't settle down. Rob rubbed his back in circles. Even then, he refused to sleep—probably since he'd woken up too late. Rob took him onto his lap and read him a story in the rocking chair before putting him back to bed. When Biyen fussed again, Rob shook his head. "No more. It's time for bed."

By the time Rob went onto the front porch for a smoke. It was almost three. Where was Laura? He couldn't hold out much longer. He must figure out what to do about Andre. They were adults now and could no longer act like reckless boys. Were they mature enough to settle their differences like grown men? Rob had never thought about himself that way— as a grown man—though if it meant he could hang on to Laura by learning how to be one, he would sure as hell try.

He put out his cigarette on the rail and went inside to watch TV. When she wasn't home at three-fifteen, he texted her. *When will you be back?* At half-past-three, when she still hadn't checked in, his hands began to shake. He went outside for another cigarette, though when he heard a familiar creak on the front step, he slipped his Camels into the pocket of his hoodie as if he were in high school and afraid of being caught. After all the years, his father's measured footsteps still carried weight.

"What's going on?" Art asked. "Where's Laura? I need to leave soon to get Helen and Ella."

Rob, unable to stop himself from pacing, told him that she and Nate were running late.

"Something wrong?" Art asked.

Rob shook his head. "Nah, I'm sure they'll be back before you need to take the car."

"Well, then we've got time." Art pulled out a pack of Marlboro Reds from his breast pocket. "Go ahead." He leaned against the porch rail. "I'll have one with you."

Dad, who hadn't smoked in front of him in years, lit up. "Your mother doesn't like it when I smoke anymore."

Laura never said anything about his smoking, though Rob knew she wanted him to quit. When he inhaled the tremor in his hands stopped. He wished he could tell his father about the predicament he was in until he remembered Art's reaction at the time of the accident. *You've done nothing wrong, son.* Dad had a way of seeing things his own way when he wanted to.

"Hey, I just wanted to apologize for my behavior at the gallery the other day with that couple from Chicago. I was suffering from an acute lack of vision. I let my worst instincts get the best of me. I'm ashamed of myself."

Rob recalled how Art had cheated the couple and then lectured him about the end of the age of King Arthur and his knights. Chivalry is dead. There are no heroes. "We all have bad days, Dad. I understand." Why was his dad apologizing now? Did he know more about Sandra's death than he let on? As an artist, he'd always been a close observer. It was a quality that Rob had learned could serve as a double-edged sword.

"I spoke to the guys at the body shop," Art said. "The van should be back next Monday. Insurance is going to cover the whole thing. If we'd had airbags it would have been totaled."

Rob took a drag. "Kind of wish it was totaled?"

Art ashed over the railing. "I think I'm all out of wishes. Sometimes you have to accept what is and move on. This way we're no worse than when we started. Maybe even a little better off."

Rob could see the sense in that. "I'm really sorry about what happened. I didn't see her until it was too late."

Art nodded. "Yeah, from the looks of the front end, she took you by surprise. An eight-pointer came at me out of nowhere like that once before you were born when Helen and I were driving home. The hood looked like it had gone through a trash compactor." Rob could picture it, though he was curious why he'd never heard his dad tell this story. "I came out of it with just a few scrapes—kind of like you. Worst thing was, Helen hit her head on the dashboard. When I looked over, blood was running down her forehead. Scared the living shit out of me."

"But she was all right?"

"Yeah, in the end. I took her to the hospital. They stitched her up, but when she started vomiting they kept her overnight for observation. Back then, they made you wait outside the room. Sitting there alone, thinking about what I could have done differently, was one of the worst nights of my life."

Art took a long drag and let out the smoke. "One thing's for sure. You can't go back."

Rob looked over to his father. "Yeah, but you shouldn't feel that bad. It was an accident. You didn't mean to crash or for Mom to get hurt."

"Let's just say, I'd had a few. I might not have been impaired but I should have let her drive like she told me. It took time, but she forgave me." Art threw down the butt of his cigarette and put it out with the hard sole of his shoe. "I never let it happen again."

"I see." Rob couldn't help but think that his dad was trying to tell him he knew what happened between him and Sandra on the bluff long ago. Rob put out his cigarette. "But Sandra died, Dad ... I held her head in my hands."

Art put his arm around him. "I know, son. I know." Rob hugged him back. They rocked from side to side. "But you and Laura have to go on living."

Rob found some solace at first though, after a moment, he stepped away. "How?"

"You did the right thing," Dad said.

"But what about Andre?"

"We all get what we have coming," Dad said.

Out on Main Street Laura neared the house. She never made excuses. One by one, Rob cracked his knuckles. She'd want him to be honest. If only it was that simple.

Chapter 33

October 24, 2016

As soon as Laura pulled in the driveway, Art came toward her and motioned for her to roll down the window. According to the clock on the dashboard, he didn't have to leave for ten minutes. "Sorry, I hope you weren't worried." She reached to turn off the ignition.

"I thought you didn't need it until four."

"No, that's when I have to be there to pick them up," he said. "You can leave it running."

Laura slipped her purse over her shoulder and took the information from the doctor off the passenger seat. According to the job description, medical assistants who worked in physicians' offices were paid a mean hourly wage of $15.37 with an annual salary of $31,960. If she started making that kind of money, she and Rob might be able to afford a place of their own.

She went around back to unload the wheelchair. Suddenly, Art got behind the wheel. Nate was still in the backseat. "Wait!"

Art stuck his head out the window. "Don't bother. Let him be. Helen has Ella's booster. He'll have enough room."

"It will just take me a minute," Laura said.

"Nah," Art said.

She didn't understand his sense of urgency but knew enough to steer clear of him when he had his mind set. Or was this something else? Once she was out of the way, he backed down the driveway. Her phone vibrated in her purse. Chelsea had texted. *Want to trick or treat? Meet here at 6 on Saturday.* It was like Chelsea read her mind. Laura couldn't wait to tell Nate. She slipped her phone back into her purse and came into the kitchen where Rob met her.

"What's going on?"

"Oh, Chelsea texted. She wants to get the kids together for Halloween."

Rob looked past her at the wall clock as if he hadn't heard a word she said. "Where have you been?"

"At the doctor's."

"How'd everything go?" he asked.

"Nate's burns are healed well enough to remove his splint and start using a boot and crutches instead of the wheelchair. He's ready to go back to school, but there are some complications. I'm going to need to talk to you about that—though, what's up with your dad? He was really uptight about the car."

"Don't worry. He'll get over it," Rob said. "The van will be out of the shop Monday."

"That's good. How did you do with Biyen?" She set her stack of papers on the table.

"Oh, fine. We went to the park." Rob pointed to the handouts. "What's all that?"

"Oh, nothing. Just something the doctor suggested for me."

"For you?"

"Yes, it's a possible opportunity. We can talk about it later."

"Why were you so late?"

"I didn't know there was a rush."

"I'm sorry," he said. "I didn't know where you were."

His tone had softened, but why Rob was acting like he didn't trust her? He'd never kept tabs on her before. "I stopped at Rosa's."

"Rosa, from the bar?"

"Yes."

"I didn't know you were friends."

"Well, we are now. I heard her play the saxophone. She's really good. You should have her play at the bar. Live entertainment might bring in some new customers." Laura looked up at Rob. His eyes were red and puffy as if he'd been crying. "Are you doing all right?"

"I'm just trying to figure out what we're going to do," he said. "About us."

She was trying to figure out the same thing but didn't yet have an answer. "I thought we agreed to give it some time."

"How much time do you need?" he asked.

"I don't know … more than a day."

"Can't you give me some kind of ballpark?"

Laura didn't like the way Rob was pressuring her. The sense of well-being she'd felt sipping coffee and listening to jazz at Rosa's was quickly wearing off. "I have no idea. This isn't a game."

"I'm sorry. I just need to know—are you going to stand by me?"

She bristled at his accusatory tone as if she were somehow in the wrong. "Rob, I'm standing by you right now. I need time to figure out how I feel. I'm not a switch you can flip on and off."

Upstairs, Biyen cried out from his crib. "I need to go to get him." She backed away from the kitchen toward the attic.

"So, you're going to avoid me until I have to go into work?" Rob asked.

"I'm not avoiding you," she said.

"Then he can wait a minute."

Laura stood and faced him. "Okay, what?"

"Andre texted me." Rob hooked his thumbs in the belt loops of his faded jeans. "Patricia told him that I hit the deer. I have to get back to him. What do you think I should say?"

Laura felt like she was being trapped in the middle of a triangle of lies. She wouldn't put up a façade, not even for Rob. "I don't know what to say, except that you should have told him what really happened a long time ago, just like you should have told me. I think he deserves to know the truth."

Rob's cheeks flushed. "I understand. I'm sorry. But what are we going to do right now?"

She didn't like him involving her as part of his cover-up. "Ask me what you really want to know, Rob. Am I going to tell Andre or the police what really happened—that's it, right?"

"Well, are you?" he asked.

"I'm not going to turn you in, but you might want to consider it. What you did to Andre was wrong," she said. "You've got to find a way to make it right."

"I promise you, Laura, I will do anything … as long as you still love me." Rob grasped her by the shoulders. "Do you still love me?"

His touch made her uncomfortable. His failure to be honest had wounded her more deeply than she could have ever foreseen. She felt empty as if she'd been gutted. "Please, Rob." She wriggled away from him. "Why would you ask me that right now? You're not being fair." She reached for her papers and took them from the table. "I really need to check on Biyen."

Chapter 34

October 24-25, 2016

Rob followed Laura toward the attic. He wanted to take her into his arms, tell her how much he loved her, and beg for her forgiveness—like he always did after they'd had a big fight—except, this situation was like nothing they'd been through before. She didn't want him to touch her and wasn't ready to forgive him. She needed time. He respected that. But if he intended to restore his integrity and win her back, he couldn't wait around and see. He needed to take action. Step up. Be honest with Andre. It was the only way to salvage their relationship unless, he worried, it was already broken beyond repair.

Fifteen minutes later, on his way to work, Rob texted him from the sidewalk outside the bar. *Explain about deer tomorrow morning. Got some back straps for you. Want to paddle board?* If there was one place they could channel their energy in a positive direction, it was out on Lake Michigan with the whitecaps. Southwest winds were in the forecast, which usually stirred things up in a good way, at least when it came to paddle surfing.

Once he turned on the lights and opened the cash register, Rob started wiping down the dozen or so glasses lined up beside the tap. He'd be lucky if he used half of them unless a group came in for Monday Night Football. Given tonight's matchup—Texans versus Broncos—that wasn't likely. Most of the tourists who'd come to hike through the fall foliage left last weekend. Fantasy Football wasn't a big enough draw and regular customers were staying home to watch the debates. Hillary Clinton was still highly favored to win. Donald Trump kept disputing the polls. Rob wanted it to be over. Discord was bad for business. He was tired of seeing Hillary's smug smile and enduring Trump's tantrums for the camera. In little more than a week, he'd be able to free up all three flat-screens for sports and things would get back to normal. Rob ran his towel around the rim of the last glass and set it on the bar with the others when a text popped up from Andre. *Yes. Meet you at the lighthouse at 9.*

Andre's response came as a relief and a challenge. Unlike Laura, Andre had never been the type to forgive nor forget. Once Andre set his mind on something, he didn't back down until he got it. He expected to be in charge and made sure everyone knew it. When they were growing up, Rob never confronted him. He'd always gone along with Andre's schemes, whether it meant sneaking out at night to drink or sneaking in pot when Rob's parents were away. The snow day changed everything. If Andre found out that Rob had betrayed him, there was no telling what kind of retribution he'd take. The truth couldn't come out unexpectedly. Risking it wouldn't be fair to Laura and the kids. He must find another way to resolve things between them. He had until noon tomorrow to figure out how to turn around his life.

When he reached the lighthouse, Rob zipped up his wetsuit. Far offshore, shielded in black Neoprene, Andre cut in and out of the strong surf under a gray sky. Andre was always most invigorated once the weather began to turn and wasn't going soft anytime soon. To reckon with him, Rob must be prepared. He stepped across the rough sand toward the edge of the water where his old friend surged into shore.

"What a rush, eh?" Rob said.

"Always." Andre flipped the board up on the wet sand and unwound the leash from his ankle. "Have at it, old man."

Cold, hard rain spat down on them and the temperature dropped. At this rate, the precipitation would soon change to sleet. "Are you sure you don't just want to go back to the bar for a Bloody Mary?" Rob asked. "I've got those tenderloins waiting. It was crazy how, right after you booked out of there, that doe jumped me."

"Yeah, so I heard. Does sound crazy." Andre looked away at the breaking waves. "But we just got out here. You can get me the cuts later. What are you now, some wus?"

Rob took off his parka and zipped up the back of his wetsuit. He couldn't refuse Andre today. "All right, dude. Game on." He picked up the board and stepped into the stirred-up waters where a wave smacked the board into his chest. The conditions were treacherous, though Rob felt strangely soothed as he submerged himself in the frigid surf. At this point, he'd do almost anything to escape Andre's wrath and regain Laura's affection.

Rob came up out of the water and knelt on the board. When he took his first stroke forward, the waves pushed him back. The timid wouldn't survive out here today. He paddled harder and popped up to stand amid the whitecaps rising one after the other. He moved himself into position through the churning seas and waited for the instant he could catch a ride. A swell formed ahead and he paddled with all his strength to get there before it crested. He dug in his paddle, swiveled around, and gave into the rush beneath his feet. For a few seconds, he almost hovered. Then he pushed his heel into the back of the board and flowed with the dark force, just as he had when he and Andre were teenagers without anything else on their radar except the next breaking wave.

When Rob came onto shore, Andre was waiting for him. Though now, as Rob looked ahead, he noticed a cop car with its lights flashing in the otherwise empty parking lot. A police officer, wide around the waistline and short on hair, stepped out of the vehicle and approached them from across the battered stretch of beach. Rob propped the board in the sand. "Dude, we've got company." Andre turned around and looked behind him just as the officer, now about fifty feet away, swept his arm around and motioned for them to come in. Rob picked up the board.

Andre didn't budge. "That's bullshit," he said under his breath.

Rob started walking. "I know, but let's just go see what he wants." Andre followed grudgingly, cursing repeatedly, until they met up with the officer.

"There's a winter weather advisory," he said, zipping up his leather jacket. "I need to ask you to come in so that no one gets hurt."

Andre, his spiked hair now flattened to his forehead, snorted and wiped away the watery mucous that dripped from his wide nostrils. "We understand the risks."

"Do you?" The officer sucked in his gut. "That's not what I've heard."

Andre spit into the sand. The officer reached for the radio strapped onto his waistband. Rob took a step forward between them. "Hey, I apologize. We're leaving right now, no problem. Didn't mean to cause you any trouble, sir. Thank you."

He turned to Andre and made bug eyes as if to say *shut up you crazy bastard. Do you want to get us arrested?*

When they reached the bar, Rob offered Andre the Bloody Mary he'd promised him earlier. Andre, hunched over on the bar, asked only for a can of PBR. Rob cracked it open for him. Andre, staring down at his hands, nursed the beer. "I can't believe the cops showed up." He shook his head at Rob. "That's the thing, it's like … once you've been in prison they're never going to stop messing with you. I'm almost twenty-seven and they're still treating me like I'm seventeen." Andre chugged the rest of his beer and crushed the can on the bar with his palm. "You're lucky you were able to stay out of it. For a while it looked like they were going to charge everybody. I think your dad was even worried. I know Patricia was. That's why she snitched." Andre nodded at Rob as if looking for approval.

Rob sipped his Bloody Mary and tried to swallow his shame. Looking back, Patricia's snitching to the cops was understandable. His silence was the real crime that sent Andre to prison. They'd both turned seventeen, a month before the accident, in December. At the time, Rob never imagined Andre would be convicted of an adult crime. More than ever Rob believed it was wrong to prosecute anyone that age as an adult. They'd both been young and stupid, never considering that someone might get hurt, much less killed. Andre, as often as he complained about Sandra, had loved his little sister. Of that, Rob had no doubt. Andre had grieved along with his mother. Why would the law punish someone who was already in mourning? Rob hadn't been strong enough to tell Andre the truth. He'd been wrong to let him take the fall and go to prison for a crime he didn't commit. Andre had served his sentence. He didn't deserve to be treated like a criminal anymore. Rob cracked open another beer and handed it to him.

Andre stared at his beer but didn't take a drink. "You know how I said I quit the circuit? Actually, I was kicked off the team."

Rob leaned on the bar. "Why's that? You were killing it this spring."

Andre shook his head. "I was, that's the thing, but the officials in Costa Rica said I cut off their dude when he dropped in on me. I had the line straight in. He came around my left side near the rocks. I held my line. He came through in front me. I continued straight. There was no way I could avoid clipping him at the very end. I won. He bit it and got pulled under into the reef, even had to be rescued by the lifeguards on Sea Doos and emergency airlifted to a hospital in San Jose. They accused me of playing dirty. Said I would always be a murderer. Al asesino. A murderer of my own flesh and blood. The Costa Rican tournament officials sided with the Costa Rican team, no surprise there, but our coaches didn't even support me. They didn't want to risk any liability, so they just cut me—said, if I didn't quit, I would be held personally responsible."

It didn't sound fair. Rob's insides burned with the knowledge that he was partly to blame. If Andre had never been convicted, there would be no reason to mistrust him, and he'd likely still be on the team. Rob couldn't deny the discrimination he'd witnessed in Sanctuary firsthand. In the eyes of the law, and most of the world, Andre would always be a felon. It wasn't just the police who wouldn't let it go. No one in town would hire him, not even the people who'd known him when he was growing up. All Andre wanted was a job. Rob had done this to him and sensed that he was only beginning to serve his sentence.

He scanned the liquor shelf behind him, pulled down a bottle of Jack Daniels, and poured them each a shot. "That rots." There was nothing more he could say about Andre's mistreatment on the circuit that would make either of them feel better. It was time for him to do something real. He could start by giving him honest work. And for the bar to stay afloat, he needed Andre's help. In July, when Andre and Patricia had taken over during Nate's stint at the hospital, they'd turned a profit like Rob never could. He'd asked for Patricia's advice, yet she wouldn't share her secrets. Rob couldn't rely on luck to get by. He needed a solid plan. His dad had taken out a second mortgage on the house to help finance the bar. If he didn't turn things around, the bank might not extend his credit line and decide to foreclose. Maybe, he and Andre could strike a deal?

Ever since Andre moved back to town it was as though Rob had been cursed. By opening up to Laura, he'd cast out a demon and was one step closer to setting himself free. But a confession now to Andre would destroy them both. Instead it was up to him to make amends for letting Andre bear all the blame. Ever since Sandra's death, he and Andre shared a stigma that had revealed itself over time. Only now could Rob fully see. In the town's eyes, Andre was the black sheep and he merely gray. Rob knew together he and Andre believed in their brotherhood. They'd needled their failings into their flesh as permanent reminders. Neither of them would ever forget Sandra. Each of them had to endure. There was no use pouring over losses anymore. At their core, they were both innately aware that the past never died; people in town would always question them, their friendship, their behavior. On that point, they agreed. But Rob would not let his low standing in the town annihilate his dreams. He and Andre must remain united. They were warriors, not victims. His five-year-old son had shown him what it meant to be fearless. If Nate could find the courage to persevere, so could he.

Rob couldn't change the past, but he could try and make up for it. Emboldened by the whiskey, he ran his palm over the lacquered counter. "Bro, I have a proposition."

Andre lifted his chin and, for the first time since they'd arrived, made eye contact.

"I've been thinking about those craft cocktails you and Patricia made this summer. People went crazy for 'em. Do you want to try it again? If I don't haul some ass by the end of the month, I'm going to get called into the bank for a sit-down in the corner office with Nicky and her boss."

Andre stayed quiet for a minute and ran his fingers along his trim beard. "There's a stiff breeze out there today."

"Don't worry about the weather," Rob said. "I was thinking about doing it Friday or Saturday with Halloween. Maybe something kind of creepy. As long as we avoid clowns, we're good."

Andre stood from his barstool. "Fuck fake holidays. I'm sick of copying shit. People here want something real, something they can relate to, you know? In the Caribbean, they have their Blue Curacao and Bahama Breezes. What about us? We ride ice waves like a couple of sinkers bobbing on heavy water that's turning to slush and trying to pull us down."

Rob poured them both another shot. "I'm following you and not. How does our experience translate into a drink?"

"I'm saying we concoct an experience in a glass that looks and tastes how we feel out there," Andre said. "A stiff one with a cold burn."

"Hard liquor is pricey," Rob said.

"We can charge ten bucks a drink. I guarantee you the profit margin on that is a lot higher than beer."

"Shut up, man. No one's going to order a Stiff Breeze much less pay ten bucks for it."

Andre extended his hand. "Wanna bet? You can keep the first fifteen hundred. My cut will be the next. If we don't clear it, I'll make up the difference."

Rob considered this, but wasn't ready to shake on it. "You're crazier than I thought you were, man."

"You're just not seeing it. We're like the directors of our own movie. The customers will act the part if we make it seem real." Andre scanned the room. "I'll need to make a few adjustments to the décor like taking down those old posters and the stained-glass light fixtures that look like they came from grandma's house."

"It's supposed to remind people of the good old days," Rob said.

"Do you even hear yourself? The tourists don't care about the history of the town and neither do half of the people who are from here. They come because they want to have fun and escape. It's our job to create a place where they can do that. We can make a shitload of money, Rob." Andre extended his hand to him again. "Do we have a deal?"

Rob felt like the curse, which had been hanging over him since Andre had returned, finally might be lifted. He took Andre's hand and gave it a firm shake. "Deal."

Andre leaned back on his stool. "You better stock up on whiskey, bro." Rob poured them each a double. When they clinked glasses, Andre met his gaze. "Salud."

"Salud." Rob savored the slow burn as the whiskey streamed down his throat. Maybe, for once, he and Andre could both come out on top.

Chapter 35

October 29, 2016

An Edison bulb radiated above Andre who stood at the far end of the counter arranging an assortment of bar tools. Dressed in black with his hair slicked into a wave frozen above his forehead, he looked like he was ready to deal out a hand of poker rather than tend bar. The Saturday before Halloween, when adults came out to act like kids and college students came home to drink like adults, was usually among the busiest nights of the year. Rob was betting it all on Andre's scheme and Andre had definitely amped up his game since the summer, but Rob remained nervous. This would be his first time serving craft cocktails and, with competition from the new brewery on the highway, the odds didn't necessarily favor the house. Still, he had a good feeling. Andre, with Patricia's help, had taken care of promotions and covered the county with flyers from tip to tail. Skip the Draft—Come for a Night of Cocktails by Craft. Rob, for one, was impressed.

The sun wouldn't set for another hour or so, but he was already getting a positive vibe from the row of customers bellied up to the bar. In the far corner facing Andre, a couple of guys in check shirts and premium denim studied the drink menu, which included not only the Stiff Breeze, but Patricia's concoction— Goodnight Dunes. "It's a takeoff on a sloe gin fizz with a wellness shot of chamomile tea," she said.

Rob eavesdropped from beside the register as the men, in hushed voices, made their selections and placed their money on the table. With his typically wispy goatee sculpted into sharp V beyond the tip of his pointy chin, Andre hadn't over-looked a single detail, including the crucial role of Patricia, who swooped in as needed. They made a good team, both of them so driven and focused on their job. Rob couldn't stop thinking about how Laura had questioned whether it would be a good idea for him to put himself in the position of working with his friends, especially when he'd be running the show. If only she could see them now, working together toward the same goal, she'd get how they could all move on without dredging up the past.

Straight-faced and holding a martini shaker in each hand, Andre was in his element. He commanded attention as if he were dealing at a high-stakes' table in Las Vegas. Though the harsh lighting accentuated his pale skin and the dark circles under his eyes, he'd never seemed more alive and lucid than at this moment as he raised the stainless-steel containers and shook them in synchronicity. The ice rattled with a ca-ching, ca-ching, ca-ching. Rob felt like he'd hit the jackpot at slots.

He couldn't help but smile, yet at the end of the bar Andre maintained his poker face as he simultaneously strained the chilled liquid from each shaker into two tall glasses. He knew how to let it roll. The men, appearing hypnotized, sat motion-less as he inserted a sprig of sage. For several seconds, Rob too was transfixed as he watched them take their first sip. There was something out of the ordinary going on and he wasn't sure what to make of it. They tried to appear unimpressed but, by the way each of them sat up a little straighter on their bar stools one after the other, their deep satisfaction was exposed. They'd come to the right place, and they knew it.

Rob stood back and watched as Andre worked the room. His body language was intimidating, but the two women approaching him didn't seem afraid. The old-timers in John Deere ball caps and suspenders, huddled around their usual table with a pitcher of beer, pointed at them and shook their heads. "Can you believe the kids will pay ten bucks for 'em?"

Rob almost couldn't believe it either. His bar, which Andre had compared to a living-history museum, had been transformed into a hip speakeasy overnight. A line of customers, waiting to order, snaked through the room. Andre had run out of elixirs. When Patricia went for refills, Andre held up a credit card for Rob to run. "Was I right or was I right?" he asked.

"It's unbelievable," Rob pinched the plastic between his fingers. "We're going to have to do this every weekend."

Andre winked without altering his expressionless expression. Rob couldn't control his rush of optimism. However, at the instant when he turned toward the cash register, his eyes grazed Andre's collar and settled on the tattoo that ran up his jugular vein to below his gauged earlobe. From beneath the black collar, Sandra's artificial blue eyes stared at him sideways. He turned away and swiped the card for twenty dollars, plus tax. Suddenly, the money that seconds earlier had been so intoxicating, held no interest. He couldn't return for a signature right now. He looked around everywhere for Patricia, yet Rob couldn't avoid where his focus was unwillingly being drawn. It was no use trying to look away. His eyes automatically locked on Sandra's. From all the way across the counter, he could still clearly make out the tattoo of her that ran the entire length of Andre's thick neck. Those eyes, once so captivating, wouldn't let him forget. He'd come too close. Money alone would never resolve the problems between him and Andre. Sandra demanded more. So, did Laura.

Chapter 36

October 29, 2016

When she reached Chelsea's front walk, Laura split off from Nate. She watched from a distance as he wheeled himself up Jacob's driveway with his pirate sword balanced across his lap. Nate had looked forward to this moment all week. Secretly, she had too. For once, she didn't even mind that they'd moved up trick-or-treating to the Saturday before the actual holiday, which was on Monday. Still, Laura didn't understand why Chelsea had waited for a special occasion to get together with the boys.

She knocked on her door. After a minute it opened a crack, and there was Brett holding the candy bowl piled up with skittles. She gave him a friendly wave. "Trick or treat."

He stood there, speechless for a second, and then looked down the driveway at Nate.

"Are Chelsea and Jacob ready?" she asked.

Brett frowned. "I'll go check."

"Mind if I take a piece of candy for Nate while we wait?" He didn't hold out the bowl, but she reached her hand in anyway. "Thank you."

He stepped back and shut the door. Wind gusted off the lake, sending shivers down her spine as she walked toward the garage where Nate was doing circles. "Why aren't they ready?"

She shrugged, unsure why Brett had been so cold to her. "I'm sure they'll be out in a minute."

Jack-o-lanterns glowed on the porch across the street as droves of masked children and their families passed by them on the sidewalk with their plastic buckets ready to be filled. A group of teenagers carrying pillowcases came by too. Shrieks of laughter filled the air. Five minutes later the garage door opened automatically. Jacob, dressed as Luke Skywalker, ran out toward Nate. Chelsea followed after him, pulling the wagon with her twins who were in coordinating Elsa and Anna costumes. "Now, everyone stay together."

Laura stepped beside her. "Hey, is everything okay? Brett seemed surprised to see us."

Chelsea kept walking. "No, I mean, yes—we're all good. I told him we were going with you before he left for Dallas. He just forgets the things I tell him when he's stressed." Chelsea shook her head and smiled. "Tonight, I think he's really just worried he'll run out of candy. He takes everything so seriously. He'll be fine. Let's go."

Nate pushed himself ahead with Jacob. Laura walked alongside Chelsea until they reached the sidewalk.

"You'll be staying with him the whole time, right?" Chelsea asked.

"Of course." Laura nodded.

Laura cringed. She'd never forgive herself for failing to get Nate sooner and putting Chelsea in a such horrible position. She'd give anything to go back and make different choices. The sinking feeling she'd experienced at the hospital when Jacob visited came rushing back. She'd hoped tonight they could all relax and have some fun, but the awkwardness remained. Since the accident, it had been so hard for them to talk. "He's still learning to get around by himself."

Laura stepped aside as Chelsea, towing the wagon, led the way to the first house. She turned into the driveway and let her girls out at the narrow path to the front door. Jacob took off. "I'll bring you back some candy," he called behind him. Still, Nate followed him halfway.

She and Chelsea waited on the blacktop. "So, what have you all been up to?"

"Oh, just keeping busy with homeschooling. Nate has to go to the doctor a lot. Rob's been working a ton. He's actually at the bar right now with Andre."

"So, Rob's okay? Brett said he hasn't seen him, except for once when he was at the gym. Said he looked pretty beaten up by that deer he hit."

"It was more like the deer that hit him," Laura said. "It was a rough night for a lot of reasons. We stayed up to harvest the deer though."

"I'm surprised he was up for going to the gym the next morning," Chelsea said.

"Yeah, he was really wiped. We both were. But we pushed through it."

"I guess so." Chelsea looked toward Jacob and her princesses who were coming toward the sidewalk with the candy in their feathery baskets.

Jacob handed a Hershey bar to Nate who held it up for her to see. "Look, Momma." He smiled at her before putting the candy in his pillowcase. "It's king size!"

She nodded distractedly. What was Chelsea trying to insinuate? As they continued to the next house, the back of Laura's neck tightened. "I'm sorry, you were saying something before we got cut off about Brett seeing Rob at the gym?"

"Oh, it was nothing. How are things going for him at the bar these days?"

In the past, before Nate's accident, Chelsea would never have talked around the subject. Clearly, the friendship had changed. "Well, Rob has been trying to help Andre get back on his feet. I guess he's had a tough time finding a job. He just confided that he was cut from the SUP-circuit. So, tonight Rob's letting him experiment with some new concept. Craft cocktails, I guess. Patricia is helping, which I'm a little skeptical about."

"I would be too." Chelsea walked ahead as if she were hurrying to get the night over with. She told the kids to skip houses where the lights were clearly on.

"Chelsea, wait up."

At the end of the next driveway Chelsea stopped and waited with her girls. Nate followed Jacob up the driveway as far as he could until Jacob left and ran to the front door on his own. By the time Laura reached them, she needed to catch her breath. "Wow, you're really moving. Did you miss your run today?"

"No."

"Oh, so that must mean I'm really out of shape," Laura chuckled.

"Well, it wouldn't hurt to check out the gym sometime."

"Ouch."

"Sorry, I didn't mean it that way, it's just that Patricia works there."

"Yeah, I know."

"And she likes to help spot."

"Spot who?" Laura asked. "You mean, Nate?"

"Could have been ... or Rob, I'm not sure," Chelsea said. "I only know what Brett saw, and Rob was hurt that day. That must be why Patricia was helping spot him."

Chelsea sped off with her girls in the wagon. Jacob ran across the yard to the next house. Laura waited for Nate—wondering what in the heck Rob and Patricia were up to. Suddenly, Nate came rolling down the driveway and over the sidewalk where the roots protruded. Laura lunged toward him, but the wheelchair got hung up and tipped sideways. She was hardly able to watch as he leaned in the opposite direction and tried to regain his balance, but he wasn't quick or strong enough to prevent the chair from falling over. He spilled out of his seat onto the grass. "Momma!"

She knelt on the ground beside him. "Oh my, god! Baby, are you hurt?"

He was lying on his side, crying. His bandaged leg was crossed on top of the other. Jacob came over and gaped. Chelsea arrived, breathless. "Jesus, Laura, what happened?"

Nate whimpered. "I just fell." Laura checked him up and down for any signs of injury. He wiped his eyes with the back of his hand. "Mom, stop it. I'm fine."

Chelsea picked up his chair and propped it beside him. Her girls waited in the wagon down the block. "Can I help you get him back in?"

"Sure, unless you need to get the girls."

"They can wait another minute."

Nate put one arm over each of their shoulders. Together, she and Chelsea lifted him onto his good foot. Without being asked, Jacob held the wheelchair for them as Nate hopped up onto his seat. Bits of dried leaves were stuck to his bandages, but otherwise he seemed unharmed.

"I'm going to get the girls." Chelsea brushed off her sequined sweater. "We could take the kids back to our house and let them count their candy, if you think he'd still be up for it."

Laura tried to regain her bearings. "Thanks, I think he would like that."

Once Chelsea left, Laura started to push him. "Mom, let go of me!"

She backed off and he went ahead with Jacob. Chelsea was coming up the sidewalk to meet her. "Everything okay?"

"I think so. He wouldn't let me push him."

"Oh, I guess sometimes things have to work themselves out."

"Yeah, I guess you're right." They kept walking and for the first time since the accident, Laura felt like she might be able to open up to Chelsea again. "I just want to apologize."

Chelsea paused. "For what?"

Once and for all, Laura needed to make things right between them. "Putting you in such a bad position. I mean it was the Fourth of July parade, I should have never let Nate stay. I hope you know how sorry I am."

Chelsea looked away. "Please, Laura, don't."

"Can you ever forgive me?"

Chelsea shook her head. For a second, Laura considered the possibility of losing her as a friend forever. "Laura, friends help friends. There's nothing to forgive." Then Chelsea nodded. "I'm the one who should be apologizing." She grimaced. "To be honest, I've been avoiding you. Brett didn't want me to hang out with you because he was worried you were going to sue us."

Laura's legs wobbled. "Why would he ever think that? You did nothing wrong." She and Rob had never even talked about the possibility of taking legal action against them. It had never occurred to her that Chelsea or Brett would think they might. What had put that idea in Brett's head?

Chelsea stared at the ground. "I didn't actually see what happened to Nate. Jacob told me." She began picking at her nail polish. "Oh, my god, Laura, I'm so sorry."

Laura couldn't breathe. Chelsea kept on. "I went into the garage to get another folding chair so I could sit down and watch them. I was only gone a minute when I heard Jacob yell: 'Stop.' I rushed back but, by then, it was too late."

Suddenly, Laura felt very cold and lost her ability to listen. Chelsea sounded as if she were speaking underwater. "I should have told you. I should have trusted myself and been there for you. Instead, I kept my secret and stayed away."

For a minute, standing there with Chelsea, Laura couldn't comprehend what she'd heard. It felt like a week ago when she was back in the attic with Rob hearing his confession. She felt like she was drowning. Laura didn't even know she'd made a sound until her cry echoed into the night.

Chapter 37

October 30, 2016

Laura cleared the last of the breakfast dishes from the dining table and brought them to the kitchen sink. Lies and more lies. That's what she'd been served. There were so many of them she wasn't certain, anymore, what was real. First Rob. Now Chelsea. Laura still couldn't explain her actions last night. She was so mortified, confused, and angry, that she barely remembered the moment when she grabbed Nate's wheelchair and left crying as if she were a child running home to her mother.

Chelsea had deceived her. How could she have told Jacob to keep quiet about it? *You must never tell Nate.* Laura couldn't even imagine what Chelsea had told her son. Who even cared if Chelsea had stepped away for a minute? It wasn't like Nate was a two-year-old. She wouldn't have blamed her for any of it. But Laura loathed Chelsea now. All these months Chelsea had misled her. Alienated her. She and Rob would never have sued her or Brett—and still wouldn't—though Laura wasn't sure she'd ever speak to her again.

She glanced in the dining room at Nate, who had hardly eaten any breakfast after binging on candy the previous night alone. He'd been so mad at her for rushing home. She could never explain to him why. He looked calmer now, more in control, but she still didn't feel like herself. Laura put John Coltrane's "A Love Supreme" in the CD player and finished rinsing the dishes. Within a few minutes, between the bang of a gong and a procession of cymbal washes, the hard thoughts running through her mind softened. Getting to know Rosa, and discovering her passion for jazz saxophone, had inspired Laura to learn more about the music. Ever since stopping over, she'd listened to something new every day. Somehow, when the music was playing, Laura didn't feel as overwhelmed. Sometimes, she even felt uplifted. Other times, like right now, she wasn't sure how she'd survive without it.

So much of what Chelsea had said was still hard to take in. Brett had seriously thought that she and Rob might sue them? And why would Rob have chosen to open up to her about his past and then be sneaking around with Patricia behind her back? It didn't make any sense. Rob had told her that nothing was going on between them. She'd believed him. She wouldn't stand for another cover-up, not now, after he'd told promised to be completely honest.

She took the leaded-glass plate from the drying rack, the one from her mother that she'd brought with her from Wisconsin. As she ran the dishtowel over the flower buds etched around the edges, Laura recalled that her mother had only brought it out for special occasions. Today, Laura had served ordinary buttermilk biscuits. She looked through the spiral grooves in the center of the plate as if she were peering into her old View Master, squinting at the past she'd nearly forgotten. The plate heavy in her hand, she remembered the countless times that she and Shenia, along with their mother, had cleaned up after meals together. For the women of the family, drying dishes had been a ritual, one that she'd found comforting as a teenager, especially on Sunday evenings after all father's guests were packed up and headed home and he'd gone out for a smoke; when they'd had the kitchen all to themselves. She could see it in the twinkle in the corners of her mother's bright brown eyes, so similar to her own. In a house of hardness, her mother's presence soothed—until her stomach began to ache and they discovered the cancer. By the time she was diagnosed at Stage 3, her condition was terminal.

The phone rang from across the kitchen and Helen answered. "Hello, Sanders' residence. Oh, yes, Laura." She frowned and nodded at the same time. "Let me get her." Laura turned off the music. Helen, covering the receiver with her hand, came toward her. "It's for you. An elderly man. It sounds like he's sick." She handed her the phone.

"Laura," he said in a raspy voice. In one word, she recognized the gravelly undertone, though he sounded hoarser than she remembered. Probably still smoking a pack a day if she had to guess. "This is your father."

When was the last time they'd actually spoken? Six years earlier, before Nate was born, she'd shared the news that she and Rob were getting married. He was skeptical from the get-go. "Married?" he asked. "You only left here 'bout six months ago."

She explained she was pregnant.

"Knocked up, 'bout what I'd expect—always making your own rules."

He declined her invitation to the wedding, saying Michigan was too far. "I bet the two a' you don't make it a year."

Despite his negativity, she'd mailed him a birth announcement with a picture of Nate—his first grandchild—and later sent photos of Ella and Biyen as newborns. At Christmas, she religiously sent a card, though she hadn't yet mentioned anything to him about Nate's accident over the summer. Why bother? He obviously didn't care about her life or have any interest in his grandkids. She was curious why he'd be calling her now. "Yes, Father."

"I need you to come home." He wheezed. "I'm not well."

He didn't sound particularly well. Coming from him, these words didn't elicit much sympathy. Still, she was concerned. "I'm sorry to hear that. What's wrong?"

"Something in my lungs." He hacked into the receiver. "They're calling it COPD. Makes me weak. I can't get around. They're making me carry an oxygen tank everywhere. I think I'm running low."

She didn't know what COPD stood for, but there was no denying he was having trouble breathing and needed assistance—and probably fast. "You're out of oxygen?"

"I think so, almost."

"Well, can you check it? Is there a gauge?"

"I don't need any gauge. I was supposed to go into the doctor on Friday and get a full tank, but then I thought it could wait until Monday. Now, I'm not sure."

"Is there someone you can call?"

"I tried Shenia, but I can't reach her."

Even if he could reach her, Green Bay was almost three hours away.

"What about your doctor, or someone else local?" she asked. "I'm sure they would come check on you and bring another tank of oxygen."

"No one's going to make no house call for me on Sunday," he wheezed. "I was hoping you could text Shenia. I have her number right here." Between coughing jags, he gave Laura the number and explained the process of texting.

"Thank you. I know how it works," she said. "I will try, but Shenia and I haven't kept in touch lately. Are you sure you don't want me to call for an ambulance?"

"No." He wheezed. "I can't afford that."

"Well, if it's an emergency, then—you have no other choice."

Suddenly, the line went silent. "Father, are you there?"

"How about you come?"

Sanctuary was nearly eight hours away, and they were still down to one car. She held the receiver away from ear. Her thoughts scattered. Could she really go home—right now? "I'm not sure. Let me try and reach Shenia, first. And, if you give me the number of your doctor, I can try and get hold of the person on call."

He hacked into receiver. "I already told you, they ain't coming. It's you or your sister."

Given his condition, she wouldn't argue with him anymore. "Fine. But even if I leave now, I wouldn't make it until dinner time."

"I ain't going nowhere."

By the time she hung up with him she'd broken into a full sweat. She had to reach Shenia. Their father could be dying.

Helen approached from the dining room. "Everything okay?" Laura nodded. They'd all been through so much lately, she hated to burden her with another problem. She twisted the towel around her wrist and shook her head. "Come on, I can see you're worried. Was that your father?"

Father. Even the sound of the word made her unsteady on her feet. "He's very sick and says he's almost run out of oxygen. I wanted to call for an ambulance, but he refused. Unless I can reach my sister, I'm going to have to go see him." She closed her eyes and hugged her arms into her chest. "I'm scared." Even after all these years, it was hard to admit the truth and reveal herself to Helen. Though her mother-in-law had opened up to her about some of her own vulnerabilities, she still felt the need to try to impress her. Not appear weak. "He's not a good man."

Helen crossed her arms. "Do you think he'd ever harm you?"

He had harmed her, many times. She recalled when she'd talked back to him once as a teenager. Laura blamed the fish in the lake for causing Mom's cancer. She'd begged him to stop using weed-killers on the lawn because of the toxic run-off into the lake. Then, right after Mom died, she refused to eat the fish he caught.

"What, you're too good for fish now?" He slapped her across the face. "You should be thankful I put food on your plate."

Her cheek burned with anger more than pain, though his blow had stung and left a bruise. He never tried to understand. He was outright cruel.

Maybe he'd changed? She couldn't say for sure what he was capable of, though she doubted he'd be much of a threat— if he was even alive by the time she got there. He needed her help. "From the sound of it, he's very weak. I'm sure I can handle it, unless I can reach Shenia. I'm going to text her right now."

Helen nodded. "Okay, do what you need to, as long as you think you'll be safe. No matter what happens, we'll be here to support you." She gently stroked Laura's hair as her own mom often had when she was a girl. She'd almost forgotten the softness of being mothered. "You can take my car."

Had Helen forgotten that the van wouldn't be out of the shop until the next morning? How would she get to work? How would Nate get to his afternoon doctor's appointment? "But if I take your car—"

Helen rested her hand on Laura's shoulder. "We'll figure something out."

She knew Helen meant what she said and would take good care of the kids, which was a big relief. "Thank you."

Still, once Laura walked into the attic stairwell she felt as if the walls would collapse in on her. She recalled their last medical crisis when they'd learned that Nate had gone into a coma. She'd reached out to Shenia then, but her sister hadn't gotten back to her until after Laura had messaged that he'd regained consciousness. Then Shenia had responded as if it had somehow all been no big deal. Now their father had an emergency. Would Shenia avoid them? *Father called. Says he is low on oxygen and needs our help. Can you go see him now? It will take me 8 hours. Please let me know ASAP.*

She went upstairs to pack her overnight bag, just in case. She would miss the kids, yet wasn't sure she felt the same about being away from Rob, who was still asleep. He'd been up most of the night working with Andre. According to his text, they'd made lots of money. He was definitely trying to make things right between them. She had to give him some credit for that, and their finances were improving too. He'd done everything possible to restore her faith in him—even helping around the house and with the kids. Yesterday, he'd changed Biyen's diaper several times without being asked. The night before last, he'd read with Ella before bed.

But now, as she prepared to leave for Wisconsin, a side of her was glad to get away from him. Since he'd broken his silence about the past, he'd been pressuring her for answers she couldn't give. Being in the same house with him was making her claustrophobic. She still wasn't sure if she could trust him to tell the truth about anything, especially after what Chelsea had told her about him and Patricia. Then again, she couldn't trust Chelsea either.

Laura didn't have time to deal with any of it. Her heart was tired of sorrow and grief. She hurried to finish packing. Then, she shook his arm. He yawned and rolled toward the middle of the bed. "Hey, wake up. I have to tell you something important."

He gave a stretch and, after a few seconds, half-opened his eyes. "Come lie with me."

Something in his casual tone struck her, and she ignored his request. "My father called. He needs me to come to Wisconsin."

"Your father?"

"Yes, he's very sick."

Rob propped a pillow under his head. "What about Nate's appointment tomorrow?"

"I thought you could take him. The van should be back by then. Your mom said I could use her car."

"When did all this get decided?"

"He just called, but he made it sound like an emergency."

"This is out of hand." Rob sat up and pulled on a pair of sweat pants. "It's that bad?"

"Yes, apparently. He's on oxygen and is almost out." Laura stared at him. "Are you doubting what I'm saying?"

He ran his hands back and forth through his hair. "No. It's just, you haven't been in touch with him for years and now you have to leave right away. That's kind of crazy, don't you think?"

"He's my father." Suddenly, all the blood rushed to her face. "Last night, I heard about something else really crazy."

"What? Everything was cool."

Laura took a deep breath but couldn't control it. "When Chelsea and I were trick-or-treating, she told me something about you."

"What?"

"Something Brett saw."

Rob squinted at her, fretful.

"You with Patricia at the gym on that first day you took Nate, remember?"

He blinked about ten times as if he didn't know what to say. She'd obviously struck a nerve. He flopped over his knees. "That guy is such a dick. I knew he'd say something. I had no idea Patricia was gonna be there. She just came up to Nate and me and started helping us."

Unsatisfied with his explanation, she waited, arms crossed over her chest, until he looked up. "Chelsea said Patricia was spotting you."

He shook his head, then stood and placed his hands on her shoulders. "I didn't ask for it, Laura. Please, believe me. I didn't want her to touch me."

She backed away. "But you let her."

He threw his hands in the air. "I was lying with my back on the bench and the bar over my head."

She stood still, considering what he'd said. First lies. Now excuses. Laura felt as if she were climbing the dunes and sinking deeper and deeper into the sand, which was collapsing on either side of her with each step. She wasn't sure she could listen to another word. "What are you trying to tell me?"

Again, he put his hands on her shoulders. "I'm telling you that I love you. Not her."

She shrugged him off her. "Well, actions speak a lot louder ..."

"I told her to leave us alone. I promise you. Come on. I'm not interested in Patricia anymore." He pulled her toward him.

She ripped herself away. "Anymore—since when is that?"

"Jesus, Laura. She's engaged to Andre."

"That doesn't matter." Laura's throat tightened. "Do you still love her?"

"No."

"Well, apparently, she still has feelings for you."

He ran his fingers through his outgrown beard. "Fine. So, now what am I supposed to do?"

"That's obviously up to you."

She couldn't think for him. He should know. It felt as if she'd been scaling the dunes all these years and now they were about to cave in on her. She picked up her bag and stepped past him.

"Come on, I don't want you to leave like this." Rob followed her onto the landing and pulled her into his arms. "You know I love you."

Laura stood stiffly. "Then make sure she knows it too." She elbowed herself away from him. "I'll say good-bye to the kids. Your mom said she'd make sure they were taken care of."

"How long will you be gone?"

"A couple days at least. But then, I really don't know."

She moved toward the stairs.

He caught her by the arm. "Don't go."

"I've got to go." She started walking down.

He called after her. "I'll miss you."

The sound of his vulnerability caught her off guard, and she paused for just a second, but didn't look back.

Chapter 38

October 30, 2016

Laura spotted the two towers of the Mighty Mac rising from the straits as she approached the south shore of the bridge that would carry her into the UP of Michigan and on toward Wisconsin. Her tires thudded against the steel grates and she peered down at the choppy waters. There, past the first tower, suspended a couple hundred feet above the narrow stretch between Lakes Michigan and Huron, Laura recalled herself six years earlier crossing the same bridge in the opposite direction. She'd been just a girl, driving with the windows rolled down, searching for a way out. Though a grown woman now and a mother, she was being forced by her father to return home. Laura wanted to jump out of her seat. Instead she rolled down her window and let the wind whip through her hair. The lashing off the lake made her cheeks burn. It was an act of desperation, she knew, but she didn't know how else to relieve her anxiety. How in the hell was she supposed to reconcile with her past when she was already so torn up about Rob? Right now, she couldn't even handle thinking about him, let alone the future of their marriage.

Laura reached the other end of the bridge and began her journey to Eagle Ridge through the dense forests of the UP. After all these years, she still couldn't believe she was really going back there—to him. Laura rolled up her window and inserted the Miles Davis CD Helen had given her for the ride. *Nature Boy* began to play. Laura's mother had loved the same song, though she'd preferred the original version by Nat King Cole. It seemed strange that a song could connect all of them through time. If only her mother hadn't died so young. Laura tried to imagine a different life with her mother in it. Lois would be a grandmother. Then again, if her mother had lived through the cancer, Laura might never have left Wisconsin? She might never have met Rob. They might never have had the kids. There was no way to go back and change history.

Now, she didn't know what to expect from her father or Shenia. With any luck, Shenia would already be there. Laura wasn't sure she could face their father without her. Deep down she missed her, though she wouldn't admit that to her sister. Shenia had let her down too many times since she'd abandoned her after graduating high school. Laura had texted her nearly three hours ago. So far, she hadn't heard anything back. Now her phone was almost dead, and from here on out—until she made it through the UP—cell service would be sketchy. She turned it off to save battery.

How could Shenia have not texted back right away when their father could be dying? Unless she didn't care. It was entirely possible. Laura had often wondered if their father had ever cared about either one of them. It was hard to fathom, but were she and her sister nothing more to him than child laborers? The more she thought about it, Laura wasn't sure if he was capable of caring for anyone, much less love in any form. Had Shenia come to that conclusion after their mom's death?

Her passing could have brought them together. Instead it created a wedge between them. Laura had thought they'd always stick together. Instead Shenia left her to fend for herself at their father's fish camp with his low-life crew of weekend warriors.

It was dark by the time Laura turned off onto the dirt path that led to the cabin. The moon was hidden behind the clouds. She switched on her brights and leaned into the wheel, prepared to wind her way for a mile through the dense forest, but after she rounded the first curve, the way home came back to her as if she'd driven it yesterday. She parked outside the garage. At the far end of the cabin, a warm light flickered in the great room where smoke rose from the chimney. Her father must be waiting for her or, then again, had he drifted off to sleep?

Laura left her car and stopped under porch light, suddenly at a complete loss. What would she say to him? Worse yet, what would he have to say to her? She'd never imagined feeling disoriented in the place where she'd lived until she was eighteen. God, she wished Shenia were here. For a minute, she stood outside in the cold and shivered, unable to move. Part of her wished he'd never called.

She came into the garage and walked up the stairs toward the kitchen door, stepping aside as she passed by a hole in the wall that marked the place where Father's wooden paddle had once hung. She slipped off her boots on the landing before going inside. Immediately, the medicinal smell of mothballs and underlying odor of must overwhelmed her. Water dripped from the kitchen sink. She switched on the light over the table. Around it, the warped linoleum was pulling up from the edges of the room. "Anybody home?" In the great room a fire crackled. "Father?"

Laura clutched the strap of her overnight bag and crossed through the kitchen into the dim hall beyond the bathroom. She wanted to duck away and hide in her old room, but instead she entered the great room where she imagined her father slouched in his wingback chair. The oak planks creaked under her footsteps and suddenly, from the edge of the hearth, a large dog with a thick coat stirred. Laura took a step back. The dog barked at her, though it didn't charge. Beside the fire, her father's chair sat empty. On his footstool, someone had left a scribbled note. She picked it up. *Took dad to the ER. Left Phoebe on guard duty. Meet us there.*

Her sister's large and looping handwriting was unmistakable. Just then Phoebe bounded toward her, jumping up and licking her nose. Instinctively, Laura squeezed her eyes shut. When she opened them, Phoebe was circling her. Laura took the iron poker and snuffed out the fire. Phoebe came to her side and began to pant. Laura ran her fingers through the dog's curls, then realized she must be thirsty.

In the kitchen, Laura found two dog bowls. She filled one to the brim and set it on the floor where Phoebe lapped up the water. The bowl beside it was empty too. One by one she searched the cupboards, but couldn't find any dog food, or much of anything else. Her father was down to a half-can of Folgers and a bag of Saltine crackers. Then she went to the fridge. Except for a few hard-boiled eggs, a six-pack of PBR, and a jar of pickles, those shelves were also bare. What had he been eating? She chopped up an egg for Phoebe. That should hold her over.

★

Laura drove straight to the hospital in Eagle Ridge. By the time she arrived at the ER, it was after nine. The last time she'd been there was the day her mother died. Now she went in to search for her father.

The attendant scanned the patient list on her clipboard until she came to his name about half the way down and looked up from her paperwork. "Your relation?"

"I'm his daughter."

The woman nodded. "I'll have someone come out. You may have a seat."

"No, if it's okay, I'm gonna stand right here. I've just driven all the way from Michigan to see him." Laura's voice faltered. "He might be dying."

"Oh, I see." She opened the doors to the ER and flagged over a guy in scrubs. "Can you please take her down there to Mr. Warner?"

Laura, not knowing what to expect, followed the man down a hall lined with empty rooms until he stopped at the one where the curtains were closed. He stepped aside and motioned for her to enter. She paused there for a second, unsure what to do since she couldn't knock. Then, with a tremble, she pried apart the shades.

Her father was propped up in a bed, but his eyes were shut. Tubes ran into his crooked nose where his moustache was left untrimmed. She knew she should get closer, but instead Laura took a step back—almost unable to resist the urge to flee. After a minute, she forced herself to approach him. His beard was scruffy and she could see how the skin sagged under his chin. Clearly, his muscles were weakened along with his lungs. When she reached his bedside, she noticed the bones of his shoulder protruding through his thin shirt. In this emaciated state, he could do nothing more than lash her with his tongue—if he was even strong enough speak. He looked much older than she remembered.

She brought over a stool and sat there a few minutes watching him, wondering when Shenia would show up and tell her what was going on. Suddenly, he let out a phlegmy cough, which seemed to jar him awake. She stood over the bed. A few seconds passed before he recognized her. "Laura?"

"Yes."

He pointed at the bedside table. "Can you hand me my glasses?" She reached for the wire spectacles, the same pair he'd worn when she was in high school, and handed them to him. His hands were cold. "So, you finally came." A brief flicker came to his eyes.

She lowered hers. "Yep. Got here as fast as I could. When did you arrive?"

"I'm not sure. After dark." His skin was as blue as the ragged hat pulled down over his forehead. She thought about suggesting that he might want to take it off but, then again, he seemed comfortable enough. "Shenia brought me when I started coughing up blood."

Laura's chest tightened. "What did the doctor say?"

Her father wheezed. "Called it a flare-up, said I probably caught some sort of virus."

Laura didn't know what to make of any of it. "Well, you should rest then. I'll stay here and wait." Her father's head sank deeper into the pillow and his eyes quietly shut, though his breathing sounded through the tubes, which looped around his ears to keep them in place. Sores had formed where they entered his nose at the edges of his nostrils.

Laura sat on the stool with her back up against the wall, wondering how her father's health could have gotten this bad without her knowing. She thought about going outside to call

Shenia, but then reconsidered. Her sister would show up when she felt like it, or not. Laura reminded herself that she couldn't control anyone's actions other than her own. They weren't little girls playing in the forest anymore. And ever since their mother died, and their father took up heavy drinking, Shenia had put her own freedom first and treated Laura with complete disregard. Nothing was likely to change now.

After about fifteen minutes, when the doctor returned, his ruddy cheeks flared. "How could you let him run out like that? He almost dropped to 80 percent."

Laura instantly stood. Why was the doctor yelling at her? She didn't even know he was sick until he'd called her that morning. She had nothing to do with this. Now she was only trying to help. "I had no idea. I just got here." Suddenly, shame welled up in her.

He crossed his arms and leaned back onto his heels. "I see. Well, you're his daughter, am I correct?"

"Yes."

"Is there any other family in the area?"

"My sister Shenia lives in Green Bay. She's the one who brought him, but I don't know where she is right now. So, what do you mean about my father? Is he going to be okay?"

"I'm not sure yet. The oxygen level in the blood is supposed to be 95 percent or higher. When it gets below 90, and down as low as 80, organs can fail. Can you stay here with him while I run a few more tests?"

"Of course," she said.

Once the doctor left, Laura returned to her stool and pushed it against the wall. She rested against it. He had no idea what she was going through. She wanted to scream. He had no right to accuse her of neglecting her father, who was now wheezing in his sleep. After the way Father had treated her, what obligation did she have? She had her own family in Michigan. She squeezed her eyes shut and held still, trying to block everything out. At that moment, she would have given anything to be back home.

A while later, Laura felt a tap on her shoulder. "Hey, wake up, sleepyhead."

She hadn't realized she'd dozed off. A vague image of the attending nurse came to mind until she saw Shenia smiling down at her with magenta lips. Before Laura could respond, she'd been scooped into her sister's arms. Shenia planted a kiss on her cheek. Laura placed her hand on the spot.

"Don't worry." Shenia giggled to herself. "It's smudge proof. All the women athletes wore it in the Summer Olympics." She covered her mouth as if in shock. "I'm sorry. Do you seriously still not wear any makeup?"

Laura let the remark pass without comment, remembering how Shenia enjoyed talking for her own benefit almost as much as baiting her—as if it were her birthright as the oldest to say whatever she wanted. Laura recalled being greeted by Phoebe. She'd had enough stress. There was no need to defend her actions. During the Olympics, spotting fashion and makeup trends hadn't crossed her mind. She wouldn't even try to explain how defeated she'd felt watching athletes like Usain Bolt and Michael Phelps. On the other hand, Nate, watching from his wheelchair, had been inspired by them.

"Maybe I can swim like that when I grow up," he'd said.

Laura still wasn't able to think that far ahead, though sometimes she wished she could. It couldn't possibly hurt as much as looking back. After being out of touch for so many years, she didn't expect Shenia to understand how much her life had changed since they'd last seen each other when they were teenagers. As far as she knew Shenia was still single with no kids and lots of time to put on makeup. She doubted that would ever change. Right now, she didn't care how many layers of concealer and lipstick Shenia had applied. They couldn't gloss over the problems with their father.

"So, you must have met Phoebe. I hated to leave her there alone like that."

"I was a little shocked when I came in," Laura said. "She seems sweet. I gave her some water, but I couldn't find any dog food."

"Yeah, I had to rush out of there. Dad was on empty. Sorry I didn't get back to you sooner." Shenia ran her fingers through her big hair, which was stiff with hairspray. "I was at work, and the manager there doesn't let us keep our phones on us. So, I only saw it at break. And when I told her I had to leave, she still gave me shit, even after I explained why. *Like seriously, I'm just going to stay there, and what, leave my father to die alone?* She'd already made me work Friday, which is why he missed his appointment in the first place. I thought he could make it until Monday when he gets his regular oxygen delivery."

"That's unbelievable. Thank god you made it. My phone ran out of battery, so I never got your message. But, I don't understand about missing his appointment. You were going to take him?"

At that instant, the doctor walked in. "Well, I'm glad you're both here now. I have a few things to explain."

He glanced down at Shenia and let out a deep sigh. "I'm Doc Nielson. I presume you're the other sister."

"Yes, that's correct. I've been coming up to see him once a week for a few months."

The doctor shook his head at her. "I'm afraid that's not going to cut it, anymore—even if you were more reliable."

Shenia crossed her arms. "I have been reliable. I just missed this one time. My boss made me work. Friday and Saturday were supposed to be my days off. I'd planned to be here."

"I hear you, miss. But realize that now he's suffered irreparable damage." The doctor lowered his chin to his chest. "After a night like tonight, he won't make it through another round."

Laura turned to Shenia, who suddenly had tears in her eyes. "I'm so sorry."

"Please." His tone softened. "I just have to keep him overnight and then he can probably go home with you tomorrow after he sees his regular doctor. But he needs a pulse oximeter to wear around his neck, so he can check his oxygen level without having to gauge it from the tank. It's pretty simple, just a matter of placing it on his index finger. As far as tonight, can one of you stay with him here and be responsible for getting him home tomorrow after his appointment?"

Shenia raised her eyebrows. "I should really check on Phoebe, but then I could come back."

Doc Neilson directed his attention to Laura. "Are you able to handle it?"

"I'll try my best," she said.

The doctor planted his hands on his hips. "We're fine then for tonight. But realize, from now on, he's going to need constant care."

"What do you mean by that?" Laura asked.

"It could be a home caregiver or he could move into an assisted living center. That's up to you two and your father."

Then the doctor glanced at Shenia. "Just ensure that he gets to his regular appointments and I don't see him like this again. I'm not saying it's going to be easy." He reached out and firmly shook their hands. "But you have each other."

Once he left the room, the gravity of their situation took hold. Laura's arms and legs were suddenly heavy. She didn't understand how to use any of the equipment. "Are you going to be able to come back and help me get him home?" Though Shenia had been caring for him, she looked equally shell-shocked. "I mean how does he get around with all that equipment and the tubes?"

"Hey, don't worry about it now. We can straighten everything out tomorrow."

"Whatever you think is best, but why didn't you tell me he was this sick?"

"Come on." Shenia threw her head back and stared at the ceiling. "You have your own family to take care of. And after all that was happening in the summer with your son, I figured you didn't need to be burdened."

"Still, I wish you would have told me. I mean, he could have died."

"You're right. I thought I had things under control. Obviously not."

"You did the best you could under the circumstances," Laura said. "But like the doctor said, it's really not a job someone can handle alone."

Shenia glanced at the door. "Are you sure you don't mind staying tonight?"

"Not at all. It'll save me from more driving."

Shenia nodded. "Thanks for being here to take the second shift."

"Yeah, no problem. I've got plenty of experience sleeping in these chairs."

Chapter 39

October 31, 2016

Laura scraped the ice off the windshield before she pulled out of the medical building parking lot. In the passenger seat, her father sat with his hands in his lap taking shallow breaths. She kept her eyes on the road, yet couldn't fully concentrate. *Irreparable damage.* Doc Neilson's diagnosis from the previous night, which had just been confirmed by Father's regular doctor, ate away at her. Chronic Obstructive Pulmonary Disease. He was going to die from the condition in a matter of months, even weeks, if he didn't receive proper care including adequate nutrition. His insurance wasn't good, the billing specialist informed her at checkout. Laura wasn't sure he had enough to cover the cost of today's visit, much less his overnight trip to the ER. What about all the appointments to come?

Shenia had finally texted her back a half hour ago. *Went to grocery store. On my way.* Funny how that always seemed to be the case, almost as if she was still trying to live up to her Ojibwa name, Shenia, which their mother had given her at birth after two days in active labor. Laura messaged back. *Leaving hospital now. Meet you at home.* Given the help of the hospital staff, who'd fitted him with a portable unit of liquid oxygen, Laura had been confident that they could safely make the twenty-five-minute trip. He didn't seem to be taking in much air.

"How are you doing?" she asked.

"I'm fine. Just drive the car."

His remark burned along with the acid in her empty stomach. She'd survived through the night on the biscuits she'd brought with her from breakfast the previous day. It was like playing catch-up. "You can't live like this."

What had she just blurted? When they were living in the same house, he'd have slapped her across the face. Never before had she dared to speak so sternly to him and didn't know where the assertive voice came from. Seated beside her, he let out a weak cough and closed his eyes without saying a word.

She recalled the exchange with his doctor. "You've got to take better care of yourself, Mr. Warner. Missing your appointment and showing up here on empty is unacceptable. Do you understand?"

Once a robust man, her father was reduced to no more than a hundred fifty pounds and was no longer in a position to argue with his doctor. "I do."

Then, the doctor had looked at her. "You too bear some responsibility."

She wouldn't waste any more time arguing. He was elderly. No matter how much she resented him for the times he'd failed to protect her and Shenia, or how deeply she loathed him for mistreating them and Mother throughout the years, she must accept that it had fallen upon her to care for him. Nothing mattered at the moment except getting him home and hooked back on his regular oxygen tank.

By the time they pulled in front of the garage twenty minutes later, it was one o' clock. She scanned the yard, expecting that Shenia already would have been there waiting for them. She could use a second hand getting him up the garage stairs and inside to the kitchen. But, since Shenia was nowhere to be found, they'd just have to work together. "Here we go."

He leaned against her. She waited, supporting him with her hand under his elbow as he got out of the car. Slowly, he made his way toward the garage and onto the first stair. "Only four more," she said. He cleared his throat and scaled them one by one. Afterward, he paused in the kitchen to catch his breath. His bedroom, at the far end of the house, seemed a long way off. They stopped again in the hallway before making their way across the great room. "I think it would be good for you to lie down."

He took a seat on the mattress. "I'll be right back to hook you up." She raced back to the car and lugged his equipment to his bedside. Then she reattached his breathing tubes and turned on the flow of oxygen as the physician's assistant had demonstrated. She slipped off his shoes and settled him in under the covers. "Are you hungry?"

"I'll rest first."

"Okay, then. Just one more thing." She moistened the raw sores around his nostrils with a dab of Aquaphor, setting the saline solution aside for later. He shut his eyes.

By the time she left his room, Laura felt as if she too might collapse. Wind rattled the front window. At least the sun had finally broken through the clouds. A thin streak reflected off the dark lake. Where was Shenia? She better hurry with the groceries before their father woke up, starving. Laura turned away and went into the kitchen. Right now, she was prepared to eat anything. She took the tin of biscuits out of her bag and then reached in the fridge for the pickles and the last hard-boiled egg. The cool shell fit in her palm and she prepared to crack it on the edge of the sink, but instead set it aside. She might need to peel it for Father if Shenia didn't show up. Gherkins and day-old biscuits, what a feast. Laura had planned to save the silverberry jam she'd made but, given the circumstances, she popped off the lid and dipped a biscuit in the jar. When she was finished, she licked the jam off her fingers and brushed the crumbs onto the floor for Phoebe.

Now, before her father needed her again, she needed to phone home. Laura left for the bedroom she and Shenia once shared, looking forward to resting on the bed and talking with Helen and the kids. But when she reached for the worn brass doorknob, Laura hesitated. What was she afraid of? She was a mother not a child. Slowly, she opened the door and stepped inside the oak-paneled room. The down comforter looked as soft as ever, though the wooden headboard didn't seem as grand compared to the countless stands of white spruces huddled outside the bare window.

Though she knew no one would be watching anymore, Laura turned her back to it before she changed into her sweatshirt and sweatpants. When she and Shenia roomed together, and the fish camp was still in business, they'd always shut the curtains and kept a lookout for Peeping Toms. Now it was strange to be alone with the forest that spread mile after mile behind the cabin. They'd explored every inch of it when they were kids as if it were a sprawling playground. She went to their dresser, which she'd taken over after Shenia left. Shenia had already put her stuff in the guest room off the main living area closer to their father. Though she knew he was too weak to physically harm her, Laura still didn't like being alone with him. Being around him stirred up all sorts of bad memories, including how he'd berated her and put her down—just as he'd done to her mom. It was always only a matter of time, minutes rather than hours, before he'd inflict the next string of insults as if were trying to get in as many hurtful words as possible before he took his last breath. Laura held hers, unsure how much longer she could wait around for further abuse. Why wasn't Shenia back? She should have at least texted.

She checked her phone, which she'd charged at the hospital, though there hadn't been any service in the facility. She'd managed to send Rob a quick text outside the doors of the Emergency entrance at about 2 a.m. when Father was moved from the ER into a regular room. *Dad ran out of oxygen, but Shenia took him to the hospital. I'm staying with him there tonight. Meeting his doctor tomorrow.*

Rob had texted her back late this morning, though she hadn't received the message until she and Father had left the hospital. *Glad he made it. Taking Nate to doctor at noon. Ella and Biyen are good but we all miss you.* She wondered if he'd talked with Patricia. But if so, wouldn't he have called her about it? Laura hated not knowing what was up with him and the kids. She must reach them somehow. Behind her, an engine revved and the snow tires of a black Hyundai gripped the drive. Laura went onto the front porch, which had been remodeled into a four-seasons room. Shenia pulled up next to the Buick and waved in her direction. In a matter of seconds, from out of the passenger door, Phoebe bounded toward the house.

Shenia stepped around to her trunk, popped it open, and pulled out a couple bags filled with groceries. Laura went outside and helped her bring them in. "What took you so long?"

"I stopped to visit a friend. How's Dad doing?"

"Not that good."

Irritated, Laura paused for a second. How could Shenia always be so chill? Then, she remembered how she'd stopped over at Rosa's on the way home from Nate's doctor appointment when she'd been stressed. Rob had gotten so freaked out. Laura took a deep breath and tried to keep an open mind. "Do you want to see him?"

"Let's unload the groceries first." Shenia set her bags on the counter. "So, what's up?"

Laura wasn't sure how to explain the situation. "We just got back from the doctor's before you came. He's in bed."

Shenia nodded. "So, he's fine."

"Not exactly." Why did Shenia talk in circles? It made Laura want to pull her hair out. "Go in and see for yourself."

"I'll talk to him when I'm finished."

Once all the groceries were put in their proper place, Shenia went to him. Laura and Phoebe followed. Phoebe came up and waited patiently at Shenia's feet along their father's bedside. Laura felt like she was ten again and her sister had put herself in charge. Why did she always act like the boss of her?

Their father gradually opened his eyes. "Shenia?"

Laura leaned against the doorframe as her sister took their father's hand. "Yes, it's me. I'm right here." Shenia patted his thin skin, which made Laura cringe. "You look good."

His cheeks and eyes lifted. "So, do you."

Shenia raised an eyebrow at her. "Can you give us a few minutes?"

Before Laura could respond, Shenia turned toward their father. What made her sister think it was okay to dismiss her as if she were still a child or hired help? Laura wanted to strangle her. "I'll go make Dad a sandwich." Neither Shenia or their father looked up. Laura left for the kitchen and wrestled with the twist tie on the bag of white bread before giving up and tearing it open. Why did Shenia treat her that way? How come she let her? She spread a thick layer of liverwurst on one piece of bread and slathered Miracle Whip dressing on the other before slapping them together. After all these years, whether she wanted to or not, she still recalled how he liked it.

Laura returned a few minutes later with the sandwich and a glass of ice water, which she set on the bedside table. Father nodded, looking up for an instant before he and Shenia continued their conversation. Laura stepped out of the room but listened from beyond the open door.

"You do need to take better care of yourself when I'm not here," Shenia said.

"Yes, I know."

She'd said the same thing, yet both of them were treating her as if she weren't capable of understanding the real issues— almost as if she wasn't a part of this family. Laura escaped into her room. She had no purpose here. Her family who needed her was in Michigan. At least now she could finally make a call to Rob and see how Nate did at the doctor. Her pulse raced as she waited for him to pick up. When no one answered, she left a message. "Hey. Just checking to see how everyone's doing. Hope Nate's appointment went well. Please let me know. I'm back at my father's place with him and Shenia. He's stabilized. Now we need to decide who's going to take care of him and how to pay for it."

Laura hung up. Feeling more tired than ever, she closed her eyes and rested her head on the pillow. After a few minutes, Shenia strode into the bedroom with Phoebe panting at her heels. "Want to take her for a walk with me?"

Laura kept her eyes shut. "I'm taking a nap."

Phoebe pawed at the floor, scratching her nails against the wood.

"Come on. You can sleep later."

Shenia must have slept well last night. Laura was exhausted and didn't want to deal with her. But the sooner they started figuring things out, the sooner she could go home. "All right, as long as you think Dad will be okay on his own."

"He's sleeping," Shenia said. "I'll make dinner right after."

Once they'd bundled up, Laura followed Shenia into the forest behind the cabin. Phoebe darted between the bushy pines, kicking up icy snow.

"She sure seems to know her way around," Laura said.

"Yeah, she loves it out here," Shenia said.

"Do you ever worry she'll run away or get lost?"

"Nah, she just seems to get it. Now, when we go back to Green Bay, I always feel bad putting her on a leash."

"I bet. This is a different world," Laura said. "Remember how we used to go out and search for ghost houses?"

Shenia laughed. "I totally forgot about that. Do you still know where they are?"

Laura wasn't positive. She thought she might recall one hidden away from the lake on the other side of their drive behind the green cottage from the fish camp. "I think so." Shenia followed as she trudged ahead over fallen sticks and branches. For Laura, it was her first time making the trek in the snow among the pines when so many of the other trees were bare. The forest seemed stark now by comparison, yet the thin clusters of birches remained familiar along with the thick trunks of the ancient oaks that rose from the frozen ground like pillars holding up the sky. Soon she found her rhythm and recalled the way to the ramshackle cabin that had always exerted a pull on her. The dog ran around them in circles.

Shenia stepped in close behind her. "How old is Nate again?"

"He just turned five, this summer, the night before the accident."

"How's he doing now?"

"He's still in a wheelchair, but Rob and I are working with him. He's making really good progress. The doctor had originally said he might never walk again, but we didn't believe him. Nate never did either. Rob was taking him to the doctor today to see if he's ready to wear a boot with crutches."

"That's good." Shenia rubbed her mittens together. "He sounds like a cool kid."

"He is. Maybe someday you can meet him. His little sister and brother are pretty cool too. Ella is four and Biyen is one." She almost couldn't believe that Shenia hadn't met them, or Rob. "Right now, we're actually living with his parents."

A clearing appeared in the distance and the outline of the ghost house encircled by evergreens came into view. With the wind at her back, Phoebe dashed toward it as if she'd known all along that it was their destination. Shenia clapped twice. About fifty feet ahead of them, Phoebe stopped and looked down her snout at her master. "She must wait for me," Shenia said. "It might be dangerous inside."

Phoebe looked back and forth between them and the dilapidated shack, which had deteriorated into little more than framing, until Shenia came beside her and clipped the leash onto her rhinestone-studded collar. They continued on together.

"Do you think you'll ever have kids?" asked Laura.

"I doubt it." Shenia paused for a second. "Ryan and I split up practically right after I left here with him." Shenia walked in the long shadows of the pines toward the shack. "Now I'm so busy with work and being on my feet all day making people beautiful, listening to their life stories, I don't need any drama when I come home at night. I had enough of family responsibilities when I was kid. Can say, though, I could run the Ulta store better than the manager they have now. Definitely not a firstborn."

"What's that supposed to mean?"

"When you're the oldest, you're put in charge whether you want to be or not." Shenia paused before she came up onto the doorstep. "I never asked to be the one who was responsible. I watched you like I was told." She peered inside the broken window beside the door. "I'm worried about Phoebe going in there. What do you think?"

Laura poked her head through the frame of the opposite window looking for any glass. There was none by the door that she could see. Two rickety chairs were arranged at the table in the center of the room, probably by hunters, she thought. "I'll go check it out."

She moved past Shenia, brushing by Phoebe, and pulled open the door. Wind gusted in from where the roof had collapsed. Snowflakes drifted from the branches of the tall pines reaching through the holes like bare hands.

"It's freakin' freezing out here," Shenia said.

"I'm not sure it's any warmer in here, though there is a fireplace." The warped floorboards creaked under each footstep but, as Laura walked from corner to corner, nothing struck her as particularly dangerous for a dog. "Looks safe enough to me."

Shenia came inside. Phoebe followed her in and curled up at the foot of the empty hearth. Laura sat in one of the wooden chairs. Shenia took the other. A tin cup was left on the table between them. Shenia picked it up by the handle and stared inside. "Remember that time you spilled grape Kool-Aid all over the velvet couch?"

"Not really. Why?"

"Well, you were asking me about what it means to be first-born. You don't remember because I'm the one who got punished for filling up your glass too high and letting you drink in the living room. No matter what happened, I was always to blame. Somehow, I was supposed to protect you. After Mom died, I couldn't take it. Dad put so much pressure on me. As if I could somehow take her place."

No one could replace their mother, and their father knew how to put on the squeeze. She agreed with her sister on that. Still, she couldn't understand why Shenia blamed her for her unhappiness. In the distance, a timber wolf howled as if it were crying. Phoebe's ears pricked up. The back of Laura's neck tightened. She hadn't heard a wolf in years and never one that sounded so forlorn. Shenia went to look out the window, though Laura had no idea why she'd bother. The wolf's high-pitched wails were echoing from miles away.

When they were kids, she'd looked up to Shenia and relied on her. Back then, in Laura's mind, no one could have been braver—especially on the day shortly after their mother's diagnosis when Shenia was fourteen and had gone through these woods to get the mail on her own. It was one of those dog days of summer around lunchtime, as Laura recalled, and their father had taken the car to town. Shenia walked for a mile through the woods along their dirt drive to reach their mailbox on the main road. Their mother, who was expecting an important letter from the hospital, asked Shenia to hurry. At the time, no one seemed to have given Shenia's safety a second thought.

However, as Shenia later told them, perhaps they should have. For soon after she retrieved their mother's letter and turned around to make her way back home, a lone wolf appeared ahead of her on the drive. With a thick gray coat and sharp blue eyes, the wolf took her in. She met the creature's gaze for a second and then looked away. She wanted to run off into the forest and hide, but then realized it could easily chase her down. There was no point in turning back, since hardly anyone traveled on the main road. Shenia, her palms covered in sweat, held onto the letter, understanding that she must move forward. Mother had trusted her to do the job, and so she would. Shenia bowed her head once to the wolf, which hadn't budged, before proceeding at her regular pace. Acting as if nothing stood in her way, she focused on the soft chirping of the birds and the gentle breeze rustling the leaves as step by step she drew closer to the wolf, which was sniffing at its heels. Coming closer still, she noticed its silvery fur swaying from side to side. Must she cross its path? Small pebbles crumbled beneath her feet. The wolf's ears pricked up. Raising its head, the wolf took notice of her. Once again, their eyes met. She didn't say a word—trying not to think about the crushing pressure of its jaw. Instead, she held the letter tightly to her side. She reminded herself of her commitment to her mother. In the distance, a branch snapped. Then, without further warning, the wolf bounded off. She watched as it picked up a steady, easy gait and loped away into the trees until she could no longer see it. The next second, she tore off toward home and never looked back.

Laura hadn't thought of the episode in years. The wolf had stopped howling, but Shenia was still staring out the window. What did she have to fear? Suddenly, through the hole in the roof, a clump of snow fell from the long arm of a pine and landed with a thump beside the fireplace. Phoebe, who'd remained still and quiet during the wolf's mournful cries, yelped and rose onto all fours. Shenia rushed over and hugged her dog around the neck.

Laura came to their side. "Is she okay?"

Shenia stroked the fur on Phoebe's ears. "She hates loud noises. It's getting dark. I think we should go."

Following Shenia and the dog, Laura was half way to the door when she noticed Phoebe limp. "I think something is wrong with her front leg."

Shenia stopped and checked. "I don't see anything." Still, Phoebe wouldn't put any weight on her right side.

"Maybe she strained herself," Laura said.

"Or stepped on something?" Shenia added.

Laura got on her knees and patted around the floorboards by the fireplace where Phoebe had been resting. "Hopefully it's just a splinter."

Shenia came beside her where a cracked mirror reflected up at them. Laura caught a warped image of her sister. Shenia's bright lipstick had smeared. "Great. She probably has a piece of glass stuck in there. Why did you say it was safe to come in here?" Shenia glared at her.

A chill sank into Laura's bones. "I thought we both agreed." She looked sideways at Shenia, who hadn't seemed to have noticed she had lipstick all over her face.

Shenia pried open Phoebe's paw, prodding around and poking it, until the dog began to whimper. "I still can't find anything."

"Why don't you let her rest for a minute and see how she does."

"Fine." Shenia let go and sat back on her heels. "But I should have known better than to take your word."

Laura shook out her hands and feet, which had gone numb. Shenia's contempt seemed to run as deep as the dark lake they'd grown up on. Had she ever wanted her around? It almost sounded as if Shenia would have preferred if Laura had never been born. After a moment, Phoebe went to the door and panted.

"She seems fine. I'm going to check on Father." Laura walked out, not waiting up for Shenia. She didn't need her sister's permission, or her protection from wolves or anything else. The wind gusted against her, but she quickened her step, wondering why she'd ever decided to come back and help. She should leave now. This was not her home. Shenia and their father could handle his affairs on their own.

"Laura, wait!" Shenia sounded breathless, but Laura didn't stop. "Please, Ra-Ra. Wait for me."

Laura almost stopped in her tracks. When was the last time her sister had called her that name for short? She hadn't even thought of it in years. Her legs burned along with her throat and chest. Still, she kept walking faster until Phoebe cut her off as if she was guarding her for Shenia.

After a minute, she caught up. "I'm sorry." She brushed off the snow and ice under Phoebe's chin. "I shouldn't have blamed you for that."

"But you always do." Wind gusted in their faces, leaving a sting. "Is that why you hate me?"

"What? I don't hate you. Why do you think that?" Shenia asked.

"Why would I not think that? You left me on my own after Mom died and haven't wanted anything to do with me since. You treat me like when we were kids, like I'm still a little pest, or worse. Even when Nate was in a coma, and I needed someone to talk to, I could tell I was bothering you, and you still just wanted me to leave you alone."

Shenia pulled up her collar against the wind. "I can't believe you would say that."

"Then why didn't you call me back when I told you about Nate?" asked Laura.

"I texted. You told me he was going to be fine."

"No, I didn't. You determined that. He still isn't fine. Nothing is fine!" Laura pulled up her hood. "I'm going back. Father could have died yesterday."

She started walking. This time, Shenia kept up. "So now after one day, you're his saving angel. Hah." She tugged on Laura's coat sleeve. "I've been coming up to take care of him for the past few months. I'm the one who's been bringing him to the doctor and getting his groceries. And guess what, I have a personal life too."

Laura couldn't stand hearing her make herself out to be the martyr. "Yeah, well, if I had known I could have helped you."

"Come on—think about it—really? Dad's problems were the last thing you needed to hear. And the way you always take everything so seriously, I didn't want to be the one to put you over the edge."

"I see, so now I'm the problem." Laura spun around to her. "So, what? You just don't tell me—not even months later?"

"It's not like you had a relationship with him."

Phoebe whimpered. Shenia stopped walking and bent down to check her paw once more, poking and prodding the tender area. Laura wished she could go back in time and replay her all the phone calls and throw all the invitations, birth announcements, and Christmas cards in her face. How could she not recognize all the times she'd tried to reach out to them—all the times they'd rejected her. "I would have been there." Her voice quivered. Now, hearing her own sense of futility, something struck her about Shenia.

Laura remembered the evening shortly after their mom died, when she'd heard dishes clattering in the kitchen sink after dinner. Then, the bang of a glass plate on the counter.

When she came in from the porch and a man with stringy hair was standing behind Shenia, pressing himself up against her backside. Shenia tried to squirm away, but he held tightly onto her hips and thrust his pelvis forward before groping her and reaching for her crotch. "Get off me!" Shenia struggled to shake him, but he took her by the shoulders and dragged her toward their bedroom next to the garage. "Let go, right now!" He slammed her back into the door to their room and reached for the knob. "No!" Shenia pushed him away.

Laura shuddered at the memory. She'd been so afraid, unable to speak. Yet she stepped toward them, and then, he saw her. "What you looking at?"

"Leave her alone," Laura said in a quivering voice.

"You go mind your own business," he said.

"I'm going to tell my father."

The man, his wide jaw clenched, glared at her with commanding green eyes. "You shut your fucking mouth, little girl, or you'll be next."

"I'm telling now." Suddenly, she recognized the man, who'd been staying at the fish camp in the green cottage. She ran out through the porch into the yard and yelled for her father to come—until she saw his rowboat far out on the lake. Even if he could hear her screams, he'd never make it back soon enough. All she could do was pretend. She ran back inside toward the kitchen. "Our father's coming right now!"

She'd only been gone a minute, but the bedroom door was shut and everything had gone quiet. She reached for a carving knife—prepared to do whatever she must—before she yanked the door open. Shenia was lying on their bed, curled up in a ball. The man who'd attacked her seemed to have fled.

Laura once again wondered what would have happened if she'd not been curious about the noise in the kitchen. An hour or so later after dark, when their father returned to shore, she told him everything. But he'd probably been drinking for hours and didn't seem to fully listen. She'd taken him to Shenia, who was under the covers.

"What did he do to you?" their father asked.

Shenia just whimpered.

"I think he ran away," Laura said.

"I didn't ask you." His nostrils flared. Then, he'd told her to get out so he could speak with Shenia.

Now, hunched over in the snow, Shenia pulled a small shard of glass from Phoebe's fleshy paw. She held it in the fading light. "It's hard to believe a little sliver like this could hurt so much."

Laura swallowed and considered how vulnerable Shenia must have felt that night. They'd been through a lot together as kids. More than kids should have to. Her bitterness toward her softened. "Yeah, do you think she'll be able to make it home?"

Shenia nodded. "For sure. Phoebe's tough. And it's not like she really has a choice, right?"

"Well, we could always carry her. I mean, if we had to."

"Yes, I guess you're right. Between the two of us, we'd probably be strong enough."

Chapter 40

October 31, 2016

Laura walked side by side with Shenia the rest of the way home, not knowing what they could expect from their father, but sensing that maybe they finally had a chance to start talking things through and figure out what went wrong between them.

Once they shook the snow off their boots and came inside, she led her into the bathroom to face the mirror. "What?" Shenia asked.

Laura stood back and watched, trying not to laugh, as Shenia's jaw dropped at her own reflection. Not only had her lipstick smeared, but now her mascara was running and her eyelashes were clumped. "Okay, I look like I've run a marathon." She poked Laura in the arm. "Why didn't you tell me I was such a mess."

Laura giggled. "You said it didn't smudge."

Shenia wiped her lips with a tissue and dabbed around her eyes. "Want some? I think I put on enough for both of us."

"You look like you're ready for a Halloween party," Laura said.

"Ya think? Zombie apocalypse witch, maybe?"

Soon, they were both giggling uncontrollably as they had more than once in church when they were kids. Then coughing from their father's bedroom carried down the hall.

Shenia leaned closer toward the mirror. "Can you check on him? I'm going to need another minute or two to get all this off."

"Or ten," Laura added.

Shenia's laughter followed her until she reached their father, who coughed into his hankie. He set it on the bedside table next to his plate where only a few crumbs remained from the sandwich she'd made him earlier. He was down to his last sip of water. "Are you feeling better?"

"I'm still breathing," he said. "Where did you go?"

"For a walk."

"What are we having for dinner?"

"I'm not sure what Shenia has planned, but we'll get something ready for you soon. Do you need anything right now?"

"No. Just my dinner."

Laura took his lunch plate into the kitchen where Shenia was standing in front of the fridge with a beer in her hand and not a speck of makeup anywhere on her face. "Want one?"

"Nah, I'm good."

"Come on, don't make me drink alone. It's happy hour." Shenia cracked open a can of PBR and handed it over. "Cheers."

"Cheers." They clinked cans. Laura sipped through the foam. She caught herself staring at her sister's bare skin, which was as smooth and supple as fine suede. Shenia's cheeks looked a little bloated from too much drinking, but Laura couldn't imagine why she wore concealer. If anyone needed makeup these days it would be her. With a fair complexion like her father's mother, after whom Laura was named, she was getting wrinkles around her eyes. Probably from too much time in the sun. "What were you thinking we'd make Dad for dinner?"

Shenia brought out an assortment of prepared food, including a rotisserie chicken and mashed potatoes. "This usually keeps him happy. I'll nuke it and he can eat it in bed."

Fifteen minutes later, once he was served, Shenia grabbed them each another beer. They sat down to eat at the kitchen table. Behind them, the faucet dripped. Laura swallowed a bite of potatoes. "It's so weird to be back here."

"Yeah, but not necessarily in a bad way." Shenia sipped her beer. "I'm kind of liking it more now."

Laura could not see why. "Really, how's that?"

Shenia set aside her beer. "Do you remember my friend Beth from high school?"

Laura thought back to when she was a sophomore, recalling the whispering that went on between Shenia, then a senior, and the skinny blonde who came to her locker at the end of the day before they drove home. "The one with the really short hair?"

"Yeah. I guess that's one way to describe her. But anyways, the first time I came up here I went into the Piggly Wiggly to buy a block of cheddar for Dad, and I noticed someone next to me with bag of cheese curds." Shenia chuckled. "The last time I ate cheese curds was with Beth. And sure enough, I look up and there she is. She recognized me too." Shenia gulped her beer. "She invited me over to have some."

"So, did you like them?"

Shenia broke into a goofy smile. "Yes, Laura, but not as much as I liked her."

Her stomach dropped. "You mean like her, like her?"

Shenia blushed. "Oh my God, you're so childish. But yeah, I like her like that."

As happy as Laura felt, she was equally concerned about how their father would react, unless he already knew. "Have you told Father?"

"No, I'd never. I mean, he'd never be able to accept it. But you know how he is—even at this age—you can't put anything like that past him. I'm sure he's onto us. He overheard us talking when I told her about being called in for a second interview at the new Ulta store and saying I might move back to be closer to him—and her."

"Aren't you afraid?"

Shenia shook her head.

"Really, you know his temper? I can't even remember all the times he paddled us."

"That was when we were kids. I'm his lifeline. He can't do anything to me now. I'm getting another beer." She started to stand. "Want one?"

"No, thanks. Don't you think you should pace yourself?"

Shenia sat back down. "What are you trying to say?"

"I mean, we still need to come up with a plan for how we're going to take care of him. I'm worried we won't be able to think as clearly as we should if we drink too much."

The kitchen faucet, leaking for years, seemed to drip faster. She wouldn't say it now, but she also didn't want to see Shenia fall into the same trap as their father, who relied on alcohol to avoid his problems—especially after Mom died. "Hey, I just want to apologize to you for that night I lied to Father and tried to get you in trouble so he wouldn't hit me with the paddle. He went so crazy on us that time."

Shenia, resting her elbows on the table, set aside her drink. "Yeah, I could see how terrified you were of him. But that was a long time ago. Don't worry about it."

"No, I should have listened to you in the first place and not run off, and I shouldn't have lied. I'm really sorry."

"Well, I forgive you. To be honest, I haven't thought about that night in a long time." Shenia braced her chin with her fists. Something still seemed to be bothering her.

At that instant, Laura again recalled entering the kitchen and finding Shenia at the sink with the man from the fish camp groping her. "Do you remember when I walked in and saw that guy forcing himself on you?"

Shenia stared at the ceiling. "Yeah."

"I'm sorry. I understand if you don't want to talk about it?"

"It's fine."

"It's just that I never knew, exactly … what did he do to you?"

Shenia swallowed and seemed to shrink in her chair as if she were once again sixteen. "After you ran for help, that sicko got me in there and shut the door. He threw me onto the bed. When he started unbuckling his belt, I kicked him in the nuts. That's when he fell on top of me and tried to get in my shorts, but I kept kicking and fighting and he never got his pants down. Then, all of a sudden you were screaming. He gave up and ran out the garage."

"What about Dad? What did he say when you told him?"

"Called the guy a 'son of bitch,' but then said I should learn to put some clothes on and some sort of bullshit about being a woman now and starting to act my age."

"Whatever happened to the guy?"

"Dad checked his cabin, but by then he was gone. I begged him to call the police. Most of all, I was afraid the perv would come back. Dad never followed through on anything, or even made a report, though he should have been able to figure out where the guy lived from his reservation. That's what really pissed me off. I wasn't able to talk about it with you, you know. It was one of those things where you were too young to understand. But if it weren't for you—" Shenia's voice cracked.

Laura swallowed back tears and reached across the table for her sister's hand, which was trembling as much as hers. "You don't need to keep things from me anymore. I'm all grown up now, so we need to protect each other. And I want to help you with Father as much as possible. Maybe, this time, we can do it together."

Shenia shook her head. "Yeah, I'm sorry for not telling you about Dad. I should have said something a lot sooner. I know you don't let people down." She squeezed her hand. "After Mom died, I should have stayed and taken care of you. I felt so bad after I left. I didn't know what to do. Then Ryan and I broke up. As time went on, I felt more and more guilty. I missed your wedding. You had Nate and I never came. By the time you had Ella and Biyen, it seemed too late. I pretended like you wouldn't really care—and didn't miss me anyway—though, I knew how much I missed you."

For a few seconds, Laura just sat there. Now she finally understood where her sister was coming from. The tension between them was broken. "I didn't know."

"You couldn't have. There were so many times I dropped the ball." Shenia looked her in the eye. "I'm sorry, for not being there."

"Well, me too," Laura said. "Seems like we have a lot catch up on."

Chapter 41

October 31, 2016

Rob restocked the liquor bottles on the shelf for Andre, almost questioning whether it was a good idea. They hadn't opened until five but, after only three hours in, the crowd was acting as rowdy as if they'd been binge-drinking for three days since the kids trick-or-treated Saturday. Clearly Andre's cocktails were more potent than beer though, inevitably, the combination of the liquor and costumes exposed the true character of more than a few patrons. Rob tucked his T-shirt into jeans, recalling the ultimatum Laura had given him before she left. He had no time left to pretend. He must make it clear to Patricia, in no uncertain terms, that he wasn't interested in her anymore and never would be. He was in love with his wife, though he wondered: Was she still in love with him?

He'd pushed her way too far. If only he and Nate hadn't missed her call earlier when they were at the hospital without service. They'd rushed to call her back. Rob held his phone up to Nate's ear, so he could tell her himself. "Momma, I rode the bike!" However, she hadn't picked up. He'd also left a message, but it wasn't the same.

Rob really needed to hear her voice. And he wasn't the only one. Helen had made an early dinner of lasagna to celebrate Nate's accomplishment, but the kids only pushed their noodles around their plates. Then Biyen had grown restless and yanked Art's hair. "I wa' Ma-ma."

Still, Rob couldn't imagine anyone wanting Laura back more than he did. She'd been gone less than two days and was busy with her father, he understood. He was being ridiculous, of course. Yet he wasn't sure how much longer they could hang on. Without her, nothing seemed to matter as much. What if she decided to stay in Wisconsin?

Rob finished stocking the shelf remembering, then, that he was short a bottle of Jack Daniels. He went around back to grab another and poured himself a shot. Just then, Patricia came around with a fancy drink in her hand. The sight of her made him unsteady, though he hadn't had a drop of alcohol.

"Put that down." She held up a mason jar filled up with clear booze and crystals of blue sugar around the rim. "This one isn't on the menu. Pure Michigan. I made it exclusively for you. It's like the lake on a calm summer day when you can see all the way to the bottom. Remember those?"

"Not really." He lied and drank the shot he'd poured himself.

She crossed her arms. "Come on, stop shittin' me. You know those were the best days of your life." She held the glass to his mouth and tipped it up between his lips. "You have to try."

He took one swallow. Sweet and smooth at the start and finishing with a kick. Pretty damn good. Damn good actually, but he wouldn't say it. Discouragement. That's what she needed. Strong discouragement. He must discourage her from ever coming near him again—even if she hated him forever.

She took a step closer. "What do you think?"

He wiped his lips with the back of his hand and knotted his mouth in distaste before he backed away. "I've had enough."

She looked up at him and blinked flirtatiously as if it were all a joke to her. "Come on, seriously? I know your taste." She offered him the glass. "One more—"

He pushed her hand away and the drink sprayed against the wall. "It's disgusting, all right?" He planted his hands on his hips. "Give it a rest. I keep trying to tell you."

Her jaw dropped and then she shook her head like she was finally beginning to understand. "What's your problem?"

"I've had enough—of you."

Her eyes narrowed and her cheeks turned as red as the blinking smoke alarm light above her head. "What? You've been begging for a piece of my ass this whole time since I moved back."

"That's not true, and I'm sick of you coming on to me. I'm not interested. I'm in love with my wife."

She pinched her glossy lips together and leaned forward like she might head butt him. "Don't even start pretending like it was all me."

"That's pretty much how I see it, actually."

"Oh, so here we go again—just like back in high school— you acting all innocent and blaming everyone else." She raised her hands in fake surrender. "You're such a liar. You even lie to yourself. You can't even admit you still love me."

"Come on, Patty. I mean, Patricia."

"Just stop. Why don't you just admit it. You loved me more back then, than you love her now. I bet you've never loved Laura as much as you loved me. Tell me if that's not the truth."

Rob was tired of her twisting up his words. "I did love you once, that's true, until I figured out all you really cared about was covering your own ass. Seriously, what did you think would happen when you told the police Andre and I were stoned and drunk? You threw us both under the bus. Now you're engaged to him and throwing that away too. Get some self-respect."

"Oh, don't even go there," she said. "I just tell the truth."

"If it weren't for you, Andre would have never gone to jail," he said.

"How dare you say that? You're such a hypocrite. It's your fault. You were right there. You should have done something to save Sandra, but you were too out of it, just like I always said. You're as guilty as ever and you know it."

"Go to hell," he said.

She stormed off. He rocked onto his heels and felt like he might pass out. He hated her more than ever, mostly because she was half right. Sandra's death was his own damn fault, and he'd let Andre take the fall. He couldn't avoid it anymore. There was no way out but the truth.

Chapter 42

October 31, 2016

Shenia was on the porch with Phoebe resting across her lap when Laura returned from their father's bedside. She sat down next to them on the glider unable to stop thinking about all they'd kept from one another. Shenia had always been strong-willed and a little hard-headed, but maybe so was she. For whatever reason the distance between them had stretched on for way too long. She rested her head against the cushion and tried to relax.

"How's he doing?" Shenia asked.

"He's asleep."

"Amen to that." Shenia giggled and pushed them off with her feet.

Laura shook her head as they glided back and forth.

"Come on, Ra-Ra. Don't look so serious."

Laura forced a smile. "I'd totally forgotten you used to call me that—until earlier today."

"Well, from now on, I'm going to try to remember the good times and stop letting the other stuff hold me back."

Laura stroked Phoebe's soft fur. Her sister had a point. The past could really drag you down. However, ignoring it didn't seem right either. "I hear you, but I'm not sure it always works that way. Please let me know if you ever need to talk— for real."

"Thanks. I appreciate that. You too."

Laura gazed up at the stars. Orion's belt stood out just as it did in Michigan, though tonight it looked magnified. Being on her own for a couple days had given her time to focus and start to see things from different perspectives, yet the unresolved issues between her and Rob again nagged at her conscience.

"It's so peaceful here right now," Shenia said.

"Yeah, feels kind of weird though, with everything so calm and quiet." Strangely, Laura felt tense. She didn't want to betray Rob by telling anyone what was happening with them but couldn't keep everything inside. If anyone could possibly understand their circumstances, it was Shenia. "Without the kids, and Rob, I feel like I'm missing parts."

"Have you spoken with them today?"

"No, we keep playing phone tag, but I've left a bunch of messages. Now Rob is working and it'll be crazy since it's Halloween and his friend Andre is bartending. He makes these craft cocktails."

"Sounds yummy. Have you tried one?"

"No. I try to avoid the bar, especially when Rob's friends are there."

"Why?"

How could she explain without giving away his secret, which was now her burden too? She'd avoided thinking about her relationship with Rob since leaving Sanctuary, though she now wondered if he'd confronted Patricia, or again let it slide. What could he ever do to make things right with Andre? "If I gave you an answer, it might take all night."

Shenia stroked Phoebe's floppy ears. "We've got time."

"Promise me you won't tell anyone?"

Shenia flattened Phoebe's ears. "We do solemnly swear."

"Seriously?" Laura asked.

"Serious," Shenia said.

Without sparing details, she told Shenia about Rob's confession and his long history with Andre and Patricia. "I only found out the truth last week." Her mouth had gone dry. "Now I feel like I can't trust him about anything anymore. I'm worried it's over between us."

"Do you still love him?" Shenia asked.

"I'm not sure."

"Why not?"

Laura pressed her eyes shut and tried to think. Lately, she'd been consumed with so much negativity about their relationship that she almost couldn't remember what it felt like to be in love with him. She'd wanted to believe their love was true, but then again, he'd lied to her about Andre. He'd been messing around with Patricia. Was their whole relationship a lie?

"Isn't it pretty obvious? I mean, he lies to me and he flirts with his ex-girlfriend behind my back—even though she's engaged to his best friend. I feel like a fool. The worst thing is, Andre still believes he killed his own sister. And I'm not sure if Rob will ever tell him the truth."

Shenia leaned toward her. "I see what you're saying, but he was seventeen when the accident happened, right? That's about the same age I was when Mom died—a kid, really. I was a different person back then. I'm sure we'd all go back and do lots of things differently if we could. I know I would."

Laura thought about how she'd rushed into her relationship with Rob when she came to Michigan when she was still seventeen. She'd put a lot of pressure on him early on. He said he'd always meant to tell her the truth about Sandra before they were married. "I guess you're right."

"Do you think he still loves you?"

All of a sudden, she remembered how he'd called down to her from the steps on Sunday when she was rushing out. Tears rose to her eyes. "Yes."

"Well, then. It seems like you've been through a lot to-gether and worked so hard to get to the truth—wouldn't it be a waste to throw everything away now?" Shenia patted Phoebe on the head. "Not to be judgy or anything, Laura, but you can be kind of rough on people."

Her back felt achingly stiff. "What do you mean?"

"Not everyone sees things as clearly as you." Shenia looked into her eyes. "And sometimes there isn't a definite answer no matter how much we want one. The truth has a way of re-vealing itself. He's found a way to be honest with you. I don't see why you feel like you have to keep punishing him. As far as I can tell, Andre is his friend—not yours—so it's up to them to settle things." Shenia got out from under Phoebe. "Anyway, it's just something to think about. I need a bathroom break."

Laura leaned back and snuggled with Phoebe. Was she being too hard on him? She remembered when they were young, picturing the flex of Rob's taut shoulders which first caught her eye when she saw him carving a path through the strong current on his board. His blue eyes had been elusive, though there was a certain softness to his gaze when he took her all in, standing before him on the fine sand in her tie-dye skirt and the swimsuit she'd crocheted. The half-smile that slipped out next from the corner of his mouth charmed her too. But what was it really? There was something more. Some-thing that happened in between when he came toward her from across the beach with his paddle board tucked under his arm. Something about the way he walked with his feet pointed outward like a duck. Yeah, he had duck feet, that was it. It seemed almost unbelievable now. She was touched by his small impairment and how he rose all the way up on his toes like he was trying to make the most of each step. Somehow, it had pried open her heart. She was probably making too much of it. For whatever reason, the memory now gave her hope for them.

She'd fallen for him in a matter of days and wanted them to share a life together in Sanctuary. He'd been so into her too as if everything she did or said was new. No one had ever adored her that way. And she adored him. Then, a few months later, she found out she was pregnant. He stayed with her. Married her. And Nate was born. Nate with those long lashes like hers and that lopsided smile inherited from him—or was that something he'd learned through imitation? Rob was the one who pulled him out from under the car and tried to comfort him with her until the EMTs took over. He was the one who waded deep into the water with Biyen in the crook of his arm when Ella jumped off the end of the dock and didn't pop back up. He was the one who came after her from the bar and held her in his arms so tenderly that cold night when they rekindled their passion among Art's fading watercolors.

She loved him when he trusted his instincts and acted on them—sometimes before thinking. But wasn't that exactly what got him into so much trouble? He was the one who rushed in to save Sandra but couldn't. Instead he saved Andre. But at what cost to himself?

Chapter 43

November 1, 2016

Rob locked the door behind the last customer and started counting the money. He counted it a second time, just to be sure, before telling Andre. They'd raked in more than three grand. "You struck again." He stacked a wad of cash on the counter in front of him.

"Guess we got something going here, huh." Andre folded up his share and stuffed it in his back pocket.

"Unreal—" Rob looked him in the eye. "Because of you."

Andre nodded. "And you."

Rob looked away. "Not so much, let's be honest." The words caught in his throat. "I mean, they all come for you. It's kind of scary, like they worship you or something."

"Whatever you say. It's just the alcohol talking. We went through three cases of Pearl Sake for that Thunder Snow. I can't believe I almost ran out of Red Bull, and Patricia brewed like eight pots of chamomile tea before she bolted out of here."

Rob's head pounded at the mention of her name. He wished he'd never have to see her again. "That's insane."

Andre put on his jacket. "Totally. I'm wiped."

"Wait. I gotta ask you something."

He raised an eyebrow. "You ain't getting back any of my take-home pay, just sayin'."

"What do you think I am, some Michigansta like Bill?" Rob could hear his own forced laugh. "After tonight, I'm all clear—for this month and next." He leaned back on his heels, wanting more than ever to call it a night. "It's about your sister." He crossed his arms so they wouldn't shake.

Andre sucked in his cheeks and started chewing on them from the inside like he had when he was a kid trying to think of a comeback to Sandra. Rob remembered how she'd lorded over him when they were sitting around the dining table smoking pot. Somehow, even though she was the youngest, she always managed to have the last word. He pictured her lying on her back in the snow, pinned under the machine, waving her arms in front of her face. If only he'd realized sooner what she was trying to tell him.

"So, when we were hunting, I went by that cross we made. Have you ever been back up there?" Andre shook his head from side to side. "Well, I need you to go with me tomorrow." His shoulders tightened like someone was trying to squeeze a sausage from its casing.

"Why's that?"

"I just think we should."

"We should, why?" Andre zipped his jacket up all the way.

Rob couldn't think of any good reason. "You gotta trust me on this one."

Andre screwed up his forehead. "All right, bro, your call. I got some wedding crap with Patricia at church right before lunch, but I could meet you there around two. Gotta say, I don't see the point though. What's done is done. We got a good thing going here."

Rob's knees locked up. "How 'bout I just see you there tomorrow."

Chapter 44

November 1, 2017

Could she accept what Rob had done and move on? That was the question stuck in her head when she watched the sunrise out her window. She couldn't sleep, though it had been a long night. She and Shenia had spent most of it coming up with a plan for their father. He must sell off some of the property, they'd decided, to cover his living expenses and pay his medical bills. Shenia had a second interview at Ulta later today, and offered to stay on a few more days until things with him got straightened out. Once they talked to him this morning, they'd agreed, Laura could go home. It sounded straight-forward, though they both knew how obstinate their father could be.

Laura pulled on a sweatshirt, bummed she'd missed Rob's calls yesterday. Nate had never sounded more excited. He'd pedaled the bike with both legs at the same time. Rob had said they'd left the wheelchair behind and that Nate was now using a boot and crutches. Nate would walk again. It was difficult to imagine.

After wanting to get away so badly, she now couldn't wait to get back. A string of coughs echoed down the hallway. She tiptoed across the wood floors. Father's coughing grew louder, though it didn't seem to disturb Shenia, who was still asleep with Phoebe resting at the foot of the bed. Laura grabbed yesterday's newspaper off the top of the dresser. Father always liked reading the news, though today she opened it to the Real Estate section. Shenia had said that Beth knew a realtor who could list the properties. She really hoped things worked out for them. Eagle Ridge was so small, though it was growing and getting more popular with tourists from bigger cities like Milwaukee.

Laura poked her head into their father's room and set the paper on his bedside table. Selling off pieces of the fish camp would be tough for him to come to terms with, but he would need to. As Doc Nielson said, he had two choices. Have a health care worker come to the house or move into an assisted-living center. Both options cost money. She and Shenia had agreed they'd do whatever it took to guide him through the transition.

Laura pulled open the curtains. Right now, it would be hard enough just to get him out of bed. He made a sour face before slipping in his dentures. He hadn't been up, except to use the bathroom, since before dinner. She must get him moving. It almost felt as if she was trying to wake the kids. "The sun is up so up with you," she said. The kids knew it was a line from Dr. Seuss, but she didn't bother sharing that with her father. She propped up his pillow. There were some things, like grandkids, that he'd never relate to. She'd let it dig at her for too long. Now she must accept it and move on. She and the kids had Helen and Art. What would she and Rob have done without them?

She helped her father get comfortable before handing him the paper. He put on his glasses and squinted at the properties for sale.

"I'm going to make breakfast. I'll come get you when it's ready, unless you need something right now?"

"I'm fine."

Laura let the eggs and bacon fry as she sat at the kitchen table, sipping her coffee. In the distance, hunkered down under the spruce trees along the water's edge, her grandfather's cottage remained. Though it had fallen into some disrepair, Laura doubted they'd have a problem selling it. Though he went by Peter, her grandfather was also known as Leading Eagle in the tribal community. And everyone, from near and far, knew that he was the real reason for the fish camp—even Father. With his keen eye, Grandfather could spot bass like the bald-headed eagle that swooped down to snatch its prey from the murky water with its mighty talons. And if he didn't succeed the first time, like the eagle, he'd make a second pass and a third, until he brought in his catch. She remembered paddling with him between the reeds until they found their spot hidden among the lily pads in the shallows. Always in a canoe. Never a motor boat. "Muskies hear you coming," he'd always said.

Only with his help, had she gained her freedom from her father. That, she would never forget. Suddenly, grease spattered in the pan behind her. She hurried over to the stove. Already, the eggs were fried hard and the bacon was almost crisp, just the way her father liked it.

She got him out of bed and helped him into the kitchen where the food was waiting at the table. He took his seat and finished a piece of bacon before she'd refilled her coffee. Behind them, water dripped from the faucet. How would she break the news about selling off grandfather's property and likely one other? She dipped the corner of her toast in her coffee. She was better off waiting for Shenia, who seemed to have a way of getting through to him.

Sunlight spread across the surface of the lake where patches of ice were forming. In a matter of weeks, it would likely be frozen solid. She'd been only eight the first time she followed her father with her fishing rod onto the ice until they reached the center and he took hold of the auger. "It must go down half-a-foot or else the fish gobble us up for dinner."

She didn't want to fall in, and knelt beside him as he bore a hole through the ice until he tapped the frigid darkness and determined it was safe to fish. She stood up. She couldn't disappoint him. With her pole in her right hand, she dropped her line with the left—watching the night crawler she'd picked out from the dirt in the foam container as it wriggled on her hook until it sank too deep for her to see. Soon, she was shivering, holding the line, waiting for a bite. Then, a flock of geese honked overhead. What were they still doing here? She watched them fly away. Something tugged on the line but then it fell slack. She jerked it sideways and found some resistance. Maybe the fish hadn't gotten away with her worm after all. Quickly, she reeled it in, but found only a bare hook.

"You know what this means—" Father rested his eyes on hers. "You go without fish tonight."

It was too cold for tears, which stung her cheeks and froze to her lashes. How come she could never do anything right in his eyes?

When he was through with his breakfast, he wiped the grease from his chin and set his napkin on the table before looking up at her. "I need you to stay and take care of me. Shenia, she's no good at it."

Laura froze in her seat. What was he saying? Up until last weekend, he and Shenia had been managing just fine without her. Now suddenly his attitude had changed. "What do you mean?"

"First off, she can't cook."

Staying with him in Wisconsin wasn't an option. She was leaving in a couple hours at most. Didn't he realize that, on the other side of the lake, she had her own family to take care of, including a son who was still learning how to walk again?

She cleared her throat. "Shenia and I were talking last night. We have some ideas for you."

"Well, that's Shenia for you. Always talking. I'm your father. I know what I need. You've got the touch."

Laura stared at her hands. She didn't want to break anyone or be broken. Yet that appeared to be what she was faced with on both fronts. "But my husband and kids need me too."

"So, you just abandon me."

"No. Shenia is trying to find a job here so she'll be nearby. We're going to hire someone to come to the house and care for you."

He sniffed. "I can't pay for that."

"That's what we were talking about. You can sell off some of the property."

He scowled. "I'm not selling off anything. You're just like your mother. You think you can tell me what to do. In my house, you live under my rules."

"That's not fair. Shenia and I have a plan. We can pay for the medical care and living expenses if you sell off grandfather's cottage."

"Oh, now I see. You came for the money."

Blood rushed to her head. "You know that's not true. I'm not taking anything. It would all go back to you, even though my grandfather earned every penny of it. As far as I see it, that cottage should have belonged to him and Mom after all the years they worked for you."

Her heart felt like it was pounding out of her chest. Why had she lost her temper with him? She knew she should have let Shenia do the talking.

Father shook his head. "I loved your mother. But she didn't understand, a wife can't be free. A husband must have control just as a father has control."

She took a deep breath but couldn't hold in her feelings any longer. "So that's how you rationalize working her to death and abusing Shenia and me."

"I never abused anyone." He coughed into his hanky and stuffed it back into his breast pocket. "I taught you how to survive. What did you want me to do, send you out of here swimming around in the world defenseless like them fish?"

He wheezed as if blocks of ice were separating in his lungs. "I tried to break your mother, but the truth is, she broke me. I took other women to show her she should be grateful. Instead, she despised me. You and your sister are the only reason she stuck around. We fell into our routines, though she hated me." He clasped his hands. "I never wanted that. I tried to explain myself, but she wouldn't forgive me."

The pounding in her chest softened. At least now they'd been open with each other. Knowing his thinking helped better explain her mother's dying words at the hospital. "Never lose hope, Laura. You'll find a way out."

Even in the face of despair, her mother hadn't given up on her. She hadn't understood it all then, but believed now that her mother wanted her to be brave enough to believe in herself and search out her dreams, even if they weren't like anyone else's. She now knew what to do.

She had to trust herself and set Nate free. Once she returned to Sanctuary, she would give him permission to ride the scooter at school. He'd shown his strength and proven himself responsible in the long months of his recovery. He'd shown her what it means to be brave. Once Nate was better, she'd find a way to go back to school. This was her new path, one, where she could help people and ease the financial burden on Rob and his parents.

Maybe Father really did think he'd been doing right by his family. That, she would never know, though she couldn't excuse his mistreatment of them. It wouldn't be honest. Still, he deserved some compassion. She had no right to be unkind. He wasn't a good man, only human. And humans were often cruel. "I understand." She reached out and took his hand. "I can't stay here, but I will come back and help. Shenia and I will make sure you're well taken care of. You don't have to worry."

Fifteen minutes later, once she'd helped her father into his seat by the fire, Laura packed her bag. If she got on the road by nine, there was a chance she'd make it home for dinner. She'd done all she could here for now. It would be up to Shenia to see their plans through. Managing their father's affairs wouldn't be easy, but Shenia knew how to manage people—she'd said so herself. Laura would stay in close contact, and make room for them in her life, though taking care of the kids remained her primary concern. And what about Rob?

Looking back at how she'd treated him over the past few weeks, she now feared she'd grown cold-hearted like her father. Unlike him, Rob had never been cruel. Despite everything, she believed he was a gentle soul. Now she finally understood. He avoided confrontation as a rule and couldn't stand up to his dad or Andre, which had led him to lie. He was only seventeen when it happened. She wouldn't judge him anymore. She just wanted to tell him it's all okay now. To be vulnerable. To ask for help. To seek comfort. She was there for him.

He'd tried to suppress his feelings and buried all the grief and the guilt and mostly the shame. Internalizing his emotions almost cost him his sanity, and she didn't want to imagine what was he thinking when she'd found him that night at the lodge holding tightly onto the cleaver. When she returned, she would tell him that she was sorry. It was up to him now. She had no right to make him feel like he had to change for her. *Be the man you are.* That's what she would say. *That's all anybody can ask of you.*

Laura snapped shut her bag and went to get Shenia out of bed, but when she entered the hall her sister was already shuffling toward her in fuzzy, oversized slippers. "Morning." She yawned and went into the bathroom. "Give me a couple minutes."

Laura went to her father, who had fallen asleep in the chair with his head slumped sideways and his mouth hanging open as he labored for breath. She covered him with a blanket. There was no room in her heart for hatred anymore. "Sleep well."

She went into the kitchen and made herself a sandwich to take with her so she wouldn't have to stop for anything other than gas. Shenia came beside her and poured a cup of coffee. "So, were you able to talk to him?"

"I think so. Are you sure you're going to be able to handle everything?"

"Somehow, I always do."

"I know. Just keep me in the loop. I can come back to clean out the cottage or whatever you need help with."

"Thanks," Shenia said. "I'll let you know."

"Maybe I can stay an extra day, so there might be enough time for me to hang out with you and Beth."

Shenia swatted at the air. "Stop. You are so far ahead of yourself. Maybe next time you can bring the kids?"

"We'll see. Or you could come visit us in Michigan."

Shenia nodded. Laura opened her arms. For the first time since they were teenagers, they held each other close.

"Just wait one minute. I have something." Shenia hurried out of the kitchen.

Laura made a glass of ice water for their father. When Shenia returned, she was carrying a pair of leather moccasins about the same size as the ones Laura had worn out. "I found these in the bedroom closet."

Laura ran her thumb over the stitches of the pucker-toe moccasins, recalling her mother's soft steps across the kitchen each morning.

"Please, take them with you. She would want that."

"What about Father?"

"I'm sure he would want you to have them too."

Laura wondered whether he could ever grasp the value of her mother's moccasins for her. She took his glass of water off the counter. "He likes ice in it by the way. I'll just bring it to him before I go, so he'll have it when he wakes up. He sleeps with his mouth open, you know?"

"Don't worry." Shenia took the glass from her hand. "I'll bring it. I'm sure your kids are anxious to see you—and Rob."

Laura smiled. "Yeah. Thanks again for listening."

Chapter 45

November 1, 2016

Rob fumbled to switch off his alarm clock until he realized the screeching noise was coming from outside the attic window where a crow was cawing. Holy shit. It was already noon. Somehow, he'd slept right through the night. Rob picked up his phone. He needed to talk to Laura before he met Andre. By now, she was probably already on the road. He called her number, but the phone kept ringing with no answer, though the bird, sitting on a nearby branch, wouldn't shut-up. He considered chucking his phone at it. There was no way he was leaving another message.

"Hello, Rob?"

"Hi. Yes, Laura, it's me." The line crackled. "I can barely hear you. The signal between us is weak."

"I know. You're breaking up too. I'm in Manistique, on my way home. I think I'll make it by dinner. Will you still be there?"

Rob stared out at the dense fog and tightened his grip on the phone. How could he explain what he was planning without scaring her? From now on, he wanted them to be completely open. Since she'd been gone, he'd felt like one of the empties he and Andre had tossed the previous night. "I just wanted to say, I love you. I'm sorry about everything. You're so beautiful. I never thought what I'd done could hurt you so much. Yesterday, I told Patricia to go to hell. And today—"

"Rob, please, don't worry right now. We can talk about it once I'm home. I—"

Suddenly, she was no longer there. "Laura?" He called her name over and over, louder and louder, even though he knew it was no use. He tried calling again. He had to tell her how he was going to make things right between him and Andre, but she didn't answer. He'd let her get away. Would he ever get her back?

Rob walked through the thick fog along the shoreline, keeping his head down, until he reached the trail into the forest that would take him to the cross. Soon after, the sandy soil changed to dirt. His foot sank into the mud. Against his best instincts, he pulled it out and continued. What could he possibly say to Andre to make him understand? Unable to see ahead through the trees, Rob blindly followed the winding path for about a quarter mile and then stopped at the spot where he thought he'd gone up to the cross from before. He scanned the side of the bluff for it, but the fog was too dense. Anything could happen out here today and no one would know. The dampness settled into his bones. There was no turning back. He must tell Andre the truth. But after all this time, would Andre ever be able to forgive him?

He had no other choice other than to ask. Rob started making his way up in the mud. With each step forward the ground gave way and he fell back. He landed on his knee and then grabbed a stick to help brace himself the rest of the way. In these conditions, Andre might bail on him. Rob couldn't stop. He was almost there. After a minute, through the fog, resting on brambles beneath the tree, appeared the cross. Beside it stood Andre.

Rob hunched over and tried to catch his breath. "That was rough."

"Yeah, man. Took me a half hour. I couldn't see shit. What are we doing here, anyway?" Andre, with the hood of his parka pulled over his head, pointed at the fallen cross. "I mean—all this—it's over."

Slowly, Rob straightened up. "No, it's not."

Andre frowned at him. "What the fuck are you talking about?"

His body went still and he recalled the split-second when the doe's eyes captured his. "When we were hunting, I was up here while you were shooting that doe. After you called my name and told me she was coming, I ran down to help. Then, it was like she came right at me."

"So, what?"

"The doe looked at me with these terrified eyes. I recognized them." Rob took hold of Andre's shoulders. "The doe's eyes were Sandra's."

"You're talking crazy, bro." Andre backed away.

"No, your sister made me remember what I'd done," Rob said. "When you crashed into the tree, the snowmobile didn't land on her chest."

Andre's eye sockets were gaunt as if the muscles had detached from the bone. "You told me she was already dead when you found her."

Rob stepped around the cross and pointed at the lowest branch of tree behind it. "No. When I got here, her right leg was pinned under the machine. The end of the blade was wedged right there."

Andre's face turned as gray as the sky. "Then what?"

"She told me to help get her out so we could find you," Rob said. "I tried."

Andre looked at him. "Tried what?"

"To lift the machine off her." Rob bent down to show him. "But I lost my footing and the blade slipped out of my hand. That's how I dropped it." Before he could apologize, Andre rushed toward him. Rob stood and raised his hands in surrender. "Please, understand. I'm so sorry. It was an accident."

Without hesitating, Andre jumped him. "Murderer."

Rob grabbed onto his shoulders and tried to fend him off, but Andre locked his hands around his neck and started to choke him. Rob couldn't breathe and tried to pry Andre's hands apart. Andre slipped in the mud, but didn't let go. They fell into the dirt. Andre landed on top of him. Then they slid down the bluff in a blur. Andre continued choking him. They broke through branches, rolled over logs, and tripped on tangles of vines, until they fell sideways and lodged against a tree with roots snaking out in every direction. Andre, his jaw clenched, dug into to his throat with his fingernails. Rob couldn't breathe. He tried to get a foothold, and push Andre away, but all his weight was on him. The best he could do was flip over. Finally, Andre let go of his neck, but then tackled him and grabbed hold of him around the chest. He tried to get up, but Andre pinned him face-down in the mud and pushed his face deep in it. "Do you know what they do to seventeen-year-old boys in prison like this?"

Rob wrestled from side to side, though he couldn't get out from under him. Andre sat up and reached under his pant leg. He pulled out his knife. Quickly, Andre cut away the collar of

Rob's fleece, exposing the back of his neck. Andre pressed the tip of the blade against Rob's skin. "All these years, you let me think I killed my sister. I always knew you were lying about something."

It was the moment he'd feared all along. He was at Andre's mercy. "I don't blame you for wanting to kill me."

Andre breathed hard from on top of him. "No, Rob. I need to kill you." He jabbed in the tip of the blade, which pierced the skin between Rob's shoulders. "I've never hated anyone so much as I hate you now."

Rob felt a sharp pain. Blood began to trickle down the middle of his back. "I don't blame you. I'm sorry. But please, just believe me, I never meant to harm Sandra or you."

Andre shoved his face into the brittle pine needles littered under the tree with the mud. "Shut up. You have no right. Persevere. That's a sick joke, man." One by one he traced over each of the letters in Rob's tattoo with the knife, pricking him repeatedly. "I was the one who had to … and I did. Beat those cocksuckers. Went to solitary confinement for it. I'd rather die than let 'em fuck with me." Andre grabbed Rob's hair, snapped his head back, and put the serrated blade against the front of his throat as if he would slit it any second. "After what you did to my sister and me, you deserve to die."

Unable to move, Rob gritted his teeth and thought of his dad, who'd always seen it another way. Rob knew better now and prepared to *get what he had coming to him* until he thought of Laura and the kids. "You have no right."

"Oh, I have every right."

"No. Andre. You don't. I would have done anything for you. You always bullied me into going along. I tried to help and I fucked up. But if it weren't for you, none of us would have been put in that fucked up situation in the first place. You're the one who took it too far."

Rob spat. "Go ahead, kill me now if you think that'll make this right. But then what will happen to you? You want to go to jail again?" For a number of seconds Andre breathed heavily, his exhalation hot on Rob's neck. "I'll do anything to help you get your life straightened out. You can come work at the bar and make a shitload of money. Just tell me what you want."

"Hah." Andre grunted. "You think this is some do-over and we can just pretend like nothing ever happened?"

"I'm not saying that." Andre's sweat dripped into Rob's cuts and started to sting. "I'll go with you right now and turn myself in, if that's what you want. You can be free. You and Patricia have your whole life ahead of you. Once your record is clear, you can go and do anything."

"Don't even pretend like you care what's best for me. I'll choose what to do with my life from now on." Andre's weight settled in his core. "Even if I turn you in, nothing will change the way people think of me. It's too late. I can never go back in time. I'm already banned from the team because they didn't trust me."

Andre twirled the blade so Rob could see. "The sickest thing is that I get sent to prison and you get married to Laura."

Andre shoved Rob's face back in the mud. "Never forget. Do you remember? That's what we said when we raised the cross. You lied to me. Even then, you were already doing exactly what you said you'd never do. I loved you as my brother and you betrayed me." Andre ran the blade across Rob's upper back. "Never forget that."

A searing pain coursed between Rob's shoulders over his tattoo. He struggled for breath. "You know I never would. I don't want to fight you ... I never did. I'm sorry I lied. I was a coward."

Andre didn't move for a few seconds. "On that, I can agree. You're also a damn fool for thinking I'd work for you for free."

"What are you talking about?" Rob asked.

"There's more than one way to open someone's wallet," Andre said.

"What the hell are you saying?"

"I'm talking about my side hustle: vikes, kickers, jackpot. I made a shitload of money at your bar selling opioids, and you were too blind to see it right in front of you."

"Did Patricia know?"

"Now, that's a funny question." Andre laughed for his own benefit. "You remember that night you came in and surprised us—when we hung after? Patricia thought you were onto us when you started asking her about the wellness shots. So, she roofied your drink to make you forget everything you saw."

Rob remembered how hammered he'd felt walking home that night to give Ella a kiss. He couldn't give up on his family now. Not for a liar and thief. Rob struggled to get up from under him. "No one gets off free, bro." Andre dug the blade deeper in between the shoulders. "I suggest you just stay down and keep your mouth shut."

Rob choked back tears. He couldn't move, under the weight of Andre, and thought he might be dying. Suddenly, Andre hurled the knife into the forest. "You're not even worth killing." Out of the corner of his eye, Rob watched the blade disappear. Then Andre stood. "Forgive me, sister."

Left alone with the cross, Rob rested his head on the ground as he watched Andre walk away through the mud. There was no use chasing after him. Only bad blood would run between them from this moment on. Rob wanted no more.

Chapter 46

November 1, 2016

When she finally reached Harbor City, Laura drove past the medical complex where she and Nate had spent so many restless days and nights. The choppy water stirred groggy memories of dozing off in the waiting room between fireworks. For weeks, she'd half-slept beside him in the reclining chair, wondering if he'd ever be strong enough to leave. Now, with the help of a boot and crutches, he was learning to walk again. She couldn't wait to see his eyes light up once she gave him permission to use the knee scooter. He'd matured so much since the accident. In a few more weeks, after Thanksgiving, he'd go back to school. By summer he might, once again, be able to climb the dunes. Keshya was right, *You must believe to achieve.*

Laura imagined herself, one day soon, entering Dr. Azzi's office—not as the mother of a patient, but as a member of the staff. Next fall, if Nate's recovery continued, she might be the one back in school.

She came to a stop at the red light. Beside her signs were posted along the beach for a new SUP-board rental and training center. Five years ago, around the time Nate was born, hardly anyone except Rob and Andre had even heard of the sport. They were practically pioneers. These days, everybody wanted to take a stab at it. Maybe Rob could help educate people and give some lessons? Heck, he could probably manage the place. She wondered what he was doing now. He'd sounded so anxious earlier, before she'd lost service earlier crossing the UP. Laura wondered why he hadn't picked up her call an hour ago when she stopped for gas after crossing the Mackinac bridge. At least Helen would know when to expect her—assuming she checked her voicemail at work.

It was almost five o' clock. Laura stayed in the left lane and turned onto the highway toward Sanctuary. As long as she didn't hit any more rush-hour traffic, she might beat Helen and Ella home. After a few miles, as Laura neared the coast of Lake Michigan, the fog rolled in and made it difficult to see around the corners. She was itching so bad for a bear hug from Ella, Laura was almost unable to resist the urge to floor it. She imagined her daughter waiting at the door, hopping from one foot to the other, ready to jump into her arms the second she got there. Laura missed Biyen, too, and yearned for the satisfaction of squishing her face against his chubby cheeks. Before Nate's accident, there were so many things she'd taken for granted. Only now, having almost lost him, did she realize how fortunate she and Rob were to have not one, not two, but three healthy children. She'd never been more thankful for that.

Laura found herself craving his touch, though the thought of seeing him again made her nervous. Finally, she felt ready to talk. From now on, she would really try to listen. Their life together wasn't always pretty, much less beautiful, but she loved him from the core of her flawed heart to the center of his gentle soul. She wouldn't be the one to tear them apart.

As Laura neared Rosa's house, fog swirled amid in the dips of the highway. Someday, she dreamed of having a place just like it—even if they, like Rosa, only rented—a cottage tucked away in the woods where the kids could run wild and she and Rob could have some privacy. Rising and falling with the road through the rolling hills, Laura recalled the melodies she'd listened to from Rosa's doorstep. Maybe Rosa was practicing right now for her debut at Sanders the Friday night after Thanksgiving? Laura imagined her standing tall, performing to a crowded room, before soaking up the applause. She couldn't wait to see her shine for real. Rosa's music emanated from her like waves that gave Laura the courage to chase her dreams.

By the time Laura came racing down the hill toward Sanctuary, the fog had formed a wall around the village. She didn't see the green light at the intersection turn yellow until she'd sped right through it. Now that she was on Main Street, there would be no more stops until Rob's parents' house. She unclicked the safety-belt, which had been choking her the entire trip. Only a half mile more, or so, and she'd be there. Beside her, the dimly lit antique store seemed to be drifting off to sleep amid the thick fog, though it wasn't yet dark. Odd, the streets were so quiet. Everyone must be worn out from partying again last night. Up ahead, along the sidewalk, only the old oaks stood guard.

When she came beside Art's gallery, Laura took her foot off the gas. Beneath his new sign hung a striking painting she hadn't seen before. She glanced at it over her shoulder. It looked like an enormous cat's-eye marble or, possibly, the magnified beacon of the lighthouse. She wasn't sure. In any case, it grabbed her attention like nothing else he'd ever created. As soon as she got home, she'd have to tell him how much she liked it. It was only a few more blocks. Though now, as she approached Chelsea's, Laura noticed a for-sale sign in the front lawn. The house looked empty. What was going on?

When she looked back at the road, a red car appeared. Almost instantly, the driver weaved across the center line and came into her lane. It took her a second before she realized the car was speeding toward her. Its headlights were beaming straight at her. She tightened her grip on the wheel. Then the driver accelerated, coming close enough for her to see the person behind the wheel. *Oh my god.* She recognized him. Andre. He was about to crash into her head-on. If she didn't do something, in a second or two, she'd be history.

She pounded her fists into the horn with the hope that he'd switch back into his own lane. He was so close now. She glared at him through the windshield. His thin lips stretched from his pointy chin toward his gauged ears. He wasn't going to stop. Her heart beat, violently, as never before. "No!" In that split-second, she swerved toward Chelsea's driveway. Laura put her faith in the oldest of the oaks, which was the only thing standing between her and Andre. Without hesitation, she slammed on the breaks. Her eyes squeezed shut. Bam! Warmth washed over her. The cloud cover opened, and an eagle with great wings swooped down and swept up her weightless body into an embrace of a thousand brown, black, and white feathers—lifting her toward the hallowed places beyond the sky to rejoin her mother and grandfather. She was gone.

After an unknown amount of time, her throat began to burn and she was startled awake by her own coughing. Fumes filled her lungs. Slowly, with muscles she could hardly control, Laura forced open her eyes. Through the smoke and fog, Andre's headlights glared at her sideways from the opposite side of the oak where the hood of his car was crushed like a beer can.

Her cheeks felt quite warm and she placed her hands there. Suddenly, she realized her face was covered in blood, which ran down the front of her coat. She rested her aching head against the seat. She must have banged it into the rear-view mirror when she'd come to a stop beside the tree. Above her, from high in the sturdy branches of the oak, she heard a piercing call that sounded like squawking. Then, she remembered. The eaglets. Poor little things were probably as shaken as her and also struggling for air. It was so hard to breathe. She felt lightheaded, like, she might pass out. Time ceased to exist as she sat there staring out the windshield unable to focus or move. Then a feather, fluttering this way and that, floated before her until it landed on the glass. Somehow, unless she was imagining, she'd received a sacred gift.

Humbled, she bowed her head as far as she could in honor of the creator and the eagle, which served as a messenger to the world of spirits where her ancestors dwelled. Raising her eyes, she remembered, then, what her grandfather had always told her. "Never be ashamed of who you are."

She finally understood the teachings he'd been trying to instill in her. There was darkness within her and others, she realized. After what she'd been through, there was no way to pretend that evil didn't exist. She could no longer ignore it. In order to survive, she must learn to manage.

They were all of the same heart. Each person could decide. Andre had given into manipulation, hatred, and revenge. She refused to give up. Through her struggles, she'd learned to believe in herself and was committed to opening her mind and seeking balance. From this day forward, she wanted to continue her grandfather's work toward shining the light. Yet, at this moment, she couldn't even get up from her seat.

Then, from up the street, she was startled by another image, hazy through the smoke and fog. Rob. He was limping toward her, ragged and caked in mud, though not as a broken man but rather as one who'd held his ground. When Rob saw her, he shuffled ahead faster. He looked badly hurt. Had Andre tried to kill him too? Laura yanked on the handle.

Just then, Rob reached her window. Through the fumes, she met his bloodshot eyes before he pulled the door open. "I thought I'd lost you."

"Nope." She reached out her hand. "You found me."

Rob, his grasp firm, drew her toward him. "What happened?"

"Andre tried to run me down."

Rob shook his head in seeming disbelief. "Oh my god, Laura. I never imagined. I'm so sorry."

"Did you tell him?" she asked.

Rob's hand tightened around hers and he held her gaze. "Yes, I told him everything." At that moment, a wave passed through her as if carrying her across Lake Michigan, the great body of water that once created such a vast divide between them.

She felt a deep release, listening, as he loosened his fingers and continued. "Andre was trying to bring me down with him and, apparently, you too. He was never going to let go of his pain. I lost myself getting tangled up with him, but I never should have doubted you. You were always the one trying to raise me up. Instead I dragged you with me to the bottom. "Forgive me, please?"

Before this afternoon, she might never have understood the depths of Andre's rage. Now that she'd been his target, Laura thought about Andre and his relationship with Rob another way. "You are forgiven." A lump formed in her throat. "Maybe we needed to sink to the bottom all along?"

Rob wiped the blood from her cheek. "I'm so lucky I found you."

Just then a plume smoke rose from under Andre's hood. "Is he—?" she asked.

With a ripple of something like remorse, Rob's upper lip wavered until it shut tight. "No one can help him now." He looked her square in the eye. "He made his choice. He can't hurt us, or anyone, anymore." She noticed Rob's back, covered in blood, as he helped her the rest the way out of the car and onto her feet. She wobbled, for a second, before taking the feather with her from the windshield. The sirens of oncoming emergency vehicles blared. "Come on." Rob led her away from the accident.

She considered going back, but then accepted that EMS was coming. She must leave those conflicts behind. Let her spirit fly free. Andre had cut his own path. She and Rob were on a new road. It might be rutted or filled with a bunch of potholes, but it was good enough. By trusting and supporting each other, she had reason to believe, they could resurface. For now, they hobbled over the concrete and collapsed onto the lawn outside Chelsea's house. Lying there, shoulder to shoulder, she sensed that nothing more could come between them, a sense not exactly of happiness but of deep gratitude for, now, they shared the same heart.

There, beside him on the frozen ground, she entered a sanctuary that emanated from within her. A beautiful space. And Laura knew, for the first time, that she'd arrived where she truly belonged. Her own place of being that she would carry with her everywhere. She raised the feather above them and embraced her ancestral teachings with her whole heart for, *To know love is to know peace.*

Acknowledgements

Many thanks to my publisher, Adelaide Books, for believing in my work and the giving me the joy of seeing this novel take flight.

Only after its sale, did I realize how the writing of this book has been a sanctuary for me. I owe a tremendous debt of gratitude to those people in my village who helped me find this place. You've made the publication of this story possible.

It's a story that began long ago, with the care, love, and understanding of my late grandparents, Theodore and Rose Czerniak, who will always be dear to me.

I'd also like to give a special thank you to Cynthia Summers, my next-door neighbor growing up and lifelong confidant, who taught me the true meaning of friendship when she stuck with me through my rhyming phase and never stopped believing in my writing even when I had my doubts. I, too, am grateful for my lasting ties to the courageous families in Granby, East Granby, and Simsbury, Conn., who never cease to amaze and inspire me.

A heartfelt thanks extends to my incredible circle of friends here in Northville, Mich., including my writing partners. Robin Gaines-Franks, you have shown me the way in writing and in life. I appreciate you being such a dear friend when I needed one most. And Paul Lewis Bancel, the power of your gentle guidance can't be overstated. Additionally, thank you to the gracious members of the Stonewater Book Club for opening your homes and your hearts. You've been a lifeline over the past decade and I wouldn't be the person or writer I am today without the camaraderie we've shared.

I'm am immensely grateful to my mentors along the way, including author Summer Wood, who shepherded me through my first master class at The Taos Summer Writers Conference and offered continued encouragement through the years with all those extra writing prompts. A mountain of gratitude also goes to mystery author Christine DeSmet, who made the University of Wisconsin-Madison a retreat that helped me remain grounded while reaching for the stars.

I am infinitely grateful for the dedicated community of writers at Vermont College of Fine Arts and my extraordinary faculty advisors: Jacquelyn Mitchard, Clint McCown, David Jauss, and Ellen Lesser. Your insights and wisdom will forever shine.

I also want to thank all the people who took a chance on me early on in my writing career, including journalist and author Mike King, who brought me aboard as a cub reporter for *The Atlanta Journal-Constitution*. Additionally, many thanks to all the wonderful, talented people at the *Hartford-Courant*, who supported me in my various writing ventures and made me feel like a valued part of the reporting team.

Finally, I'd like to thank my family. I am forever appreciative of my in-laws, Joan and John Crabb and their extended family, for their support and belief in me and my writing endeavors. I also owe a tremendous debt of gratitude to my parents, Joanne and John Knape, who supported my education, from early on, through high school and college. Mom, you succeeded in instilling me with the will to achieve my goals.

Dad, thank you for all the boat rides and passing on your love of the Great Lakes. I'm also grateful for the love of my sister, Jennifer Marie Chiodini, and to her husband, Victor, for being such a good sport about answering a barrage of deer hunting questions.

And, to my three daughters: Thank you for your patience. I couldn't have done this without you. You are what *Love is ...* to me. Kayleigh, I will forever cherish our philosophical debates and your appreciation of those times when I just couldn't "turn it off." Clara, thank you for always being there to share a laugh, or a tear, and for knowing when I really needed a hug. Hadley, thank you for brightening my day. With your many talents, strength of spirit, and kindness of heart, I know you will rise to the challenge and overcome any adversity you may face. And, lastly, to my husband. Greg, you are the reason. I don't know how you managed to put up with all my talk about writing this book. You deserve a "major award." Thank you for being at my side—even when it meant being apart. You've supported me in every way possible and then some. Thank you for never giving up on us. Your love means everything.

About the Author

Cheryl Crabb is a fiction writer and accomplished journalist. She recently earned her MFA in Writing from the Vermont College of Fine Arts. She also has a master's degree from the Medill School of Journalism at Northwestern University and has worked for fifteen years with newspapers including the Atlanta Journal-Constitutionand The Hartford Courant. A Wisconsin native, Cheryl lives with her husband and their three daughters in metro Detroit and has contributed as a guest columnist to the Detroit Free Press. She's a member of the Association of Writers & Writing Programs (AWP) and Detroit Working Writers. Cheryl and her family frequently visit northern Michigan where they enjoy jumping the waves and hiking the dunes. The Other Side of Sanctuaryis her debut novel.

Made in the USA
Middletown, DE
12 January 2020